# WRATH & RIGHTEOUSNESS
## [Episodes One and Two]

## CHRIS STEWART

**MERCURY**
RADIO ARTS

**MERCURY**
**INK**

NEW YORK      DALLAS

Mercury Radio Arts, Inc.

1133 Avenue of the Americas

New York, NY 10036

www.glennbeck.com | www.mercuryink.com

Original Edition © 2004, 2005 The Shipley Group Inc.

(Published by Deseret Book Company)

Condensed Edition © 2013 The Shipley Group Inc.

(Published by Mercury Radio Arts, Inc. under license from Deseret Book Company)

First Mercury Ink paperback edition July 2013

Cover design by Richard Yoo

ISBN: 978-0-9892933-1-0

*And where the Spirit of the Lord is, there is liberty.*

*2 Corinthians 3:17*

*How art thou fallen from heaven, O Lucifer, who didst rise in the morning!*

*Isaiah 14:12*

# WRATH & RIGHTEOUSNESS
[Episode One]

# Prologue

*In war there are no unwounded soldiers.*

*José Narosky*

It was calm. Peaceful and sweet. Like that brief moment in the morning before waking and thoughts settle in, before the dim light filters through and the morning winds blow. It was the calm of nature, a peace that man cannot produce, like the silent roll of dark clouds before the coming storm or the calm of glassy water before the first raindrops fall. The peace seemed to come from above and below, from the sky and the ground, as if the Earth itself paused as it took a long deep breath.

It was the last peace, the great peace, the deep breath before the storm. The Golden Age was closing and the heavens paused and waited for the long plunge ahead.

Some people saw it coming.

But they were few.

## Arlington National Cemetery—New Annex
## (Formerly Alexandria National Cemetery)
## Alexandria, Virginia

It had rained all night, thunderclouds rolling in from the Blue Ridge Mountains, the dark clouds boiling with power as they met the moisture from the sea. Lightning and heavy rain pounded the night, then suddenly stopped as daylight drew near. The first line of storms moved off to the Chesapeake Bay and lingered over the sea, caught between the rising sun and the musky coastline behind. But the rain wasn't over. What was already the wettest spring in a century had much more to give.

The day dawned cold and dreary. Another band of dark clouds gathered in the morning light, moving in from the west, blowing over the hill that loomed on the horizon. Heavy mist hung in the air until the weak morning breeze finally carried it away.

The grass around the freshly dug grave was wet and long, with tiny drops of moisture glistening from the tips of each blade. The pile of dirt next to the grave was dark and rich, loamy with many years of rotting vegetation and now soaked and wet. A patch of Astroturf had been placed over the pile of dirt and pinned down on the corners to keep it from flapping in the wind. A sad arrangement of plastic roses and baby's breath set atop the Astroturf.

Only recently had Alexandria been designated as the annex to Arlington National Cemetery, which had been destroyed. Although smaller, it was just as beautiful, nestled on the west side of the Potomac River. But like the rest of Washington, D.C., it had been destroyed, too. Rows of elms and oaks stood over the graves, but the trees' bark facing north were burned, and soon the trees would die.

Within the confines of the cemetery, the world was peaceful and quiet. Indeed, the cemetery appeared much like it would have a few months before. But outside the cemetery gates, there was appalling evidence of how the world had been thrown on its back.

Underneath the heavy clouds, the sky was heavy from the dust and ash that had been kicked into the air. Above the clouds, there was a layer that blocked out much of the sun and turned the moon blood red. Every night was ablaze with the aurora borealis, sheets of green and blue that, for the first time in history, reached as far south as the tropics. Outside the cemetery gates, there were a few people walking—even a man on a horse—but no operating motor vehicles could be seen anywhere. The roads were littered with cars, buses and trucks that had not moved since the moment of the event, all of them remaining where they had rolled to a stop, their metal carcasses cluttering both sides of the streets. In the skies above the cemetery, no aircraft could be seen descending toward Reagan National Airport. Indeed, all across the nation, there was no air traffic at all. And that was not the only modernity that was no more. Postal service, banks, electricity, communications, refrigeration, modern travel . . . the list of things that had disappeared was very long.

In the median that separated the highway, a desperate group of people who now called themselves a tribe was working the ground with a plow that had been improvised from a sheet of metal and piece of rope. Two men pulled while another man guided the makeshift device. It was slow and painful work, and barely suitable, for the plow barely turned the earth. But they were desperate to till the ground in any way they could. If they didn't plow, they couldn't plant the few seeds they had been given by their benefactor—a foreign government. If they didn't plant, they didn't harvest, and if they didn't harvest, they didn't eat.

The world was back to the 1880s.

It was not a good place to be.

*******

The six-man color guard waited by the grave. Their uniforms were so crisp they almost cracked as the men moved. Their polished boots reflected the gray light from the sky. The sergeant in charge stood in front of his men, giving them one final inspection before the mourners appeared. "Gig line!" he hissed to a junior non-commissioned officer. He glanced at his chest and aligned the buttons on his shirt with the zipper cover on his pants. "Cover," the sergeant whispered as he moved down the line. A young corporal adjusted his headgear, pulling it down uncomfortably over his eyes. Satisfied, the sergeant moved to the end of the line, put himself into position, then glanced at his watch. It was 2:56 p.m. The service was scheduled to begin at 3 p.m. It would begin exactly on time, of course. Perfection was the standard when it came to paying respect to their dead.

The sergeant heard the soft clip-clop of hooves coming up the narrow strip of asphalt that wound through the National Cemetery. Glancing to his right, he saw a single mare, old but proud, her dark mane perfectly curried and braided to the right. She emerged from around a tight bend in the road, drawing a small carriage behind her. Black and shiny, with wooden wheels and a leather harness, the carriage carried a single bronze casket on its sideless bed. Seeing the casket, the sergeant took a deep breath and straightened himself. "*Ten-HUT!*" he whispered powerful from deep in his chest. His soldiers drew themselves straight, their shoulders square, their chins tight, their hands fists. They looked straight ahead, their faces without expression as they stared at some unknown object on the distant horizon.

As the funeral procession approached, the sergeant placed his right foot exactly behind his left foot, his right toe pointing down, barely touching his left heel, and turned right with perfect mechanical precision. He faced the approaching wagon, staring at the metal casket so as to never make eye contact with the mourners who followed. The dark horse walked with high steps, her flanks glistening with sweat.

As the wagon drew close, the sergeant felt his heart quicken. This one was special and he wanted the funeral ceremony done right.

The wagon passed by a huge oak tree and he caught a better glimpse of the casket, a dark bronze box draped in an American flag.

Atop the flag, an enormous ring of flowers, freshly cut and beautifully arranged, had been placed over the center of the casket.

Twenty-four roses. Twelve red and twelve white.

White roses for virtue. Red roses for blood.

Seeing the flowers, the sergeant had to swallow against the catch in his throat. Although he felt a severe sense of pride in each funeral ceremony that he participated in, he knew this dead soldier's story and he felt unprepared for the emotion he suddenly felt welling inside.

Next to the roses, glistening in the humid air, a copper medallion with a blue ribbon had been carefully draped over the stars on the flag. For the first time in his life, the sergeant saw the Congressional Medal of Honor, the most sacred tribute a nation could bestow upon a man. Ten thousand soldiers could die in battle and not one of them would earn the privilege of receiving this award. It was rare, it was sacred, and too often it was given posthumously.

The sergeant's color guard stood stone still as the funeral procession approached, the mourners following the carriage as it moved toward the grave. And though the sergeant didn't focus on the family, he couldn't help but see her out of the corner of his eye.

She was small, maybe six or seven years old, with blond hair, slender arms and pale eyes. She glanced around anxiously, bewildered, fear and pain bleeding through the tight look in her face. Her mother walked beside her, a perfect reflection of the child: blonde hair, dark features and blue eyes. She was tall, slender and dressed in a simple white dress. No dark colors, the sergeant noticed—no black dress or mourning veil. And there was something strong and wonderful about her. Even in their sadness, the mother and daughter were beautiful.

The child approached the grave like it was a terrible monster, a dark gaping passage leading into the next world. Thunder broke and rolled through the trees. Deep, sad, and somber, the sound echoing across the wet ground as another thunderclap rolled and slowly faded.

A cold breeze blew at the sergeant's neck, raising the hair on his arms. "Please," he prayed, "give this family twenty minutes before You let Your rains fall."

With a flash of lightning, another thunderclap rolled across the rolling hills. But the rains didn't fall.

The sergeant had performed a hundred ceremonies over the past eleven months; indeed, this was the third funeral ceremony he had presided over on this day. But as he watched the black wagon and proud horse, as he saw the small child grasping her mother's hand and the Congressional Medal of Honor over the flag, he couldn't stop the emotion boiling up inside him. A single, salty teardrop rolled down his cheek to settle on his jaw before slowly sliding down his neck.

Too many funerals. Too many good men. Too many young children and too many wives.

*White roses for virtue. Red roses for blood.*

The family approached, stepping across the wet grass while staring into the darkness of the open grave. An army chaplain reached out and took the mother by the hand to direct her to a set of wicker chairs. The mother and child sat down carefully, the young girl gripping her mother's hand as if she was holding onto life. A crown of white flowers had been braided through her hair and she tugged at them gently to keep them in place.

The funeral procession formed a half circle on one side of the grave. The deceased soldier's parents stared solemnly at the casket. A man reached down and placed his hand on the widow's shoulder, and she leaned her face against his hand. Six generals watched and waited. To their right, two army captains stood in their dress uniforms, a shadow on their faces that seemed to age them somehow. A young woman with dark skin and long hair waited behind the others. A foreigner, Middle Eastern maybe, she was one of the most beautiful women the sergeant had ever seen. A small boy stood beside her; dark-haired, olive skin, darting eyes. Behind him, at least a dozen bodyguards blended among the heavy trees, all of them keeping a careful eye upon their charge. The young boy glanced quickly at the little girl, then lowered his eyes to the dirt, his face clouded with shame. One of the young officers noticed his reaction. He knelt down and whispered to him but the little boy didn't respond.

The chaplain nodded to the color guard leader and the sergeant commanded under his breath, *"Element, post!"* The six men moved forward in perfect step toward the carriage, three on each side. Without verbal commands, the men reached out, took the casket by the metal handles and lifted together. The casket was light, for it was nearly empty. The men turned crisply, carried the flag-draped casket forward and placed it over the nylon straps that had been stretched across the grave, and then stepped out of the way. The chaplain leaned over, whispered a few words to the widow, and then stood.

In that brief moment of quiet, one of the young army officers took a short step toward the casket. Looking around bashfully, he knelt and placed his hand on the flag. "You are my brother," he whispered through his tears. "I will love you forever. And none of us will forget . . . ." His voice trailed off. "We will always remember what you did for us . . . what you did for them." He knelt there a moment, his forehead touching the flag, then forced himself to stand and walk back.

The young mother reached out as he passed. He touched her hand with his fingers before stepping back in place.

Everyone fell quiet as they waited for the service to begin.

The chaplain straightened his uniform before he offered his final words. He spoke of simple things—duty, honor, bravery, truth, the obligations that came with freedom and the price that had been paid to keep people free. Then he nodded to the young widow and lowered his voice. "In a moment such as this, there is little comfort I can give you," he said. "Indeed, were I to say too much, my words might only diminish your loss. Only time and the Lord can ease you of this pain. But though I don't have the answers, this much I believe. All men will die. All of us will be called upon to pass on to the other side. But only a few special men are given the honor of dying for a cause.

"In this life, especially in these trying times, all of us will be called upon to make a sacrifice. When, or in what manner that sacrifice may be required, only God knows. All we can do is wait and prepare and pray that when our time comes, we will be ready to complete the task He gives us. All we can hope is that when our sacrifice is over, we might look to the Lord and say the same words that He said: 'I have fought a good fight, I have finished my course, I have kept the faith.'"

The chaplain paused and looked again at the widow. "I am so grateful there are still men like your husband in this world," he said in a low voice. "He fought for the freedom of others. That is why we fight wars. We don't conquer other nations; we don't occupy other lands. Indeed, the only foreign soil our nation has ever claimed have been tiny spots such as this where we seek a quiet pasture to bury our dead.

"So I speak for a thankful nation when I tell you that we are not only grateful to your husband, we are also grateful to you. We are grateful for your sacrifice and the price that you and your daughter have paid. Your sacrifice is sufficient. Your husband is now home. And I pray the Lord will bless you until you are together again."

With that, the chaplain took a step back and nodded to the color guard. Two of the soldiers stepped to the casket and lifted the American flag. Another sergeant marched to the side of the dark oak and watched over the grave. The sergeant lifted a silver bugle and began to play.

*"Day is done, gone the sun,*
*From the hills, from the lake,*
*From the sky. . . ."*

The sound of "Taps" was low and mournful and it trailed through the trees and across the wet grass, melting over the graves of the American dead. As the bugler played, the two solders reverently folded the American flag into a perfect triangle, tight and firm. The junior non-commissioned officer held the folded flag, clutching it with crossed arms at his chest. The sergeant took two steps back and stood at rigid attention, then quickly drew his fist from his thigh and up across his chest, extending his fingers as his hand crossed his heart, then moving upward until his finger touched the tip of his brow. He held the salute, the last salute, for a very long time, then slowly, almost unwillingly, lowered his hand.

Stepping forward, he took the flag from the junior non-commissioned officer, then turned crisply to the young wife. "On behalf of a grateful nation," he whispered as he handed her the flag.

She reached out and took it, placing it on her lap. The soldier passed her the Congressional Medal of Honor, and she clutched it in her hand. Then the soldiers turned together and moved to the side. The bugle faded away and the silence returned.

And with that it was over. The service was done.

At least it should have been. But no one moved, for it seemed as if there was something left unsaid. Every eye turned to the widow and her child. The young mother glanced down at the little girl and nodded. The mother smiled encouragingly and the little girl stood, moved slowly to the casket then turned hesitantly to her mother, who nodded again. The crowd waited in breathless silence. It seemed as if even the Earth held its breath.

The little girl stood for a moment, and the clouds seemed to part. The wind turned suddenly calm and the thunderclouds paused. The girl placed her hand on the casket, then lifted her head. "Daddy, I want to tell you something," she said in a quivering voice. "I want you to know that I'm going to take care of mommy, just like you asked me to do. I will make her cakes for her birthdays, just like I promised that I would." Her voice trailed off and she quickly looked away then turned back to the casket again. "I love you, Daddy. I want to believe the things you told me. But daddy, I'm scared. I miss you, I miss you! And there's so much I don't understand . . . ."

She fell silent, lowering her head in frustration then closed her eyes. Crossing her arms, she held herself as if in an embrace. No one spoke. No one moved. There was a reverence in the moment that no one dared to break.

How much time passed, no one knew, but the little girl eventually lifted her head. And when she did, something had changed. Something was very different. Her face was calm and peaceful. For the first time in months, her eyes were bright and clear.

Her mother pulled her close.

Then the little girl broke into a smile.

*******

Behind the thick veil that separated the natural and the supernatural worlds, other souls observed the funeral scene from the shadows of the trees. They were the dark and evil spirits the mortals never saw but often felt.

As had been the case since the beginning of man, these dark ones watched and listened, they studied and they plotted, their evil wafting like a heavy stench upon the world. And their power—Satan's power—was growing, their devastation having already brought the world to its knees.

A lean-faced spirit named Balaam stood among the unseen crowd. One of the darkest of the evil spirits, he was aggressive and mean. But despite his aggression, he was also insecure, for he had failed his master a few too many times before. Now, he only thirsted for more. More blackness. More evil. He was never satisfied.

As the group of evil spirits looked upon the little girl, seeing her courage and her smile, as they looked out on the strength of her mother and the bravery of the soldiers who stood so near, the dark and evil swarm could not hold back their pain and fear.

Together, they let out a scream of hate so clear it echoed across the wet grass into the very bowels of hell.

Balaam howled loudest among them, for he hated what the mourners represented the most.

# ONE

**Eighteen Years Before**

Prince Abdullah al-Rahman lay slightly inebriated on a beach on the southern tip of France. Behind him, the *La Villa de Ambassador II* rose above the shoreline, one of the finest resorts on the Mediterranean coast. The water was clear and a perfect blue sky shone overhead. Cyprus trees swayed in rhythm with the wind and the sand was so even it looked as if it had been raked. The grass above the beach was perfectly manicured, the air was clean and the water sparkled with a million diamonds from the Mediterranean sun. Behind him, on the other side of the wrought iron security gates that surrounded the *Ambassador II*, the beautiful resort towns of Monte Carlo and Nice lay equidistant, one city to the east, the other to the west. It was late afternoon as Prince al-Rahman sat alone on the sand, staring out at the sea.

Prince al-Rahman and his entourage had leased the entire *La Villa de Ambassador II* for the week; all 225 rooms, three gourmet restaurants, spa, golf course and private beach. For the next seven days it all belonged to him and his group of 97: bodyguards, concubines, wives and friends. Al-Rahman and his family had come to France to shop and get away from the desert heat, which meant that in addition to the cost of the resort, one of his wives had transferred several million dollars into their petty cash account.

But Al-Rahman wasn't interested in shopping. He had other things on his mind.

At twenty-five, the prince was young and trim, with a finely sculpted face and almost European features, thanks to his mother, an Italian beauty herself. He had a fine nose and strong eyes over thick lips. And unlike most Arabs, the prince didn't consider facial hair an indication of his manhood or his devotion to Allah, so he kept his face clean, his beard never more than three or four days old.

One of the wealthiest men in the world, Prince al-Rahman was the second oldest son to King Faysal bin Saud Aziz, monarch of the House of Saud, grandson of King Saud Aziz, the first king of modern-day Saudi Arabia. As a royal prince in the kingdom that held the largest oil reserves in the world, he and his family were unbelievably wealthy. There was no whim or desire, no pleasure or need that the prince could ask for and not have it given to him; and along with his wealth, the royal prince held the reins to great power, for the world economy revolved around oil and the politics of oil revolved around the Saudi Arabia peninsula.

Yet despite all his power and wealth, the prince was unsatisfied and always wanted more. It was as if he had an insatiable hunger, an unquenchable thirst. Like a starving man in the desert who was forced to eat sand, no matter how much he ate it did not satiate what he craved.

And now, what he had been given was going to be taken from him! His idiot father was going to pack up the kingdom and give it away. In the name of democracy, a completely foreign concept in this part of the world, his idiot father, King Faysal bin Saud Aziz, was going to destroy everything his ancestors had worked for in almost 300 years. He was going to give up the kingdom and institute a democratic regime.

All of it gone, in one generation, destroyed! Like a wisp of black smoke, his family's wealth would disappear.

He had to put a stop to it!

But how? What to do? The prince was completely distraught.

Then he thought of his older brother, the Crown Prince, and his blood boiled even more. Could he trust him? Would he support him? He really didn't know.

He cursed violently as the bitter rage grew inside him, a hot, burning furnace of equal hate for his father and lust for what he might lose. If it were not for his father . . . if al-Rahman had played his cards right he might have been king one day.

But his father wouldn't let him.

He was going to give the kingdom away!

The prince pushed his hands through the sand as he sipped at his beer. He was frustrated and angry, more so than he had ever felt in his life. The day before, as he was preparing to leave for France, the prince had fought with his father, a bitter argument that had turned so angry three of the king's bodyguards had been forced to step between the two men. And though the prince had argued and pleaded until he was blue in the face, his father hadn't listened, but instead cut him off.

"Leave me, Abdullah!" his father had screamed in a rage. "Leave me *right now* and never speak of this again! I do not have to justify my decision to you. Now go and forget it. I will not discuss it again!"

And so it was that al-Rahman found himself on the beach, fuming, his dark heart growing cold, his mind constantly racing, trying to develop a plan. His father was a fool. No, he was worse than that, he was selfish and stupid, a conceited old man! He cared not a whit for his children! He was a slithering fool, a spider in the corner, a poisonous snake in the grass.

The sun moved toward the sea as al-Rahman raged, leaving a blood-red horizon above the hazy waterline where the prince sipped his beer and kicked at the warm sand.

Then he looked up and saw a withered old man. Al-Rahman had not heard him approach, and he stared up in surprise. Cursing angrily, he pushed himself to his feet. He looked around for his bodyguards, but they were nowhere in sight. The old man stared at him and grinned.

"How are you Prince al-Rahman?" he asked in heavily accented English. His voice was weak and raspy, and he smelled of cigar smoke and dry breath.

The prince glared with contempt. "Who are you?" he demanded in a sour tone.

The man smiled weakly. He looked old and decrepit; fine white hair and large teeth were his predominate features, but he moved quickly and with an energy that belied his small frame. His eyes seemed to glow yellow from some inner furnace and al-Rahman wondered quickly how old the man was? He could have been 60 or 100, it was hard to say, for his face was blotched with liver spots but his eyes were young and intense. And though his face seemed ageless, he flashed a fast smile, his white teeth jutting brightly underneath a bony nose.

The old man pointed a slender hand to the east. "Your father is a fool," he said without introduction.

Al-Rahman glared but didn't answer. The old man waited, then ran a withered finger across his lips, wiping away a line of dried spit.

"Speak not evil of my father!" al-Rahman sneered angrily.

The old man scoffed, looked away, then glanced down the beach. "Al-Rahman, please, don't play the loyal son with me. There's no need to impress me. I know what's in your heart, and I don't have the time or inclination for role-playing right now. We need to focus on our enemies, those we both need to bring down."

Al-Rahman shook his head uncertainly, then shot a quick look back at the resort. Three men stood at the top of the trail leading from the beach to the pool. Large men. Caucasian. Determined. Dark glasses and dark suit coats to hide their sidearms. None of the faces were familiar and he swore to himself. It was suddenly very quiet, as if the sound of the street traffic on the other side of the hotel had stopped. He glanced east, down the beach to a line of low trees and saw another stranger standing in shorts and an oversized shirt. An enormous beach towel was draped over his shoulders and al-Rahman knew where his pistol was concealed. Behind him, in the distance, barely a bird on the horizon, a gray helicopter hovered above the coastline.

He glanced left and right, feeling naked, his gut tied in knots and his underarms sweating. For the first time in his life, he knew he was alone.

Where had his men gone? Cowards! He would have them shot!

Al-Rahman glared at the stranger, then nodded toward the hotel. "Who are they?" he demanded.

The old man looked up and hesitated, as if he didn't know.

Al-Rahman growled, "Come on, old man, tell me!"

The old man glanced at the bodyguards. "They work for me. That's all you need to know."

"Where are my people?"

"It seems they have left."

Prince al-Rahman shook his head in disbelief. Could it be true? He *will* have them shot! The old man watched him, then reached down and adjusted his loose T-shirt, pulling it down over his bony hips. "Don't blame your men," he said softly. "They did their best. My people are better, that's all."

Al-Rahman felt the panic rising, a knot of fear growing tight in his throat. His eyes darted up and down the beach, thinking of how he might escape. Another man appeared near the tree line. Al-Rahman looked in the other direction where a small schooner had planted itself on the beach. The two men who worked the small anchor kept a focused eye on the intruder.

His mind began racing. Was this a kidnapping? A murder? One of his rival cousins? He swore and looked down at the sand, then glared at the old man.

The stranger read the look on his face. "No harm, no foul," he said calmly. "You are not in danger. Your men are not far away. So relax and forgive me, but I wanted to speak with you alone."

"Who are you?" al-Rahman demanded. "What do you want?"

The old man smiled, then reached into his shirt pocket and pulled out a stick of chewing gum. He unwrapped it quickly and dropped the blue wrapper on the sand. "I want the same thing as you do," he answered simply.

"How do you know what I want?"

The man smiled again, his glowing yellow eyes burning bright. "I know the hearts of most men. I know how they think and I know how they feel. I know what they desire and what they are willing to do. That's what I know. And that's what I know about you."

Al-Rahman was quiet as the fear began to subside in his heart. He glanced past the old man. "How *did* you get past my bodyguards?" he asked. The old man dismissed the question, but waved a bony finger in front of his chest. "We need the royal family to hold on to power," he said. "Your father, the monarch, must not go through with his plans. The last thing we need is another democracy in the Middle East. I'd say the filthy Jews are enough, don't you agree?"

Al-Rahman certainly did, but he still didn't answer, and the old man wet his dry lips again. "Your father will ruin everything unless we stop him," he said.

Al-Rahman snorted in disgust. "My father is a fool," he answered bitterly.

"No! You are wrong. You might as well say the sun comes up in the west as to call your father a fool. The king is a *visionary*! The most dangerous kind. But he is no fool, I promise, and until you understand that you will be useless to me."

Al-Rahman stood silent. He wouldn't quibble over words. *Fool. Visionary.* "Whatever," he said.

The old man studied the prince, knowing he had not understood, but he also saw the fire of hatred and that was enough. "Your father isn't the only enemy you have, Prince al-Rahman!" he continued. "You have more enemies than you know of, and I'm not talking about jealous brothers, bitter cousins or betrayed friends. I'm not talking about any man in the kingdom who could do you harm. I'm talking about the only real enemy you have, the only real force that could take from both of us what we most desire in this life."

Al-Rahman stared at him. "What are you talking about?" he answered bitterly. Al-Rahman always spoke sharply—being raised as a prince made one prone to be rude—but his tone had changed now. His voice was soft and clearly interested.

"We can change things," was all the old man said.

Simple words. Certainly not threatening. No indication of menace or obvious harm. But something inside the young prince trembled. *We can change things.* Yes, that was something he would like to see!

The prince thought a long moment, then pushed the trembling feeling aside. "Who are you?" he demanded in a demeaning sneer. "Who are you, old man, and what can you do?"

The man cocked his head toward his left shoulder. "Oh a few things," he offered simply. "Like, I don't know. For example, we caused the American invasion of Iraq. OK, I overstated. We didn't cause it, at least not literally, but we certainly *facilitated* the natural progression of events. That's no big thing, I suppose. Nothing, except for what did it lead to? Twenty *trillion* dollars of economic contraction. Governments toppled. Governments on the edge. People rethinking their expectations for the next entire generation. A reordering of the security relationship between citizens and governments all over the world. The U.S. government is certainly among those who have been affected, taking advantage of the crisis to reorder things, at least as much as they could, with the men that were in place."

He paused, glancing toward al-Rahman. "Not bad, for a first step." His voice was sarcastic and disdainful. "And we could do it again. In fact, there's a chance that we will."

Al-Rahman turned away when the old man looked at him.

"As to who we are," the old one concluded, his dry spit bridging a white line between his lips. "Look where all the money goes today. Trillions of U.S. dollars being moved here and there. I know, I know, the saying is trite and overly simplified, but in this case it is at least partly true. *Follow the money, and the power.* That will tell you who we are."

The prince didn't move, the stiff breeze blowing back his hair. Although the fading sun shone upon him, he trembled again.

The old man turned to stare out on the water. "Now, do you want me to show you how to stop your old man?" he asked

Al-Rahman glanced around him, then was silent again.

The old man nodded. "Yes, I thought that you might. Now quickly. Come with me to the airport and I will show you a few things you need to know."

\*\*\*\*\*\*

A short flight later, the two men sat in a rented car parked on a side street, half a block from the American Embassy in Paris. It was dark and warm, and the Parisian streets were busy around them. Cement barricades blocked the street twenty yards in front of their black Mercedes-Benz SUV, and a contingent of *gendarmes* guarded the security booth near the barricades.

Prince al-Rahman shifted nervously in the back seat of the Mercedes Benz. A driver and another bodyguard sat in the front, but a dark, bulletproof glass separated the front and back seats. The old man sat beside him. Al-Rahman still did not yet know his name. The old man glanced at his watch, then began to explain. "The American ambassador is hosting a reception for the Saudi OPEC delegation," he said. "You probably know that. It has been in the news. The public explanation for the reception is to strengthen the American ties to the lead OPEC nation, but the real reason for the meeting goes far beyond that."

The prince shot a look toward his new friend. "What else?" he asked.

The old man shifted, moving himself forward in the seat. "The U.S. secretary of state will be at the meeting. They will sign a document that will guarantee the Kingdom of Saudi Arabia will not reduce its output of oil for at least the next five years. It will also guarantee Saudi Arabia will exert its influence to ensure that none of the other OPEC nations will reduce their production as well. In exchange, the U.S. military will reassign the First Marine Expeditionary Force to the military base outside Dhahran. See, your father, King Faysal, knows the transition to democracy may be difficult at times and having a U.S. military presence established again in the kingdom will likely reduce the threat of bloodshed and instability. So everyone gets what they want. The United States secures its desperate need for oil as well as a reestablished military presence in Saudi Arabia, and the king gets the stabilizing influence of U.S. forces for the next twenty years. That is the essence of the secret deal that will be signed here tonight. No one will ever know."

Al-Rahman nodded gravely. He had already heard rumors and he wasn't completely surprised.

The two men were silent and the night grew darker around them. The old man reached to the console between them and pulled out a package of cigarettes and lit up, the orange-yellow glow illuminating his scrawny face. He offered one to al-Rahman, who took it and lit up with his own silver lighter. The old man pointed to one of the *gendarmes* who stood near the cement barricades. "Do you see the young sergeant there?" he asked. "The one in the black hat?"

Al-Rahman moved forward on his seat and nodded.

"He has twenty pounds of plastic explosive strapped up and down his legs," the old man explained.

Al-Rahman grunted. He didn't believe it. The old man stared at him, reading the dull expression on his face. "You have a question?" he asked.

Al-Rahman grunted again. "Your guy does not have any explosives on him," he said.

The old man looked hurt. "Why do you say that?" he asked.

Al-Rahman pointed to two guards with German shepherds standing at the barricade. "Sniff dogs. If your guy had explosives, they would be going crazy right now."

"Hmmm, of course you're right. But you see, Prince al-Rahman, earlier this evening the dogs were exposed to a 50 parts per million whiff of hydrogen sulfide, a strong enough dose to destroy their olfactory abilities for the next ten days or so. Truth is, you could throw those dogs a stick of dynamite and they would happily retrieve it and drop it at your feet. Those dogs couldn't smell a skunk if it climbed on their faces and rolled on their noses."

The old man took another drag then continued, "In five minutes, at exactly 9:15 p.m., the young sergeant, our man in the black hat, is going to walk toward the embassy and talk to the canine guards at the door. He will be cleared to enter the embassy to use the restroom, but he will have to use the service entrance on the south side of the building. It will take him just more than three minutes to get inside. Once inside the building, he will make his way through the kitchen, toward the service elevator. The reception for the OPEC delegation is being held on the second floor, just above the main reception hall. He can get to the main hallway from the service elevator. Once he is in the main reception hall, he will detonate the plastic explosives that are strapped to his legs. Most of the east side of the building will come down in a grand fireball." The old man spoke as calmly as if he were announcing the future demise of rats. "We estimate forty or fifty casualties," he concluded. "Most of them will be Americans, but there will be many Saudis as well."

Al-Rahman turned toward him, his face stretched in surprise. "You're going to kill them!" he cried.

"No, al-Rahman. *You're* going to kill them. The decision is yours," The old man answered calmly.

Al-Rahman shifted, his eyes wide with sickness and fear. "But why? What is the purpose? What do you hope to do?"

"Our only purpose, Prince al-Rahman, is to test you. We want to know who you are. We want to know what you value and how far you will go. That is the only reason we're here. Now we have chosen to strike the Americans, but that hardly matters to us right now or at least in this case. Our only purpose in this exercise is to see if you will go along with us and find out who you really are."

"But," al-Rahman stammered, "if you kill the U.S. secretary of state . . . ."

"Relax," the old man answered as he pulled another drag on his smoke. "The secretary of state isn't scheduled to appear for another hour or so. He's not a target. This is just our little test."

Al-Rahman gasped, his heart slamming in his chest. "I don't understand," he sputtered.

"Oh come on, al-Rahman, it's not that difficult. Say the word, say one simple word, and the entire operation is called off. One word from you and *poof*, not a thing happens here. Say the word and that's it, we call the entire thing off. You and I say goodbye. You'll never see me again. I drop you off at a private airport where one of our executive jets is waiting to fly you back to the beach. You forget me. I forget you. This whole things becomes a strange dream, nothing more. Just say the word and you save the lives of your countrymen and some American civilians as well.

"But if you decide you want to join us, if you decide you want us to show you how to hold onto power, then don't say anything and at 9:21 p.m., fifty people will die, many of them Saudis, your countrymen, even friends. Many more will be injured, but I can't say how many for sure."

Al-Rahman remained silent, his heart slamming his chest in shock and fear. "I don't believe it," he stammered.

The old man studied him by the glow of the street lights. "Have you ever seen the result of a suicide bomber?" he asked.

Al-Rahman shook his head.

"Hard to explain what it looks like. Bloody . . . really bloody . . . a horrible mess. Pieces of bodies, bowels, heads, and ears. I've seen the face of a child lying on the street. No head, no bone, just the face, as if it had been surgically removed from the skull. I've seen dead hands reaching for something that was no longer there. Teeth and burned toes scattered on the sidewalk. And the smell, oh the smell! Burning flesh and charred hair! Smoldering bones is a smell that you will never forget!"

Silence for a moment.

"Everyone who dies here will be innocent," the old man then observed in a suddenly sympathetic voice.

Al-Rahman stared at his hands.

The old man looked at his watch, then looked harshly at al-Rahman. "You've got to decide," he commanded. "What are you going to do? Join us, and we help you. I can guarantee you power. Join us and I promise you will be the next king. Or say no and we forget it. We call off the mission and just drive away."

"I need time to think!" al-Rahman hissed.

"No, al-Rahman. You are young! I am old! I'm the only one who needs time!"

The prince frowned and cursed violently.

"I know it may seem a little awkward," the old man continued, "but you've got to decide now. This is how we do it. This is how we find out what's in your gut. If we give you time, you will think, you will rationalize and consider. You will weigh the pros and cons and come to a decision in your head. And that's not what we want. We want to know what's inside of here!" The old man reached over and tapped the prince on his chest. "We have learned this is the best way to know what's inside a man's heart. Will he kill? Will he flounder? Will he hesitate to act? Or will he move with the commitment we hope that he will? Trust me, Prince al-Rahman, this is a very effective test.

"If you really want to join us, you've got to have blood on your hands. If you don't want to get bloody, then we're not interested in talking to you. If you're not willing to go the extra mile, if you're not willing to sacrifice innocent lives, then you're not ready to work with us and we will say goodbye.

"But if you think I can help you, then you have to be willing to take a chance. You have to be willing to get bloody. And that's why we're here. So what's it going to be? You've got to decide, my new friend."

Al-Rahman was silent as his eyes darted widely in doubt.

The old man glanced at his watch. "Thirty seconds," he said. "Tell me what to do. It's up to you. Say you will do it or we say goodbye."

"No! Not right now! Give me a little time!"

"No, *Prince al-Rahman,*" the old man sneered his name now, "you must decide *now*. Join us and we can show you a way to be king, King of the House of Saud, one of the most wealthy and powerful men in the world. Join us, and we stop King Faysal's foolish plan. Join us, and we save you, but understand this as well. You will be joining a battle that goes far beyond what you see. You will be joining a battle that goes far beyond the simple struggle for power inside the Kingdom of Saudi Arabia. We have a much larger battle, a much greater war, a much longer vision and a much longer plan. And you will have to fight those battles with us if we fight this battle for you. Now that is all I will tell you. What are you going to do?"

Prince al-Rahman sat speechless, his mouth hanging wide, his cigarette burning to a long, gray ash in his hand.

The old man's voice rose, a snarl in his chest. "Fifteen seconds," he cried as he stared at his watch. "Commit now to join us! Tell me to kill your countrymen! Prove to me we can trust you! Now what are you going to do!?"

Al-Rahman leaned suddenly toward him, his eyes burning with fire. "You swear to me, old man, that I will be king!"

"I swear it," the old man cried shrilly.

"Swear you won't fail me!"

"I swear it, al-Rahman!"

Al-Rahman swallowed, then smiled and the old man stared at him. "Swear to me you will join us!" the old man hissed to the prince.

Al-Rahman didn't hesitate. "I swear it," he said.

"You will bring down this building?"

"Kill them all!" the prince sneered.

The old man looked at him a long moment, then smiled and relaxed. "So be it, al-Rahman. And welcome, my new friend."

The old man leaned forward to tap on the glass and the driver started the SUV and turned it around.

*******

As the black SUV drove away, the *gendarme* in the black hat stood and stared at its red taillights. He knew it was a go and he sighed wearily, the massive dose of Valium the only thing that kept him calm. He was a dead man anyway, he might as well go in a sudden explosion instead of being tortured to death. If he tried to hide they would find him, they had already proven that. He had a debt. They wanted payment. It was simple as that. So he had agreed he would do this so he could go without feeling pain. In return, they would take care of his daughter and the debt would be satisfied.

He sighed again sadly, then turned away from the receding taillights of the car.

At exactly 9:15 p.m., the guard turned and walked toward the embassy door.

*******

The SUV was two miles away and driving down *L'Infante Boulevard* when al-Rahman saw the flash of orange light behind him. He didn't hear the explosion or feel its expanding concussion, but the flash and rising fireball was strong enough to light up the night.

# TWO

Two days later, the old man and Prince al-Rahman sat together at a small café on a narrow and crowded sidewalk in the *Place du Casino*. The golden square of Monte Carlo sparkled around them, a sensory overload of beautiful sights, smells, and sounds. Both men had checked into the *Hotel Hermitage* the night before and were rested and comfortable in the morning air. They wore summer suits and dark shirts and they smoked as they talked. Native peace lilies, roses, and daisies created a natural bouquet around them and the air was heavy and warm with the smell blooming flowers. It was a lovely spring day and the flower shops, boutiques, art galleries and small cafés bustled with tourists, most of them overweight working stiffs from the continent and United States who had come to bask vicariously in the reflected glory of the young and beautiful. A few locals hurried through the crowd on their way to their minimum wage jobs that couldn't buy them a closet in the city, let alone an apartment or small home. Because it was Monte Carlo there was constant wealth on display, and the prince and the old man mingled comfortably with the ostentatious crowd.

More than a dozen security men subtly worked the sidewalks and streets, some of them Prince al-Rahman's, some of them belonging to the old man. The two sat at a small table on the sidewalk near a flowing fountain. For almost three hours they sipped French coffee and nibbled tiny pastries, deep in conversation. The old man did most of the talking. Prince al-Rahman sat straight, his eyes intense, sometimes incredulous, sometimes unbelieving. Yet, despite his eyes, he smirked constantly.

Al-Rahman had made a good decision. The old man had a plan. Just hearing his ideas was worth the "small" price of the blood on al-Rahman's hands.

"You will be responsible to liaison with our Pakistani agent," the old man gave his final instructions. "We have planted the seed, but it will be your responsibility to nourish it and bring it along. It will take several years of your undivided attention. We will take care of the security, but the rest will be up to you."

"And the objective?" al-Rahman asked. The old man had been talking around it for hours now and the prince was growing impatient.

The old man smiled smugly. They had finally arrived. It was time that the prince knew. The old man leaned across the table and whispered the objective, his breath dry and foul.

The Saudi prince listened, then pushed away from the table, his mouth hanging open, his eyes smoldering. "Impossible!" he sneered. "Do you think you are the first ones to try this? It has been tried many times before. All of them failed. And you will fail, too."

The old man snapped angrily back in his chair. "Are you stupid?" he asked, like irritated father scolding his child. "Haven't you been listening? Haven't you heard *anything*?!"

Al-Rahman slowly nodded. "I have heard every word."

"Then how can you doubt us?"

"I don't doubt you, my friend."

"Of course you doubt me. Isn't that what you just said? Have I completely misjudged you? Haven't you heard anything!?"

"Friend, I only wonder have you thought this thing through? Many of the best men have tried, and *all* of them failed. There are too many countermeasures, too much security. Everyone who has tried it has ultimately failed. And I'm sorry to say this, but it is my objective judgment that you will fail, too."

The old man thought a moment, then softened. "I don't think so," he said.

"But why not?" al-Rahman prodded eagerly. He wanted to believe him. He really did.

"Because we are patient," the old man explained. "Because we invest in the *future*. We don't demand results right now. Because we know it will take time, maybe ten or twelve years. Maybe more. But trust me al-Rahman, we will succeed. By then I will be old, I will be a dying old man, but I will live to see it. I will live to see our success." The old man sipped at his coffee, then took a deep breath and leaned forward again. "*I will live to see the burning glory*," he smirked sarcastically.

Al-Rahman shook his head. He couldn't help smile. "The burning glory," he repeated, almost laughing. "Yes, that's good!"

The old man laughed with him and then turned serious again. "Take care of our man in Pakistan," he commanded. "That is your only job. And you must learn to be patient. This will take many years. But the payoff will be worth it, I assure you of that."

A little more than three weeks later, Prince al-Rahman made his way to Karachi, Pakistan. For five days he explored the city, traveling anonymously, moving through the slums and markets, staying in a classic yet modest hotel. He was an oil supply businessman from Riyadh hoping to land a $500,000 dollar deal. He camped out at the *Hotel Karachi,* an old brick-and-marble structure that dated back to the colonial era, one of the very few centers of international commerce in Pakistan. He brought with him only four bodyguards, and he never talked to them or acknowledged them in any way, though he noticed them around him from time to time as he walked.

It was the first time he had ever been in Karachi and he found it nearly as despicable as he had been told. It was noisy. It was hot. It was the murder capital of the world. The men and women relieved themselves in the open, right out in the street, squatting over rusted holes drilled into the sidewalks before moving on. The children looked hungry and thin, and everything smelled; the food, his hotel room, the taxis and streets, there was a permanent odor of humans, animal feces, garlic and sweat in the air. Standing beside his bed, he sniffed at his suit. He would have it burned the second he got back to Saudi Arabia. He looked out on the street at the poverty below. How in the world did *these people* develop the technology to build a nuclear weapon? It was an incredible irony he could not understand!

But they had. And he hadn't. And so he was here.

For five days, he moved around Karachi, feigning low-level business meetings, looking and watching, wondering when it would come. He knew the other party was watching him, testing his patience while making certain he wasn't being trailed. So he waited, passing the time as convincingly as he could. By the third day he was growing impatient. By the fifth day he was furious. Who did this old man think that he was? Didn't he know with whom he was dealing? Didn't he have any sense?

He had been told they would make contact and until that time, there wasn't a thing he could do. He was completely at their mercy. But the whole thing made him furious and he raged like a chained bull inside.

Then, on the evening of the fifth night, Prince al-Rahman was sitting alone in a small bar in the back of the hotel. It was quiet and growing late when a small, mustached gentleman approached his table and nodded to him. "Come with me," he commanded without introduction.

Al-Rahman glanced around. Two of his security people sat and talked at the bar. He caught one by the eye and the bodyguard turned away, though al-Rahman could see he was still watching him through the smoky mirror behind the bar.

Al-Rahman didn't move. "Excuse me," he said.

"My master would like to speak with you," the stranger answered curtly.

"And who is your master?" al-Rahman replied, his heart skipping suddenly as he drew a quick breath.

The stranger lowered his voice. "Dr. Abu Nidal Atta, deputy director, Pakistan Special Weapons Section, principal advisor on national security to the Pakistani president."

Al-Rahman nodded slowly. This was why he was here.

He glanced toward his bodyguards, then stood and followed the man.

The meeting took place in a small room on the fourth floor of the hotel. It was a short discussion, direct and all business, and both men left satisfied.

It would be a very long time before Prince al-Rahman would see the Pakistani scientist again. Although they would work closely together, they agreed they would never meet face-to-face, always communicating through intermediaries, a very few men they could trust.

At the end of the process, both men would get what they wanted most. Prince al-Rahman would have his nuclear warheads. And the Pakistani scientist would become one of the richest men in the world.

# THREE

*The two men were not alone in the Pakistani hotel suite.*

*Lucifer had always been and he would always be among the mortals, standing close enough to whisper his lies in their ears. He walked and talked beside them, interacting with mortals through his temptations of violence, lust, betrayal, and a ravenous hunger for the dark things of the world. Those he didn't have, he tempted. Those who fought against him, he sought to destroy. Those he had already won, he directed, turning them into his servants in his quest to devastate the world.*

*And he certainly had al-Rahman; his body and his soul.*

*Lucifer, prince of all the evil in the world, watched the conspirators shaking hands and smiled before emitting a violent snarl from his throat.*

*Then silence.*

*Outside, the sky was growing dark and sandy, the wind kicking up dirt and dust before the coming rain. Standing in the shadows of the musty suite, Lucifer embraced the darkness of the night as the storm clouds gathered near. But he didn't stand alone. Behind him, invisible behind the thick veil that hid them from the mortal world, a cluster of other fallen angels waited for his command, rage upon their faces, cold stones of death within their sullen eyes, all of them dark and loathsome warriors in the battle to destroy. They seemed to sway together in agitated and filthy swarms; chanting, hissing, seeking strength from one another in their desire to kill, a stinking mass of the wretchedness, their faces dead and callow from their desire to destroy. Having sold their souls for nothing, having followed Lucifer into the depths of darkness, they had but one desire now: to share their pain and misery; to bring death; to steal any love, hope or happiness from the world's dying embers.*

*Balaam stood at Lucifer's side. At one time, Balaam had been one of Lucifer's most trusted lieutenants, a member of his inner circle, one of the most evil and powerful. But over the past few moments of eternity, Balaam had fallen from Lucifer's grace. Too many botched ideas and operations. Too many good things gone awry.*

*After his fall, Balaam was desperate to climb back up the ladder, willing to do anything in order to get closer to Lucifer who he hated with every fiber of his damned soul. It was ironic that he wanted to please the one he hated, but Balaam didn't care. Power and ambition drove him like an overheated furnace ready to explode.*

*Glancing in Lucifer's direction, but careful not to catch his dreadful eye, Balaam noticed the spider web of creases that ran from the corners of his mouth. Lucifer's masculine face was angry and unpredictable, his eyes pale and piercing and incredibly intense, questioning and suspicious behind a dark stare. His long fingers were elegant, though in the penumbra they looked bony and weak.*

*If there were one word to describe Lucifer it was cold. Cold skin, cold hands, cold smile, cold heart. Like an exquisite ice sculpture, yes, there was some beauty there, but there was nothing in his presence that invited an embrace. He was a bitter winter morning, ice chips running through his veins. There was no warmth or good within him. Like a dead and dried out insect, he had a hard and brittle shell. But inside he was empty, hollowed out with hate.*

*Over the years, Lucifer had taken on several names, some respectful, some offensive, some old and some new. In the ancient times, long before the creation of the mortal world, they had called him the Son of the Morning, but he hated that name now. The connotation was insulting. So he had taken on other names; Lucifer, Satan, Dragon, the Fallen, Rahab, the Deceiver, the Father of Lies. Sometimes he was called Master Mahan, but only in whispers, and always in the dark, when the angels weren't watching and the wind wouldn't carry the name.*

*But whatever they called him, one thing was clear: Lucifer was miserable. Balaam knew that. All his fellow demons knew it, too. Lucifer was powerful. He could work miracles to deceive or appear as an angel to the mortals; he could cite Scripture to make mortals unholy, believing they were on the right course while he soothed, manipulated, cursed and controlled. He could stir secret combinations, murder and sinister works in the dark. But he could never be happy. He was beyond any of that now. He was a dismal wretch, dark, ugly and perfectly miserable.*

*The only purpose that he had now was to destroy the mortals and their freedom, and then drag them down to hell.*

*Behind him, the dark angels continued chanting. It excited them to see the great plan of destruction take shape, the possibility of destruction pouring fuel upon their fire.*

*Lucifer felt the heat of their breath, the rage of their despair. He felt their power. It was his power. Without them he was nothing! And they had come so far!*

*A few more steps, a few more victories, and he could claim this world.*

*Lucifer snarled at his accomplishments, then looked upon the mortals once again.*

*It would take a few years. What they were planning wouldn't be quickly put in place. But he was patient. He had learned that lesson. It took time to destroy an entire world.*

*Thinking of what was coming, he felt the thrill of death run down his spine. His plan would kill a hundred million mortals. And not just any mortals, but the very worst kind, the filthy ones who lived in the land of freedom, stretching their sickening light of liberty across his world.*

*But he could kill them. Their country and their freedom. He could kill it all. That's what it all came down to. That's what the fight was all about. Simmering in the memory, the hated words slipped again into his mind.* And there was a great battle in heaven, Michael and his angels fought with the dragon, and the dragon fought and his angels: And they prevailed not, neither was their place found any more in heaven. And that great dragon was cast out, that old serpent, who is called the devil and Satan, who seduceth the whole world; and he was cast unto the earth, and his angels were thrown down with him.

*He remembered it very well; the defeat, the humiliation, every tear and battle scar. The war had taken place long before the mortals were even placed upon the Earth, but even now, the things that they were fighting for remained the same.*

35

*Liberty. Individual rights. The worth of a soul. Their ability to determine their own path.*

*"And that great dragon was cast out[.]"*

*Yes, they had cast him out. They defeated him! Humiliated him! But now, after eons of waiting, he had a chance to fight again, a chance to destroy everything that the Enemy had built, to destroy His kingdom and His glory, the freedom of His children, the liberty that a million souls had died for. He could destroy it all.*

*And that was something that was worth waiting a few more years to do.*

\*\*\*\*\*\*

*Balaam watched Lucifer quietly, then bowed and approached him in a quiver of fear. He hated Lucifer. They all did. But Lucifer was all Balaam had now and he worshiped him with every fiber of his damned soul.*

*"Master," he begged in a whisper.*

*Lucifer glared at him and snarled.*

*"Master," Balaam repeated while bowing so low his head and shoulders were parallel to the floor.*

*Lucifer waited a long moment, keeping his servant bowed. "What do you bother me with, servant Balaam?"*

*"Master, if I could . . . ."*

*"Say it, slave!"*

*"Master, I was thinking . . . sometimes I wonder . . . ."*

*The Dark One turned toward Balaam and pulled his hair to lift his head. "You interrupt my rejoicing, servant Balaam? It will be much better for you if you have something meaningful to say."*

*Balaam quivered but did not turn away. What he had to say was important, and Lucifer would see that once he had a chance to explain. "Deceiver, there are some children. They are young now . . . ."*

The brief moment of jubilation over what the mortals had agreed to do immediately fled from Lucifer's damned soul. "Children! What are you talking about?" he demanded in a terrifying voice.

"There are young ones," Balaam started. "Young, but strong. I think . . . I believe the Enemy has saved them to be born into this day. They seem to be the best, so capable, Master Mayhem, able to bring failure to our world. But if we can find them . . . identify them, we could destroy them before they grow stronger."

Lucifer stared at his servant as if he were going to snap him in two. Then he suddenly stopped and took a step back.

Could it be that Balaam was right?

Lucifer stood there, his eyes fading, as if he were looking upon another world, his vacant stare dark and empty as his face tightened up with rage. He stared into the distance for a long moment, searching the corners of the earth.

In his mind, he saw them; the good and faithful of the world. So many of them were coming. It made his skin crawl. He hated them. His stomach rolled, a magma of anger that was impossible to control.

The young ones. The great ones. Full of faith and destiny. Some of them were already here. Willing to fight and pay the price for freedom.

How dare they fight against him? How dare they intrude, with the final battle almost here?

How long had he been waiting?! How long had he been scratching and clawing for this day?! Too long! Far too long!

The end was growing near, the final crisis at long last here. But the outcome hung in the balance and nothing was assured. No one knew how it would end.

But this much he did know, for he had learned it in hard lessons fought since his downfall.

The final result wouldn't be decided by the presidents or within the mighty kingdoms or the great capitals of the world.

It was the ordinary people that had the power to save the world.

*Much as he hated to admit it, that was the bitter truth.*

*He knew it. His servants knew it.*

*The question was, did the mortals know it, too?*

# FOUR

Major Neil S. Brighton stared through the large plate glass window of his home office on Chevy Chase, Maryland. The old plantation house, a classic two-story brick Victorian with lots of polished wood and white paint, was large and quiet and smelled of pine. The house was almost 125 years old, but exceptionally well-maintained; and from where he stood, the major could look south and see most of the downtown Washington, D.C., skyline. The house sat atop one of the highest hills inside the Beltway, and from his second-story window it offered an exceptional view. The National Mall and national monuments were a little more than seven miles away. The George Washington Memorial, a pointed pillar of white bathed by enormous floodlights tracking skyward, jutted up to the east of the George Washington bridge. Even from this distance, he could see the glow of the lights that surrounded the National Mall. He jogged there daily; four miles, every afternoon come rain, sleet or shine. His secretary *always* cleared his schedule between 4 p.m. and 5 p.m. It was the only time he ever had to be by himself, which made it the most productive hour of his day. And as a former college boxer, he considered it a big deal to stay in shape. When asked how many pushups he could do, the answer was always the same: "At least one more than you."

And though he couldn't see it from his second-story window, he knew the White House was less than a mile to the north of the National Mall. He envisioned the security fences around the White House lawn, the covert bunkers for Secret Service personnel and the hidden surface-to-air missiles on the government buildings next door.

The major was very familiar with the White House. He worked there daily. Which was bad news and good news. Bad because it was a competitive, cunning, cutthroat environment, one that wore him down unlike anything he'd ever done before. Good because it certainly was exciting, the brutal hours aside. *"I work at the White House,"* he sometimes found himself thinking. *"How freakin' cool is that!"* The adrenaline kept him going. At least it did for now.

Before stepping out of his office, he checked his wall safe, armed the security system, pulled the tab to synch up the secure telephone to the next code of the day, flipped off the overhead light, then walked from the room. His wife had turned on the nightlight in the hallway so he wouldn't have to stumble to bed, and he started unbuttoning the buttons on his Air Force jacket, stiff with rows of ribbons, as he walked down the hall. *When was the last time Sara and I went to bed at the same time,* he wondered? Too long. And it made him sad. In the old days—the old days being when he had been blissfully happy flying combat jets, before he had been indentified with the *"audacity, initiative, and tenacity to make an excellent general officer,"* as his performance report had read—they would frequently lie alongside each other and talk well into the night. But now he was so busy with his new assignment with the national security staff that he hardly had time to think, let alone lie next to her and talk in bed. Truth was, nothing had prepared him for the demands of his job. Flying combat was a piece of cake compared to the political combat that took place inside the White House.

After undressing in the dark, he slipped into bed, exhausted. Sara didn't wake as she rolled onto her side. He laid his head on the pillow, but sleep didn't come. He tried to close his eyes but something compelled him to stare at the shadows that flirted through darkness.

The night was quiet, the moon hovering above the western horizon. Then a sudden wind blew, whistling with unexpected violence through the trees. Brighton listened carefully, something catching his attention in the sound of the wind. The windows rattled with each new gust, the fall leaves ripped from their dry branches to beat against the house. The wind picked up in intensity, seemingly coming out of nowhere, fierce and without direction. But it was a stormless wind, for moonlight continued shining through the venetian blinds, showing the skies were clear. He rolled to his side, watching the shadows of the blowing branches a few feet beyond his window then sat up on the side of the bed.

Like the wind, Brighton was agitated. He had been agitated all day. He'd been agitated for a week. *Something was coming.* He could feel it deep in his bones. Something *moving,* something *watching,* something that was bringing evil change.

He shook his head to clear it, but the feeling didn't go away.

He glanced at Sara, who remained asleep, her blond hair tossed about, the streetlight on her face. He watched her sleep a moment, her breathing heavy and slow, then she seemed to wince and pulled back, as if in her dreams she felt it, too. Neil reached out to touch her, placing his palm on her cheek and she leaned into his touch. But she didn't fully wake and soon was in deep sleep again.

Neil felt tight; a sprinter ready to explode from the starting blocks. He shook his head again, but the fear only settled deeper into his chest. The blackness seemed to consume him. He'd felt nothing like this before. He glanced at his wife, then, angry at the frustration, he pushed himself up from the bed.

He walked down the hall, pausing at the top of the stairs. He placed his hands on the rail, feeling the beautifully carved oak. He listened for a moment to the grandfather clock ticking at the bottom of the winding stairs, then took a deep breath, fighting the anxiety. He stood a long moment, alone, in the dark.

Then he thought of his sons, who mere children still. A feeling of fear sank into him and he turned suddenly for their room.

He opened their door just enough to let a crack of light cut into the hall from the nightlight by their junior beds, getting a whiff of baby oil and sippy cups half filled with milk; the musky smell of little boys he knew so well. He looked across the toys and picture books scattered across the floor, toward the wooden beds.

Ammon, eleven minutes older than his brother, lay sprawled across his small mattress, his hair, like his mother's, a blond tousle on his head. Luke, dark haired and lean, opened his eyes to look at him without really seeing, then lay back and went instantly back to sleep.

Having been driven from his bed by a dark power that seemed to move across the land, Neil looked at his children and wondered for the thousandth time, "*Who are you, really? Where did you come from? What are you doing here?*"

Although they were still so young, his sons were better than he was. He knew that already. They were more clever, more . . . he didn't know, but there was something about them that he couldn't deny. Something strong. Something . . . *focused.* It was as if they understood things he didn't, things they knew but couldn't tell.

Yes, they were stronger than he was.

But he was afraid for them now.

In a flash of foreboding, he imagined their future, so dangerous and unsure. The world was tipping; he could feel it, ready to roll onto its side. It wouldn't come at once, it would take a few more years, but things were going to change. A feeling of fear and uncertainty exploded in his chest. He wanted to take a step toward them but the sinking feeling almost dropped him to his knees.

"My sons," he whispered. "What is your world going to be like? What challenges, what heartaches, are you going to see?"

\*\*\*\*\*\*\*

*Balaam heard the father's words of doubt, recognizing the agonized expression on his face. He had seen it a million times before. Indeed, he was the one who had planted the fear within the mortal's soul. Now that he had planted it, all he had to do was make it grow.*

*He jumped into his lies, well-practiced from thousands of years of having been repeated. "There is no hope for them!" he whispered into the father's ear. "The world is too uncertain! They have nothing to look forward to, but doubt and fear. There is no good now, only worry, and that will only grow with the years."*

*The father paused, sensing the blackness of the lies that had been planted in his mind. He seemed to look around, then fell silent in the dark.*

*"They are not strong enough. You think that they are special, but there is nothing great or extraordinary about them. They are common! Merely common! What chance do they really have?"*

*Brighton grasped the doorknob, his fist tight around the metal. His sons seemed to grow restless in their sleep, both of them turning onto their sides.*

*Balaam pressed his cunning lies, sharing the darkness of his world. "Your country is growing weak now. What you're seeing is the beginning of its great decline. Chaos will follow! The world will come apart! Most of the world already hates you, and there is much more hate to come. Your economy will continue to crumble! The best days are behind you. Nothing but unrest and bitterness lies ahead."*

*Brighton gripped the doorknob tighter, feeling the anxiety well up in his chest.*

*"Your sons have no future!" Balaam almost cried now, his voice filled with bitterness and hate.*

*Brighton felt Balaam's influence so near that Brighton actually repeated the words: "No future . . . no future . . . ."*

*"The world is too dark now. And it will only get worse. Your sons have nothing! You have nothing! There is no more good or hope in any of your futures. This is my world. I have claimed it. And you would cry and quiver if you could see all of the misery I have in store!"*

# FIVE

*Allah is greater than any description*

*I testify that there is no god but Allah*

*I testify that Muhammad is Allah's Messenger*

*Hasten to prayers*

*Hasten to deliverance*

*Hasten to the best act*

*Allah is greater than any description*

*There is no god but Allah.*

*From the Adhan*

*(Muslim Call to Prayer)*

**Agha Jari Deh Valley**
**Twenty kilometers southwest of Behbehan, Iran**

Later that night, the same moon looked down upon another man who was about to become a father, too.

This one thought of himself as a fallen king, but that wasn't really true. He was not fallen, but denied, for fate had kept him from ever climbing upon the throne.

The young Persian was tall and slender, with brown eyes, a clean face, and short, wavy hair. He was handsome, almost regal, with a fine Roman nose, high cheekbones and widely spaced eyes of a prince. Indeed, in another time, under different circumstances, he would have been one of the kings, for the royal blood that ran through him was a thousand years old, and the fact that he wasn't was but a twist of timing and fate. Had he been born a few generations before he would have sat on a throne, along with his cousins and uncles, all of them tracing their roots to the trunk of that great royal family tree.

But it wasn't so. Instead, Rassa Ali Pahlavi was a Iranian sheepherder and sod farmer, a man who scratched out an existence, living from one season to the next, praying for rain, then praying for sun, praying for a harvest that could carry him through.

Here, in his country, the royal family name meant nothing at all, nothing but memories of disappointments and the failures of the generations long past.

So despite the fact that Persian royal blood ran through him, it bought him no advantage and he preferred to keep his lineage a secret, unwilling to be reminded of how his ancestors had failed. His own grandfather, the Great Shah Pahlavi, last in a line of Persian monarchs dating back to Cyrus in 559 B.C., had, through arrogance and corruption, lost the claim to his kingdom and been expelled with his family, leaving behind but a few, all of whom where stripped of any prestige, money or power. Thinking of the royal family's exile, it was as if Rassa could picture the ancient royals of Persia packing up their caravans and slipping into the desert. His family, too, had packed up their wealth and slipped into the night, transferred enormous sums of money into overseas accounts, loaded their jewels and their paintings, the riches of their kingdom, and sulked away with their caravans of wealth, disappearing into the dark. With the fall of the shah, his family's power and wealth—and worse, their ambition—had slipped into the desert and completely disappeared. Most of Rassa's family lived in far-away lands; fat and discontent, but too scared to come home.

Yet Rassa was not like them. He was neither fat nor discontent. And he was certainly unafraid.

Still, it appeared there was no turning back the clock. The age of Greater Persia had passed. The Rule of Pahlavi was gone. The timing of his birth had ensured he would live his life in the mountains, herding sheep and plowing fields, and never sit on a throne.

It seemed ironic to Rassa that so much was left up to fate. Fate and the Master. Timing and place. They could all be so cruel, the young man had learned.

But still, life was good. Rassa said those words to himself daily. It wasn't perfect, there was sadness, and no, he was not a prince. But that was all right. It mattered not. Life was *always* worth living, and worth passing on.

And on this night, at this time, that was his only concern. His young wife and their child. That was all that mattered to him now.

Rassa Ali Pahlavi, twenty-six and broad-shouldered, walked along the narrow trail that led through the trees, away from his village. Twilight fell quickly, and the shadows under the canopy grew dark as he walked. The jungle of trees along his path formed a perfect canopy and the air was musky and wet, almost salty from the wind blowing in from his back. Behind him, the briny salt flats ran parallel to the shore of the Arabian Sea, some twenty-one kilometers to the west, and the evening air carried the smell of salt water and decaying brine shrimp. The terrain between his village and the sea was steep and rugged, with narrow valleys and foothills rising from sea level to meet the peaks of the great Zagros

Mountains, the mountains that acted as a barrier to the mighty storms that rolled in from the Persian Gulf, a wall over which the clouds couldn't climb without dumping their load, leaving the valleys on the west side of the mountains rich, green, fertile and wet.

As Rassa moved off the trail and from under the trees, the evening light broke through. He climbed a grassy embankment that looked over his village, a neat square of squat, clay houses, wood fences and tidy courtyards surrounded by brick walls. The barnyards were filled with white and brown goats, dark-skinned children, gnarled plum and fig trees and tangled grapevines, a hundred years old. To his back, the mountain rose above his village; rich green grass and gray rock, with tiny pockets of snow in the highest crevasses left behind from the winter snows. The terrain sloped up to the mountain from his village in a near perfect half-bowl, rising ever more steeply until it merged with the rocks. An enormous wedge of granite, like a huge piece of rock pie, jutted at the peak of the mountain, almost 12,000 feet up. Lower, on the southern tip of the bowl, a thick forest lay, with large oaks and tall pines swaying in the dim light.

Standing atop the rolling crown of the hill that looked over his village, the young Persian looked back to the east where the rising moon was now low, a huge blood-red orb on the distant horizon. He could see the haze and humidity rising off the warm waters of the Persian Gulf. The moon soaked through the wet warm air.

Blood red and warm. Yes. That was right. Blood red and warm. Like the birth of his child.

Rassa thought quickly of his wife, Sashajan, a woman he loved more than he wished to live. She was young, she was beautiful, she was everything to him and as he stood there in silence thinking of her young face and anguished cries, as he pictured the consternation in the midwife's dark eyes and the feel of her arms pushing him toward the door, he felt a shudder run through him and the anxiety rose again.

His child was coming. On this night, it would be born.

Then he fell, his knees buckling, his arms heavy and weak. He put his hands together and bowed until his forehead touched the dirt.

He hunched there, unmoving as the evening grew still.

*******

It seemed to him as if time stood still. He wasn't asleep, but he saw it as if it were a dream. The vision was bright, but still misty, as if he were watching through a great gulf of distance and time. There was a sheen to it all, as if wet from heavy rain. He saw shimmering trees, wide and gentle, and an enormous stone gate.

She stood alone at the gate. He almost gasped out loud. She was so beautiful! Young. Strong. Dark hair. Black eyes that seemed to dance with light. Anticipation and excitement in every motion of her hands.

He watched her intently.

Did she see him, too?

She took a careful step toward the gate, a gaping hole leading to some unknown world. She paused and trembled, and then Rassa understood. She was excited, but scared, maybe even terrified. Yet she continued moving forward, unwavering, strong and confident!

And he knew, somewhere inside him, that *this was his child!*

She stopped and glanced toward him. Staring through the distance, she looked directly into his eyes. Then she smiled and nodded. *"Yes, it is true!"*

He gasped. It was a moment of joy so intense, so powerful and *pure* that he almost couldn't breath.

She nodded to him again then stepped through the stone gate.

*******

The vision faded quickly and soon it was gone. Rassa felt his chest tighten and a rush of blood flow to his head. A shadow fell over him and the enormous space between them seemed to grow suddenly more vast and powerful.

He found himself kneeling in the darkness, his head touching the ground. The night had settled around him and the hilltop was now dark. The evening wind blew, chill and dry from the mountain, and he felt a cold shiver run up his spine. Looking up, he stared at the dark night. Then he saw the shooting star. It flamed from the north, stretching across the entire evening sky, trailing a stream of sparkles that seemed to reach toward the ground.

*An angel falling from the heavens . . . falling to the mortal world . . . .*

He didn't move, his eyes closed, his head touching the soft grass. Finally, he took a deep breath, bringing himself back to this world.

Then he heard a voice speaking to his very soul.

*"This thing that is about to happen, know that it is my will."*

A deep sense of brooding seemed to seep into his soul.

*"This thing that will happen, know that it is my will."*

He held his breath and listened to hear the cry of his child. Hearing nothing, he pushed himself to his feet, turned and ran through the night down the hill.

# SIX

Rassa Pahlavi ran through the streets of his village toward his home. The half-moon had climbed, a burnt orb in the eastern sky just barely above the rocky peaks of the mountains. The air was calm. The sky was crystal clear and the stars were shining brightly, for the dark had settled in. Dogs barked as he passed, and he could hear the sheep bells tolling from the pastures to the east, but the baked brick and stone streets were deserted and dark.

He paused on the cement step outside his front door, then let himself in. He found three neighbors there, all old men, village leaders who had come to bless his home, bringing gifts for Rassa and Sashajan. He hugged them all, pressing his face against their cheeks, their beards pressing against the fine hair on his neck. He walked through the simple kitchen, past a set of wooded chairs and old table, a worn vinyl couch and small television, then stopped at the door to his bedroom and listened. He could hear movement and the sound of water being poured into the steel basin, then laughter, and hushed voices, then the cry of a child. He bowed his head and took a breath, then pushed back the door.

Sashajan was sitting up on their bed holding their child in her arms and he moved quickly to her. Her face, though drawn and weary, could not hold back her joy as she leaned to the side, her cheeks touching the top of her daughter's soft hair. The midwife worked around them. Rassa glanced to her as she pulled a clean cotton cloth across a small mattress and placed it inside the wicker crib that Rassa had constructed from dry reeds he had pulled from the banks of the stream that ran through the center of the village. He caught her eye and mouthed a quick "Thank you," then turned back to his wife and child.

Sashajan smiled, her dark eyes beaming brightly. She drew a contented breath, then held out her hand and Rassa touched her fingers lightly as he sat on the edge of the bed. The smell of talcum powder and olive oil rose from his new baby's body. The child was sleeping, her lips puckered into a tiny circle, her hands clenched into tight fists at her chest, as if she were bracing from some unseen blow. She was wrapped in a cotton blanket, her legs tucked tightly against her body. Her head was covered in dark hair, thin as silk, and the midwife had already pinned a tiny white ribbon on the crown of her head.

The young parents stared at the baby. Neither one of them spoke. Rassa felt a shiver run through him as the peaceful feeling settled again.

Sashajan looked at him, thirteen hundred years of tradition pressing heavily on her mind. "You have a daughter," she said, her voice quiet and apologetic. It was, after all, a wife's duty to produce a fine son.

Rassa stared at the child, thinking of the vision he had seen. "Yes, I know," was all he said.

Sashajan began to question, then glanced nervously to the midwife, who had stopped her work and placed her hands on her hips, ready to defend the young mother if Rassa were so foolish as to say the wrong thing. Sashajan turned from the midwife and dropped her dark eyes. "You wanted a son!" she said simply.

"No!" Rassa answered. "I want *this* child."

Sashajan looked up quickly, her eyes filled with relief. She squeezed the tip of his fingers. "Thank you," she whispered. There was far more meaning in her expression than most could understand, for it was a seal of their commitment, a commitment which surpassed the boundaries of their culture, the boundaries of their people's traditions or time.

Rassa stared at the infant that slept at Sashajan's breast. Reaching down, he lifted her carefully and pulled her into his arms. The baby remained still, and he bent and whispered quietly into her ear. "*I witness that there is no god but Allah, and I witness that Mohammad is the messenger of Allah.*" Words from Mohammad himself. It was the desire of all Muslims that these would be the first words a child would hear from their father's mouth as well as the last words that they would utter or hear before death. Rassa repeated, "*I witness that there is no god but Allah,*" then pulled his head back to look into his child's face.

She slept peacefully, taking shallow breaths, light as a bird sleeping in the palm of his hand. He placed his little finger inside her palm and the baby girl instinctively grasped it, her tiny fingers unable to extend around his finger. Then she opened her eyes and stared at him blankly. Her eyes were dark and deep, her face calm and unmoving, as if she were intent on keeping her thoughts to herself. Rassa stared at her and wondered how much was going on inside her head? Did she understand things . . . did she remember things? Is that why God made His infants unable to communicate? Did a child only watch and learn, or did they already know? Was she learning or forgetting during these first few days on earth?

Sashajan watched Rassa, then moved closer to her child. The infant turned toward her and it seemed that she smiled. Her lips turned upward, her eyes brightened, and her face seemed to beam. "Did you see that, Rassa!" Sashajan cried in delight, "she smiled at me, Rassa. I know that she did."

Rassa didn't answer and Sashajan glanced toward him. "Do you think she knows I'm her mother?" she asked.

Rassa answered slowly. "I don't know, Sashajan."

Sashajan lifted her finger to touch her new baby's cheek. Rassa watched her a moment, then lifted the child to his face. He dropped his mouth to her neck, feeling the softness and warmth of her flesh on his lips. "I saw you," he whispered so that Sashajan couldn't hear. "But where did you come from? I do not understand."

Sashajan glanced up, a questioning look in her eyes. "Rassa?" she asked him, "what are you saying?"

Rassa looked at his wife. She looked so young and so small, as if she had shrunken from the experience of delivering their child. She was pale and shaking, and Rassa knew that she was weak. He turned back to his child. "We will call her Azadeh Ishbel," he announced, lifting her to present her to the heavens. "*Freedom is my oath to God.*"

Sashajan leaned forward and placed her head next to his. "'*Freedom is my oath to God.*' Yes, Rassa, that is a good name. There is something about her—it seems to fit her perfectly."

Rassa smiled. "She is beautiful. She is Azadeh. Thanks be to God." He lowered his arms and kissed the infant's brow and she unconsciously tightened her lips into another tight circle. "Azadeh, I love you," he whispered as he placed the child in her mother's arms. "And though I don't understand where you came from, still I welcome you here."

*******

Before she left, the midwife pulled Rassa into the next room and spoke to him in a low voice.

"It was a difficult birth," she said wearily. "She is young, but not strong. It was very hard for her."

Rassa looked worried. "What do I do?" he asked anxiously.

"Let her rest. Keep her warm. *Don't* let her out of bed. I will come by first thing in the morning and see how she is."

Rassa felt his knees weaken. "She will be fine, though?" he asked anxiously.

*"Insha'allah."* "If God wills it."

The midwife studied the deep worry lines on Rassa's face, then patted his arm, her hands heavy and strong. "I have seen many women worse," she offered as she gathered her things. "Birth and death. Death and birth. The cycle of life carries on. Who are we to intervene in the will of God? But she is young and there is no reason to assume she will not mend in the next day or two. But she needs time to rest and recover from all the life she has lost. I can't do that for her, Rassa, and neither can you. But if you let her rest and keep her warm, she will be fine, I am sure."

Rassa swallowed hard. The midwife swept through the room one final time, then her work was complete, she let herself out the door.

Rassa returned to the bedroom. Sashajan opened her eyes as he walked in. "We are a family," he muttered as he sat beside her on the bed. "God has blessed us. We have reason to rejoice."

Sashajan nodded wearily. "I love you, Rassa," she whispered as he gently stroked her hair. She fell asleep almost instantly. Rassa sat on the bed and held her hand as the child, wrapped in her soft cotton blanket, slept at her side. Sashajan eventually rolled away from him and he tucked the covers around her back, then placed the baby beside her so that she could nurse. For a long moment he watched them by the moonlight, the night so quiet that he could hear Azadeh breathe.

He was a man. He had a daughter and a beautiful wife. And one day he was certain that he would also have a son.

Life wasn't perfect, but on this night at least, it was very good.

After some time, Rassa moved away from the bed, stripped off his clothes and pulled on a nightshirt. Moving carefully, he lay down close to the child, eager to keep her warm against the cool mountain air. As he lay on his back and wearily closed his eyes, he suddenly remembered the silent words again.

*"What is about to happen, know that it is my will."*

He felt his chest tighten and his mouth seemed to grow dry. It was a warning, he realized, and for the first time he grew scared.

He lay tense; his eyes open, staring into the dark, wondering again what God was trying to say. But eventually sleep overcame him and he slept restlessly.

He woke at the first light of the sun. Moving carefully, he pushed himself out of bed, then turned to look at his wife and daughter. Azadeh was staring at him, her eyes dark and wide. She followed his movements as he walked around the bed. Sashajan was still asleep and he bent carefully to kiss her cheek. It was cold, almost clammy, and he carefully studied her face. Her lips were tight and so dry that they almost looked blue. He placed his hand on her forehead and felt the shiver of cold. He panicked, his heart racing, as he bent to her side. "Sashajan!" he whispered, trying to wake her.

But a blood clot had already lodged firmly in her brain.

She never regained consciousness and by afternoon, she was dead.

*******

After the spiritual rituals and cleaning of the body had taken place, Rassa led a procession of mourners up a winding, dirt trail. Behind a small hill, ancient stones had been set into the soil in an intricate pattern, establishing the area as holy ground with the same rights and benefits as a mosque. Tucked away in a small dell, the cemetery was a little square of grass completely out of sight from the village. Although it was small and almost 800 years old, there was always enough room for one more. The mountain villagers were practical people, having been taught by hard life, and they accepted death easily. Out of sight, out of mind, was their thinking when it came to their dead and once the mourning was over there was no need to be reminded of those who were no more.

But Rassa wasn't like his people. And he didn't accept Sashajan's death. Like his ancestors, the ancient Persians, he was romantic and soft-hearted, and he missed her so much that his heart ached in his chest, each beat pounding at him like a drum of pain and despair. He hardly saw the sunlight around him, so thick was the blackness inside.

And though he didn't see it, it was a beautiful day, warm and sunny, with a light breeze from the sea. The sycamore trees were in full color, and the grass was still green and full. In another month, the cemetery would be covered with dead grass and brown plants, but for now it was beautiful, alive and green.

Rassa led the mourners while desperately holding his child. Dressed in a white gown that flowed from her head to her feet, she was a sparkle of light in a sea of black turbans, long robes, dark scarves and long veils.

Rassa laid Sashajan to rest, somehow believing he would see her again, then dropped a handful of dirt on her pine casket and walked away, following the winding path that led to his home.

That night, he held his newborn baby in his arms while feeding her a bottle. She watched him intently and he couldn't help but smile as she stared into his eyes. "What are you thinking?" he wondered. "What emotions are you hiding behind that deep stare?"

Azadeh looked away, then yawned deeply, clenching her fists to her side. She fell asleep quickly and Rassa held her tight. The house grew quiet and dark, the rocking chair creaking on the wooden floor. Rassa kissed her cheek then sang in her ear:

*"The world that I give you
Is not always sunny and bright.
But knowing I love you
Will help make it right.
"So when the dark settles,
And the storms fill the night,
Remember I'll be waiting
When it comes,
Morning Light."*

\*\*\*\*\*\*

Two weeks after the funeral, Sashajan's sister came to him and insisted that she be allowed to take the child. "It is not a man's job to raise her," she demanded.

Rassa turned away and looked at Azadeh sleeping contentedly in her crib. She had grown full and healthy in her first few days of life and the formula that he fed her seemed to keep her satisfied. He watched her a moment, then shook his head.

Allah had sent her to him. She was all he had left. He would keep her and raise her. It was Allah's will.

\*\*\*\*\*\*

The next day came and then passed, then another after that. A week, then a month, then another month came and went. It was summer, it was fall. The snows came, and then the spring, then another spring after that.

Rassa fell into a routine. And though he had opportunities to remarry, he never could find the heart, for the image of Sashajan's face never quite left his dreams. Every year, on the week of the anniversary of her death, he left the child at Sashajan's sister and disappeared for a day of private mourning. No one knew where he went, though a few of his friends tried to guess, and when he returned he always brought wildflowers, which he placed on her grave.

Azadeh grew into a stunningly beautiful young woman. Rassa continued to love her more than he loved anything, for the emptiness inside him seemed to disappear when she was near.

And the time that passed soon slipped into years.

# SEVEN

Eighteen years had passed since the night Major Brighton had stood outside his son's bedroom door, listening to the frightening wind while fighting the silent fear.

Since that night, he had left his assignment at the White House to lead a fighter squadron in Alaska, came back to Washington, D.C., to be fill the dreaded staff job at the Pentagon, then down to take command of the First Fighter Wing at Langley Air Force Base, where he earned his first star. From Langley, the new general took an assignment at NATO, then back to the Pentagon (very happy that he and Sara had decided to keep the old house), then on to Central Command where he'd overseen aerial operations over Southwest Asia, the most hostile and war-torn region on earth.

The day he earned his second star, he got another call from the White House. A new president had come to power. The president knew of General Brighton.

It was time for him to come back to Washington, D.C.

*******

Major General Brighton stood at the office window of his home in Chevy Chase, the old plantation house that had been the family home for almost half of his military career. Everything about it was familiar. The smell. The old wood. The creak on the stairs. The slope of the basement floor. Although they had moved every couple years, it seemed they always ended up back here and his family considered the Victorian house to be their permanent home. It was full of happy memories and he was glad to be back in the old house.

He looked out on the city, seeing the glow from the lights on the National Mall, thinking of the huge floodlights that illuminated the grounds around the White House where he worked once again. He had a slightly larger office than he had before, though it was still tiny compared to others he had occupied throughout his military career. The underground parking lot was larger now, the environment more chaotic, the security procedures he had to go through every day far more thorough.

He took a deep breath and wondered for the thousandth time, "*Who am I kidding? I'm just a farm boy from Texas. What am I doing here?*"

He stood still for a moment, thinking on the passing years. Since his first assignment at the White House, so much had changed. The world was different now. So much had gone wrong.

At 45, Brighton was still tight and lean, with a strong jaw and laugh lines on the corners of his mouth, but over the past couple months his hair had taken on a hint of gray. His job was prone to do that. Truth was, he hadn't slept a full night since returning to Washington, D.C.

The thrill of being a White House insider had long since faded away, suffocated by the stress of working in the most demanding environment on the planet. A military officer inside a very *civilian* White House. Staffers viewing him as an enemy at every turn. A boss who was as demanding as Genghis Khan, the weight of the world upon his shoulders. The world going crazy all around him. He remembered a time when working at the White House, the *White Thrill* as staffers called it, made up for the sacrifices he had to make. But those days were long gone, leaving little that he enjoyed about his job.

He glanced at the old English clock on the faux mantel. Almost midnight, and here he was, still dressed in his air force blues, the formal uniform he wore to work every day. As military liaison to the national security advisor, one of the most demanding jobs in the entire Department of Defense, he hardly had time to think. He took his secure cell phone with him to the bathroom, the shower, running, outside while working in the yard. He kept it by his bed at night. It was like his pants and underwear, he felt utterly naked without it. And it didn't just ring with an emergency every once in awhile. It rang every day. Sometimes every hour. Nothing was as demanding as the job he held now; not flying fighters, not commanding a combat wing, not masterminding an air war—nothing compared with the pressures he dealt with daily. Eighty-hour workweeks were the norm. He was exhausted all the time. He knew his family was suffering. Surely his sons resent it! How could they not? But he didn't know what to do.

His only comfort, his only consolation at all, was that his wife had assured him that he was doing what he was supposed to do. *"Don't worry about me. I'll take care of things at home. What you're doing is important. I think it is part of the reason you were brought into the world. Besides, someone's got to do it. And I really believe that no one else will do it as well as you."* Sara had written the words of encouragement on a yellow slip of paper and tucked it in his uniform pocket one morning several months before. After reading the note, he had folded it up and kept it in his wallet. He was certain she didn't even remember writing it, but during the most difficult times he found himself pulling out the wrinkled slip of paper and reading her words again.

He stretched, feeling the stiff fabric and the pressure of all the ribbon bars on his chest. He missed wearing his flight suits, they were much more comfortable, and he certainly missed flying, especially after days like today. His morning had started with a private meeting with his boss, the national security advisor, after which he had suffered through no less than 14 appointments, then ended with a reception at the Libyan

Embassy, a typically stuffy and formal affair, the kind his wife enjoyed and he absolutely despised.

Then he remembered how beautiful Sara had looked in her black dress and suddenly the evening didn't seem like such a waste. *"Sara, oh Sara,"* he thought to himself, *"when I asked you to marry me, did you know I would drag you from one corner of the world to the next? Did you envision the challenges of the life we would choose?"*

He wondered, supposing not. It had been a wonderful journey, but not without cost.

"Sometime soon," he frequently promised himself, "things are going to change. Life will slow down."

The general breathed deeply, knowing it probably wasn't true.

He glanced at the clock again, then turned to check the wall safe and security system before turning off the lights. He had to get up in five hours and it was time to get some sleep.

As he was reaching for his bedroom doorknob, his secure cell phone started ringing, stopping him in his tracks. "Please go away!" he mumbled. "It's late. I am tired. Let it wait until morning."

But the STU-IV secure cell phone continued ringing and he turned to pick it up, noticing on the digital screen that the call was coming from the CIA. "Yes," he said as he put the phone to his ear, the delay from the encryption providing a noticeable delay.

"Sorry to bother you, boss." Brighton recognized the voice of a junior member of the security team. "Colonel Jensen and the night watch have a little problem with the PDB."

Brighton shook his head. The *Presidential Daily Brief.* Every morning at the White House. The president attended. *No* screw-ups were allowed. None. No forgiveness. Another beast that had stolen his life away.

"Do we need to take care of it tonight?" he asked, trying to keep the impatience from his voice.

"The watch supervisor said it can wait until morning, but they need you in by four."

"OK. I'll be there." He glanced at his watch. Then he remembered. "No, no, I almost forgot. I'm leaving for Saudi Arabia day after tomorrow. I've got briefings with the guys at the Pentagon in the morning to wrap up a couple things before I go. You're going to have to call my deputy."

"Of course, sir. The watch supervisor must have forgotten. I'll give Colonel Hampton a call."

"Tell him I'm sorry, but he's going to have to handle it." Brighton wasn't worried. Important as it was, the PDB was one of the least of his concerns. "Anything else?" he asked.

"No sir. Sorry for bothering you. Have a good trip, sir."

"Thank you, Patty. Good night." Brighton hung up the phone.

He had barely turned out the light again when the secure cell phone started ringing a second time. He stared at it in anger. "Brighton!" he said abruptly as he jammed it to his ear. He hadn't noticed the call was coming from the White House.

"Major General Brighton?" a communications specialist asked.

"Yes."

"Sir, this is Sergeant Bendino at the CIC communications center. I have a call from Prince Saud, crown prince of Saudi Arabia. We have traced and authenticated the phone number to verify it is coming from Riyadh, but voice recognition has not confirmed his identity. He wants us to patch him through."

"Crown Prince Saud bin Faysal?"

"Yes, sir. That is who he says."

"Then of course, patch him through."

"Sir, do we need to notify the operations desk?"

"No, Sergeant Bendino. I suspect this is a personal matter. I have known the crown prince for a very long time."

"Yes, sir. But you realize, of course, that as with all communications with foreign heads of states, these communications will be recorded and monitored."

"I understand, sergeant. Now please patch him through."

The secure satellite line clicked and then buzzed and then fell silent again. "Neil?" he heard the prince's deeply accented baritone.

"Your Highness! How are you? I hope everything is OK?"

"OK? Yes, of course. Everything's fine."

Brighton considered the differences in time, knowing it was early morning in Saudi Arabia. "It's good to hear from you, Prince Saud. It's been a long while."

"Too long, general, too long. Listen, I know it is late there, and I don't have much time, but I heard you were flying over to meet with some of my air force leaders. I would hope we could get together. Nothing special, just an hour or two to catch up on, how do you Americans say it . . . older times?"

"Old times, Prince Saud."

"Old times. Of course. Anyway, could we try to get together?"

"I'd be honored, your Highness."

"Excellent, Neil. Now listen, I'm going to be in Medina for most of the week, but I'm going to fly back to meet you in Riyadh. I'll have my people give your staff a call and work out a schedule. Will that be all right?"

"Of course, Prince Saud. Whatever you want. But let me ask, is this important? Anything formal? Do I need to do bring my staff or do anything to prepare?"

The line was silent a long moment, and Brighton could hear the prince breathe. "Nothing important, Neil," he finally answered, "It is a personal matter. That is all."

The general sensed the hesitation and was about to press but the crown prince spoke before the general could say anything. "Same number at the Pentagon?" Prince Saud asked.

"The switchboard will always get you through."

"OK, then my friend. I look forward to seeing you."

The phone clicked and went dead and the general pocketed the secure cell phone in his pants. He turned again for the bedroom door.

# EIGHT

*During the millennia that passed since Balaam had been cast to earth, he had claimed many souls; a million, perhaps ten million, he really didn't know, for once he had destroyed them he never thought of them again. And though he and his fellow fallen angels had mastered the art of destruction, it was not always easy, and this one lesson they had learned: never give up. Everyone had a weakness. Even the great could fall. Think of Cain. Think of Judas. Think of King David and a million other souls. Many of the strongest had been taken and everyone was fair game.*

*Through the years, Balaam had seen it all until he reached the point where there was no pain or disappointment, no depravity or torture, no betrayal, hate or hurt he had not mastered. He had been there and cheered when Cain had lifted the stone. He had witnessed Abel's blood flow and learned the power of greed. Soon after, he and the other fallen angels realized the astonishing power of lust and its incredible potential to destroy. It was a short step from lust to far greater sins. Soon, there was no aberration or depravity they had not introduced to the world.*

*Over time, Lucifer's followers had developed a real love for the blood and horror of war. How many battles had they started, then watched the outcome with glee! Armies were their playthings, the cries of the dying sweet music to their ears. In his mind, Balaam could smell the smoke from the fires and the stench of dead flesh. He could hear the cries of broken mothers as their children had been tortured and taken as slaves.*

*In one particularly brilliant display, Balaam had convinced a young mother to sacrifice her own children to a pagan god, a moment they all remembered with particular pride. And they had called it religion! Even Lucifer had laughed. On another night, Balaam had laughed while Judas put a rope around his neck, promising the mortal he'd keep on fighting to the end of the world.*

*Looking down on the Iranian village from the hills up above, Balaam thought of all of the millennia that he had wandered the Earth, considering all of the changes*

67

*he had witnessed. He had seen great cities rise and great nations fall. He had seen deserts grow out of marshlands and the seas flood their coast. But now Earth was growing old. He shook his head in anger and snarled a hot stench of breath. So much time had passed!*

*Short! Time was short! And still so much work they had to do!*

*Yet, as he stared down on the Iranian village, he felt the pull of something large. Something strong and great and powerful. Something that brought him great fear. It was here. Something dangerous lived in the village.*

*Someone who could hurt him.*

*He had to discover who it was!*

# NINE

The ground above the Agha Jari Deh Valley rose sharply to the west. There, on a rocky spot looking over the haphazard village, an ancient guard tower rose like an arm and fist from the ground. The tower was made of stone cut from the mountain and stood almost sixty feet above the sloping terrain. The base of the tower was some forty feet wide, the granite walls six feet thick, with a large and high-ceilinged room inside. A single metal door allowed access to the ground floor room and a narrow set of wooden stairs along the back wall wound up to the top of the tower. In ancient days, the tower was manned constantly to provide warning to the villagers when an attack was imminent. In the early years, or the lean years, when the population of the village was small, most of the village's women and children could be crammed inside the base of the tower. There they would huddle while they listened to the sounds of the battle outside.

The tower, known as *el Umma*, or the community, had through the years fallen into deep disrepair. The huge metal door was nearly rusted off its hinges, and the steps were so dry and rotten they sagged mightily under even a little weight. But the tower was one of Rassa's favorite places to think, and through the years he had retreated there many times to ponder and pray.

The day before Azadeh's eighteenth birthday, he got up early and hiked the steep trail that led to *el Umma*. It was spring, but the hay was coming near to full, and his day would be busy for there was much work to do.

Rassa entered the tower just as daylight was beginning to break. Inside, el Umma smelled of mold and dust and ancient, rotting wood. Four-inch slits in the rock walls provided light to illuminate dimly his way as he climbed the stairs and every ten or twelve feet the walls were scorched and black from where oil-soaked torches had been attached to the walls, suspended by steel latches that were embedded into the mortar and stone. He climbed carefully, testing each step, though he was familiar with most of the weakest boards. The sun was just rising between two of the highest peaks when he emerged at the top of the tower. A round rampart with a short wall provided a barrier to keep him from stepping into space. Rassa knelt, facing Mecca, and bowed his head for prayers, then sat back and leaned against the tower, the rising sun to his back.

He kept his eyes open, looking out on the sea. The sky was clear, and a cold front had moved through in the night, clearing the air of haze and humidity. From where Rassa sat, he could see most of the eastern coastline of the Persian Gulf, the dark waters stretching north and south, lapping at the brown sands and dry foothills that made up the Iranian coast. The sea was hazy and gray, and sparkled in the rising sun. Looking north, he could clearly make out the oil platforms and pipelines that crossed the shallow waters of the gulf. Further out, he could see the drilling platforms and pumping stations of Khark and Ganaveh, the heart of one of the richest oil fields in the world. A row of tankers, perhaps four in all, lined up at the Bandar-e Bushehr offshore pumping station to take on their load. Even from this distance, he could see those that were already loaded with oil, for they sat much lower in the water than those that were waiting to be filled. After filling their holds with Arabian crude oil, the tankers would steam south and east, through the Straits of Hormuz and into the Arabian Sea. It would take the tankers several weeks to reach their destinations in Japan, Taiwan and the southern U.S. gulf ports. Rassa watched with only casual interest, for the Iranian oil fields meant very little to him. He benefited not at all from the incredible wealth that was generated through Iranian oil production, and because he had been watching the oil tankers since he was a child, there was little there he had not seen before.

Yet as he stared to the west, something did catch his eye. Far out at sea, maybe twenty kilometers off the coast, a monstrous ship steamed into view. It started as a gray dot on the southern horizon, but grew quickly, and Rassa watched it carefully. As the ship moved closer, he saw the deck and the enormous, steel mast, and he knew it was an American aircraft carrier. The carrier cut through the water, its sharp bow slicing through the three-foot seas, and made good time as it cruised to the north. If it hadn't penetrated Iranian coastal waters, it must have been very close. Minutes later, Rassa saw one, and then two, aircraft launch from its deck, pointed-nose fighters that disappeared for just a fraction of a moment below the carrier's deck, then formed up together and turned to the west. Rassa could tell from their shape of their wings that the aircrafts were F-18 Hornets.

The fighters accelerated, then pulled their noses steeply into the air and disappeared beyond a high strand of gray clouds. Rassa watched them, curious, then something else caught his eye. To his right, along the mountains, he saw two Iranian fighters, old Iraqi MiG-29s that Saddam Hussein had sent over the border to Iran during the first hours of the Gulf War and which the Iranian government had never returned. The MiGs screamed in from the north, low and fast, following the contours of the mountains before turning toward the brown sands of the coast. The MiGs always stayed away from the international waters, and certainly never ventured near the American carrier as they circled over the coast, though one made a feint for a U.S. destroyer before quickly turning away to fly back over the coast. They were flying very fast and they soon disappeared behind him, heading back to their base, already running low on fuel. Like everything made in Russia, the fighters were loud and fast, but they drank fuel like an elephant drinking water from a glass.

Rassa watched with interest. He had seen the game of cat and mouse before; an American carrier group would move up the coast, flanked by escorts and destroyers while launching their Hornets on combat air patrols. The Iranian (or, in the old days, Iraqi fighters) would follow the American ships, watching and teasing in their own show of force. Rassa wasn't a military man, but he suspected if the U.S. fighters ever got serious, if they ever made a turn for Iranian fighters, his brothers would run. It was one thing to tease. It was another to get blown out of the air.

As Rassa watched, he realized such scenes were far more common over the past several months than they had ever been before. And he had witnessed other things, things which worried him and were only whispered about by a few. The government was very close to maybe six nuclear warheads. Such would be a game changer, everybody recognized, even poverty stricken people in remote villages such as his. And with unstable governments springing up throughout the region, everyone was on edge, including his masters in Tehran. Now there seemed to be a constant line of army convoys moving up and down the coastal highway. Some said these army units were there to act as a barrier to the constant flow of insurgents and foreign fighters who hid out in the Iranian deserts, where they had established base camps from which they would train and prepare for strikes into the struggling Iraqi democracy. Some claimed the Iranian army wasn't there to stop the rebels, but to provide them training, as well as food, money, ammunition and aid. Rassa had also recently seen many more American warships than he had ever seen before. Normally, the Americans would keep their battle groups much farther to the south, rarely venturing much farther north than the northern coast of Bahrain, but lately the American ships regularly docked at the Iraqi ports near Umm Qasr, as well as the ports at Kuwait. And there seemed to be many more western oil tankers in the Gulf. He glanced again to the offshore loading docks at Bandar-e Bushehr. On any given week, he might see one or two tankers load up at the port, but over the past year or so, and especially over the past several months, the number of American tankers had doubled, even tripled. And Rassa wondered why.

As he watched, the American aircraft carrier turned forty degrees to the west and was soon out of sight, though an escort trailed behind, staying between the carrier and the coast. There were no longer any fighters in the air, and Rassa shifted against the tower to look on his village below.

Agha Jari Deh was an ancient town, with maybe a little more than four thousand people, a number which hadn't changed much over the past couple centuries. From where he sat, on the top of the tower that was uphill from Agha Jari Deh, Rassa watched his town come to life. He saw a pair of *mutawwa*, the religious police, walking the streets dressed in their black turbans and white robes, ready to enforce the morning call to prayers. In the center of the village, a new civic center was being built, a modern brick building going up alongside ancient mud huts reinforced with palm leaves and logs. The *suq*, or village market, was exactly as it had been for almost five hundred years. The money changers were out, already clinking their coins to advertise their business as the merchants set out their wares—flour, copper, peaches, fine rugs, ancient spices (catalyst of too many wars), coffee, tea, sugar, holy water from Mecca, pistachios, goat meat and finely thin cuts of lamb—everything needed for daily life could be bought in the market. The streets were busy with pedestrians, bicyclists and motorcyclists, but there were also many more automobiles than there used to be, including Mercedes Benzes and Land Rovers brought in from Europe. Islam had never preached that it was a sin to grow rich, and many of the villagers had grown relatively wealthy working the offshore oil fields or trading with those who came to the market daily. From where Rassa sat, he could see the fault line that ran almost straight through the middle of the town. Every hundred years or so, a powerful earthquake shook apart his village, but afterwards, whatever houses or shops that were shaken down were quickly rebuilt. His people were not easily rattled and what they lacked in resources, they made up in tenacity, patience and reduced expectations.

The sun was rising now, and it was quickly growing warm. Rassa felt drowsy and peaceful, and he considered for a moment his home and life.

Rassa was a simple man, but he was not unlearned, having been educated in one of the finest private schools in the region (one of the few benefits of being a descendent of the shah) and he knew this place where he stood truly was unique in the world. He surveyed his village, a place whose roots dated back almost 2,500 years, back to the days when men were first learning to plow, when they realized an ox could do more work than a boy, back to the age of the Old Kingdom in Egypt, the first great civilization that was to rise to the Middle East. He knew that some of the world's greatest warlords and emperors had stood in this place. From the first nomadic tribesmen to the Persian kings, from the Roman senators to the Muslim caliphs, Russian czars, and British generals—many of the greatest leaders had fought for this ground. How many men had died, how many wars had been fought, how many empires had risen and settled over Persia, this fertile piece of land that he called home?

Persia. The White Pearl. Treasure of ancient days.

The world had been changed here.

Might Persia change history once again?

Rassa had a feeling that it would. This feeling, this thing he had felt since he was a child, had been one of the reasons he had chosen to stay. In the years following the fall of his grandfather the shah, most of the royal family (and they had numbered in the hundreds) had accepted luxurious exile in various nations outside of the Persian Gulf. There they had retired with their millions, their servants, aides, butlers and wine. But in leaving, they had forgone any influence on their nation, as well as any hope of a respectful return. But Rassa's father, now dead, had chosen to stay, and Rassa had followed his lead; even if anonymous, even if poor, he wanted to remain in this land, for he believed a time would come when the glory of Persia would rise once again. And he wanted to be here when that great day arrived.

As Rassa stood in the rising sun, he sensed a sudden rush of both good and bad; the passing of time, the passing of history, of dreams and disappointments, of birth and death. The emotion passed over him like a warm wind. Bending over, he ran his fingers through the two hundred years of dirt that had settled on the stone bulwark at the top of the tower. It was black, like the soil below it, and he let it sift through his fingers, then lifted his hand and smelled the richness there. He turned in a slow circle, looking from the forest to the mountain, then back to the valley below. Where else could man stand and look down upon more than two thousand years of civilizations, the tracings of wars, long forgotten, but which had shaped the world's history?

As he stood alone at the top of the tower, he pondered the birth and death of nations, the birth and death of peoples, the birth and death of his ancestors who had lived here for so many years.

Then he thought of the birth of his daughter and the death of his wife, the only women he had ever loved.

Thinking of them, he shrugged. Who was he to understand the cycle of life? Who was he to question what it was for? He could ponder, he could ask, but he could not comprehend.

Might he know it one day?

*Insha'allah.* If God wills it.

# TEN

Rassa heard heavy footsteps echoing up from the base of the tower. Soon, Omar Pasni Zehedan emerged at the top of the stairs.

"Rassa," he offered simply as he moved to his side. From where Rassa had been sitting, it would have been impossible for Omar to have seen him from the ground, for the low wall around the embattlement would have hidden him from view. But it wasn't uncommon for the two to meet here, and the neither of them was surprised to see the other there.

Omar sat next to Rassa and leaned against the cold stone. Rassa was quiet as he settled down.

"You see the aircraft carrier?" Omar asked after catching his breath.

Rassa nodded and hunched his shoulders toward the sea.

"There were also a couple of our fighters up north."

Again, Rassa nodded.

Omar pulled out a crumpled pack of unfiltered cigarettes and stuck one between his fat lips. He was a huge man, with legs like tree trunks and a thick, hairy neck. His hands were round as grapefruits and he had a steel vise for a grip. Father of fifteen children, husband of six wives (the Qur'an only allowed for four wives, but he didn't count the two who had failed to provide him with offspring), Omar was wealthy, cynical and wise. As a young man, he had grown rich through illicit trade, selling black-market supplies to the Iranian army, smuggling dollars and various European currencies (without which little business could be done), selling passports, bribing the port tariff managers to export rare Persian rugs, running drugs, alcohol and guns—there was little he hadn't bought, sold or traded at one time or another. But he was far more conservative now, for he had much to lose. He had many friends, about as many enemies, but all in all he was as well-connected and financed as anyone Rassa knew.

Their relationship went back many years. Their fathers had fought side by side in the Iran-Iraq war, cringing in sandy trenches while chemical warheads had flown overhead. Upon the death of Rassa's father, Omar, twenty years older, had taken him under his protective wing and over the years they had become loyal friends.

Omar spit a piece of tobacco off the tip of his tongue. Rassa watched him shift his weight from one hip to the other, knowing the cold stone exacerbated his arthritis. Omar cursed and stretched his legs. "I drove up to Bandar–e Mah Shahr yesterday," he then said. "It normally takes me two hours. Took me almost four. I was stopped at three roadblocks. There used to only be one. I passed an army convoy that must have been three miles long. I made note of the unit, their commander proudly, and stupidly, had his unit flag waving from his staff car." He spit once again. "They were the Twelfth Special Security Forces," he announced, as if he were breaking important news.

Rassa stared blankly. It meant little to him.

Omar was silent as he lit up his smoke. "The Twelfth is normally posted to the central headquarters in Tehran," he continued. "So I did a little reading." Omar was well traveled, but far more important, he had a computer *hooked up to a phone line!* Access to the Internet meant access to an entire world of information. Many times, Rassa and Omar had spent until the wee hours of the morning learning things for which they could be hanged.

"They are posting the Twelfth to protect the oil fields to our east," Omar concluded.

Rassa glanced toward him and shrugged, "Protect them from what?"

"One begs that question, it would seem. I don't see enemy navies ready to invade our shores. I don't see an enemy ready to knock down our doors. It seems the mullahs and bureaucrats are growing both suspicious and bold. They don't see an enemy, they see us. But it appears they intend to protect their theocracy, even with Muslim blood."

"You knew they would, Omar. How many times have we said the same thing?"

The older man growled and shifted his weight to his other oversized hip. He adjusted his turban and glared to the south, then reached under his robe and pulled out a curved knife from a leather sheaf strapped to his leg. Extracting a peach from his pocket, he cut it in half and extended a piece toward Rassa, using the end of his knife. Rassa took it and thanked him as he took a healthy bite.

"Too much is going on," Omar answered. "Too many rumors. Too many whispers of war. Too many army units on highways and too many threats from the mullahs who hide in Tehran. But the enemy isn't the Great Satan like we used to think. The enemy comes from within. And there is a darkness, a mist, spreading like smoke in the air. I don't like it, Rassa. It is calm now, I know that, but I feel it is the calm before the crashing storm."

Rassa nodded weakly. "Yes," he agreed.

The world was changing, even here in Iran. There was too much information, too much travel, too much talk, for the ultraconservative *unmans* and mullahs to keep their people in the dark. Rassa had heard all their arguments, all of their bile and fear. Having been raised in the swamp of their loathing, how could he have not heard it all before? But he knew it wasn't true. The ayatollahs were lying. The men who ran Iran, the mullahs, the local district leaders, the policemen, teachers and bureaucrats, all of them hated the United States; it was a part of their jobs, one of the qualifications they were screened for before they even applied. But not everyone shared in their hatred and there was a growing sentiment, especially among the educated and the young, that the Iranians had a decision to make; enter the 21st century or step back five hundred years. Take a step toward freedom or toward the Dark Ages once again.

Omar glanced to Rassa, expecting to see him roused with anger. The two had conspired many times, and Omar knew how Rassa felt about the Iranian government. But Rassa's face remained passive as he stared at the calm morning sea.

Omar crushed his cigarette and turned his eyes to the rising sun.

A long silence followed. Omar started talking, then fell silent, then shifted his weight against the rock once again.

"*Should he tell him*," Omar wondered? "*Should he tell Rassa of his dream about his daughter?*" Truth was, he wanted to forget it, to drive it from his mind. But he had always been a dreamer and his dreams had always proven true!

He glanced uneasily at his young friend. "And Azadeh, how is she?" he asked. It would have been considered very rude to ask about another's daughters or wife had he not been a close friend.

Rassa didn't see the flash of concern in Omar's eyes. "She is growing restless," he answered, a look of pride on his face. "She wants to leave to go to school."

Omar pushed himself up to his feet, eager to get off the cold stone. "You know, Rassa, I have nine daughters," he said. "Some of them are goat ugly. I don't mean to be unkind, but I am an honest man and I know what I see. There aren't enough blind men in the valley for my daughters to marry. But thankfully *some* of my daughters look like their mothers and not me. Some of them are beautiful, Rassa, I am proud to say. But I tell you now, Rassa, there is something in Azadeh. She has a beauty that goes far beyond the eye."

Rassa smiled proudly. "Thank you, Omar," he said.

"I'm not just being pleasant, Rassa. She is a vision, an angel who fell from heaven. Sometimes angels fall among us. Where angels fall and why, Allah does not reveal. But Azadeh is an angel and she has fallen here."

Rassa nodded slowly. "Our children are like angels in our midst."

"Yes, Rassa. But this generation, these children, I don't know . . . there is something about them, something I don't understand. They are better than we were. They are better than we are now. And we are all the time speaking of how our children need us, but I have come to believe that before this time is over, it is us who will be needing them." Omar glanced down at the village and rubbed his hand over his face. He felt himself tremble and he was embarrassed. He was a hard man, a businessman, a man of great wealth and means. But this dream, this cold warning, it had cut him to the bone. And he loved Azadeh as much as he loved his own.

He turned to the younger man. "Take care of her," he warned him. "I'm worried for her, Rassa . . . ," his voice trailed off.

Rassa rose to his feet, his eyes hurt and intense. "What are you talking about Omar?" he demanded.

Omar started to answer, but the words didn't come. He remained silent for a moment, his mouth open, then turned away and shrugged, wishing he hadn't said anything. What could he tell him? How could he make him understand? "*Your child is in danger Rassa, for I had a dream!*" He would sound like a fool if he tried to explain!

"I just worry for her, Rassa," he finally said. "She is young, she is special, and you have been left to care for her yourself. She needs a mother, like we all do, and you need a wife. I worry for you both. That's all I meant to say."

Rassa watched his friend's face, knowing there was more, but Omar waved his hand and moved toward the steep steps. "It is nothing, Rassa. Nothing. I must go. It is getting late and we both have work to do."

Omar stopped short of the stairs, then turn and lowered his voice. "There is a meeting tonight," he said

Instinctively, Rassa looked around. "I can't come," he said. "Tomorrow is Azadeh's birthday."

Omar grunted, "Yes, yes, of course."

Omar started down the stairs.

"Be careful," Rassa whispered to him as he disappeared.

# ELEVEN

*Balaam found Lucifer in a dark room, casting his temptations over his flock, draping them in a cold and passionless blanket of sin and despair. "Master," he whispered as he crawled to his side.*

*Lucifer turned toward him, his eyes cold as wet stones. Balaam looked away, unable to look into Lucifer's dark eyes. Normally, Balaam wouldn't have bothered Lucifer, but this was important. Maybe very important. Balaam had identified one of the great ones who had the power to change the world. So he whimpered one more time. "Master . . . ."*

*"What are you doing here?" Lucifer sneered.*

*Balaam almost quivered from the rage in Lucifer's voice. It hurt him, burning like a hot knife in his chest. "Master Mayhem!" he pleaded, his head almost touching the ground, "I have located a girl. She is only a child, but I know her, I can feel it, she is important to the Enemy's plan. She will do things, she will accomplish things, that haven't been done before. But . . . " Balaam hesitated, suddenly feeling unsure, "but if we destroy her, Master, before she is able to make a difference, it will help us over time."*

*Lucifer seemed to hesitate then stared deeply into Balaam's eyes, bent on reading his thoughts. Balaam almost quivered, the knife cutting deeper into his chest, feeling the power of Lucifer's cold stare. "Yes," Lucifer finally answered when he was finished rummaging through Balaam's mind. "Yes, we must destroy her. Now how do you propose we do that?"*

*Balaam thought desperately, his mind racing. Lucifer was asking for his opinion! He wanted to know what he thought! It was a glorious moment of recognition. He could share with Lucifer some of the magnificent things inside his head.*

*Then he froze, his heart thumping!*

*His mind went utterly blank.*

*Nothing. He had nothing.*

*What was he going to say?*

*Lucifer glared at him, waiting.*

*Balaam's mind raced through a dark fog.*

*Lucifer snarled, then turned away. "It is as I thought," he muttered. "You bring me a problem but no answers."*

*Lucifer stared at his feet as he thought, then turned back to Balaam, gesturing over his head. "There is another angel who works this village. His name is Roth. He is slow, weak and lazy, but he might be the only choice I have. I want you to find him. Talk to him. Tell him I need him to kill her. Tell him he will do this for me and I will reward him graciously." Lucifer cocked an eye to Balaam before twisting the knife. "Tell him that I trust him." He waited as he smiled.*

*The words cut so deeply Balaam had to catch his breath.*

*"But tell him not to fail me," Lucifer went on, "or his punishment will be swift and sure. And you know about that, don't you, Balaam? You know about my wrath. You can warn him of my anger as well as anyone."*

*"Yes Master, I will find Roth," Balaam muttered, trying to hide his disappointment and disdain. "Yes, Roth will do it. I will tell him Master. I will do anything you say."*

# TWELVE

The morning broke orange and yellow over Washington, D.C. As the sun rose, the winds shifted to a light breeze from the Chesapeake Bay that smelled of brine and wet marsh weed, humid and cold. Traffic started early as it always did in the city, the legions of government minions and private sector bloodsuckers heading into the district to fight their unending battles over government money and power. On the surface, everything looked as it always did; a steady stream of airliners took off from Reagan National Airport, the Metro line ran on time, and the I-495 Beltway had bumper-to-bumper traffic, same as it had been for more than forty years.

Nothing had changed. But there *was* change in the air, a tension and expectation that had finally risen to the surface after bubbling underneath for a generation.

The continuing economic uncertainty had stirred the pot of insecurity and resentment, the great American machine never throttling up to full power. Instead, it had limped along until it had created a new normal of expectations very far below what generations of Americans had anticipated before. Bit by bit, one disappointment and frustration at a time, the American Dream had slipped away until it had been redefined to mean nothing more than mediocrity among all the turmoil in the world. And it didn't end there. The sputtering economic system that seemed to be always standing on the edge of a cliff was just the beginning of . . . *something.*

And more was coming. People sensed it in their bones.

Washington, D.C., was a tense city. It had always been high strung, for the people who lived and worked there were by their nature ambitious and cutting edge. But over the past several years, it had changed from nervous to neurotic, the growing global tension having completed the transition from uneasy to scared. The truth was people who lived and worked in Washington, D.C., knew they were the primary target, the most likely to burn, and they seemed to have grown used to the stress of the bull's eye on their backs. How many other American cities had so many police barricades? How many had surface-to-air missile batteries hidden on the tops of their buildings or secret "sniffer" units that scanned the highways and ports, searching for the telltale radiation emitted by a nuclear device? How many other American cities had already suffered an anthrax attack, revived their underground shelters or had their hospitals drill regularly for a mass-casualty attack?

Such was business as usual in Washington, D.C. But something even more was astir now, a dark expectation that had been building for years. The people felt the pressure growing, a dark, rising cloud that was ready to burst, until there was an almost fatalistic acceptance that it was only a matter of time. A week, a year, maybe longer. Disaster was coming. It was just a question of when.

*******

General Brighton woke early, showered and dressed quietly while Sara slept. When he sat on the chest at the foot of the bed to pull on his shoes, she stirred and held out her hand. He stood and came to her, kissing her on the cheek, then sat next to her on the bed.

"The boys are going rock climbing this morning," she told him, glancing at the bedside clock.

Brighton nodded. He had heard them getting breakfast downstairs.

"You were up late," she then said.

"I had some papers to review."

"I think I heard your phone ring. Did you get a call on the secure telephone?"

"A couple of them, really."

"Anything important?"

Brighton almost laughed. "Everything is important."

Sara nodded, understanding.

"Prince Saud called from Riyadh. He wants to get together when I'm in Saudi Arabia."

"Prince Saud? How is he? You haven't seen him in a long time."

Brighton paused, thinking of the strain in his old friend's voice. "He seemed a little anxious," he answered. "But I can understand that. He's sitting on a powder keg, and most of the people around him are striking matches and tossing them on the floor."

Sara sat up and brushed her blond hair from her eyes. Brighton watched her and wondered how she could be so beautiful, even in the morning, even barely awake.

"And the absolute secrecy of the kingdom only makes things worse," he went on. "They are private and protective to a ridiculous degree. It's like looking into a dark well, trying to discern what is happening in their world. You drop a rock and listen, hoping to pick up a bit of information from what you hear echoing back. But it's difficult . . . no, impossible, to really know what's going on. Prince Saud opens up from time to time, but believe me, those times are very rare."

Sara's blue eyes, pale and shining, narrowed as she thought. "Prince Saud is a good man. I have always said that, and it's not because I'm overly impressed that he's the crown prince."

Brighton nodded, knowing that was true. With an advanced degree in philosophy, and having lived in some of the most sophisticated capitals of the world, Sara moved comfortably among the elite. She had met presidents, ambassadors, senators and kings, but she was hard to impress and unafraid to speak her mind, even to argue, if the opportunity presented itself. He remembered a reception at the White House about four months before when she had had a strained disagreement with the French president's wife over the inherent difference in the nature of boys and girls. Raised a traditional Catholic (meaning she actually believed what the Church taught) and educated in private schools in Boston, she had become what she called a motherhood feminist, a vocal advocate of homemaking as a legitimate career.

Sara watched her husband. He looked worn out, even more so than usual. "Anything going on at work?" she asked sympathetically. "You look a little tired."

Brighton didn't answer. The truth was, something was *always* going on at work. Always. Forever. It would never change. He felt like the kid holding his thumb in the dike. He only had ten fingers and there were hundreds of holes, gushing cracks in the dam, all of them spurting powerful streams of dark water. He could move to the worst breaks, but more popped up every day. Pakistan was in shambles. Russia was moving into Chechnya again. North Africa was on fire. Syria hanging by a thread, its leader shooting his own people as if they were at war. Lebanon, the same. Oman. Yemen. Bahrain. Egypt had been taken over by Islamic fundamentalists, all in the name of democracy, an irony so fresh it would have been hilarious if hadn't been so sad. The Arab Spring of years past was now a distant memory. Their friends in Europe had abandoned them, then sat back and laughed, hoping the Yanks would finally fail. Argentina had just reelected a socialist government that immediately announced they had developed the first nuclear weapon in the Western Hemisphere outside of the United States. The new Brazilian government was courting ties to Cuba and Venezuela, the bastions of communism that sat at their door. And North Korea! *North Korea!* He hardly had time to even think about that! Afghanistan was a mess. No, it was much worse than that! After years of near-civil war, the people appeared incapable of governing themselves. The Mullahs in Iran were growing bolder, taking courage in the mess they had helped create in Iraq. According to the Threat File, they were only months away from testing their first nuclear warhead, maybe a year, if they were lucky. Would the United States have to go in? Would Israel act on its own? Then there was Hamas, Hezbollah, al Qaeda, the Fetaheen—all of them spewing more bloodshed and hatred toward the United States than any one nation could absorb. Israel, their only democratic ally in the area, was isolated and terrified, the United Nations demanding sanctions for their refusal to honor the 1967 boundaries, an order which would have resulted in national suicide. Their enemies didn't grow weaker—they grew stronger. There was no way to reason with them, absolutely no common ground. General Brighton sometimes felt they were more likely to reason with a snake than negotiate with these radicals, for a snake, if it were to see an option that would benefit its position, would at least consider the move. But not these people. Brighton had seen it enough to be completely convinced. They cared not about improving their position, their people, their children. They only cared about one thing and that thing was death. Death to their enemies! The glorious death of a martyr. Death in the jihad.

To the radical Islamist, the Americans weren't human, they were *jahili*. Barbarians, subhuman. Decadent and soulless. Without value to God. They had rejected the one True God and so indignity and death. And whereas Westerners fo cultures or societies, it was not so for the Islamis

Western culture completely devoid of value, populated by savages with whom they could not coexist. Which explained why it was acceptable to kill their children. They *were not* innocent. They would grow up to be barbarians. Was a young scorpion less deadly than the mother who gave it life? Was there any law that insisted they couldn't kill their enemies until they were strong enough to fight?

Brighton had seen such thinking illustrated a thousand times before. They were not true Muslims, for Muslims didn't believe in such hate. No, the men he fought were not religious in any way. They were nothing but religious hacks, evil men who had hijacked a religion to further their cause, men who were as likely—even more likely—to kill their fellow Muslims as an American if it furthered their cause.

Brighton understood now that this wasn't a contest of religions or philosophies. At its core, it wasn't even a battle between cultures or nation-states. It was a battle for freedom. It was simple as that. Good against evil, black against white.

And it was a battle they were losing. At least that's how he felt.

Of course, he believed in God. He believed in mercy and redemption. He believed in faith, optimism and hope in the future. But this was beyond that. He had read the Threat File. He knew they were in trouble. Which is why he didn't sleep at night.

Give him another day, another small victory, another chance at hope and he would regain his optimism. He had been down before and he had always scratched his way back up. But his faith was growing fragile. The battle had worn him out and he was getting scared.

Brighton thought quickly of a copy of an instant message the CIA had intercepted just the day before, an exchange between two Iraqi brothers who had forced their younger sister to participate in an uprising in the Iraqi central town of Ramadi. The message was crude and halting, and translated loosely, but the meaning was clear:

> **Al-Anbari:** All of the people in the area have started to move. I put our sister in the crowd and thrust my AK-47 in her hand. I see other mothers push their children into rioting crowd. I didn't think that the people in this area were so heroic. And she was only nine!
> **Kamal:** Whatever God wants! Blessed be the Almighty!
> **Al-Anbari:** She just tried to come back, but I shut the door. I told her I would kill her if she dishonored our name.
> **Kamal:** Oh God! God is great!
> **Al-Anbari:** It is done. She was killed by our brothers, our own Iraqi police. But we will avenge her. We still have others we can put in the fight.
> **Kamal:** Do what it takes, al-Anbari. You strengthen my pride.

Brighton thought of the captured exchange and wondered how he should answer his wife's question about *"How things were at work?"*

Truth was, they were losing. They knew, all of the agents and officers he worked with, that they couldn't stop it. It was coming some day. So yes, he was tired. He was worn to the bone. He was weary physically, mentally and emotionally. Even his spirit was worn thin, like a sheet that had been laid on for too many years. There were too many battles. Too many enemies. He had to protect the country; he had to protect the president! It was his responsibility to advise him on what he had to do. But there weren't any answers! At least not enough! Their enemies were like rats climbing over the wall. They were shooting them one by one, shooting as quickly as they could, but there were so many! The rats kept spilling over. Which meant he was failing. But what more could he do?

He glanced at Sara sadly, then forced a smile. Like he did everyday, he pretended everything was all right. "Got to go," he said as he kissed her hand. "Want to talk to the boys before I leave."

"See you tonight then," she said to him. "Are you going to be late?"

"Hopefully not, maybe even early. I'll let you know."

He bent down to kiss her forehead and left the bedroom.

*******

Brighton walked down the winding staircase and into the kitchen where he found his two sons, Luke and Ammon, sitting at the table dressed in baggy shorts and oversized T-shirts. Overflowing bowls of cold cereal sat before them and he noticed the spilled Lucky Charms on the floor. "Morning guys," he said as he walked to the refrigerator and poured himself a glass of orange juice. He glanced at the bowls of cereal. "You could cook some eggs. Or there's frozen waffles in the freezer."

Ammon looked up as he spooned in another mouthful of sugar and bleached wheat. "That's OK, dad. We're in kind of a hurry, you know."

"You are going down to the river?"

"Yeah. Carderock."

Brighton poured himself a small bowl of rolled oats, added some milk and placed the bowl in the microwave. "Carderock? Is that at Great Falls in McLean?" he asked as he punched the buttons on the microwave.

"Yeah. It's a good rock. Plenty of handholds, but if you don't climb it just right you can find yourself hanging under some pretty awesome outcroppings."

Brighton knew his sons could climb like flies. He was pretty good himself, but he couldn't even come close to keeping up with them. But sometimes they made him nervous. It was one thing to be aggressive, another to be stupid, and sometimes the line was a fine one, and blurred. "How high is the rock?" he asked.

Ammon shot a quick look to his brother, who paused eating long enough to hunch his shoulders.

"I don't know, Dad," Ammon answered, "maybe fifty feet or so. It's not the highest climb in the area, but because of the angle and outcroppings, it's one of the hardest."

Brighton pressed his lips as he pictured Luke and Ammon hanging from their fingers, their hands gripping the tiny ledges that extended from the rock, their feet and legs swinging through the emptiness as they pulled themselves up and over the sandstone outcroppings by only their arms.

He opened the window blinds that looked out on their back yard. "You don't have any classes this morning?"

Luke poured himself another bowl of cereal. "Ammon's got labs this afternoon. I've got calculus at ten. That's why we're in a hurry. We want to get in a couple hours climbing before I have to get to class."

Brighton watched his sons slopping in their cereal as he sipped his juice. Something was up. He knew his sons too well. "Why are you climbing on a Tuesday? Why not wait until the weekend when you won't be in such a hurry."

Again they both paused. Ammon shot a knowing look to his brother, then ducked his head.

93

Although only older by minutes, Ammon had always been more responsible and it made his father nervous to see the guilty look in his eyes. It was Ammon's nature to take things a little more slow, and if he was nervous, then his dad got nervous too. Luke, on other hand, was a full speed ahead, let's-give-it-a-go kind of guy. If he left a wreck behind him . . . no, *when* he left a wreck behind him—he would apologize for the trouble, then speed off to the next crash.

When neither son answered his question, Brighton asked it again. "What's up guys, how come you're climbing today?"

Ammon took another spoonful of cereal. "Nothing special, Dad," he answered. "A couple guys we met last week want to come with us. They're a couple big-shot climbers from California, at least they think that they are. They were bragging about all the rocks they had climbed out West. We told them there were some pretty good climbs around here, but they didn't believe us."

Brighton sipped again as he filled in the blanks. Luke liked to talk. Talked a little too much. So he had met some new friends from California where there were lots of natural climbing walls and had talked himself into a situation where he not only had to prove there were good rocks to climb along the Potomac River in northern Virginia, but that he was the master of them all. Now it was time to make good. And Ammon was going along to keep his brother from killing himself.

How many times had he seen this before? Still, he had to smile. "You're going to class though, right?" he asked as he sat down.

"We'll make it, Dad."

"You know how much tuition cost me?"

"Ah . . . yeah Dad, it seems like you might have mentioned that before. And you're only paying half."

"Still, I'm getting my money's worth, right? You're not *just* screwing around? Sometimes you go to class? Sometimes you actually learn something, right?"

Quiet for a moment. "We're learning lots, Dad," Ammon finally said.

Luke looked up suddenly, "Oh, yeah, that reminds me Dad, my history professor wants to know if you will come in and speak to our class. He's a flaming idiot, I tell you. Revisionist history, through and through. It was his idea to have you come as a guest lecturer, but I was thinking maybe you could set him straight . . . ."

"Have him contact my office. He'll have to schedule through them."

"It would really help me, Dad, if you could come. I'm afraid I might have . . . ah, I don't know, made him a little bit defensive, maybe. Sometimes I argue too much."

"Can't imagine that, Luke."

Luke lifted his bowl and drained the milk, leaving a white mustache on his upper lip. Ammon looked at him and laughed and Luke wiped it with the back of his hand. "Dad, don't worry about us missing class," he said. "We both have partial scholarships—saves you boatloads of money, no, really, it's OK, no need to say thanks—but we're kind of thinking we might head out west to school after our freshman year anyway. Maybe UCLA."

"No way," Luke shot out. "California beaches suck. What's the point? Me and the real men are heading to Texas A&M."

"Whatever," Ammon answered before turning back to Brighton. "What I'm saying, Dad, is that we're both probably going to switch schools next year. So we're trying to keep things cool, you know, enjoy things our first year and all."

Brighton nodded slowly, a sense of sadness passing over him. His sons were as comfortable in one place as another, but they didn't call anywhere home. They were happy and adaptable, they could make friends in weeks when others took years, and they wouldn't have had it any other way, but they had no roots to speak of, there was no doubt.

It was one of the prices his family paid for his military career.

The general finished his orange juice and straightened his uniform. "Hey guys," he said. "If you're going to go climbing, I don't think that sugar crap is going to be good enough. Hang on a minute and I'll make you some eggs." He pulled out a large skillet and placed it on the stove.

"No time, Dad," Luke answered quickly. "And you've got to get to work, too."

"It will take me three minutes. Put some bread in the toaster. You'll be glad you did."

Luke hesitated, then walked to the toaster and dropped in four slices of bread. Brighton pulled out an egg cartoon and scrambled six eggs, dumped in some bacon bits as the skillet grew warm, then poured the eggs and stirred them while watching his sons.

Ammon sat at the table, reading the sports page while grumbling about his Wizards who had started 1 and 10 (bottom of the division again!), while Luke grabbed his calculus textbook and started cramming his way through some problems that, no doubt, should have been done the day before. How Luke managed to keep his grades up, Brighton would never know. So far as he could tell, he and his youngest son took very different approaches to life. While he believed that preparation was 90% of the battle, Luke seemed to think that true inspiration came only under great stress, and self-induced stress was the most inspiring kind.

Although they were twins, his sons were different as any two brothers could be. Both were freshmen at George Washington

University, but Ammon was tall, a little more than 6'2", with broad shoulders and long legs while Luke was shorter and stockier, with thick arms and thick legs. Ammon had his mother's blond hair and fine eyes while Luke had his father's dark hair and Roman nose. Ammon was smooth as Georgia cream; he could talk himself out of any situation, manipulate any teacher, make any friend. He always knew what to say (even if it wasn't always *exactly* the truth). Luke, on the other hand, was extremely straightforward; there was no pretense to him. He didn't sugarcoat the situation, just the opposite in fact, he sometimes made things worse just to liven things up. With Luke, what you saw was what you got and if someone didn't like that, that was OK with him.

Ammon had been named after one of Brighton's great-grandfathers, a gambler who had discovered his purpose in life soon after finding a young Alabama blonde and bringing her out to the Wild West. After going straight, Grandpa Ammon had gone on to become one of the most feared lawmen in West Texas, a sheriff who was known for getting his man dead or alive. It apparently mattered not a whole lot to him. Luke was named after the missionary who had baptized his great-grandfather, bringing him religion after a hard life of imposing the law.

Watching Luke and Ammon, Brighton knew he had probably mixed up their names. Luke was the gunslinger, the fearless lawman with the "get 'em or kill 'em" attitude. Ammon, on the other hand, was the mediator, the smooth-talking ladies man. But he was proud of them both, and loved them as only a father could love his sons. If they had any faults, and both of them did, he often found the same faults in himself, and knew that was where most of their weakness came from.

Brighton looked down to see the eggs were cooked and he spooned them onto two plates, buttered the toast and set the plates on the table.

The two sons dug in, stabbing at the eggs as if they hadn't eaten in days, their stomachs apparently forgetting the multiple bowls of cold cereal they had just wolfed down. Ammon scooped his eggs onto a piece of toast, took a large bite then turned to Brighton. "Sam called last night," he said.

Brighton perked instantly. "You're kidding!"

"Yeah. He's in Germany this week."

"He's out of Afghanistan?"

"For a while anyway. He has two weeks in Europe for R&R."

Brighton stared as he thought. Sam, his adopted son, the lost sheep of his fold, the young man he loved as much as he loved his natural sons, was off on his own now, having joined the Army right out of high school. No college, no hesitation, just a jump into life. But ever since joining the Army, his relationship with his adopted family had become distant and it seemed they heard less and less from him now. "Did he say anything?" Brighton prodded.

"Not really. He was in kind of a hurry."

"How is he?" Brighton asked eagerly.

"Seemed OK. I told him you were on your way to Saudi Arabia this week. He wanted to know if you were stopping in Germany to refuel. If you are, he wants to hook up."

Brighton frowned. Much as he'd love to, it'd be very difficult to make it work. "How's his unit in Afghanistan?" he asked, eager to hear Sam's report. He kept a very close eye on the status reports from the Special Forces units operating in Afghanistan, but word from the theater was hard to come by, especially from the Ranger units who were working with the CIA.

Luke smiled. "He was glad to get a hot shower and sleep in a bed, but you could tell he was really satisfied. He said he's making a difference. It sounds really cool!"

Brighton eyed his son. "It's not as cool as you think, trust me, Luke. Sleeping in tents. Every meal an MRE—cold soup and spaghetti out of plastic bags. Sharing a latrine with fifty other filthy men. It's muddy, cold and extremely hard work. Don't even think of enlisting! You've got to be an officer! So do what I say, Luke, enroll in an ROTC program. And for heaven's sakes, don't be a grunt. Why would you join the Army when you could learn to fly jets! You talk about cool, but what could be cooler than that?"

Luke didn't answer. They had had this conversation before. Flying? Yeah, he thought it would be OK. But it seemed the Air Force took their best pilots and jerked them out of the cockpit and into staff positions long before they were ready. And besides, there was something else, something greater, a feeling that the real men fought their wars in the blood and mud, not from some sterile cockpit at forty thousand feet. But he had never told his dad that. And he never would.

Brighton moved to the hallway and returned with his flight cap and briefcase. "When is Sam taking his R&R?" he asked.

Ammon and Luke were gathering their climbing gear. Ammon hesitated, then shook his head. "He didn't say. But he said he could meet you at Ramstein if you layover there."

"Did he talk to your mother?"

"Only for a minute," Ammon answered. "She was on her way to meet you at the embassy reception. And he was in a hurry, too; he said he wanted to call his old man. He hasn't seen him in a couple years and apparently the old bag isn't feeling too well."

Brighton shook his head. "Don't call him that," he said.

Ammon hesitated. "He doesn't deserve any better. After what he did to Samuel, he deserves a lot worse."

"Doesn't matter!" Brighton answered, his voice growing sharp. "It doesn't help Sam when you call his father that."

"You should hear what *he* calls him!" Ammon replied.

Brighton looked stern and Ammon shut up. This wasn't an argument he was going to win. And his father was right. It's just that he hated Sam's natural father so. All the things he had said, all the things he had done, how could Sam want to talk to him, let alone still call him dad!

The three were silent, then Luke headed for the door. "Come on, Ammon," he shouted. "We should have left fifteen minutes ago."

Ammon stopped at the built-in locker in the back hallway of the old Victorian house and pulled out a pair of gum-soled climbing shoes. "See you tonight, Dad," he called as they walked out the door.

# THIRTEEN

Rassa was silent during the evening meal. Azadeh cleared the table, washed the dishes, then sat down beside him as he smoked by the fire. A biting wind blew down off the mountain to claw at the clay shingles that lined their low roof. Azadeh could feel the cold draft as she passed by the window to sit beside her father.

Rassa turned to her, looked away, then turned to her again. "Let's go for a walk," he offered in a low voice.

Azadeh stared at him, her eyes bright with anticipation. It wasn't like her father to offer such a thing. More, it was cold and blowing. A hard storm was coming and the weather on the mountain could be violent and unpredictable. Still, he stood and pulled his coat on. "Come with me," he said. "We'll go to the market and walk around for awhile."

Azadeh's heart flipped. The market? At night? She had already completed their shopping. They had milk and eggs, cooking oil, and honey. They did not have to go shopping for another couple days. In her mind, she pictured the market, its shops crowded with people, merchants displaying their wares to the wealthy that had come up from the valley. She thought of the multicolored lanterns that would be hanging to light the night.

Going to the market at night when they didn't need supplies? It could only mean one thing! He had not forgotten her birthday. He was going to buy her a present! Her heart leapt with joy!

Azadeh quickly draped a dark shawl over her shoulders and flipped the hood over her long hair, pulling it forward to protect her eyes as she followed her father out the front door. He waited for her and she ran to catch up as he turned toward the town square. She glanced down the dark streets toward the lights in the distance. They burned with an intensity she had not seen before.

Of course he had remembered! He would not forget. But the fact that he always remembered her birthday didn't mean there was always a celebration. In a culture that never ran short on reasons to celebrate—birthdays, weddings, Mondays, anniversaries, leap years, government holidays, untold religious celebrations, it seemed they celebrated anything—there had been precious few presents or parties in Azadeh's life. "No money," her father would explain in a pained voice. It hurt him and she knew that, but the truth was there was rarely so much as an extra rial to spare. Although he was one of the ex-royal family, Rassa was nearly penniless, an anonymous and struggling farmer who had to scratch out a living just like everyone else. And it had been a brutal year. The cotton had nearly wilted in the fields from the lack of spring rain and then several flash floods had washed away some of the best cows in their herd.

Still, as they walked toward the market, Azadeh stepped quickly with hope. Could it be her father had somehow managed to scrape a few rials together? Might there be some extra money? Some unknown fountain of which she was unaware?

Tomorrow was her birthday. And not just any birthday, she was turning eighteen! In a few hours, her childhood would be left behind her. It was supposed to be a great celebration, a time to celebrate the passing of the young ways and the coming of the responsibilities that came with being a woman.

She shivered from excitement as she clutched her father's hand.

He looked at her, then pulled away uncomfortably. The *mutawwa* would be angry if they saw them holding hands.

If Azadeh had been forced to be truthful, she would have admitted that there had been times in the past when she felt her birthday had become more a day of mourning her mother's death than a day to celebrate her birth. Sometimes Azadeh wondered if her father realized that she felt lonely, too. And though she wanted a present terribly, what she really needed was a token, some kind of sign that her father loved her as much as he had loved his wife. She needed a symbol of his affection, some indication that he realized that she missed her mother, too.

She lowered her head against the wind and didn't look up again until they were almost at the market.

She knew what she wanted. She had eyed it in the market some three months before. But it was no article of clothing, piece of china, or something for her dowry. No, this was something more.

In her mind, she pictured the only photograph that she had of her mother, a faded black and white taken on her mother's wedding day. She thought of the bright dress, her mother's eyes peeking above the white veil that covered her face. She thought of the golden headband woven through her black hair, the single diamond centered just above her eyes. Simple in design, it was beautiful and elegant.

It was nothing but a dream to think that she might own something so beautiful one day. Far too expensive. It was ridiculous. It was for too much to even ask.

But they *were* walking to the market. And it *had* been his idea. Who knew what he was thinking? Perhaps a miracle was in store!

The market was not crowded, the coming storm having chased most of the people away. But the wind had died down now and it was no longer cold. The lanterns cast multicolored shadows in every direction. Rassa moved toward a small booth with handmade dresses hanging in display, a clash of lace and colors. Azadeh hardly looked at them. These dresses were for little girls! Her father watched her reaction, checked the price, hunched his shoulders and moved to the next stall. They worked their way around the market. Dresses. Handbags. Shoes. Denim pants from the West. A silver flute. He checked the prices carefully, occasionally lifting some less expensive item as if to suggest it to her before placing it carefully back on its shelf. Azadeh tried to show interest, but her heart felt faint. They were moving in the wrong direction! The birthday present she wanted was on the other side of the market, almost a block away.

Rassa lifted a set of small gold earrings, holding them next to Azadeh's cheeks. "These are beautiful," he said hopefully

Azadeh smiled and agreed. "They are beautiful, Father."

"How much?" he asked the merchant.

"Forty-five thousand rials," the merchant answered. Five American dollars! Rassa's eyes dropped in a look of despair. Azadeh watched him, her heart breaking. She heard the sound of the coins clinking in his pocket and she knew he did not have enough. What might he be holding? A few thousand rials? Not enough for the earrings. Not enough for anything.

She would not get a present. But she didn't care about a birthday gift, at least not any more. She only cared about her father and how he must feel. What a failure he must feel like. How disappointed and embarrassed! She watched him carefully and for the first time she saw it, a look of complete despair. Everything he had, he had given to her. But it was not enough. He looked away in shame.

She leaned tenderly toward him. "It doesn't matter, Father. I know we don't have any extra money, but that is all right. Come on, let's go home. It will be OK."

Rassa looked at her sadly. "I'm sorry," he said. "It has been a bad year. The cotton. The cows. We'll do better this year. And then I will get you . . . ." He gestured toward the shops and the brightly lit kiosks with their playful displays. "I'm sorry, Azadeh," he repeated as he lowered his head.

She took his hand and pulled him toward their home. "It's OK, Father. I really do understand."

They walked in silence, making their way up the dusty roadway that led to their home. At the top of the hill they stopped and turned back, looking down on their village. The wind had swept the skies clear and the moon was bright and orange, a large ball rising over the mountains. The lights from the village shone in the clear air and a huge bowl of stars shined over their heads. The Milky Way was full and fat, a bright band of stars. They looked at each other and Azadeh forced a quick smile.

"She is up there," she whispered.

"Who?" Rassa asked.

"Your wife." She hesitated. "My mother."

Rassa shook his head slowly. "I hope so," he said.

They looked at the sky a moment longer then turned again for their home.

They were just coming under the light of their front porch when Rassa turned and said. "You wanted something special, didn't you?" he asked.

Azadeh shook her head. Her father watched her, then pressed. "I could see it in your eyes. I could see it in your actions. Did I even come close to guessing what you wanted? I don't think that I did."

Azadeh was silent, hoping she would not have to tell him what she had been hoping for. "It was nothing, Father," she answered softly.

"This is a very special birthday. I know you had your eye on something. I have tried to figure out what you hoped for, but I had no idea. Fathers are not good at these sorts of things. This is where you need a mother. She would know what to get you. But I couldn't even guess."

Azadeh was silent.

"What was it?" her father prodded.

She kicked her sandaled feet through the dirt, then whispered in an embarrassed voice. He nodded slowly, a look of great sadness clouding his eyes. It would have been far too expensive. "I'm sorry," he apologized for the last time.

"I still love you, Father," Azadeh teased in reply.

*******

After Azadeh was asleep, Rassa sat alone for a time, then pushed himself up from his chair and walked to his bedroom and stood by his bed. Leaning down, he pulled out a small chest from under the headboard then extracted a hidden key from a chain around his neck. Opening the chest, he extracted two American silver dollars, the only wealth he had ever accumulated in his entire life. He fingered the coins. They were heavy and firm. He held them tightly in the palm of his hand, then closed the chest and pushed it back under the headboard.

*******

Azadeh woke early. The sun was just breaking over the mountains and the dawn was pink and purple from the clouds overhead. She heard her father working in the kitchen and smelled his special jellyrolls, her favorite treat. She lay on her pillow and smiled. He was the best father in the world. She knew that she was blessed. It really was enough.

She lay there a moment, enjoying the laziness of lying in bed, then threw back the covers and put her feet on the floor.

She saw it on her bedside dresser and her heart almost stopped. The gold headband had been laid on a purple cloth, the delicate links having been carefully arranged into a nearly perfect circle that glittered in the morning sun.

She didn't move. She *couldn't* move. For a long moment she just stared, her heart slamming in her chest. She glanced toward the door, then back to the beautiful gift again. She reached out for the headband then pulled her hand back. For now, it was enough just to look at it and know that it was there.

She held her hand to her mouth, then jumped out of bed. She ran into the kitchen, slamming back her bedroom door. Rassa turned in surprise as she burst into the kitchen. She ran toward her father and fell into his arms. Pressing her face against his shoulders, she cried like a baby in his arms.

# FOURTEEN

Sara Brighton watched her husband pack as she sat on the edge of their bed, legs crossed, her nightgown pulled tightly around her knees and tucked under her feet.

Like all military officers, Brighton had spent much of his career on the road and it only took him minutes to pack for the trip. One suit bag and one carry-on, the general had it down to an art. His travel bag was like his schedule, tight and precise. And he always traveled light; no fluffy bathrobes, extra clothes or personal pillows. The only non-essential item he would carry would be whatever history book he was reading at the time. For the major items he kept a pre-packed military suitcase in the back of his closet which contained a fully packed toiletry bag, underwear, dark socks, Air Force shirts, two dress uniforms, dark leather dress shoes, a long overcoat and athletic gear.

After joining the National Security staff, Brighton was surprised to discover how often he had to travel with only a few moments' notice. (He had to laugh at seeing the look on his neighbor's face the first time a military helicopter set down in their cul-de-sac to whisk him away. In a town that lived and died by perks, even the Armani-suited attorney had trouble matching *that* power play.) Because of the short notice requirements, Sara had learned to launder his clothes and repack his bag immediately upon his return, for neither of them knew when he would have to head out again.

As Brighton stuffed military papers into his briefcase, Sara watched in silence, twisting a strand of light hair in her fingers. She frowned, then adjusted her nightgown, pulling it over her knees.

"How long will you be gone?" she asked intently.

"Couple days," Brighton answered. "Three days in Saudi Arabia. A quick hit and go." Overseas trips like this were no more unusual for him than a trip to the mall.

"Saudi Arabia is a long way to go for just a few days," she said.

Brighton pressed his lips and nodded, but didn't say anything.

"You say you have some meetings with the Saudi military commanders?"

"Yeah. We've had a little problem with some of our joint operations we need to iron out."

"Joint operations? As in command and control or operational missions?" After years of being married not only to her husband but also to his job, Sara had the basic concepts of military operations and lingo down.

Brighton dropped to his knees and looked under his bed. Pulling out *A Short History of the World*, he shoved it into his briefcase. "There are some operational options we're looking at," he explained.

Sara considered. Operational missions with the joint Saudi forces. She knew what that meant. If one read the daily papers, especially the *Washington Times,* one could add two and two together and come up with a pretty good estimation of the top-secret information that was briefed to the president in his *Presidential Daily Brief.* For weeks now, even months, the *Washington Times* had been saying that King Faysal was preparing to move against many of the terror camps that had sprung up along the Iranian border across the Persian Gulf, many of which were, ironically, funded originally by the Wahhabi fundamentalists that ran his own kingdom. Many of these terror camps had been used as the operations centers from which they attacked targets within the kingdom, and the king had decided he had no choice but to act. A house divided will not stand, and the terror these Islamists were wracking within his own kingdom had to come to an end.

Sara thought, formulating in her mind some of the issues her husband would discuss with the Saudi commanders. Would the United States provide military or intelligence assistance? Almost certainly. Air assets? Without a doubt. Ground operators? Probably Special Forces, but nothing that would ever be mentioned in the press. All in all, she knew there was no way the Saudis moved without significant U.S. support. How would that play with the government in Iran? Iraq? Bahrain, Egypt and Qatar? Perhaps the better question was how would it play if they didn't act? If the United States partnered with the already weakened Saudi king, might that more likely lead to his downfall, something that was a tremendous concern in the West? How would the Iranians react if they suspected the United States had aided the Saudi attacks on Iranian soil? Worse, how would they react if they perceived the Americans as too weak to take action in a case that so clearly had national security considerations at stake?

Sara bounced the possibilities back and forth, grateful for the thousandth time that she didn't have her husband's job. It was a lose-lose proposition. Indeed, most of the issues he dealt with had little positive potential but were bottomless pits when it came to the downside.

Which explained why he was so tired and on edge all the time.

She counted the months until the next election. A little more than a year. If the president wasn't reelected, something that looked likely now, the new administration would bring in their own team. Although ideologically Brighton would be much more aligned with the new administration, he would still be reassigned. At that point, they would have—no, they would *get*—to move on.

She approached the possibility with very strong, mixed emotions. Personally, nothing would make her happier. It would be like casting off irons, her family would be so much better off without the stress of Neil's job. But both of them would miss being in the middle of the fight.

*The fight.* Funny how the word seemed to capture the mood now. And funny how it was something that she thought about all the time.

While Neil seemed to concentrate on the battles overseas, it was the battles that were taking place at home that had her more on edge.

It was certainly different than it used to be. The tone of society's dialogue had become so emotional and ill willed. The sides were evenly split, and both of them hated each other. There was very little common ground between them. Everyone ascribed the worst intentions to their political opponents, to the point that the loyal opposition had been replaced by characterizing the other side as the *enemy*. The president, the man her husband had made a commitment to serve, had been the first to coin the phrase, she hated to admit. Worse, it seemed as if there was an open and visceral opposition toward anything that was good, even against those who had sacrificed so that others might live free. *"Dumb Jock Killed in Afghanistan,"* a small but influential newspaper headline had read in reporting the death of a well-known athlete who had volunteered for the war. Sara had printed the article from the Internet and pasted it in her journal. As a sign of the times, nothing seemed to say more.

But after years of life in Washington, she knew her way around and wasn't fooled by everything that she read in the press.

They could still keep things together. Things weren't completely hopeless, and that was her job, to keep her husband buoyed up. To give her young sons hope.

Sara considered in silence, completely lost in her thoughts, until the sound of the ticking clock brought her back to the room. She looked at her husband, who was staring at her.

"Did you say something?" she asked him.

"Do you know where my security badge is?" he asked for the second time.

"You left it on the counter downstairs. I tucked it the zippered pocket in your briefcase."

"Thanks," he answered quickly as he checked to make sure that it was there.

Sara pulled the two pillows and leaned back against the headboard. "So you're coordinating some operational issues with the Saudis?" she asked again.

Brighton nodded quickly but didn't offer more and she didn't press. He always told her what he could, which wasn't much anymore, and she had grown used to his silence about the things he was involved with at work.

She shivered lightly and pulled her arms close to her body. A cold front had moved through and a fall chill filled the air. The house was quiet around them. Luke and Ammon had gotten up early and were already gone.

Something strange happened yesterday," she murmured.

"What happened?" Brighton asked.

Sara hesitated. "Well, you know the Burkoughs at the end of the block?"

Brighton hesitated. He didn't know his neighbors well. "He works for State?" he asked.

"No. Other side of the street. Young black family. He's an associate in one of the law firms on D Street."

"OK. I know who you mean."

"Great family. I like her a lot. She works for the Red Cross."

"Yeah," Brighton answered absently. The comings and goings of his neighborhood would never be of much interest to him.

"They have two daughters," Sara continued. "The oldest girl, I think she's seven, put her hand in a nest of black widow spiders yesterday. It gives me the willies just thinking of it. She was bitten at least six times, I was told. She's in the hospital. They think she will make it, but she is a *very* sick little girl."

Brighton's eyes narrowed. "You're kidding!" he stammered.

Sara only nodded.

"A nest of black widows! I've never heard of such a thing. They are predatory insects, they don't nest together, they eat each other, I thought."

Sara shivered and looked around their room as if she expected to see spiders crawling up the walls. "I don't know, Neil. But she isn't the only one who was bitten. A couple kids at the school have been bitten too. They say it's the warm winters we've been having. Warm winters, no snow or freezing temperatures to kill the spiders like the normal winters would. I was listening to the radio. They said there's an infestation of black widows that reaches throughout the South." She shivered again. "I want to get our house sprayed," she said.

"Do it," Neil said. "Call the exterminators first thing this morning."

"I already did. They are swamped. Can't be here for three weeks."

"Three weeks!?" Neil replied in surprise. "You're kidding."

"No honey. I wish I was." She looked around the room again and pulled the blanket up. "Yuck again. A ball of black widow spiders! I tell you, I'm not going down to the basement until the exterminators come."

"Have you seen any spiders?"

"No. But I haven't been looking until the past couple days."

Brighton thought. "OK," he said. "Stay out of the basement. And keep your eyes peeled anytime you're outside or in the garage. This is an old house; there are too many dark places for them to hide. And be careful in the garden. Check your shoes and gloves. I'll spray the house and yard first thing when I get back. That will get us through until the exterminators come."

Sara nodded. "OK. I'll be careful. But the first time I see a ball of black spiders rolling toward me, you'll find me somewhere in Maine where the winters are *very* cold."

Brighton smiled and reached down to kiss her cheek. "It's a really nasty thought, isn't it? It would give anyone the creeps."

He checked his watch. He had a day packed with pre-departure meetings. His military executive jet was scheduled to take off from Andrews Air Force Base a little after 4 p.m. He had a pile of work he would complete as they crossed the Atlantic Ocean, then they would stop and refuel in Germany before heading to Saudi Arabia where he would arrive early the next evening. "Got to go, babe," he said as he stood from the bed.

"All right, General Brighton. Have a good trip, SIR!" she teased as she pretended to salute.

Brighton looked through the open doorway to the twin's room down the hall. "Where are the boys?" he asked.

"I don't know. Intramural football practice, I think. But they both told me to give you a goodbye kiss for them."

"Cool. I like it when you kiss me. No offense intended to the guys."

Sara smiled and stood up, put her arms around his neck and kissed his forehead wetly. "That's for Luke," she said then kissed his right cheek. "And this one's for Ammon."

Brighton grinned in pleasure. Puckering his lips, he closed his eyes. "And from you?" he asked expectantly.

Sara looked at his closed eyes then took his hand and shook it. "That's from me," she said.

He smiled and pushed her back, making her fall on the bed. "I don't think so," he laughed as he tickled her bare feet.

She giggled then sat up and kissed him once goodbye. Before she let him go, she looked at him for a long time, holding his face with her hands as she stared into his eyes. She looked at him like this every time he went away and had done so since his first combat deployment during the Persian Gulf War.

"Couple days, right?" she confirmed.

"Five days. Three in Saudi Arabia, a couple days enroute."

"I always miss you."

"You know I'll miss you, too."

She took a step back and let her arms fall to her side. "You're going to see Crown Prince Saud bin Faysal?" she asked.

"Yes, we're going to get together after my other meetings."

"Where are you meeting?"

"At one of his homes in Riyadh."

Sara looked worried. She knew something was up. The crown prince didn't call in the middle of the night just to set up a time to get together for a chat. She studied her husband. "I think he's in trouble," she said.

"The entire freaking kingdom's in trouble! Everyone's in trouble. It's the times that we live in."

"Yes, I understand that. But he is particularly vulnerable. And he is a good friend."

Brighton nodded quietly as he wondered if Prince Saud was still a friend. Things changed quickly within the kingdom and it had been so long since they had talked, and in a world of constant turmoil, he had learned to never assume anything. Allegiance could be as shifting as a desert wind.

Sara chewed on her lip. She was more believing, more willing to keep her trust in old friends. "Tell Prince Saud I send my regards. Tell him I love him. Tell him to be strong."

Brighton only nodded then reached for his black bag. Lifting the strap over his shoulder, he turned to face her again. "Sam's in Germany, you know. His unit has two week's recuperation time."

"Yes. I'm so relieved to have him out of Afghanistan for a while!" she answered.

"How was he when you talked to him the other night?"

"We only talked a few minutes but he sounded pretty good. He sounded happy. But he didn't say much. He was in a hurry and didn't have much time to talk." She looked at Neil hopefully. "Maybe you could see him while you are over there?" she said.

Brighton shook his head. "Don't think so," he answered. "Very tight schedule."

"He's staying not far from Ramstein." Her voice was hopeful, almost pleading.

Brighton put his bags down and looked at her. "I'm only in Germany for a few minutes. I won't even get off the airplane except to stretch my legs."

"But it's your flight. You're the boss. They will do what you want to."

"Yes, Sara, I understand that, but I have meetings scheduled every minute I'm gone. We haven't given ourselves any dead time; it's over and back, sleeping on the aircraft, eating sandwiches for lunch. I wish I could see him, but I just won't have any time. Next trip, I promise. I will schedule a few days."

"But he won't be Germany. He'll be back in Afghanistan, or Pakistan, or one of those other Ickstans by then. This is your only chance to see him. Don't you even have a few hours?"

Brighton hesitated, then shrugged. Truth was, he had already been thinking of it, trying to figure out a way. "I'll try," he answered meekly.

But Sara knew that he probably wouldn't have time. Her husband's schedule was completely outside of his control. He was at the mercy of his superiors and his staff.

She walked to him and put her hands around his neck again. "Will you please try? If you have even a moment, will you please try to see him? He needs you. He needs us. Will you please try to see him if you can?"

Brighton took her hands. "I promise," he said.

Sara dropped her eyes to the floor. "I really miss him," she muttered. "I wish I understood. I really just wish I understood what he was thinking."

"He's happy. He's doing his duty. God, duty, and honor. We can be proud."

"We are proud! But that's not the point! Why has he withdrawn from us? Why has he made it so hard?"

Brighton shook his head. He had asked the same questions at least a thousand times.

The two stood in silence a moment. "Got to go," he finally said, not eager to talk about Sam anymore. Turning, he walked toward the bedroom door.

"Hey Neil," Sara called to him and he turned around. "Can I remind you of something, babe?" He waited patiently. "What is the purpose of life?" she asked him.

The question took him completely by surprise and he paused a long moment as he thought. "I don't know, hon. To do some good, I guess. To do the best we can."

"That's right, babe, that's right. That's what this is all about; to do a little good. To take care of our families. Our responsibilities. To do the best we can. That's all you can do, Neil. But if you do that, it's enough. You might not be able to save the world, though sometimes you think that you can. There are things you can do, and lessons I suppose that you must learn, but you might not be able to stop what is coming, not like you hope to anyway. You might not save our country, they have to save themselves. Sometimes you forget that. And you carry more of the burden than I think you should.

"So just remember why we're here. Anything you do more than that is gravy. Try not to sweat things too much. It isn't healthy, general, and you're getting too old."

Brighton stared at her, mouthed "I love you," then smiled and walked out the door.

# FIFTEEN

*Lucifer stood in the center of Rassa's village square, flanked by two of his servants. Balaam stood close, but the small one kept back. His name was Roth. He was a bent and broken spirit who had lost his lust for the fight and spent most his time now sulking about the things he had lost while toying with some of the mortals who had already fallen to their side. Roth had reached a point where he didn't much care if he destroyed any more souls, for he was more interested in finding ways to pass the eternities of time, seeking any pastime that would provide a moment's respite from the torturous knowledge that his misery would never end.*

*The black enternity loomed forever before him. This was it. Forever. This was all he would have. This misery, this darkness, it was all he would ever know. Endless eternity. His misery would never end.*

*But . . . maybe, just maybe, if he could get in the good graces of his master . . . if he could climb into the inner circle, then he could grab a hold of real power.*

*Turning, he eyed the lean one they called Balaam, his face growing cold. If he had to destroy him in order to scratch his way into the inner circle then that was what he'd do.*

*Lucifer watched Roth out of the corner of his eye, knowing what he was thinking. He smiled at the jealousy between his servants, one of his most useful tools. And though he knew that Roth was dumb and lazy—he'd be used then thrown away—if he could use him to frighten Balaam, then that was a useful thing to do.*

*The truth was Lucifer hated most of his followers. But he hated Roth more than most. He considered him lazy and childish, a spirit who couldn't be counted on, a spirit who was more interested in his own diversions than bringing souls to his side. Yet Lucifer had made a decision not to deal with his slothful servants now. One day, when it was over, when the final battle was through, he would deal with Roth and the others that were as lazy as he. When that day came, he would punish them for their lack of service, for if there was one thing Lucifer hated, it was disloyalty. Lucifer smiled at the thought. When the time came, Roth would suffer in ways he had never even dreamed about.*

*But the time was not yet. Lucifer had more important work to do. He would have all of eternity to deal with lazy servants like Roth.*

*Lucifer turned back to Balaam. Like Roth, Balaam also had grown pale and thin, with bony fingers, thin arms and a long, slender neck. His face shimmered with darkness, like the reflection of water on a moonlit night, leaving a pale shadow that almost made him look dead. And there was tension and anxiety in the movements of his head, as if he was always hungry, always looking for something, starving for the taste of joy, love or success, but forever feeling famished. Like all of the dark servants, Balaam could never be satisfied.*

*Lucifer turned away from his servants to study the village around him. He remembered it well, for he had been here many times, going back to the days when men were just emerging from their primitive shells. Many times he had caused suffering in this place. Indeed, he had fond memories of this very square.*

*The market was crowded with shoppers. Children played in the streets, women walked by in dark scarves, only their eyes or faces exposed. On the corner, a group of young men talked while they tossed a small leather sack between them, kicking it expertly with their feet. Throughout the market, men haggled over prices, their voices rising until the deal was done. Lucifer turned in a slow circle, taking in the ancient market, the mud and brick shops with their small apartments above, the dirty brick streets and tangled electrical wires strung overhead. He noticed the tattered banners that denounced the Great Satan, the old movie posters, and the corner latrines that were holes in the ground. Everything was an earthy brown; the dirt, the cobblestones, the houses and shops. To his back, the great mountain rose over the village. The peaks were still capped with snow, but the hills that sloped up to the rock were covered in deep grass. He turned away, preferring to look at the shabby, manmade structures than the work of his Enemy's hand.*

*Balaam stood in silence beside him. Roth remained in the background, his lower lip trembling, his eyes wide in fear. Like all the dark angels, he was used to being sad and alone, for they hated each other as much as they hated themselves, and most preferred to be apart.*

*He cursed Lucifer's name. Lucifer noticed and glared at him, then took a quick step toward Balaam. "Where is she?" he demanded.*

*Balaam pointed toward a gentle hill on the south end of the village. A row of small houses lined the road along the top of the hill. "She lives there, with her father."*

*"And her mother?" Lucifer wondered.*

*"She died shortly after her birth."*

*Lucifer sneered. "So she doesn't have a mother. Well isn't that sad?" His face broke into a sharp grin, his lips curling upward, exposing his teeth. "That should make your task a bit easier, won't it, Roth?"*

*Roth looked away. So far it hadn't, but he didn't reply.*

*Lucifer took in the dirty village, enjoying the sight of the rundown shacks and dirty streets. He knew some of the things that went on here, behind these dusty doors and tattered walls. He knew there were few other places where the people were so hopeless, so robbed of free will. Was there evidence of freedom in anything around him? Evidence of any liberty or self-government at all? No, everywhere he looked, it was dark and brown and ugly and he couldn't help but smile.*

*What man built, he brought down! What they created, he destroyed! If there was anything beautiful, he defiled it. If there was anything innocent, he despoiled. If man were free, he brought bondage; where there was love, he brought lies. If he could not have happiness, then neither would man have it. This was the thing that drove him to work so hard.*

*He thought again of the girl. "She lives on the hill?" he repeated with a snarl.*

*"Yes, Master Mayhem."*

*"And what do they call her?"*

*"Azadeh Ishbel."*

*Lucifer looked surprised and then swore, shaking his head in disgust. "You don't see it, do you Balaam? You don't see it either, do you Roth? Both of you are so stupid that you don't understand the significance of her name!"*

*Balaam stared blankly, the knot in his gut growing tight.*

*"Ishbel is the Greek variation of Elizabeth," Lucifer announced with revulsion. "Her name stands for freedom! That hardly seems like a coincidence! Was her father inspired? Did he hear the whispers from the Enemy?"*

*Balaam shook his head, for he had not realized the significance of her name, and though he considered himself a master of every language, able to tempt and deceive with just the right word or phrase, the ancient meaning of her name had completely escaped him. He looked down, embarrassed and was reminded once again why Lucifer would always be the master. Bowing toward the fallen Son of the Morning, he said, "Master, why her father selected her name, I could not say with any authority. I have only recently found her. I would have to spend some time . . . ."*

*Lucifer growled, a familiar animal sound from his throat. "But it doesn't matter, does it Balaam? In a short time, she will be dead."*

*Balaam only nodded.*

*"Now where is the mortal that you brought me here to see?"*

*Balaam nodded toward a man who sat on the curb of the street. He was tall and lanky, all arms and legs, with a rough face, long nose and a wild, bushy beard. His hair rolled in greasy locks over his eyes, and he leered at the passing women from underneath the dark curls. He sat on a stool beside a small cart of poorly packaged cigarettes. A handwritten sign advertised his wares, "Cigarettes! Tobacco! Rolling Paper!" A small metal box sat at his feet, and every few minutes he would open it up and count the money, as if some unseen hand might have stolen from him. Three boys ran up and one extracted an orange from under his dark shirt. The man took the orange, shook his head in disgust, then reached to his rack and tossed them three cigarettes, which the boys took and ran.*

*Lucifer studied the stranger, thinking back, knowing he had seen him before, but in this place or somewhere else, he could not remember. Balaam stepped toward Lucifer and kept his voice low. "His name is Abd al Rahman al Than," he said.*

*"I don't care who he is! I don't care about his name! Just tell me the things I need to know!"*

*Balaam nodded eagerly, then jerked his head toward the evil spirit Roth. "He talks to him. He can get into his mind."*

*Lucifer turned toward Roth, who kept his eyes low, then nodded toward the mortal. "I'm not impressed," he said as he jerked a hand toward the man. "He is stupid. He is lazy. He's just like you, Roth! What can he offer us? What influence can he have?"*

*Balaam shot a cold glare to Roth. "Be silent!" he seemed to scream with his eyes. Roth nodded and stepped back into the shadows.*

*"The mortal will listen to Roth," Balaam explained. "He listens for his voice. He even tries to make contact with him."*

*Lucifer kept his eyes on Roth. "He will listen to you?" he demanded.*

*Roth glanced toward Balaam, then nodded eagerly. Lucifer moved toward the trembling devil and drew up to his full height. He stood majestic, even beautiful, his black hair falling to his shoulders, his face dark and alive. Roth fell to his knees at Lucifer's splendor. Balaam cringed, but just a little, for he knew Lucifer could hide his ugliness for only a short time.*

*"So tell me, Roth," Lucifer mocked. "What have you ever convinced this man to do?"*

*"Master," Roth stammered in reply, "I am but a humble servant. I don't claim to have the powers that you do."*

*"Yes, of course. But what have you done? Quickly now, Roth, and don't waste my time?"*

*The fallen angel fell back, unable to respond and Balaam moved forward, standing at Lucifer's side. "May I speak for him?" he begged. Satan sneered at Roth,*

123

*then turned toward the senior servant. "The mortal is not particularly bright," Balaam began. "I think we all can see that. But we don't need a smart one for what we want him to do. As I said, Master Mayhem, he will listen to Roth. They have a special relationship, one that is unique. The mortal is deviant. He has a dark place in his heart for any kind of pain. He loves to inflict it. Animals. Small children. He has done many things. Brutal things. Knives, rape and torture. And the society that he lives in allows it, for the fear he instills in his victims keeps them quiet. And this mortal knows Roth's voice. We can use Roth to get him, then turn him over to you to do what you may!"*

*Lucifer narrowed his eyes and took a step toward Balaam. "All right!" he sneered, his voice piercing and mean. "I will give him a chance to prove he can be useful. I will give you a chance to prove you can do something right. But I will not be patient! Don't let me down, Balaam. I am counting on you!"*

*Balaam backed up, feeling the cut in his chest. He had his instructions and he was not going to fail.*

# SIXTEEN

The day following Azadeh's birthday, it started to rain as a foul-weather front moved in from the coast—wet, soaking, misty and cold. The ground became saturated and muddy, and a thousand tiny rivers of runoff spilled down from the mountains to join the stream that ran through the center of the village, swelling it to a frothy and muddy torrent of broken branches, silt, and debris. It rained hard all day, and by the time Rassa pulled in for the night, he was soaked to the skin, bone-tired and shivering with cold. He had spent the day moving his small herd of cattle into a lower pasture to inoculate and brand the heifers, work which had to be done to keep the cattle from getting hoof rot from the mud. By early morning, his raincoat had been soaked through and he had abandoned all pretense of trying to stay dry, spending his day wet and shivering from cold.

Azadeh was waiting for him at the kitchen table and she looked up as he walked into the room. She smiled, her face brightening as if a light had come on, her eyes wide and happy, her teeth flashing bright. Rassa stopped and looked at his daughter. How it warmed him just to see her! Her dark hair fell down to the middle of her back, and she was tall and strong. She had her mother's olive skin, his eyes, and her grandfather's strong cheekbones. Jumping up from the table, Azadeh ran to the stove and turned up the heat. "Poppa, I have some tea for you," she said.

Rassa took off his wet coat and shook it out before hanging it by the oil furnace to dry. Then he sat on a three-legged stool and pulled off his leather boots. Azadeh worked over the stove, boiling some rice in water. "I would have had supper for you Father, but I didn't know what time you would be in," she said.

"That's fine, Azadeh," Rassa answered wearily. Shivering, he pulled off his wet shirt and grabbed a rough towel to dry his hair, then stood by the heater, reaching for its warmth. Despite almost being summer, it was cold outside, but that wasn't unusual for the mountains had a mean streak when it came to weather. The higher elevation caused wide swings in the temperature and the rain might stay for days, even weeks, before finally pushing over the highest peaks to provide needed moisture to the dry valleys on the other side.

Rassa seemed stiff and unusually tired. Azadeh watched him for a moment then pulled off a fist-sized piece of bread dough from atop a warming pan she had placed near the stove, flattened it to the size of a dinner plate, then tossed it against the burning-hot side of the stove. The dough stuck to the dimpled side and immediately began to cook to a crisp and airy piece of pita bread. Two minutes later, she pulled the toasty bread off the side of the stove, cooked the other side, then cut it open and stuffed it with spiced beans and goat meat. She threw another piece of bread on the stove which they would eat later with honey and butter, selected a Lebanese orange from the copper bin, as well as some raisins and dates, then seasoned the rice with salt and butter, sliced some cheese and set the food on the table.

Rassa watched with pride but also sadness as she worked. It hurt him to come into a dark house and find her alone. She was alone far too much. She needed a mother. And little brothers and sisters to care for. She needed to spend more time worrying about her friends and less time worrying about him. She was so thoughtful of others, it was almost a fault, the way she jumped up, always willing to serve, and though she seemed content, Rassa knew that she wasn't and it saddened him that she felt such a responsibility to keep her loneliness inside. She had fought the melancholy from the time she was a child, though she tried to be happy, always forcing a smile even when one didn't come naturally.

"Men are that they be happy," he remembered her saying one day.

Rassa had looked at her and then asked, "Where did you hear that, Azadeh?"

She thought a moment, then shrugged and pressed her lips. "I don't know," she replied.

As Azadeh grew, Rassa came to believe she would rather have needles driven under her nails than show him the sadness she hid inside.

But Rassa knew it was there. He was not so blind. He had noticed it even while watching her play with her dolls as a child (something every little girl did, no matter where they lived in the world). Azadeh would comfort her babies, sometimes crying for them, telling them that she loved them while holding them tight. As Rassa watched, he realized she was acting out all the things she had hoped her mother would have said to her if she had lived. And she not only mothered her babies, she mothered every child that she met, as well as every stray dog or cat that wandered into the village. One day a few years before, Rassa had made the mistake of bringing home a live rabbit from the market for supper. Azadeh had burst into tears and hidden in her room, refusing to come out until he had agreed they would let the creature live. Walking hand in hand to the fields behind their house, the rabbit inside a brown sack, they had set the rabbit free.

And though the memory made Rassa smile, it was a sad memory just the same.

Azadeh spent long hours writing poetry and stories, few of which she would let Rassa read. But one day he had found a letter she had written to her mother and hidden inside her small desk. Feeling guilty, he had read her letter, the words burning in his mind.

*Dear Mother:*

*It's been awhile since I wrote a letter to you, but I just wanted you to know that I still miss you. Sometimes I feel so alone. Father tries so hard, and I love him more than my heart can express, but I miss you, Mother, and I wish that you were here. And though I know you are gone, sometimes I feel you might be close. And sometimes I wonder; if we could talk, if I could hear your words, what would you tell me? Would you say that you love me? Would you say that you are proud? I hope that you are Mother, for I have tried so hard.*

*Your loving daughter,*
*Azadeh Ishbel Pahlavi*


Although it tore Rassa's heart to read what she had written, he cherished the beauty of her words.

And there was one thing of which he was certain; Azadeh's mother would have been very proud. And if she was somewhere in the heavens, he hoped that somehow, through some miracle of Allah, that she might see the treasure she had created when she had brought Azadeh into the world.

*******

As Azadeh finished preparing the meal, Rassa slipped into his bedroom and changed into dry clothes and warm stockings, then sat at the table and sipped his tea. Azadeh put the food on the table, then sat down beside him. Rassa reached out and took her hand. "Thank you, Azadeh," he said.

She bowed her head politely. "You're welcome, Father."

The two ate slowly, talking little, both of them hungry. Then, full and warm, Rassa stood to help Azadeh with the dishes. He had recently installed a new hot water heater, and they savored the steaming water that poured from the tap instead of the luke-warm dribble they would get before. Rassa washed while Azadeh dried and put the dishes into the painted wooden cupboard.

"You know, Father, my friends would die if they saw this!" Azadeh teased as she set a plastic cup on the lower shelf. "A father doing dishes! What is this world coming to!"

Rassa only smiled, knowing it wasn't as unusual as Azadeh might think. Once inside the home, the workings of a family were not what they always appeared to be. He also knew that many of the *mutawwa* who strolled through the village with their black sticks and frowns were more henpecked at home than they would have ever admitted.

Azadeh began to prattle as they worked. She would complete her final year of school in a few weeks, and she could talk of little else. "Father, might I one day go down to *El-hiram* to the School of the Masters?" she asked again. "That is where you went to the university, Father. Might I go there, too?"

Rassa lifted an eyebrow. "What have I always said?" he answered slowly.

"But I, too, am a Pahlavi, Father, same as you! Great-granddaughter of the shah. I need a good education! And I am capable . . . ." Her voice trailed off. She wanted to be careful. "Sometimes I think, Father, that even now I know as much as my teachers do!"

Rassa smiled. It probably was true. "*Insha'allah*," he replied.

Azadeh frowned in frustration. That's what he always said. But she knew not to push it. She was young, but not foolish, and she knew when to hold her tongue.

He leaned closer to her. "How are your English lessons with Omar's son coming?" he asked in careful voice.

"He says I am his best student," she answered in a whisper. Both of them knew the danger of learning English, and they couldn't help but glance toward the windows.

"Hmmm," Rassa seemed to think. "And do you find your teacher . . . acceptable?" he asked.

Azadeh looked away. They had talked about this so many times before.

Rassa waited, hoping for something more, then moved to the worn vinyl couch, pulled out a book he had already read a dozen times and started to read it once again.

Azadeh watched him, then moved toward her bedroom. "Think about the School of the Masters!" she called over her shoulder as she turned the light off in the hall.

\*\*\*\*\*\*\*

The night fell cold and dark with a steady drizzle that seemed to soak up the light. The quarter moon, low and yellow, was completely hidden above the thick clouds, and the wind blew in sudden gusts, pushing the drizzle through the trees.

The stranger waited in the darkness beyond the lights that fell from the house. He watched them from the shadows, peering through the window while stomping his feet impatiently. He had killed their dog already and he smiled as he remembered the wet cut of the knife across the mangy dog's throat.

The first kill of the nighttime. Other kills lie ahead.

"*That is fine. Take your time,*" the dark voice whispered in his head. "*I have prepared you for this moment. Now you must do as I say!*"

"I will, Master Mayhem," the slender man cried. "I promise, Master Mayhem, just tell me what to do."

The angry voice hissed inside him, dark, evil and mean. An agreement had been made between them. Now it was time to act.

The man hunched in the shadows, rainwater dripping off his hair and down his neck to soak the thin shirt on his back. His face was thin and hungry, his eyes dark and narrow. His nose flared with each breath, misting the air. He waited, then started humming an old chant from many centuries before, an oath of the dark ones who ruled the earth with blood and terror. His eyes glinted, cold and dark in the freezing rain. He was nearly mad, almost drooling, completely out of his head.

But the dark spirit that possessed him didn't care about his weakened state of mind. Would he do what he was commanded? That was all he cared about now.

*******

The hours passed and eventually the house fell dark and silent. The rain stopped, the clouds broke, and the dull moon emerged overhead. Still the man waited, his legs cramped, his feet cold, his hands numb and clammy inside his coat pockets. He fingered the knife as he waited. The entire village was silent. "*It is time*," the voice inside him finally said.

The man emerged from the shadows and moved silently toward the house. He approached the back door, staying near the shadows of the trees that lined the courtyard. His eyes had adjusted to the darkness and he saw well enough without using any light. Stepping over the dead dog, he moved to the back door.

It was open. He knew it would be. No one locked their doors in the village. He cracked the door, then waited, listening in the dark. He pushed another inch and waited, then stuck his head inside.

A fire was burning in the oil heater and the room was almost steamy warm. A small light glowed from the other end of the hallway, casting long shadows across the kitchen. He sniffed the air and listened. He must be careful. He must not fail.

"*Kill it . . . kill it . . .*," the chant started inside his head. "*Kill it . . . she will hurt us! Kill it! We want her dead!*"

The man stood without moving, only his head and shoulders inside the house, then slowly pushed the door back and stepped into the room. He pulled the knife from its sheath and, even in the dark, the nine-inch blade glistened red with the dog's blood. He tried to wipe it off, but it was dry, so he licked the blade to wet it, then wiped it on his pants as he stepped toward the hall.

"*Kill it! Kill it!*" the voices kept chanting in his head. "*Kill her. Take her. Feel the warmth of flowing blood!*"

The man narrowed his eyes and kept on walking. "Lucifer," he whispered without realizing it.

He stopped at the first door in the hall and held his breath. Which was the father's bedroom? Which was the girl's? He had to get it right. Pressing his ear against the door, he listened, but didn't hear anything. The light shone from the end of the hall, a small bulb glowing yellow, and he turned and walked toward it with light feet. A single 20-watt bulb burned in the bathroom and he quietly pushed the button to turn it off. Thick darkness enveloped the interior of the house and he waited without moving until his eyes had adjusted once again, then moved back toward the first bedroom. He sucked in a breath and held it, then slowly, almost imperceptibly, moved the doorknob. The door creaked as he pushed it open just an inch. Inside, he could hear the man breathing, deep and heavy. He slowly pulled the door closed and moved to the bedroom down the hall.

He held the knife ready, then placed his hand on the handle, turned it gently and pushed the door back. The room was dimly lit from a nightlight on the other side of the small bed. He listened, then moved inside the room, holding the knife in both hands.

She was asleep, her dark hair spread out across the pillow, the covers tucked almost up to her chin.

"*Kill it . . . kill it!*" the voice started chanting louder. More urgent. More hungry. Full of lust and hate. "*This is what I brought you here for. Do what I tell you, and you will be mine. We will be together! Forever! Now do what I say!*"

This wasn't the first time the man had listened to the evil voice that growled from time to time in his head. But this was a new voice. And this was the first time it had asked him to do something so . . . *permanent*. The man hesitated a moment. Could he do it? Could he kill her! Could he really plunge the knife?

But the devil inside him had become his best friend. He was his comrade, his companion, the only ally that he had, and he would do as his new friend told him for he really had no choice.

"*Look at it!*" the voice hissed. "*Look at it sleeping! It is innocent now, but it won't stay that way for long. Believe me, it will fight us, it will hurt us, it will haunt us one day. It will grow strong and wise. We must kill it while we can! So take your knife and do it. Kill it before it is too late!*"

The man hesitated as he looked at the girl, seeing a glimpse of the good that lie within her soul. He could barely make out her face in the darkness, so peaceful and calm.

He faltered a moment. How could she be dangerous! She was beautiful and childlike. What threat could she bare?

"*KILL IT!*" his master screamed. "*Do what I tell you or you will die!*"

The man slowly raised the knife.

"*KILL IT!*" the master cried a final time.

The man sniffled, then grimaced. He would do as he was told.

Moving forward, he held the knife in a death grip and it trembled in his hand. He reached up to steady it with the other and took another step toward the bed. Having made up his mind, he was moving faster now, sweeping through the darkness.

Then he saw it. He froze mid-step and hissed in dread. A tiny light, like a star, began to shine over the bed. The light grew from a soft glow to a shimmer as an angel appeared, surrounded by fire, heat and an overwhelming power that filled him with dismay. The angel was dressed in a white robe with a silver hood pulled over the crown of his head. A single star, like a diamond, shone from a golden headband, identical to the one lying beside Azadeh's bed. He lit up the room with his power and the flaming sword in his hand. The light hurt him! *It hurt him!* He wanted to turn and run!

"I know who you are," the angel said in a voice that tore with power and thundered through the night.

The mortal was filled with terror. *The light hurt him. He had to flee!* But the Dark One held him, not letting him go. "And I know you," the Dark One answered, his voice escaping like hissing air from the mortal's throat. "But what have I to do with you? I only want the girl."

The angel rose in power and lifted the mighty sword. "You will not touch this child," he commanded. "She is worthy of my protection, and she is my friend!"

134

The mortal seemed to shake off the dark inside him and he cowered toward the corner. "I *must* kill her!" he then whispered. It was the mortal not the devil who was speaking to the angel now. "I must or he will hurt me. *He will hurt me!* I must do as the master says."

The angel took a position over Azadeh and raised his sword again. "*YOU WILL NOT HARM THIS CHILD!*" he commanded. "Now go back to your master! Go back to your hell!"

The angel grew suddenly taller and more brilliant, shining with a fire that was brighter than the sun.

The mortal felt the heat and fell back in pain. The fire seemed to surround and consume him! The angel shook the silver hood from his head and his fine hair trailed back, blowing over his shoulders from an invisible wind. His blue eyes were so piercing they seemed to cut through the mortal's soul. "Go now!" he commanded and the Earth seemed to shake. "In the name of Jesus, I command you to leave."

The evil inside the mortal immediately recoiled, then cried out, cursing in a foul tone and then fled. The man felt the dark world falling all around him, the crushing weight of having been deserted and the emptiness of despair. He was alone now. His master had departed. He was on his own.

He stumbled backward like a coward, reaching for the bedroom door. The angel lifted his arm and pointed at him, and he squealed in wrenching pain, scrambling like a rat through the door and out into the night.

The next day, a fisherman found his body floating in the swollen river, twenty miles downstream. Having spent his life in the service of his master, the mortal had closed his final deal by jumping into the cold darkness of his master's world.

# SEVENTEEN

General Neil Brighton stood outside the famous Lelas Bar and Café, a small brick and mortar joint at the back of an alley off of *Schandelberg Strasse*. After finding out his flight would be delayed for a few hours due to mechanical problems, he'd taken the opportunity to call his son, Sam, and arrange for a quick lunch meeting. Sam had suggested Lelas, and the general had been very pleased to have a chance to visit his old hunting grounds. All through the Cold War, when there were more ex-pat Americans in Germany than anywhere else in the world, when the U.S. Army was massed and ready to drive back the Soviet hordes by defending the Foulda Gap, Lelas had been a popular U.S. joint. During the wars in Afghanistan and Iraq, U.S. forces in Germany had been built up once again. On any given night Lelas was crammed to the walls, smoky and warm from the open pit grills, and bustling with U.S. soldiers and young German women looking for American husbands. Seven nights a week, Orleans blues could be heard wailing up from the basement bar from an old American jazz band that had somehow ended up in Germany and now played for tips and beer. The food came heaped on huge plates and for seven American dollars, one could eat until he was stuffed.

But though General Brighton loved Lelas for the food, there was another, much more important reason he was so fond of the place. This was the place where he had first met his wife. Sara was touring with some friends from college. He was a young pilot assigned to Ramstein. The fates had brought them together here and they had never looked back.

General Brighton stared at the old brick building, hearing the noisy crowd and the music pounding through the small windows and ancient wooden door.

It all seemed so long ago. A different life. A different world. So much had changed since that rainy day long before.

He took a step into the café and quickly summed up the crowd. It was a rough looking group, and he was surprised not to be able to pick out any other Americans there. He listened to the voices, but heard no English being spoken as he made his way through the crowd and sat down at a round table near the back of the bar. He felt suddenly uncomfortable in his uniform, his dark pants and blue shirt with pilot wings on his chest. The café was smoky and warm, just like it always used to be, but the music wasn't familiar. Instead of the blues, European techno blasted from speakers over his head. He ordered three house specials; two to eat in and one to take back to the crew chief, then sat back and waited for Sam.

He thought back on the unlikely events that had brought the boy into their lives almost eight years before.

*******

Brighton and his family were living in southern Virginia where he was the commander at the First Fighter Wing, the oldest and most prestigious fighter wing in the U.S. Air Force.

The phone call came late one Sunday afternoon. "Neil," his friend's voice boomed through the phone. A huge black man from Mississippi, Gene was direct as a sledgehammer, with an equally powerful voice. Brighton had met him at a community luncheon (the kind of thing he hated, but was required to attend) and the two had hit it off. Brighton wished all of his pilots were such fighters. Gene wished that all the men he worked with cared about their families like Brighton did.

"Hey Gene, what's going on?" Brighton replied.

"You military guys ever going to figure out all this world strife and warring crap?" Gene boomed back. A Child Protective Services employee (and part-time preacher) who had spent his life working with at-risk kids from some of the worst areas in Hampton, Virginia, a job that had gotten infinitely more difficult through the years, Gene was not impressed with Brighton's military rank. Make him president for a day, and he'd shut the military down. Divert the funds to the hungry and homeless, those who could really use the help.

"Yeah, we're figuring it out, I think. The answer is bigger bombs. More money. Faster jets. The usual thing. Speaking of money, you ever going to pay up your poker debts?" Brighton answered.

"Soon as the state gives me that pay raise they've been promising me for years."

Brighton didn't touch it. It was a sore spot to his friend. He waited but Gene was quiet until he finally asked, "What can I do for you?"

"Got a little problem, Neil. Need your help."

"What's up?" Brighton asked, already preparing himself.

"Got a boy I was hoping we could send over to spend a few days with your family."

"You've got a what?" Brighton asked, trying to keep the panic from his voice.

"I just placed a foster child with another family, but it isn't working out. He's a good kid, but he's had a real lousy start. Abusive home. Alcoholic father. Mother hardly ever around. He's been with this other family for a couple days and, I don't know . . . it just seems they haven't hit it off like we all hoped that they would."

Brighton's chest tightened. "What has he done? Tried to burn their house down?"

Gene chuckled, his laugh as powerful as his voice. "Nope, nothing like that. Like I said, he's not a bad kid, never been in trouble in his life. He's OK with this family, but it just doesn't *feel* right if you know what I mean? As I've been working with them, I've had a clear impression. Now you might think I'm crazy, but I've come to the conclusion there's been a terrible mistake. This kid should be in your home. And just between you and me—and I'm not saying this as a representative of the state, so don't you ever think that or repeat this to anyone, this is just between us friends—but I think that's what the good Lord intended all along. We just had to take a detour to get there. Now what do you say?"

Brighton shook his head. "Look Gene, this isn't a stray puppy you're asking me to take in. We've never even considered . . . ." He was stammering now. "We're not foster parents. We're not prepared!"

"Life is full of surprises. And are we ever really prepared?"

"But Gene," Brighton floundered.

"I could fast track all of the paper work. Get you and Sara qualified."

Brighton shifted uncomfortably from one foot to the other. Inside, his gut grew tight and his heart skipped a beat. But something Gene had said kept on rolling through his head.

*"There's been a terrible mistake. This kid should be in your home."*

The sound of Gene's breathing filled the silence on the phone. "Neil," he said, his voice softening now. "Forget everything that I just told you. Forget any of what the Lord intended, OK, that's not fair of me. Put all of that aside. I've got to find this kid a place to stay, even if it's only for a couple days. Now will you please consider it? Just for a few days. That's all that I'm asking for right now."

Brighton heard Gene talking but his voice seemed a long way away. The words rolled again and he felt a shiver down his spine.

*"There's been a terrible mistake. This kid should be in your home."*

Another long moment of silence. "How old is he?" Brighton asked.

"Thirteen. A couple years older than your boys."

"He's a good kid?"

"He really is, Neil. The problem isn't him; it was the cards he was dealt. He's never been in trouble. He has a good heart. I've got a good feeling about him."

Brighton cleared his throat and shifted his weight a final time. "I'd have to talk to Sara."

"Of course, of course. And it's just for a few days. Meanwhile, we'll keep working with social services to find him a permanent home."

"OK," Brighton answered. "Let me talk to Sara then I'll call you back."

"Great, Neil, thanks. If we could, we'd like to bring him over tonight."

"Tonight," Brighton answered. "That's kind of quick, don't you think."

"The Lord works in mysterious ways, but he ain't got nothing on the state. Now go talk to Sara, then give me a call."

"Hey wait," Brighton stopped him. "What's his name?"

"Samuel Casey. He goes by Sam."

\*\*\*\*\*\*\*

The little boy stood in the doorway, clearly as hostile as he was terrified. He was thirteen, but small framed and he could have passed for ten. He was grim and firm-faced, with the demeanor of a boxer, someone who had fought his way through life. Sara knelt down beside him. "Hi Sam," she said.

"Where do you want me to stay?" he answered curtly while grasping a small suitcase in his left hand.

Sara stole a quick glance at her husband. "We've got a room upstairs for you," she answered.

"Should I leave my bag here or take it upstairs with me?"

Sara hesitated, understanding his subtle point. "Don't you want to unpack?" she asked him.

"Won't be here that long."

"You could still unpack your things and make yourself comfortable."

"It's hard to be comfortable in someone else's home."

Sara straightened herself and reached for his hand. Sam didn't take it and kept his eyes on the floor.

Brighton studied him from the foot of the stairs. He saw the bruised cheekbones and the cigarette burns on the back of his hands. He boiled inside. Who could do this to him? He knelt down beside Sam and took the suitcase from him. "Come on, Sam. I'll show you around. We've got a swimming pool at the officer's club across the park. Do you like to swim?"

The young boy's eyes widened in fear and he pulled back instantly, pressing against the wall. "I can't swim," he said. "Please don't make me get in the pool!"

Neil shook his head quickly. "We won't! We won't! If you don't like swimming, that's OK, too. You don't have to do anything you don't want to do."

The young boy continued to cower, his face tight with fear. Sara bent down beside him and took both of his hands. "Listen to me, Sam.

We're glad that you're here. It's a pleasure to have you with us. We have two sons upstairs. They're eager to meet you. We want you to feel at home."

He looked at her defiantly. "My dad beats me at home. Are you going to beat me, too?"

Sara saw through the manipulation and didn't react. She already understood him better than anyone in the world. "No Sam," she said softly, "we're not going to beat you and you know that. That's not the way this thing works."

She took his hand and he pulled back again, but she held to him firmly as she led him up the stairs.

Later that night, Sara and Neil stood by the kitchen sink and talked in quiet voices. "He's a cute kid," Neil said as he sipped a cup of tea.

Sara merely nodded as she stared out the window, seeing her reflection in the darkness outside. "What did Gene say when he called you?" she asked. Her voice and eyes were far away, absorbed in her thoughts.

Neil grunted. "Not much. Said he needed our help for a day or two. Said the other family was having problems. It didn't feel right to them, I think was how he put it."

Sara listened intently. "Isn't that strange." She was quiet for a moment.

"Sam didn't give them problems?" she then asked.

Brighton shook his head. Sara bit her lower lip. "What do you think it means?"

Brighton hunched his shoulders. Truth was, he didn't think it meant anything, at least not yet.

But Sara saw it differently, that was clear from her face. "He's supposed to be here," she whispered, more to herself than to him.

Brighton sucked a quiet breath. He had heard those very words before. Yet he hadn't told Sara what Gene had said.

"I feel it," she continued. "There's something going on. This is a pivotal event. It will change all our lives and I'm not prepared, but I'm as certain of this as I have been of anything in my life. Samuel was sent here. We have to try and help him. I know that in my heart."

Neil stared at her a long moment. "Are you certain?" he whispered.

Sara nodded, her eyes clear, her face intent with conviction. "I know it," she told him. "And you will know it too. Until then, you've got to trust me. We *have* to make this work."

Brighton stared at his mug, slowly shaking his head.

*******

It wasn't easy. A kid, even a good kid like Sam, couldn't have been raised the way that he was and not carry a boatload of baggage on his back. There were long hours in counseling, long hours at school, long hours in the bedroom listening to Sam cry in his sleep along with thousands of dollars in court costs and untold other bills. There was heartbreak, frustration and occasional hate-filled accusations from out of left field. The progress came slowly, but it came, with milestones of progress achieved along the way. No more crying at night. No more tantrums of anger. Better health, better grades, more friends at school. More affection, more laughter, more smiles.

Time proved there were two turning points in Sam's life.

The first came when he had been with the Brightons for only eight months. He was still small, vulnerable and utterly confused as to who he really was or what he wanted out of life. He knew he didn't want his mother to shoot drugs or his father to burn him with his cigarettes anymore, but little else was clear in his adolescent mind. He knew that he liked his foster family, but they were so . . . *good* sometimes he felt like he would never fit in.

It all came to a head one day after school. Homework, helping with the chores, showing respect to his foster parents, saving his money and not playing football on Sunday afternoons—it all was too much. Sam decided he had had enough. He up and left, screaming, "I hate you!" as he slammed his way out of the house. He took off without taking anything but the shirt on his back and whatever money he had in his pockets.

Neil and Sara searched frantically for two days, along with the police, but Sam seemed to have melted into the underground of throwaway kids that hung out on the dirty beaches and rundown boardwalks that lined Norfolk and Hampton.

On the third day, Sam showed up, unexpectedly knocking at their front door. Sara stood there, her face pale, her cheeks stained from tears. Ammon and Luke stood behind her, holding their breath, not knowing if she was going to let him in.

"I'm sorry," Sam told her as he stared at his feet. "I want to stay here. *Will you please let me come home?*"

Sara reached out and he took a slow step toward her, then rushed into her arms. Luke and Ammon ran forward and slapped him on the back. "Hey, Sam," Ammon said as his foster brother turned toward him. "Leave us again and I'll hunt you down and drag you kicking and screaming back home. Brothers don't leave each other. And we are brothers now."

Sam smiled, his lip trembling, then wiped his hand across his red eyes.

Yes, this *was* his family. He really was home.

\*\*\*\*\*\*\*

The second pivotal event occurred when Sam was sixteen years old.

He had been living with the Brightons for most of three years. Because his runaway mother had refused to consent to termination of her parental rights (she would lose food stamp money and state subsistence if she let him go), and though his old man didn't care one way or the other, the juvenile courts had directed that Sam would spend one weekend a month with his parents. His dad, a former high school football star who still hung out at games on Friday nights, a sometimes charter fisherman who rented his cruiser for fifty bucks an hour (forty if the client was willing to furnish the beer), lived in a ramshackle clapboard house near the fishing docks in a small town called Poquoson at the mouth of the Chesapeake Bay. Sam's mom, an attractive blonde who was just thirty-three, lived where she wanted from one month to the next, wherever the party was or a new friend could be found.

One court appointed weekend, Sam was at the old house. It was a hot fall afternoon with a strong wind blowing through the trees. He and his dad were in the backyard patching the fiberglass hull of the boat, the old man pounding beers. His mom hadn't been around for four months. Last Sam had heard, she was out in Las Vegas dealing cards at some low-rent casino on the outskirts of town; at least that's what she claimed she was doing but Sam had his doubts, for the pockmarks on her arms suggested a habit that was much more expensive than minimum wage and drunken tips could sustain.

His old man, Jody (as Sam called him now with very little affection), cursed as he applied the liquid fiberglass sealant, a burning cigarette in his mouth. He rubbed at his left arm, tracing a four-inch scar, the reminder of a vicious knife fight in some unknown bar.

"You had a birthday last week, didn't you?" the old man said.

Sam looked at him, surprised. It wasn't like Jody to remember such a thing.

"That makes you what . . . fifteen?" the old man asked.

"Sixteen."

"Hmm . . . ," Jody thought, then took a step toward him and grabbed the bare bicep on his arm. "Not much there," he miffed at Sam's supple arm.

Sam looked at his bicep and frowned. His dad stood before him and spread his feet wide. He was a tall man, still solid, with thick arms and thick legs. And he was quick with his hands, able to pick a fly out of the air or slap his mother so fast that she never saw it coming. Sam watched his father, a sinking feeling in his chest.

"Can you take care of yourself?" Jody demanded in a sour voice.

Sam looked away before he answered, then quickly recognized his mistake. He turned back to his father and stared him in the eye, trying to hide any fear. "I do OK," he answered defiantly.

His dad snorted angrily. He knew better.

"I can't teach you a whole lot, boy, but I can teach you how to fight. And there's only one way to learn. Just like with swimming, you've got to jump into the pool. And not on the kiddie side, you need to jump in over your head. So I'm going to help you, Sammy, and one day you'll thank me for this."

Sam looked at his father, his eyes wide. The older man took a short step toward him, a shadow passing over his face. He was six inches taller and weighed at least a hundred pounds more. "You're going to need to know how to do this!" Jody explained as he lifted his fist. "There's only one way to learn. It's time to jump in, Sammy. And I ain't the kiddie pool."

Sam stumbled backward. "No, Dad!" he cried.

The old man moved forward. "No son of mine will be a coward!" he sneered.

*******

Jody beat his son so severely that he knocked him unconscious. Stepping over the crumpled body, he dragged him under a tree, then turned back to the boat and started slapping on the paint.

Sam came to later on. He lay there a long time, trying to clear his head, then forced himself to his feet, washed from the hose and stumbled into the house.

His dad eyed him warily, then slapped him on the back. "You'll learn," he said as if they were old friends. "You've got to keep your hands up to cover your face. And you've got to bulk up, you've got the muscles of a fly. I'm not asking that you be a jock like I was, heaven knows there's no hope of that, but I won't raise a kid who can't take care of himself. And I bloody sure won't have a son who is afraid of a fight."

Sam only grunted.

"This is for your own good. I'm not raising a woman. I'm raising a man!"

"You're *not* raising me!" Sam cried as he backed away from his dad.

Jody froze as if he had taken a sucker punch. "Bloody straight I'm raising you," he sneered, reaching out slap him again. "I am your old man! And don't you ever forget it! I gave up everything just to have you, without nothin' in return. This is a tough world, don't I know it, and I'm gonna teach you to survive."

Sam stared at him and nodded.

The old man was probably right.

*******

"What happened!" Sara blurted when he drug himself into the house, her hand shooting to her mouth.

"Fell off the boat," Samuel lied as he held a rag to his split lip. Neither Sara nor Neil believed him, but he wouldn't say any more. They considered calling the authorities, but they knew Sam would never forgive them, for he followed a code of silence when it came to the old man.

That night, as Sam lay on his bed, his entire body screaming, he made a decision. His old man wanted him to learn how to fight. Then by hell, that's what he'd do.

Next day he spent every dime he had on a set of weights and started pumping iron. He started working out with the boxing coach and running five miles a day.

Six weeks later, the old man took notice. "See there, boy, I'm helping you already," he said as he thumped Sam on the chest. "Feel that," he mocked. "The kid is building a six-pack of his own. Well, let's see what he's got now!" Jody peeled off his shirt and flexed his biceps.

Sam held his ground. His eyes were unafraid. "I don't want to fight you anymore, Jody. You made your point, OK. I got it. I learned my lesson. Now let's just let it go at that."

"Who knows if you've learned anything? You ain't proved nothing yet!"

"No one says we have to do this!"

His old man took a quick step forward and spit on the ground.

The fight only lasted eight seconds. Three hits; a right to the midsection, just above the kidneys, a left to the jaw which broke a back tooth, then a right to the eyebrow that sent his old man's brain rattling in his skull. It was over and his father went down. He was flat on his back, his eyes open, his jaw gapping up and down like a fish. Sam went to the hose and turned it on to soak the old man.

"You satisfied?" he sneered as his father shook his wet head.

His old man nodded, his eyes unfocused, his breathing coming in grunts.

"Have I passed your stupid little test then?"

The old man grunted again.

Sam leaned down to face him, looking into his bleary eyes. "Then let me tell you something, Jody. You touch me again, and I'll kill you! You understand that. I don't want to fight you. Not ever again. But if you come after me, I promise, you won't wake up in this world. And the same goes for Momma. You touch her, and I'll find you. So grow up, old man."

Sam threw the hose down and walked away. He left his dad sputtering and never looked back again.

That night he locked himself in his room, refusing to speak to anyone. He ignored Sara's gentle knocks on the door as he cried into his pillow.

He knew it was time to start over. Really start over. Screw the old man and old lady. It was time to move on.

He had a chance at another life, a chance to do something more. He had a chance to be *normal*. A chance to make something of his life, a chance to do something besides drink beer, watch football and look for another party or the next sleazy lover who could provide a few thrills.

From that day forward he quit thinking of his biological parents as his mom and dad. Sara and Neil were his parents, the only true parents he would ever have. And he loved them with an emotion that could only be borne from the depths of despair, a depth of loyalty which came from a man who had been thrown a lifesaver in a sea of loneliness and fear. And he knew that they loved him too. Why they did, he didn't know. It was a great mystery, something he would never understand. But they really did love him, they weren't just saying the words. And they had saved him from a life of constant bitterness and self-inflicted wounds.

So despite the court's directions, it was almost a year before he saw Jody or his mom again.

*******

Sam continued to work out every day. He grew strong and fast. And he also grew smart. His senior year of high school, he went from a struggling C and B student to making almost straight As. He tried out for football and became a star running back.

"I'm too much like my real dad," he once said to Sara as they sat at the kitchen counter after one of his football games.

She looked at him a long time. "Who *is* your real dad?" she asked.

Sam looked away guiltily. "I'm sorry," he said. "What I meant was my biological father. I saw him at the game tonight. He used to play football, too. I'm too much like him." He stared at his tight hands.

Sara's eyes softened. "You were given a bad deal, Sammy, there's no way around that. But I really think that it's not so much the hand we've been dealt that matters as much as what we do with our cards. We have to play the best game; play the best way we know how, and that's what you've done, Sammy. Your dad and I are proud. We're as proud of you as any person we've ever known."

*******

During his senior year in high school, Sam and Jody seemed to patch things up a bit and he started hanging out at the old home on the weekends every once in a while. His mom came back from las Vegas and took a few steps to clean up her life. She and Jody got back together and they settled down in the old house on the bay and took to the slow life. They expanded their business, taking it seriously for the first time. She drove the boat. Jody ran tackle and cleaned the client's fish. Both of them attended Sam's high-school graduation. They even gave him a present—a hundred dollars cash and a pair of black leather Italian shoes. Sam held them up, the soft leather shining in the afternoon sun, then looked at his dad.

"One day, you're going to be someone," his old man explained. "You're gonna need to look good. And a good look starts with the right shoes."

It was one of the happiest moments of Sam's life.

*******

Sam stayed with the Brightons for six weeks after graduating from high school, a period of discontent and frustration. But Neil and Sara didn't push him, knowing Sam just needed a little time to sort things out. He spent much of his time wandering around the house, reading in his bedroom or puttering in the garden. And though Sam had always loved working with the earth, even this seemed to cause him frustration. He frequently commented on how he was planting seeds that he wouldn't be around to see grow.

One afternoon Sara walked into her bedroom to see him standing in front of the mirror wearing one of Neil's suits. The leather shoes Jody had given him shined under the loose cuff of the pants. He turned from side to side, looking at himself in the mirror, Sara watching him with pride. "Wow, you look great," she said as he adjusted the tie. "There is something about a suit. You really look good."

He looked a second longer, then shook his head. "I don't think so, Mom. It feels too tight."

Sara walked to him and tugged on the shoulders. "It fits you just right."

He looked at her and smiled. "That's not what I meant," he answered. "But thanks anyway." He disappeared into his bedroom to change out of the suit.

Sara understood what he was saying, so she waited until he was dressed. "What are you going to do then, Sam?" she asked when he reappeared from his room.

He hesitated, and for an instant she saw a young child there; a thirteen-year old boy, small, beaten by circumstances. She saw all the misery and anguish of the past years. But she couldn't change that. It was now up to Sam to decide what he was going to do.

"I'm sorry," Sam muttered, "I know you and Dad want me to go to college. Get a degree in business or go to law school or something. But I can't do it, Mom. Maybe I'm just a bad seed. Maybe I don't have it in me. Look at my old man, and I think we'd agree there's not a lot to be optimistic about. I want to be like you and Dad, but I'm just like my old man instead."

Sara felt her chest crunch. She remained speechless, her throat tight. "You are who you choose to be," she told him.

The way that Sam looked at her indicated he didn't know if that was true.

"What are you going to do then?" she asked again.

Sam clenched his jaw. He had made his decision the night before. "My old man taught me to fight," he answered. "That's something I'm pretty good at. I guess that's what I'll do."

"Neil will be disappointed that you don't go to college so you can be an officer."

"Yeah. I understand that. But that's the way it is, I guess."

\*\*\*\*\*\*\*

Six weeks later Sam left for army basic training. Twelve weeks after that, he graduated number one in his class. He was indeed a fighter. Very good at his job. Upon graduation, he was accepted to Rangers school and once again finished in the top of his class. He was then assigned to the 101st Airborne and eventually sent to Afghanistan to fight the remnants of the Taliban and al Qaeda.

Two years after joining the Army, Sam received a hand-delivered invitation from his unit commander. He opened it eagerly. He had been waiting for months.

The invitation was short and direct. The Delta Force, the U.S. Army's elite counterterrorism experts, were looking for a very few men. Did he want to apply? Sam stared at the invitation. A shot of adrenaline ran through him and he almost jumped in the air.

Delta Force are the *crème de le crème*, the most disciplined and highly trained soldiers in the world. They are part of the U.S. Army Special

Operations Forces, and they conduct covert missions that were so highly controversial and dangerous that many of the team members had long hair and wore civilian clothes as they roamed around with CIA agents in the hellish spots of the world.

Fifty of the army's very best men, those who had already proven themselves on the battlefield, would be invited to Delta training. Three, maybe five, would make it through.

Sam was one of the proud ones. Neil attended the low-key graduation, smiling proudly from his VIP seat. Sara wasn't allowed to attend, but it didn't matter, she would have only cried anyway.

Sam then spent a hellish twenty months crawling through the spider web of caves that lined the eastern Afghanistan border, hunting down and killing various enemies of the United States. During this time he finished college, getting a degree in International Relations, with a minor in Arabic and Urdu. Again, he graduated with honors. Then came a commission as an officer, a thing which made the general *very* proud.

# EIGHTEEN

Five minutes after placing his order, Neil's adopted son walked through the door.

Samuel had put on weight, twenty pounds, all of it muscle in his shoulders and arms. His hair had grown long and sun-bleached and it hung in bangs in his eyes and over his ears. And he was tan, almost dark, from the vicious Afghani sun. Brighton noted his goatee, which was so tightly trimmed it was barely a shadow of stubble. Dressed in dark jeans, a tan T-shirt and leather hiking boots, he looked more like a European than an American. He certainly didn't look army and though Brighton knew the Delta's often worked undercover, as a traditional soldier it was a little unsettling. He expected a GI Joe in a tight haircut and USA T-shirt. What he saw was a Hell's Angel who has just slipped off his Hog.

But these were the new warriors. And he thought that it was cool. He stared a proud moment then stood and waved to his son.

Sam picked him out and moved through the crowd toward his table. Brighton stood to embrace him and they slapped each other on the back before they sat down. "Sam, it's good to see you!" Brighton said in delight.

"No kidding! This is great. How are you, Dad?"

"A little nervous, actually."

"Why's that?" Sam cocked his head.

"I was only scheduled for a 40 minute refueling stop at Ramstein," Brighton answered. "I didn't think I'd have time to get together with you, but your mother was so determined that I see you, I'm thinking she snuck onto base and sabotaged my aircraft before I took off. Now I'm wondering what else she might have done. Is my airplane safe anymore?"

Both of them laughed then stared at each other, a proud father and proud son. "You look good," Brighton offered, "but I've got to tell you, that isn't what I have come to expect from a soldier."

Sam pushed his hair back. "Welcome to the Deltas. This is how it is now."

Brighton pointed to the long hair and rough clothes. "They wouldn't let our Air Force guys get away with that," he answered.

"Your boys jet around like Space Rangers. They don't play down in the mud with the men."

"I guess not."

"And remember, Dad, we have to work with the locals. It helps us to blend in, which is a good thing."

Brighton nodded. He knew that. "Things in Afghanistan OK?" he asked.

"Doing good, doing good."

His father leaned toward him intently. "Really?" he asked.

"Well, Dad, I'm not really sure what you want me to say. For one thing, you're a senior member of the president's national security staff. Anything I say could be used against me. I'm not going go there, know what I mean. If you want information on operations in Afghanistan, I refer you to my commander, General Brighton, sir."

Brighton cracked a thin smile. "OK, Captain Brighton. Duly noted. Now, just between you and me, how are things going in Afghanistan?"

"It's a hole. Hot. Dusty. Too many idiots who hate the United States. Too many donkeys and not enough rain. The whole country smells like an outhouse in the summer. Chiggers and sand fleas. What more do you want to know."

Brighton shook his head. "I'm sorry," he said.

"Sorry! Are you kidding? I wouldn't have it any other way! I can't wait to get back there. It's a miserable and lousy mission, but we're killing more of the enemy than any other unit in the world. We're shooting out the brains of those guys bent on destroying their own country and killing their own people. So no, I'm not complaining, I'm just doing my job."

"You should have listened to me. You could have gone to the Academy and learned to fly jets."

"And miss getting shot at while taking a piss over the side of an eighteen thousand foot cliff? Why would I ever do that?"

Brighton shrugged. "What was I thinking?" he answered sarcastically.

"And remember, Dad," Sam continued, his emotion on the rise, "these guys don't just want to destroy us in some vague or ambiguous way. They want to kill us. To hurt us. To cause us any kind of pain. Give any one of them a dull knife and they'd happily cut your head off, all the time laughing while they hacked away. Give them a nuke and they'd take out D.C. in a heartbeat, smiling and laughing while counting a million people dead. And if anyone doesn't believe that then I think them a fool. If they'd seen what I've seen, then they wouldn't have any doubt."

"Hey Sammy, you're preaching to the choir here."

Sam quit talking, but even in the dim light his blue eyes burned bright. Brighton lifted his water and tilted it toward him. "I'm proud of you, Sam."

Sam lifted his Perrier. "Thank you, general," he said.

*******

The five Germans watched the two American soldiers intently while sipping their ale. They were all in their thirties and had missed most of the U.S. glory days. More, they considered Miss Lelas a local joint, off limits to the American riffraff, and they thought that had been made abundantly clear from the old BUSH IS HITLER poster hanging near the front door. And if that didn't do it, the upside down British flag over the bar should have made their feelings clear.

Besides being angry at the world, the five men had been unemployed for going on three years and were nearly drunk despite the early hour. So they watched the U.S. officer and the local kid (probably selling secrets about the anti-war movement), whispering and cursing all the time. They quickly decided they detested the Yankees more than the sight of spilled beer.

"Look at him!" the largest German sneered. "Big shot American cowboy, just like Bush used to be. On his way to kill Afghans. That's all they do is kill!"

His buddies shook their heads in agreement. Stinking Americans. All cocky and proud.

"You remember Wolf?" one of them asked. The other men stared. "You know, Wolfgang Struttger, runs the printing service downtown. He married an American, some woman who got a divorce from her soldier when she got over here. Then she dumped old Wolf and took off with most of his cash. Cleaned him out completely, then made off with his son. He's seen the kid but one time since she left. She's back in the United States now, but he doesn't know where."

The other buddies swore. "Filthy, arrogant bitch!"

They stared at each other and sipped miserably at their beer.

"He shouldn't be here," the largest man finally sneered to his friends. "This is *our* place. Our country. None of *them* should be here.

They bring only death and destruction. They only care about war! They only fight when there's oil they want to get their hands on! They only fight when it suits them. And have you ever noticed, they always fight *against us*. Look at all the wars of the past hundred years. Did the United States ever help us? No! Never once. They claim they're our ally, but isn't it funny how we always find ourselves looking down the barrel of their guns!"

His buddies all mumbled, boiling even hotter with rage.

"Jew-loving *Amris!*" the leader hissed. "Arab-hating scum. Closed minded bigots and self-righteous crusaders is all that they are. How many nations have they exploited and crushed through the years!"

The other men mumbled, content to hate from afar. But the fat one had had too many beers. "I'm going to get him!" he said, pushing himself to his feet. "I hate these stinking Americans and it's time I let them know."

*******

General Brighton and Sam were working hungrily through a heaping plate of sausage and sauerkraut when Brighton saw the men approach out of the corner of his eye. Four of them followed their leader, who was a large man, tall as he, but at least 50 pounds heavier. He had a dark beard and short hair and he wore common work clothes. They all looked to be in their 30s and for a second Brighton thought they were coming to talk to him about flying. Back in the old days, it wasn't uncommon for the locals to want to talk about the air force or what it was like to live in the United States. Then he saw the angry looks on their faces and realized these men were not in a talking mood. These men wanted trouble. And they were coming for him.

159

"Heads up," he whispered to Sam as the five men approached.

Sam had already seen them coming. "I've been watching them," he answered.

Brighton put his glass down.

"This isn't going to look good," Sam whispered. "A general and his son cracking a bunch of local guys' heads."

"We're the ones who might take the cracking. We're outnumbered pretty bad."

"No prob, Dad," Sam answered as he slowly pushed his chair back. "Just remember, strike to do damage. You've got to take them out of the fight. If the only thing you do is hurt them, then all you've done is piss them off."

Brighton glanced around quickly, wishing he had brought his bodyguard, not because he was scared, but it would have made it much easier to get out of the café without trouble. Although he had popped a head or two in his early days, and been a pretty good boxer in college, he still swallowed tensely. General officers weren't supposed to get into a fistfight with the locals. It was . . . *unbecoming* of their rank. And if the German press got wind of trouble, they would have a field day. He could almost see the headlines. *White House Military Officer Brawls in Local Bar.* His boss would freak. And Sara would faint!

He cursed himself silently. How had he gotten into this mess? He shot a quick look to Sam. "You OK?" he asked.

Sam only nodded.

"If this gets ugly, stay together."

"I've got your six."

"Don't challenge them. Keep your head down and maybe they'll leave us alone."

The five men drew near. Sam cut a hunk of greasy sausage with his fork and lifted it to his mouth. Keeping his head down was the last thing on his mind. A soldier *always* watched his enemy as they approached.

Brighton heard a deep growl from over his shoulder. "*Er sieht so hungrig aus. Er kommt sicherlich von dem tÖten vielen Irakishen kindern ʒÜureck,*" the huge German mocked.

He struggled to translate, pulling the German words from way back in his mind. "Look at him, so hungry. He surely comes from the killing of many Iraqi children," or something close to it, the German had said.

The five men laughed as Brighton looked up and smiled weakly, feigning ignorance.

The German shot a dark look to Sam as if to say "get out of here boy," then turned back to Brighton, summing him up. "Big shot," he sneered in German to his friends. "Fancy stars on his shoulders, but not smart enough to learn German. Another ugly American soldier, that's all we have here."

Brighton turned away. He felt his back tighten and his chest muscles grow taut, but he kept his head down and his eyes on his plate.

Sam looked up and smiled. "Hey guys," he said in English, "we're just having a quick bite to eat. We don't want any problems. Give us a few minutes and we'll be out of here."

The thug nodded to his buddies then reached out and tugged on Sam's hair. "You need a haircut," he sneered, leaning across the table toward him. "I've got a knife in my pocket. Do you want me to cut it for you?"

Brighton leaned across the table, putting his arm between the fat man and Sam. Sam shook him off angrily, pushing his hand away. Brighton stared at the strangers and nodded. Five against two. Hardly a fair fight. And they probably had weapons, which made it much more dangerous and far more difficult.

The German leaned across the table and stuck his fat fingers in Brighton's food. "Looks good," he snickered. "Don't mind if I do." He swirled his fingers through the meat juice then licked them and wiped his hand on Brighton's shirt.

His buddies laughed loudly, prodding him on. The German turned to Sam. "Why don't you leave," he said. "This isn't about you. This is between this U.S. soldier and me and my buddies here."

Sam pushed himself away from the table and stood. "You got problems with Americans," he snorted in anger.

"Sit down," Brighton told him, then turned quickly to the man. "We don't want any trouble," he said softly, being careful not to give any excuse for offense.

Their leader bent toward him. "You're in Germany," he sneered, spit spraying on Brighton's face "We don't speak English or wear cowboy boots here!"

"We were just leaving . . . ."

The German stood in his way. "I said speak to me in GERMAN, or I'll cut out your Yankee tongue and shove it down your throat!"

"Get him!" his buddies taunted. "Take him out, Freidrich. You can do it!" they cried.

Brighton breathed deeply as he shot a look to Sam.

"You don't want to do this," he told him.

"Yeah, pig, I do."

Brighton sighed again and the German sneered. "No stomach for a fight, boy. You just want to kill babies. Is that all you do!"

The German shoved the American's shoulders and Brighton caught a glimpse of the knife sheath underneath his oversized shirt. He shot a quick look to the others, wondering if they too were armed. The German poked a fat finger in his ear. "I'm talking to you, Pigdog," he shouted. "ARE YOU NOT HEARING ME!!"

"Walk away," Brighton warned him.

"No way, *Amri*, not till I have some fun!" The German grabbed Brighton's shirt and cocked his fist back.

Brighton bolted to his feet, sending the small table crashing to the floor. He grabbed the German's wrist and twisted, almost breaking his hand, then swung him around and jerked his arm up behind his back, forcing the man to squeal in pain. His nearest buddy pulled a knife from his pocket and lurched toward Sam. Sam grabbed the metal fork from his plate and slashed it down on his arm. The man cried in agony as the fork penetrated to his bone, just below the shoulder, digging four prongs into the muscle. It stuck from his bicep and he dropped his knife to the floor. Sam kicked it aside and waited for the next assault. The other men hesitated, then rushed him as one. Sam stepped back and twisted, kicked his right foot high in the air. He smashed his boot in the lead man's throat and he fell back, grasping his shattered Adam's apple, sucking desperately for air. The third man grabbed Sam's hair and jerked his head back while another approached him with a small knife in his hand. Sam grabbed the German's arm and twisted, bringing all of his weight against the elbow while extending his hip and pushing down. There was a soft *crack* and a cry as the man stumbled backward, holding his broken arm.

Three down. Two left standing. It was all even now.

Brighton held the huge German and jammed his arm upward again until he felt the muscles in his shoulder begin to tear. The fat man screeched in agony, then pulled away violently, using his weight to try and knock Brighton to the side. Brighton moved with the German, using his momentum against him, then smashed his forearm across the

German's face, forcing his chin to one side until his neck almost snapped. Reaching under the German's shirt, he gripped his collarbone and held it, using it as a handle to keep pressure against the German's face. The fat man shrieked again, almost fainting, then fell suddenly still. It was too painful to scream. It was too painful to move. Brighton jerked the German's switchblade from his sheath, flipped it open and tossed it in the air, then caught the handle. He held the knife loosely against the German's neck and felt him grow limp with fear.

There was only one other German standing. He froze, his buddies rolling on the floor around him, all of them crying from their pain, then made a weak feint toward Sam before stopping again.

Brighton tugged on the fat one's collarbone and whispered in his ear. "Look what you've done to your buddies. Some of them got hurt. I think you should apologize!"

The huge man huffed in pain. "I'd die first, Pigdog."

"Your choice!" Brighton waved the knife in front of his eyes. The German cried in pain. "I'll kill you!" he screamed.

Brighton almost laughed. "Now what is there in this situation that would lead me to believe that!" he asked. "I'm mean, look at this Freidrich! Help me understand."

Sam took a step toward his father. "Don't kill him!" he stammered. "Don't kill this one, General. Just let him go."

Brighton felt the German's knees buckle and he jerked his arm again. "But I haven't killed anyone this week," he shot back to Sam. "Not a single Iraqi child! I *need* to taste some blood!"

"But you're on your way to Iraq. You can kill someone there!"

"Oh yeah," Brighton answered and the German realized they were jerking his chain.

"Help me!" the fat one coughed, but his buddy didn't move. He wanted no more of this. Sam took a quick step toward him and he cowered again.

"You think I'm a killer!" Brighton hissed. "Should we find out if you're right!"

"*Nein, nein!*" the German cried, his eyes wide in pain.

"I just came here for a quiet lunch. Now is that too much to ask?"

The German groaned in agony. "*Nein, mein herr, nein.* That is not too much trouble. No sir, not at all!"

Brighton swung his hand sideways, crashing the switchblade into the brick wall. The knife blade broke at the hilt and he dropped the handle on the floor. "Now perhaps we have an understanding," he said in a calm voice. "You don't want trouble. I don't want trouble. It seems we agree."

The German nodded eagerly. "I don't want any trouble, no sir."

"Then I'll make you a deal. I'm going to let you go. Then you and your buddies are going to get out of here. I think your wives are calling. Is that what I hear?"

"Yes, sir, they're calling. It is time to go."

Brighton relaxed his grip and the German almost fell to the floor. He crawled away from the general, holding his hands to his neck. Brighton nodded to the waiter, who was standing wide-eyed by the bar. "How much I owe you?" he questioned.

"Nothing there buddy. Just get the hell out of here."

Brighton stared at him, then nodded. He and Sam walked past the fallen Germans and through the front door.

They stood alone in the alley. Sam looked back at the café. "That was interesting," he said.

Brighton stared back at Lelas and shook his head sadly. "I shouldn't have done that," he whispered.

"Hey, Dad, let's get this straight. We didn't ask for a fight. And that guy would have killed you if we had given him the chance. He was too drunk and too stupid. And they all were carrying knives. You didn't do anything wrong here. Those goons were looking to fight us before I even sat down."

Brighton looked ashamed, then turned quickly to Sam. "Not a word of this to Sara. She would die if she knew this. Not one word, right."

Sam smiled and patted his shoulder. "No worries, Dad."

Brighton watched him, then turned. "Let's get out of here before those goons call their friends."

Sam followed him to his car. "You know, Dad, that was pretty good work back there. If you ever decide you want to join the Deltas, I know a few people. It's a pretty tight club, but I think I could get you in."

"No thanks," Brighton answered. "I'm too old for this."

"Apparently not," Sam answered, glancing back to the café.

"I just held my own. You did all the hard work."

Sam just shook his head. "You've got to go?" he asked his father.

Brighton glanced at his watch and nodded. "I was hoping we'd have more time to talk."

"Next time, I guess."

"Next time," Brighton answered.

The two men stood in silence. "When are you going back to Afghanistan?" Brighton asked as he unlocked his car.

"A couple days, from what I'm hearing. By the end of the week."

Brighton looked at his son intently. "Be careful," he told him.

"Always, Dad."

Sam stepped back and saluted. "General," he said.

Brighton braced himself and returned the salute. "Captain," he replied.

# NINETEEN

Two days after the fisherman dragged the bloated body of Azadeh's assailant from the river, another stranger pulled into Rassa's village, equally mystifying, though certainly not insane. He moved comfortably through the crowded streets, for he had been in the village before, several times, in fact, in the previous two weeks alone. He was a large man, well kept, though he wore unexceptional clothes. His face was hidden behind dark glasses and a neatly trimmed beard. He drove a Swedish sedan, which he parked on the south end of the open-air market, then spent a couple hours walking through the village, taking everything in. He talked to each shopkeeper he visited, asking a few questions and occasionally even writing things down, then browsed through the market, testing several wares before buying some potatoes and garlic sausage for breakfast along with a cup of thick tea.

It was Saturday morning, the start of another workweek, and the market was noisy and smelly from the usual crowd. After the first call to prayer, Rassa and Azadeh made their way through the market, collecting the supplies they would need for the next couple days. Rassa bought two liters of goat's milk and some sugar, then fifty nails and some wire to repair the fence around his yard. Azadeh picked out some fresh fruit and cabbage, then eight small carp. The fish were wrapped in old newspaper and tied with rough string. She dropped them in her basket, then ran to her father's side.

The stranger watched them intently, always staying a comfortable distance behind and acting with care so as to not draw any attention to himself. As the sun rose, the air grew warm and the marketplace became oppressive. Their shopping completed, the father and his daughter left the market and walked the dusty road toward their home.

168

The stranger watched them go, then melted into the crowd and walked back to his car. Climbing in, he locked the doors, started the motor, then pulled out an encrypted satellite phone and dialed a number in Riyadh.

"I will speak to Crown Prince Saud," he said after his call was put through. He grunted and waited. "Muhsin al-Illah," he gave as his name.

Then he waited, his breathing heavy, his hands sweaty and cold.

"*Sayid*," he said when the prince finally came on the phone. "I have been watching the target. There is nothing new to report."

The Arab waited, then answered. "They appear to be of little means, *Sayid*, though they do have their own home, a small brick and mud house on a hill looking over the village. It is small but well kept."

The large man fixed the air vent to blow on his face as he listened, then answered again. "Yes, your Highness, I agree. I have come to the reluctant conclusion that it might work. It seems that no one knows, or at least no one cares any longer, that Rassa Pahlavi is a grandson of the shah. He lives a quiet life, a simple life. And though I pray it never happens, and I hope you are wrong (blessed be your name, your Royal Highness, for I do not mean to ever disagree!), but from what I have seen I believe your plan could possibly work. *If* we are careful. And if we are left with no choice."

*******

A little more than seven hundred kilometers to the west, the crown prince of the House of Saud, future king of Saudi Arabia, thanked his loyal servant then hung up the phone. He stared a long moment, considering what he should do.

Was he that close? Was it real? Was the danger as near as he feared?

He knew that it was. And there was no time to hesitate any longer. He needed to put his plan into action.

He huffed with emotion, then picked up his secure phone again. "When will General Brighton be here?" he asked.

# DARKNESS OF THIS WORLD
## [W&R: Episode Two]

*For we wrestle not against flesh and blood,*

*but against principalities, against powers,*

*against the rulers of the darkness of this world...*

*Ephesians 6:12*

# ONE

**Karachi, Pakistan**

The Palestinian moved through the crowd easily for he was comfortable here. Although he was not among his own people, the sounds and scents were the same. He felt the constant press of flesh against him, the movement of the crowd, the chatty voices of women and the terse growls of men, too busy, too arrogant, too grand to respond to their wives. He smelled the tang of old bodies and felt the gritty dirt on his feet. He felt the uneven pavement beneath him and the white hot, oppressive glare of the sun, wringing great drops of sweat from under his arms and around the small of his back. Everyone sweats in Karachi; they sweat to keep cool, and they sweat to survive. No one was clean in Karachi. It was just the way it was.

The Palestinian moved around a brown and rusted cement hole in the sidewalk, one of the public toilets that was built without the benefit of even a curtain for privacy. He moved through the crowd, working his way toward a small open-air market half a mile down the street. In the distance, he heard a series of gunfire and a replying series of gunfire, but he paid no attention for it was almost a full block away, and gunfire in Karachi could be heard daily. In any given day, six people lost their lives to petty thieves, gang wars, drug runners, hate or revenge. The slave trade that flourished on the outskirts of the city fed the dangerously high murder rate, but also a significant contributor to the local economic machine. Teenage Afghan, Chinese, India and Pakistani captives were harbored in Karachi before being shipped off to brothels throughout the Pacific Rim. Even as he walked, the Palestinian passed a group of three teenage girls bound together. For thirty *dinre* he could have bought any one of them.

Stopping on the corner, the Palestinian waited for the traffic. He glanced quickly around him, turning his back on the street to look in the direction from which he had come. To his side, a roughly mortared brick wall sported an old movie poster. Tom Cruise smiled at him, his long black hair drooping over his eye. The Palestinian frowned, and turned around. A break came in the traffic and he crossed the street.

Ten minutes later, he sat down at a wooden table at an outdoor café. The owner moved toward him, then recognized his face and instead turned for the kitchen. Seconds later, he emerged with a mug of hot *cheka* tea in hand.

"Amid," the owner said as he placed the small cup on the table. "God be blessed, you are safe. It is good to see you again."

The Palestinian, a tall man with dark eyes and enormous ears, nodded to the restaurateur. "How is your fish?"

"Very fresh, *Sayid,*" the owner lied.

The Palestinian grunted and pointed to his plate. The restaurateur nodded and moved through an open door and into his kitchen.

Minutes later, the Palestinian was eating his meal: a charcoaled slab of sea trout, with its head and bones still intact, and a bowl of white rice with hot mustard sauce. The crowd thronged around him, moving up and down the street. An occasional automobile passed by, forcing pedestrians onto the narrow sidewalk and around the small tables of the outdoor café. A group of children played in the street, gleefully chasing each other. A mule pulled a decrepit wagon with one wheel on the sidewalk and the other on the street.

Halfway through the Palestinian's meal, a Pakistani man emerged from the crowd, approached and sat down without saying a word. In contrast to the Palestinian, who was dressed in a traditional flowing *dakish*, the Pakistani was dressed in black slacks and an open white shirt. Neither of the men was distinguishable in the crowd.

As the Pakistani sat down, Amid looked up and held his fork to his mouth.

The Pakistani lit up a cigarette. "Amid Safi Mohammad, how is your meal?" he asked.

Amid Mohammad didn't answer, but pushed in another forkful of fish. The Pakistani watched him chew, then leaned forward in his chair. Mohammad pulled away as he caught the whiff of cologne. He studied the Pakistani, then wiped his mouth with the back of his hand. "Brother, I have to disagree with you on this meeting place," he said in a heavy voice. "I don't believe it is wise." The Palestinian paused and glanced to the sky, almost as if he expected to see an American satellite hovering there. His eyes darted down the street. "The rats have eyes, eyes like spiders, they can see everything."

The Pakistani nodded. He appreciated his fellow warrior's fear. But they were in his territory now, and he was not concerned. This was his city, his territory, his tribe controlled everything and he knew every movement of the American spies. His crew had identified every one of them and kept each under a close watch, and yes, the Americans got around, but he also had evidence that they were not watching today.

He dramatically crushed out his cigarette. "Mohammad, you have to trust me," he answered knowingly while nodding almost imperceptibly to the roof of a squat cement building on the other side of the street. "The Great Satan has many eyes, but this is my lair. We are safe here, I assure you, my people are near. That is, of course, unless you allowed yourself to be followed . . . ," the Pakistani's voice trailed off. The accusation was clear.

"No, no," Amid Safi Mohammad quickly replied. "I was careful.

I followed your instructions to the letter."

"All right then." The Pakistani sat back and picked at his teeth. "Now, let's get it done."

Amid Mohammad pushed his dirty plate aside. "This will be our last meeting. Our work is almost complete."

"Good. I agree. It has been a dreadfully long year."

"You have done very well, doctor. My people are pleased."

The Pakistani only nodded. If Mohammad only knew! If he had any idea what the Pakistani had gone through! For more than eighteen years, he had lived on a knife's edge, a simple breath away from being discovered. He wanted this over. It was time to relax and enjoy his money. He took a deep breath and forced a thin smile. "The arrangements for the final delivery have been made," he said. "All we have left to do is to transfer the money."

The Palestinian nodded. "How is your memory?" he asked.

The Pakistani frowned. "Not good, as you know."

"Then get a pencil."

The Pakistani reached quickly into his pocket and pulled out a small pencil. He grabbed a napkin as the Palestinian started to speak.

"The payment will be deposited into an account drawn on the Soloman Bank of Malaysia. The account number will be forwarded to you by private messenger later tonight. The withdrawal instructions and authentication codes are authenticate zulu, one, four, whiskey seventy-nine—that's seventy-nine, not seven nine—then today's date and my birthday."

The Pakistani scribbled furiously.

"The money will only remain in the account for three minutes," the Palestinian continued. "That's three minutes, Dr. Atta, not one second more. If you haven't transferred the money out of the account within the three-minute window, we will repossess it and move it ourselves, and if that happens, it is over. Our business is done. We will have the hardware and you won't have anything."

The Pakistani looked up and frowned. "That will not be necessary," he answered defiantly. "I will make the transfer, don't you worry about that."

The Palestinian glanced down the street. "I'm not worried, Doctor Atta, but the instructions from my client are clear."

The Pakistani nodded. Amid went on. "Our people at the bank will be monitoring every transfer. Once the money has been deposited into this first account, you will immediately move the money into another account at the same bank. A second messenger will provide you with the specifics pertaining to this account. Once again, the money will remain there three minutes. Three minutes to make your transfer or we take possession again. From there, you will move the money into twelve separate accounts drawn on various banks in the Philippines. After that, you are on your own. We wash our hands of the paper trail."

The Pakistani looked up from his paper. "And the messengers?" he asked.

"Same men as before. You will recognize them both."

The Pakistani sat back and pulled out another cigarette. "Fifty million?" he confirmed.

"As we agreed."

"And the final installment?"

"Upon delivery of the last nuclear warhead," the Palestinian wet his cracked lips.

The Pakistani tightened his fingers around the butt of his brown cigarette. Suddenly, without reason, he began to sweat like a pig. He pressed his lips together and folded the paper napkin into a small square.

He studied his client. "So that is it?" he concluded.

The Palestinian nodded. "I believe that it is."

"We will not meet again."

"There is no reason."

"So tell me, before we separate, I would dearly like to know. Where did you get your money? One hundred million U.S. dollars is not a small sum. Who is your financer, I'm dying to know."

"A poor choice of words, Dr. Atta. Be careful what you ask for or you might get your wish."

The Pakistani scowled. "I have provided you with nuclear warheads, not an easy thing to do. I am taking an enormous risk, more than you could ever know. I control many generals, but I do not control every one. I have put my neck in a noose here. Don't I deserve to know who is financing this operation?"

The Palestinian pushed himself away from the table. "Too many questions is not a good thing. The money will be delivered. That is all you need to know. We want the last warhead by Friday. Now our business is done."

The Palestinian dropped a couple dirty *dinres* on the table and moved for the street.

*******

Two days later, a rusted container ship loaded with barrels of refined kerosene, lubricants, and refurbished electrical generators, left the port at Karachi bound for the Straits of Hormuz. It only took three days to reach the port of Ad Dammam, the huge Saudi port on the eastern shore of the Persian Gulf.

On the burning pavement of the seaside dock, three large but non-descript crates were loaded onto the back of a two-ton army truck. The truck pulled away from the warehouse and turned to drive south. Overhead, two helicopters followed its path.

That night, the third, fourth and fifth nuclear warheads were placed in an underground storage facility on the Saudi air force base of Al Hufuf.

*******

Twenty hours after the last warhead was delivered, Dr. Abu Nidal Atta, deputy director, Pakistan Special Weapons Section, principal advisor on national security to the Pakistani president himself, didn't wake up after his customary afternoon nap. When his wife couldn't rouse him, she immediately called for his personal doctor. He arrived within minutes, but it was already too late. The doctor's heart had ruptured. There was nothing he could do.

An autopsy was requested by the physician, but the president of Pakistan turned down the request. Following local tradition, the body was cremated before sundown that day.

*******

Prince al-Rahman smiled when he was informed of the news. He waved his advisor out of his office and immediately picked up the phone. "Get my money back," he commanded. "I want every dime."

# TWO

**Riyadh, Saudi Arabia**

A little more than four hours after taking off from Ramstein Air Force Base in Germany, Major General Brighton's C-20 lined up on final approach at Riyadh's civilian airport. Upon landing, he met the local staff and immediately went to work, attending endless meetings, conferring with the ambassador and his military staff, the CIA station chief, and six others involved with trying to keep the kingdom from falling off the cliff. He slept four hours that night, then got back to work.

Late that afternoon, after completing his official assignments within the kingdom, Brighton stood on the balcony of his suite of the grand Al Faisaliah hotel, waiting for his car to pick him up and take him to his appointment with Prince Saud. Standing next to the glass rail that surrounded the balcony, he looked down upon a city that glistened in the brilliant setting sun.

Riyadh sits in the middle of the Arabian Peninsula. It's an exceptionally modern city, with a stunning architectural mix of glass high-rise buildings and ancient desert mosques. The skyscrapers ascend like something out of a children's drawing book: sweeping arches, enormous space-saucer shaped coliseum, forked skyscrapers made of steel, glass and glistening chrome. The streets are tree-lined and well-lit, and swept daily to keep the blowing sand at bay. Desert browns, whites, and pastels are the dominant colors, and though the city is considered one of the modern wonders of the world, traditional Arab influence can be seen in the arched doorways, dome-topped mosques and caliph-inspired city center. Enormous highways sweep through the city, the cement having been laid over the trails where Bedouin camels used to trek.

The capital city of the kingdom, with a population of almost five million people, Riyadh was derived from an Arab word meaning *place of garden and trees.* Ancient wadis run through the center of the city and the surrounding soil is fertile and rich. Powerful electric motors pump fresh water from deep underground aquifers to keep the manmade oasis green and desirable.

To the west and south of the city, the terrain rises gradually for four hundred miles until it suddenly juts upward at the rocky Midian Mountains. To the east, the land descends through the Summan, gradually transforming from barren desert to rangelands to the fertile crescent that borders the Persian Gulf. A constant wind blows from the desert and the flies seem to swarm when the night cools down, especially when the date trees are bearing fruit. To the south lies the *Rub'el Khal*—the Empty Quarter—a land so bleak and brutal few humans have ever trekked across its sands; a land so desolate the Saudis were more than happy to give most of it to Yemen and Oman.

Overhead, the sky is almost always a deep gray-blue, a huge open saucer sitting over the land; cloudless and so deep in color it seems as if one were looking at the edge of space. The air is clean and clear, and the lights from the city can be seen for hundreds of miles on a clear desert night. Spring storms can bring violent rain, and the sandstorms can be deadly if one is caught in the open, but for three hundred and forty days a year the weather is monotonously predictable. Hot and dry in January, searing hot the rest of the year.

Like the city, the entire Kingdom of Saudi Arabia is a bewildering example of contradictions and extremes.

Much of the nation is an entirely inhospitable desert, yet the oases that dot the country are lush, wet and brimming with life. The cities are bright, beautiful and more contemporary than any in the world, but beyond their city limits, the Bedouin nomads live much as they have for almost two thousand years. The Royal Family jets around the globe, meeting with Hollywood celebrities and foreign heads of state, headlining cultural conferences and human rights events, while the women in some localities are not even allowed to learn how to read. The Saudi infrastructure is modern in every way, but the Kingdom still denies basic freedoms of expression and many human rights. The *Qur'an* teaches love and peace, emphasizing the need for discussion and the give-and-take of discourse, yet the royal family allows no opposing political parties; indeed there are no political parties in the kingdom at all, and the royal family was certainly not a party, but a close-knit, manipulative and fortified group of relatives who guard their family secrets above everything else.

It is as if the government straddles two ice floes that are moving apart; one foot in the West and one foot in the desert, preaching progress and equality while denying the same. Any expression of anti-government activity is unthinkable. Women cannot drive or even appear in public without a male family member as escort. Use of corporal punishment is the rule. In fact, the punishment for various offenses is precisely prescribed in Saudi law—beheadings for rape, murder, sodomy, or sorcery; amputations of the feet or hands for robbery; and public lashings for offenses such as public drunkenness.

All of the media, including the eight daily newspapers, are owned and controlled by one prince or another. The government maintains the Royal Decree for Printed Material and Publications with a list of topics that are prohibited to be written about or discussed. The Saudi Communications Company controls the backbone network through which access to the Internet must pass, and the list of approved sites is very short indeed. The *mutawwa* are tasked with enforcing the Wahhabist interpretation of Islam by scouring the culture for immoral teachings or immodest dress. Every public facility, including Western businesses like McDonalds or Starbucks, must enforce a kind of sexual apartheid, with separate entries and facilities for women and men. The men's sections are lavish and comfortable, while the women and family sections are often dilapidated and neglected, sometimes not even offering seats.

It is appalling to those who aren't familiar with the culture. But it is the way it's been in Saudi Arabia for hundreds of years.

Until now.

Now there were a very few of those who felt it was time to make a change. A few men within the royal family who felt it was time to turn the monarchy over to the forces of democratic power.

His Royal Highness, King Faysal, Monarch of the House of Saud, was one of those men.

King Faysal knew it would take several generations for the transition to be complete, but he was convinced that democracy and the teachings of Islam were not mutually exclusive ideals, and it was time for the kingdom to take the first step. Which meant it was time for the monarch to give up much of his family's great power. It was a radical heretical and insane idea! But King Faysal had already begun. Over the past twenty years, he had reined in the *mutawwa*, set up civil courts with professional judges, authorized city councils outside of the influence of royal patronage, and, for the first time, named men to senior government positions who were not his nephews or sons. The next step was to free the press. A national assembly would follow, though that was still ten or fifteen years away.

Fighting two hundred years of tradition, the courageous king had instituted the first steps of reform.

But to say there was resistance among the princes would have been a colossal understatement, for they knew what they would lose. All of their money and power was at risk. They were the richest family in the world. It was a lot to give away.

The king understood their anger, for he wasn't a fool. Still, after a long life of laying the foundation, King Faysal intended to accelerate the transition to democracy by appointing his first son, Crown Prince Saud bin Faysal, to take his place on the throne, and Crown Prince Saud bin Faysal would be the last king, for he had already made a covenant with his father to complete the transition to democracy.

The only problem, of course, was that there were other sons.

And they were far from convinced that Crown Prince Saud should be king.

*******

On the outskirts of the great city, at the end of a tree-lined road that abruptly stopped at a cement barricade, behind a wall with hidden towers and razor wire, was one of the three dozen homes the Crown Prince of the House of Saud had. The future king was a large man with dark eyes and broad shoulders and short, curly hair. He was forty-seven, but looked younger, though there were days he felt very old. With a degree from the Kennedy School of Government at Harvard, the crown prince was decisive and sharp-tongued with his subordinates, but warm and easily manipulated by his family and friends.

The prince sat quietly at the end of an enormous mahogany table. To his side, sat the American general. They were the only two men in a room so large it could have accommodated a group of a hundred or more. Brilliant tapestries, some five hundred years old, hung on the walls. The floor was imported Italian tile, the doorframes were rare and unnamed woods shipped from the Indian forest. The ceiling moldings were gold plated. Crushed glass had been mixed with the pastel paints on the walls, giving the room a brilliant radiance from the desert sun that reflected through the twenty-foot windows.

The general stared for a brief moment, taking in the beauty of the room. The prince didn't notice. He had a lot on his mind. He needed a smoke and he fidgeted nervously as he tapped on his pack of American cigarettes. Moving his chair across the tile, the prince leaned his arms on the table. "Coffee?" he offered.

The general shook his head.

"I've got some beautiful teas I've brought in from Oman. The leaf is so thick, it will, how do you say it . . . knock your feet off."

The general smiled. "I think you mean knock your socks off, Prince Saud, and no tea, but thank you." He smiled again, knowing the prince was teasing him now.

"How about a Coke then, General Brighton?"

"Yes. That'd be great."

"Diet? Caffeine free?"

"Regular Coke is fine."

"Oh, you crazy fool!" the prince scolded, trying to hide the smile on his face. "Get you away from Sara and you *really* cut loose! Next thing you know, you'll visit my kingdom and take home another wife!"

The general shook his head adamantly. "You know Sara. I don't need to say any more."

"Yes, yes, General Brighton," the prince finally smiled. "If all men were so lucky! And frankly, good friend, I don't understand how she fell for you. You are like a Bedouin camel herder who married a princess. Despite all your failings, God has smiled on you."

Neil only nodded. The crown prince was joking, but he knew it was true. "And how is Princess Tala?" Neil asked.

Saud nodded happily. "Beautiful as ever! And did you know we were expecting another son?"

Neil smiled happily. "Congratulations!"

Prince Saud clapped his hands in a gesture of gratitude, then touched a hidden button under his desk. A young Indian man hurried into the room holding a silver tray over his head. He poured soda for the American and tea for his master, then laid out a silver tray of sugar cookies and pastries and hurried from the room.

The crown prince studied his friend and smiled with satisfaction. "How long has it been, Neil?" he asked.

"I don't know, Crown Prince Saud," Neil replied. He never called the prince by his first name. "Sometime just before the fall of the Prince Basser. We saw each other at the U.N. Liberation Conference. That's been, what, almost a year now?"

The prince grimaced slightly at the use of the word *Liberation*. Well, maybe. Depending on who one was talking to. He sipped at his tea. "You are too busy now, Neil," he said over his china tea cup. "We never have time to talk! I used to see you regularly until you earned your first star."

"Life has picked up a little, there's no doubt about that."

"And you have grown so quiet, my good friend. Tight-lipped and secretive. Are you never going to tell me about what you do now?"

"Your Highness, you already know. I work for the NSA. Long days, piles of paperwork, endless meetings, buckets of mindless reports, huge egos and office politics more bloody than war. There, that's my job. Not much excitement, I assure you of that."

The crown prince huffed in sarcastic reply. "I think that's not true, my good friend. Not now. Not in these times. Not with the battles raging against rising tides. You're the military liaison to the White House national security advisor! You are the tip of the sword. *Everything* runs through the NSA! Every proposal, every war plan or decision is vetted through you. It is a *very* important position. High visibility. Very fast track. You personally brief the president almost every week. I'd say, my good friend, you are on your way to the top. Chairman of the Joint Chiefs. Doesn't that have a good ring?"

The general didn't answer, but picked up his glass and took a drink of his soda.

"I think you are involved in quite important decisions that you can't talk about," the prince prodded. "*Which was exactly why I brought you here,*" he quickly thought to himself. "*If you will just listen! If you will read between the lines. If you will think and remember what I tell you today!*"

The prince tapped the pack of cigarettes as he thought to himself. "How are your sons?" he then asked. "Twin sons! Allah has blessed you. How old are they now? They must almost be men!"

"Luke and Ammon turned nineteen last winter, and Sam, do you remember our adopted son? He's in the Army. I'm proud of them all. "

The prince smiled happily. "I am happy for you and Sara. You are good parents, I think, even in your old age."

Brighton laughed. "Remember, Your Highness, I am two years younger than you, and you don't seem to be slowing down in your parenting despite *your* old age. Didn't you just tell me Princess Tala was about to have another son."

"Yes, well, it is one of the responsibilities of a king. I'm just doing my job." Both men smiled before the prince continued in a much more serious tone. "As the crown prince of the House of Saud, the royal line runs through my veins, leaving me the obligation to produce future kings, and though I have eight daughters, I have only three sons. All of my younger brothers have more sons than I do. It leaves me in a position of weakness, I'm afraid."

The crown prince peered at the general, an intense look on his face. *"Listen to me, Neil! See the look in my eye! I can't say it out loud, so remember my words. I have only three sons. My brothers have many more. My oldest son will be the next king, but only IF they let him live!"*

General Brighton watched the prince carefully as an uncomfortable silence developed. The prince was worried about something. He sensed it and frowned, not knowing what to say.

The prince stared at him a moment, then sipped at his tea. *"Is this room also bugged,"* he wondered? *"Do they listen here as they listen everywhere?"*

Brighton pushed his chair back from the table to cross his legs, then brushed his hand through his hair. "You know, Prince Saud, for a short time we had the most exquisite decoration hanging over our fireplace at home. A silver-and-gold emblem of the House of Saud. Two crossed swords and a palm tree. It was simply the most beautiful thing we ever owned."

"You enjoy it?"

"Of course!" Brighton answered as he thought of the gift from the prince. Three hundred thousand dollars worth of gold, silver, diamonds and pearls! (He had been forced to appraise it before turning it over to the government.) He shook his head. "It was too much, my good friend!" he said.

"Are you kidding? To celebrate the coming of age of your sons? It was too little, I assure you, and it was but the smallest token of my affection for you and your wife. When a son reaches adulthood, it is reason for celebration. I just wanted you and Sara to know I was thinking of you."

The general sipped his soda. "Thank you again, Your Highness.

Still, you are too generous, and of course, as you know, I had to register the gift with the Pentagon Ethics Division. They actually own it now. It is property of the U.S. government. They let me keep it for awhile, but it is not really mine. Conflict of interest. I hope you understand."

"I understand, I understand. I even suspected that might be necessary. When you retire, I will send you another one just like it that will truly be yours."

"Your Highness, perhaps it would be better . . . ."

The prince waved a dismissive hand. "Please, Neil, it is a tiny thing to me and I want to do it, OK? Now instead of worrying about the complications of gifts and ethics, let's pretend for a while, OK? Let's pretend we're fighter pilots again. Let's pretend we don't have the weight of the world on our shoulders. Let's pretend time hasn't changed us and the world is more simple and less dangerous, like it was before. Let's pretend we are back at fighter pilot school, back when you weren't so impressed that I came from the royal family and I was more impressed with your flying, and please, will you not call me Your Highness? When it's just you and me, and no one else is around, can we go back to the way that it once used to be? Let's go back to our call signs. I'll call you Gameboy and you call me Sultan."

The general laughed at the memory of when they were young pilots learning to fly the F-15, a couple young lieutenants slicing the air like thunderbolts through the skies. They felt like Greek gods! They had the power of flight! Nothing could destroy them! They were invincible!

Both men smiled as they relived their private memories. Then the prince spoke, "General Brighton, over the years, you have always been a good friend. We see each other so rarely, but it always seems like nothing has changed."

The American general nodded. "I was thinking the same thing on my flight over. It's been, what, more than twenty years since we first met at Eglin. Remember that place, Prince Saud? I used to complain about the heat. You complained about the cold. Playing golf until midnight with those stupid glow-in-the-dark balls, then staying up to study until 3 a.m. Life was simple. Those were truly good days."

"We didn't have so much responsibility, that's for sure. Now here I am, the crown prince, and you, one of the youngest generals in the Air Force. We both carry heavy burdens. It's not quite like the old days when the only thing we worried about was crashing into each other or running out of fuel." The prince fell quiet, then added, "You know though, I have pretty much proven I am a better pilot than you."

The general had to laugh. "Are we really going to have this conversation again?"

"No, no really, Neil. Think back to when we first met. As I recall, you made a pretty big deal about how American fighter pilots were the best in the world. I took exception. Now I think it's time to lay down our cards and see what we have."

Brighton looked down and pressed the dark blouse of his Air Force blues. "You know, Prince Saud, we're never going to settle this until we strap on a jet and call 'fights on' in the air."

"No, no, no, that's not true. We have twenty years' worth of flying to back up our claims. Now, let me see, how many enemy fighters have you shot down?"

"Not fair, Saud! I was working on the staff during the war. No one was more disappointed than I was that I was not flying!"

"Yes, my sympathies, OK. Now back to my question. I had two confirmed kills. Really had three, but the gun camera jammed so I couldn't confirm that last kill, and you know the rules, no gun camera footage, no kill. Either way, I'm not selfish. I'll let the other one go. So let's see, that's two, really three, as I just said, and you have, ah, how many enemy jets have you shot down in your career . . . ?" The prince's voice trailed off but his eyes twinkled brightly.

The general shifted in his seat. His face remained calm, but he clasped his hands. The competitor inside him started to rise.

The prince looked for the white knuckles. He knew his friend well. "OK, OK, let's not talk about that," he said. "You're right, that wouldn't be fair. I mean, it's not your fault you were forced to be a staff boy when the big show came to town. Let's take another measure, ah, flying hours. I've got almost three thousand. More fighter time in the Eagle than any other pilot in the entire Royal Saudi Air Force."

"Got you there, Saud," Brighton replied. "I'm pushing almost three thousand five hundred flying hours."

"Really? That is impressive!" The prince settled back in his chair. "But you know, of course, that I'm not including any of the time I've logged as an F-15 instructor pilot. Can't count sitting in the backseat, watching some lieutenant jerk the control stick around. That's not real flying, keeping some insane student pilot from killing himself! Real pilots do it. Watching doesn't count! Now Neil, you're not including your instructor time, are you, because if I were to do that, I'd be up around three thousand six hundred hours." Again, the prince smiled. Game and match!

The general struggled a moment, then shook his head and laughed. "OK, you win, Your Highness. But let me add, even if I could beat you, do you think I would be so foolish? Show up the crown prince of Saudi Arabia, the next in line for the throne! Can you image the diplomatic crisis such a lapse of judgment would create! So I will hold my tongue."

The prince shook his head, then stared at his glass. A still silence followed and the lawn sprinklers could be heard from outside.

"Prince Saud," Brighton said, "it's good to be here, and it's always enjoyable to remember old times with you. But I know there's a reason why you invited me. I can see there's something on your mind."

The prince lowered his eyes, then looked again at his friend. His face was suddenly serious and Brighton could see the deep crow's feet that lined his dark eyes. The prince pushed up from his seat. "Come, let's walk," he said.

# THREE

**Along the Potomac River, northwest of Washington D.C.**

It would be their most difficult climb. In fact, it probably was impossible to make it to the top. It wasn't that the rock was too high, or the way the granite jutted outward to create an inversion near the top, a jagged ledge that thrust into space. Nor was it because the face of the rock was so sheer. The thing that was going to make the climb so challenging was that there were so few protrusions to place their feet on or cracks to grab a hold of. It would be exhausting to make it to the ledge, then crushingly difficult after that.

Still, they looked up in hunger at the challenge.

At least one of them did.

Luke and Ammon stood at the bottom of the rock, the sun shining behind them and warming their shoulders with its early morning light while several birds sang around them; sparrows, mockingbirds and robins calling to each other from the trees that lined the riverbed. The air was crisp and smelled of dead leaves and wet sand. The Potomac River ran low as it always did in the fall and swirled behind them, the water twenty feet from the shoreline where the sand and brush met the rocky cliffs. Above them, a sheer wall of rock rose up from the river, the remnant of some geological aberration that had piled the sand and sediment then crushed it into stone before a million of years of running water cut the softer sediment away from the harder rock.

Luke reached out and touched the cold wall. It was wet and slimy from a small crack that wept from the underground aquifer. The water ran clear and formed a mossy trail that ran down the stone. He pressed his finger into the moss then tasted his finger as he looked around the falls.

The Great Falls of the Potomac is one of the most spectacular natural landmarks on the entire east coast. Above the falls, the Potomac narrows from a wide and meandering river to a powerful ribbon of water that cuts through the Mather Gorge with incredible force. The river drops nearly eighty feet in little less than a mile, crashing over a series of twenty-foot waterfalls and cascading rapids before splitting into multiple frothing fingers running through the rocky channels that make up the lower part of the gorge. For the past ten thousand years, the Potomac has cut through the bedrock, eroding the falls and the riverbank into a moon-like terrain while leaving rock formations that are sheer and jagged and perfect for climbing.

Luke pressed the mossy dribble of water again then moved a few feet to his right, where the stone was dry and bare. Ammon glanced at the trail that led from the riverbed up the side of the steep bank.

"Is there anything in the world that is better than this?" asked Luke.

"Ahh, let me think. Got one. Girls. Yeah, girls are definitely better that this."

Luke shook his head. "I mean other than that."

"Ahh, steak. Yeah. Both steak or lobster is better than this."

"OK. Two things."

"Yeah, and sleep. Sleep is *much* better!"

"Be quiet, OK? This is great. Winter's coming. This might be our last time to climb before it gets too cold."

"Wait, I'm not finished . . . television's better . . . yeah, I think I'd rather watch televison than get up at five in the morning just to climb rocks."

Luke looked dismayed. "OK, I'm sorry I dragged you out here, all right!"

Ammon smiled and cracked his brother on the back. "Just kidding you, dog. You know I'd rather be here with you than anywhere in the world."

"A little early for sarcasm."

"Just trying to get things going, you know, lighten things up a bit." Ammon smiled again and picked up the rope and climbing harness.

Luke studied the wall, lifting his head to the top of the cliff almost fifty feet overhead. Near the top, a sheer ledge jutted outward from the wall at a sixty-degree angle. He studied the cliff for handholds, then pointed to a trail of tiny cracks leading up to the overhang. "I could climb up to that ledge," he said, pointing to where the rock jutted outward from the sheer wall.

"Yeah, and then what?" Ammon asked.

Luke studied the overhang. "It looks like there might be a few holds," he took a few steps back, "there . . . ." he pointed with his right arm, using it to guide Ammon's eyes toward a tiny crack in the rock. "If I could reach behind me for two feet or so, I could jam my hands in that crack."

"Yeah. Then all you'd have to do is hold on to that ledge with your teeth."

Luke glanced at his brother. "You don't think I can do it, do you?"

"No, Luke, I don't think *anyone* can do it. You'll be reaching out a full arms length above and behind you while hanging on with only one hand . . . no, correction, you'll be hanging on with only your fingers. I don't care how strong you are, no one could reach that far behind them and get their hand into that crack. Not while hanging on the wall anyway."

"But I could if . . ."

197

"Even if you do reach the crevasse, Luke, what are you going to do then? It's a vertical fissure; it runs *up and down* the rock, not across. You'd have to jam your fist in there then let go of the wall and pull yourself up by only one hand. No one could do it, not even you, Luke."

Luke kept his eyes up while he nodded. "You're probably right," he said in disappointment.

"Of course I'm right."

"Probably no one could do it."

"It'll probably *never* be done."

"Certainly no one's ever done it before now."

"Certainly not."

Luke continued staring above him. "Cool," he muttered under his breath.

The outcropping was a little more than forty feet up the wall. Forty feet. Four stories. A long way to fall. He lowered his eyes from the ledge and surveyed the scattered pile of boulders and rocks that had been strewn by the river at that base of the wall. Some were as big as his fist, some the size of small tables. All would hurt equally if he were to fall.

Ammon nudged his brother and pointed twenty feet to their right. "There's our spot," he said. "See that, there's a good crevasse we could jam our feet in, and plenty of handholds. We could climb the first forty feet there, then move to our left, come in above the overhang and go up from there." He took a step back. "Once we're above that ledge, it's easy climbing from there."

Luke looked up and saw where his brother was pointing. "Yeah, that's a pretty good plan. But you know, Ammon, I'd really like to try climbing up *here*."

Ammon grumbled. He knew what his brother was thinking. "Luke," he said, "let's not waste our time. There's no way you're going to get over that ledge. Look at it, Luke! It juts out at least six feet, and there's nothing to hold onto. So you're going to make me climb up the back side of the cliff to secure the rope, you'll spend twenty minutes climbing the rock and who knows how long trying to get over that ledge, then you'll have to give up and come down. By then you'll be too exhausted to try anything else. So we'll waste an hour for nothing. Come on man, let's just climb over there. There's enough cracks that I won't have to go up the backside to secure the rope, we can use the fissures to secure our own nuts, set our own safety devices as we climb. You can climb first, then I'll take a shot. We'll both get in a good climb before we have to go."

Luke was still studying his path up the rock to the overhang. "If I can get a good grip on the crevasse, I could pull myself to the edge of the overhang. Then I could hold onto the lip, swing my legs up and pull myself over the top."

"Come on, man. You don't have to do this, OK. All you'll do is waste our time."

"I know I don't have to. But I want to try."

"Let's just . . . ."

"I know what you're going to say, let's just climb over there. But you know what I was thinking, Ammon?"

Ammon grunted and didn't answer as Luke pulled on his thin leather gloves.

"I was thinking about Sam. If he were here, you *know* what he would do? He'd want to see if he could climb over that ledge, and if he didn't make it today, he'd come back tomorrow, and again the next day, and the next day after that. He'd figure a way to get up and over that ledge! You know that he would. He'd try a thousand times if he had to, but he'd figure a way to get over that outcropping up there."

Ammon shook his head. "Sam's a stubborn fool."

"Stubborn? Maybe. I guess. But is stubborn bad? Because when I watch Sam put his mind to something and never give up, it doesn't seem like such a bad thing, you know."

Ammon shook his head again. "I just want a nice, normal gut-wrenching climb. I want to get a good workout, then get back to school. You, on the other hand, want to prove something to yourself. You want to prove something to Sam, and he's not even here."

"I don't have to prove anything."

"Then let's climb over there where it isn't so dangerous and we won't be wasting our time!" Ammon shot back in exasperation.

Luke was strapping his climbing harness on. "I'm going to try it here, Ammon. Now will you go up and secure the rope, or are you going to make me do it?"

Ammon huffed in frustration, then picked up the rope and started up the trail that led up the backside of the cliff.

*******

*Balaam and Roth stood very close to the brothers, their faces contorted in burning jealousy and hate. Lucifer stood beside them, but he stayed out of the way. After their failure to destroy the girl in Persia, he knew his servants were desperate for even a small victory. So he kept the pressure on them, throwing glares of suspicion and belittlement in their direction. "Let them work," thought Lucifer. "Let them compete with each other. Keep them motivated by jealousy and desire to push the other out of the way."*

*Balaam turned toward the mortals, his eyes narrowing with fear. These young men had the power to threaten them. So they had to be destroyed.*

*Glancing toward Lucifer, Balaam caught a glimpse of his own ugliness reflected in Lucifer's dark eyes and stepped back. Like Lucifer, Balaam was pale and deadly, a corpse suspended in the air, his face so lifeless and dreary he couldn't stand the sight of himself. He was hideous and he knew it, but he no longer cared. But unlike Lucifer, who could still hide his repulsiveness if someone was willing to believe in his lies, Balaam was dark, cruel and ugly, and pretended to be nothing else.*

*Lucifer walked in a circle around the young men, listening to them talking while thinking to himself. Balaam watched him carefully, but remained still.*

*Lucifer was dressed in his normal garb; braided sandals, a red sash and a flowing gray robe, dark as smoke but with a light sheen, as if there was some unseen power there. His hood fell over his shoulders and his hair flowed down his neck. His feet were as worn and sullied as any vagabond who walked the earth.*

*Balaam studied Lucifer from out of the corner of his eye, noting the growing strength of his shoulders and his powerful arms. Lucifer's dark hair seemed to shimmer and his eyes burned with fire. He stood in great arrogance, almost reeking in power while basking in the glory that his hateful lies had produced. The world was more evil than it had ever been; more brutal, more carnal and more sinful, and the more the world bathed in evil, the more powerful Lucifer had become.*

*But there was growing good among the shadows—these young brothers, for example—and Balaam was troubled. Like tiny points of light that penetrated the darkness, the great spirits had arrived to make their mark on the world, and they too were growing powerful, more pure and more clear. That made Balaam wonder . . . .*

*He kicked at the ground with unease.*

*Lucifer turned to look at him suddenly, as if he had read his mind. "You see them too, servant Balaam?" he asked in a deadly voice.*

*Balaam nodded slowly.*

*"You think they grow stronger? And you think that I grow weak?"*

*Balaam swallowed and bowed. "No Master Mayhem," he pleaded in a trembling voice. "You are the Great Master, king of this world!"*

*Lucifer dismissed him with an angry wave of his hand. "That is right,*

*Balaam. I am the king of this world! I am its glory and splendor, its magnificent power! And I am still rising! My day is soon to come! And as my glory grows, the veil between my angels and this world will come down. A few see me now, but in time all will see. I will stand in my dark glory before them and they shall see me as I am! I appear unto a few now, but the time is soon coming when I will appear unto all. I will step forward in power and claim this world for my own! And then they shall know, and their mouths shall confess, that it is my glory that burns bright in this land!"*

*Balaam nodded eagerly but said nothing, his gut crunching into a tight ball as he lowered his eyes, knowing they would betray him if Lucifer saw. Balaam wanted to believe, he wanted it desperately, but he felt in his heart that it simply wasn't true. He felt his gloom rising as the final battle approached, the day when he would be stripped of his power and brought to his knees, when Lucifer's kingdom would be shattered and his minions destroyed.*

*The Deceiver watched Balaam, noting that he kept his eyes down. "Do you believe me, Master Balaam?" he sneered.*

*"Master Mayhem, I want to believe!"*

*"If you ever had faith in me, Master Balaam, then you'd better have faith in me now. You are tied to my future. I am all that you have. So when you pray to me, Balaam, you had better believe your own words!"*

*Balaam began to tremble in terrible fear. He had seen Lucifer angry, and the last thing Balaam wanted was to feel Lucifer's anger now! Balaam quivered, then dropped to one knee. "I believe, Master Mayhem!" he cried in a loud voice.*

*The Deceiver grunted in disgust, then turned away once more.*

*Lucifer moved a step toward the brothers and faced them, looking them straight in the eyes. They moved and talked around him, completely unaware that he was standing so close that he could plant thoughts into their minds.*

*Staring at them, the vaguest of memories came flooding back. It was lost in fog—it had been so long ago—but as he concentrated, it came to him.*

*Long ago . . . another place . . . . they stood in a dark stairway in Lucifer's old world. It was black and suffocating, and smelled of rot and wet soil. A cold rain pelted the rock structure and the wail of Lucifer's followers lifted through the air.*

*A few of those who fought against him stood before him at the top of the stairs. Lucifer stepped toward them, cursing as he moved. "I will remember what you have done here!" he screamed. "I will curse you forever if you cast me down to earth. So look at me! Remember me! Because I will remember you!"*

*Lucifer's eyes burned with emotion as the memory flooded back.*

*Then he looked at the two brothers, his eyes red with hate. Looking at them, he realized the power that they held. The things that they would do! The men they would become! The people they would touch and the lives they would change!*

*He fumed, his eyes burning. But what could he do to stop them?*

*"If I could, I would kill them," he sneered to his slave. "I would torture them, beat them and cause them great pain. I would make them cry for mercy, then beat them some more. Give me a chance and I would teach them everything I know about misery and despair!"*

*Balaam only watched Lucifer. Balaam had heard it all before.*

*Lucifer fumed a long moment, pacing side to side. Then he suddenly stopped and smiled weakly, exposing his teeth.*

*He peered at Luke for a moment.*

*Each mortal had a weakness and he remembered now what failings these young mortals had. Sometimes Ammon wasn't careful, and Luke had too much pride. So that's where he would begin. "I may not be able to hurt them," he hissed, "but maybe I can get them to hurt themselves. If we can distract them, if we can convince them to be careless, then that might be enough."*

*Balaam slowly nodded. Careless. Yes, careless. It was a tool that had been used against the young so many times before.*

*The Deceiver muttered angrily as he walked toward Luke. "He is young. He is foolish. There might be a way . . . ."*

*Balaam watched Ammon pick up his rope and begin to walk up the trail.*

*"Stay with him," Lucifer commanded. "Try to distract him. Do anything that you can. Make him act foolish. Concentrate on his anger. Shout distractions in his head!"*

*Balaam bowed and followed Ammon as he walked up the trail.*

*Lucifer watched them go, then moved toward Roth. "Play on his pride," he commanded as he pointed to the younger brother. "His pride has the power to destroy him if you work him just right."*

*Roth nodded, then bowed and ran toward the mortal.*

*Positioning himself near Luke's head, Roth leaned toward him, whispering into his ear. "You're the best. This will be easy. You're good enough, there's no reason to be careful anymore."*

# FOUR

The two men stood and walked through an open glass door looking out on a garden that stretched for acres behind the villa. They walked through the garden slowly, following the rock path that led to a gushing waterfall.

"The world is changing, General Brighton," the prince said as they walked. "Indeed, in many ways it is too late. Too much has changed already! You now have many enemies throughout the world."

Brighton glanced sideways at the prince. "Our friends are few, but that has always been the case," he answered calmly.

"No, Neil. This is different. From the east to the west, you are nearly alone. Europe hates you now unlike ever before."

"Old Europe, perhaps," the general interrupted. "But the new Europe, the emerging Europe, they are on our side."

The prince shook his head. "Maybe. It doesn't matter. Not now anyway, and what I said is still true. Most hate you now for your strength and the effect you have. They see you as a soaring eagle. None of them can stand to see you so powerful, and the effect of your decisions! I don't know if you realize how much influence you have. Your economy sneezes, and nations catch pneumonia. You go into the Great Recession and people starve throughout the world. You languish through a recovery no one believes is real, and more people die from the economic shock that started on your shores. You develop a foreign initiative and entire governments fall. You institute a new policy and by the time it reaches your allies, it is the tip of a whip that snaps at their heads. You are *so* powerful, but yet *so* naïve. Like a clumsy giant, you wander across the globe, crushing everything under your feet without looking down. Is it any surprise so many would like to see you brought to your knees?"

Brighton considered a moment. "Perhaps. But a gentle giant is a better description, I think, and all this talk of the United States seeking world domination is completely absurd! Just the ranting of societies who have failed and need someone to blame. Some people despise us, we know that. Much of Europe. Many Middle Eastern nations. Dictators and tyrants. We have enemies. But there are a few who seem to be in our camp."

"Hmm!" the prince scoffed. "I wouldn't be so sure. There are enemies rising, many foes in the world, and this is very important, Neil, so you must listen to me! There are many kinds of enemies that one needs to fear. Those you know and can identify, they are the very best kind. You see them, can study them, can counter their moves. But there are other enemies, far more deadly, those who plot in secret places but hide in the light. There may be friends, even loved ones . . . ." Prince Saud's voice drifted off.

General Brighton watched him a second, seeing the sadness on his face.

*Friends. Even loved ones.* Why was he so afraid?

"There are those," Saud continued, "who harbor secret hates and ambitions, those who have taken to the darkness and feel comfortable in it now, those who seek to destroy freedom or anything else that is good."

The general turned to his friend. "What are you saying, Prince Saud?" he asked nervously.

The prince looked around, then stared for a moment at the sky. "I am saying there is great danger lurking. Great danger to me and great danger to you." He lowered his face to look into the general's eyes. "My father intends for me to transform the kingdom. You know that, we have discussed it, but there are many who would stop me. I don't know how far they will go."

"You've got to be more specific," Brighton prodded anxiously. "Are you talking of your neighbors? Syria? Iran?"

"Those would be too obvious! You're not listening to me, Neil! I'm talking of my family. I'm talking of *your* friends!"

The prince shook his head in frustration. *Was it so hard to understand?*

"General Brighton, do you believe that I support the concepts of freedom?" Saud asked. "Do you believe that my goal is to move the kingdom toward democracy and closer ties with the West?"

"Yes, Prince Saud, I believe that is true."

"Do you believe that I am your friend?"

"I know that you are."

"Do you believe that I am a friend of the United States as well?"

The general paused. That was more difficult. The prince had many allegiances, many voices demanding his ear. Many opposing forces were hanging on him as he balanced on the tightrope and nothing was ever simple when it came to the tug and pull of international relationships. After thinking a moment, Brighton replied, "Yes, Prince Saud, I believe that you are a friend to the United States."

"Do you believe there are those who would like to see our friendship destroyed, those who would see the kingdom rise up and become an enemy of the United States?"

Brighton needed to be cautious. Although this was a personal conversation, he still represented his government and he had to choose his words carefully. But he had always been honest with the prince and he would be honest now. "There are some in my country who think that has happened already, some who believe, and with some evidence I might add, that fundamental Islamic groups carry far too much favor within the kingdom."

The prince considered before he answered, "There is no doubt that is true. But there is a fine balance, a delicate subtlety we must seek daily. Have we made mistakes? Yes we have, and my father has taken steps to remedy any errors that might have been made. But that's not what I'm speaking of. I'm not talking of radical terrorist groups. I'm talking of others, some within my government, some from opposing nations, *some within your own country*, who would like nothing more than to see the relationship between our two nations destroyed."

"I understand, Prince Saud. We see those forces at work daily."

"Do you see those forces within your own country? Do you see them within your own government? Can you see them, Neil, because believe me, they're there!"

The general was silent, then sadly nodded.

"Then listen to me, Neil. Take this moment and freeze it in your memory so you'll remember what I say!" The prince took a step forward and narrowed his eyes. "I believe we are approaching the crossroads of a mighty war. And I'm not talking about a clash between religions or clash between nation-states. This isn't Muslim against Christian, Islam against Jew, and it isn't a war between democracies and totalitarian regimes. I'm talking something far deeper and far more deadly now, a clash between two fundamentally different sets of beliefs; a clash between groups who defy normal cultures or rules. Our enemies are not contained by borders and when this is over we will find them everywhere.

"I'm talking about a fundamental conflict between those who believe in basic freedoms and those who would make all men their slaves. I'm talking about ruthless enemies who seek to destroy all free nations and free ways of life. I have seen a glimpse of the future and you've never had a nightmare that compares with their plans.

"We are rushing forward, heading for what the *Qur'an* calls the

Great War, and this war will be different than any we have ever fought before. It will be a war against an enemy that holds no territory, defends no population and respects no moral law. Such an enemy cannot be deterred. It can only be destroyed."

The prince stopped, moving his eyes down the path, then turned back to Brighton. "This enemy seeks your country's destruction above anything else. As long as you stand, then you stand in their way. So they have to destroy you. But in order to destroy you they will come after me first."

Brighton looked away as he thought, his eyes clouding with dread. He had never heard a government leader speak so frankly of his fears. And though he kept his face stoic, inside his gut grew tight.

*******

The call came through on his satellite phone, a phone that could reach him anywhere in the world.

The younger prince, handsome and thin, flipped the phone open and quickly punched in his security code. "Yes," he said simply when the call was linked through.

"*Sayid*, Crown Prince Saud is meeting with the American general," a deep voice replied.

"Where?" the prince demanded.

"His personal office."

"You are listening?"

"Of course, *Sayid*.

"Has he said anything to the American officer?"

"Nothing of note, *Sayid*, only small talk."

"He hasn't warned him?"

209

"No, *Sayid*, God be willing. But they have walked into the garden where we are no longer able to listen."

Prince al-Rahman pulled anxiously on his chin. "Where is Princess Tala?" he asked.

"She is preparing to leave the mountain. They will be on their way in just a few minutes now."

"And the children are with her?"

"*Sayid*, they are."

Another moment of silence, this was longer and more uncomfortable. "Your team is in place?" the younger prince demanded.

"They are ready to move."

"All right, Khilid. You know what to do."

# FIVE

It took Ammon ten minutes to climb the trail that led up the backside of the riverbank to the top of the rock. As he walked, he became angry, thinking of Luke. He was always so prideful, so conceited! It was never enough just to have fun; everything had to be a grand competition. Proving who was toughest, who was strongest, and he had to always be the best.

Balaam walked beside him, shouting and sneering, planting angry thoughts into his mind. *"Why is Luke always like this? He's just wasting your time, trying to climb this impossible rock!"*

Ammon moved up the trail, using his hands to pick his way up the steep path that led around the backside of the cliff. The trail was littered with broken rocks and he slipped back a time or two, grabbing the brush at the side of the trail to keep from falling back.

"What a waste of a morning," he mumbled, "standing at the bottom of the cliff, holding the rope so Luke could prove what a great climber he is."

"I really should be studying," he thought. He had a test in a couple hours. But no, he was going to spend the morning watching Luke climb an impossible rock. What a waste of time. He should have stayed in bed.

The longer he climbed, the madder he got, and the madder he got, the more distracted he became. Balaam continued working beside him, whispering scornful, angry, irrational, emotional, envious thoughts in his ear. *"Luke is better than you are. You know that and he knows that too. He's just rubbing it in, just trying to prove it again. The only reason he's doing this is to make you feel like a loser. He just wants to bug you, to put you down a notch or two. Why can't he just give it a break? It's always me! Always me! Everyone look at*

211

*me! Aren't you growing sick of it? Will he ever change?"*

Balaam kept it up, a constant barrage of vile thoughts in Ammon's head. And the more Ammon heard it, the angrier he became. The thoughts were illogical and selfish, but Lucifer's temptations rarely made any sense. Yet still people listened. Driven by emotion, the human heart sometimes doesn't let the human head think.

Ammon climbed, his head down, the bottled up emotion building inside.

Yeah, he loved his brother, sure, and they got along great most the time, but once in a while he could be a jerk.

He suddenly realized he was at the top of the hill. He stood there a moment, catching his breath, glancing at the beauty around him. He wanted to take in the view, to enjoy it for a moment, but he knew that Luke would be waiting impatiently at the bottom of the cliff.

*"Always about Luke!"* Balaam sneered into his mind again.

Looking around, he saw that because the wall had not been climbed before, there was no anchor that he could use to secure the climbing rope to. For a moment he thought of tying it to a nearby tree then changed his mind. Taking out a stainless steel anchor and undersized hammer from his backpack, he located a small crack in the rock, placed the bolt inside and secured it, driving it deeply into the crack at the top of the cliff. Finishing his work, he pulled on the anchor to check it, jerking it back and forth.

The rock around the bolt began to chip away and he leaned over to take a closer look.

Balaam leaned toward him, knowing this was his chance. Intent on his work, his eyes grew dark and mean. *"Don't worry about it,"* he hissed. *"How many times have you done this? A thousand. Maybe more! Has a bolt ever broken? No! Not once. Not a single time has one of the bolts you set in rock pulled away. So why are you worried? Luke is waiting! You've got to hurry! Why are you being so cautious! You've done this so many times before!"*

Ammon jerked on the bolt a final time.

*"IT'S FINE!"* Balaam screamed.

The bolt seemed to hold so Ammon clipped a carabineer through the anchor and screwed the safety clasp to ensure it couldn't open. Then, standing, he turned and glanced over the top of the rock. It was a long way to fall, and he felt a little dizzy. Truth was, he wasn't keen on heights. One of the reasons he loved climbing was to tackle the gnaw of fear.

From where he stood, he couldn't see Luke, who was hidden from view underneath the ledge. "Luke," he called out, swinging the rope in his hand.

Luke stepped away from the wall to where Ammon could see him. "Rope," Ammon called as he let it fall. Luke caught it, trying not to let it touch the ground where the sand would weaken it and make it less safe.

Ammon ran his end of the rope through the carabineer then secured it to his climbing harness and brake. He pulled on his gloves, then looked over the edge of the cliff.

"Ready!" he called down to Luke.

Luke checked the rope through his own harness, then tightened the slack. "Go for it," he called back.

Before backing over the cliff, Ammon looked one last time at the bolt he had driven into the crack.

*"It's fine,"* Balaam whispered, this time soothing instead of urgent. *"It's fine. No need to worry. Come on, go for it!"*

Ammon didn't move. He focused on the tiny cracks in the rock around the stainless steel bolt.

"*Luke's waiting!*" Balaam sneered. "*He's looking at you, wondering what you're doing. He's not a boob. He wouldn't worry. He wouldn't freak out like this . . . .*"

Ammon knelt down and brushed the dirt away from the bolt. The sandstone was weak and crumbling from a thousand years of rain and wind, but the bolt seemed to be firmly driven into the rock. Standing, he pulled against the rope, giving a final jerk.

"*It's OK!*" Balaam whispered quickly, keeping a steady chatter in his ear. "*Go on. Have some fun. The bolt will fine. What are the chances anything will go wrong?*"

Ammon nodded, agreeing with the whispered thoughts in his head, and because he was young, naïve, angry, distracted with thoughts about school, and hadn't been hurt by inexperience before, he trusted the evil whispers and didn't check the bolt carefully.

He stood at the edge of the cliff. "Rappelling!" he called down.

"Rappel on!" Luke called back as he braced for the pull of Ammon's weight.

Ammon turned and walked off the top of the cliff. It was a sheer drop below him and he easily bounced his way down, rappelling to the ledge ten feet below the top of the rock. Hitting the overhang, he moved to the tip of the ledge, then pushed forcefully out and away from the wall while feeding out ten feet of rope. The rope tightened, then swung him like a pendulum into the wall and he bent his legs to absorb the shock.

Above him, the bolt slipped, moving against the cracked stone. But Ammon didn't feel it as he swung into the side of the cliff. He pushed again. His weight jerked the rope and the bolt slipped again, pivoting thirty degrees. A small crack spread in the rock.

But still the bolt held.

*******

Ammon stopped his descent directly under the ledge. Hanging there, he looked over his head, his body off balance, his torso hanging back.

The outcropping had more handholds than he could see from the ground. And the ledge wasn't quite as steep as it had appeared. The crevasse they had looked at might provide a pretty good grip, *if* Luke could reach it, which was a very big *if,* for it was a good three or four feet away from the face of the cliff. Ammon examined the overhang for thirty seconds or so, then let off more rope, bouncing from the rock as he made his way down. The last of the descent was almost a free fall through space, for the overhang kept him away from the wall and he had to balance himself carefully as he moved to the ground.

Luke was waiting, an anxious look on his face. "What do you think?" he asked quickly.

Ammon stared up at the overhang as he loosened the straps on his harness. "I'm not sure about the bolt," he answered, ignoring the intent of his brother's question. He jerked on the rope and suspended his weight on it by dropping to his knees as he pulled.

The rope held firm and Luke waved at the air. "Come on, Ammon, the bolt is secure. In all the times that we've done this has a bolt ever broken away?"

Ammon looked up, keeping his weight on the rope. "I don't know," he muttered. "It just didn't feel right. Sandstone is notoriously weak, you know that Luke, and though I found a good crevasse, part of it broke away when I drove the bolt in."

Luke hesitated. "Come on, Ammon. It's fine. You just don't want . . . ."

"No, Luke, really. I just want to be sure."

"Come on!" Luke persisted. "Nothing's going to happen. You're turning into Mom, always worrying."

Ammon ignored him as he jerked again, suspending all of his weight. The rope held firm and Luke huffed impatiently.

"All right," Ammon finally said. "It seems to be OK."

"Yeah, it's fine," Luke answered. "Now what about the overhang?"

Ammon looked up. "It's going to be even harder than it looks," he answered, lifting his arm and pointing as he talked. "There, you see that," he motioned toward the leading edge of the overhang, "that crevasse you're counting on to provide a handhold, it looks to be only a few inches wide, just enough to get your hand in and get a good grip. But it's a lot wider than that, Luke, I'd say five inches or so, and it slopes downward much more than it looks like from here. You're not going to be able to use it for a handhold like you thought that you could."

Luke studied the small fissure and said, "But it's got a pretty good lip there that I could hold to."

Ammon nodded. "You could try. That's all I can say. But listen, Luke, why can't we just move down the rock fifteen feet or so?" Ammon pointed to his right. "Its got better handholds, it's even, and we wouldn't have to mess around with that overhang which is just going to make you fall."

"So what if I fall? That's what the safety rope is for."

Ammon flipped the climbing rope in his hand, eighty meters of nylon and cotton. Designed to stretch under pressure, it was a good rope, expensive, and had saved both of their lives many times. He pulled on the rope as he studied the wall. "One more thing," he continued, still hoping to talk Luke out of trying this climb, "because the rope has to extend over the edge, it will hang away from the wall. That's going to make it harder for me to keep a proper tension on it. No big deal, I can handle that, but if you lose your grip and fall, the ledge will leave you dangling five or six feet away from the wall. Which means you'll have to trust me to lower you to the ground."

"No big deal, Ammon. It won't be any harder than you repelling down."

Ammon hesitated, then tried one last time. "I just think it's a waste of time to try and climb over that ledge," he concluded. "You can't do it, Luke. No offense, buddy, but no one can pull themselves over the top of that ledge. No one. Can't be done. So I'll sit here for an hour and watch you try, then you'll be exhausted and come down, and that will be it."

"But you'll hang with me, right? You'll give me a chance?"

Ammon watched his brother. "You're not going to pull a Sam on me, are you? Because both of us know what Sam would do. He'd hang on the wall and keep trying to pull himself over that ledge until he either starved to death or we pulled him down. He wouldn't give up as long as he had any strength. He would literally fall from exhaustion before he would quit. Now, you're not going to do that, are you? Because I really have to get to my lab this afternoon. If I'm going to be here all day holding the safety rope for you, then tell me now so I can go and buy me some lunch and a couple sodas before you get on the wall."

Luke smiled. "I'll give it a reasonable try. If it doesn't work out, I'll admit defeat, come down and we'll try somewhere else."

"I'm serious, Luke, I'm not going to stay here all day," Ammon warned. "I'll tie the rope to a tree and leave you if you drag this thing out."

"Got it," Luke answered.

Ammon nodded, checked his harness, then flipped the rope, moving it a couple feet to his right in order to position it where Luke wanted to climb.

******

As Ammon released his weight and flipped the rope, the bolt he had driven into the rock reseated itself and cocked again to the side. The rock had cracked from the pressure of Ammon 's weight, weakening the sandstone and causing microscopic fractures where the bolt had been set.

******

Luke moved to the base of the fifty-foot sandstone wall. Ammon stood behind him, the safety rope secured to his harness. The rope ran over the top of the wall, through the carabineer he had secured to the bolt then back down the wall where Luke had tied the other end to his climbing harness. Luke glanced behind him. "Belay on?" he asked.

Ammon flipped the rope to make certain it curled on the small carpet he had laid out behind him, then pulled out the last of the slack. "On belay," he answered.

Luke moved to the wall. "Climbing," he said.

"Climb on," Ammon replied.

Luke stretched his hands over the rock, feeling for the tiny crevasses and finger holds that a non-climber would have never seen. His gummed-soled shoes were like fly paper, giving him an extraordinary sense of security against the rock. He stretched, reaching over his head and pulled himself up, using his feet and legs to support his weight as much as he could to help save his upper body strength for the ledge. As he climbed, he was extraordinarily aware of his body and used every part; his knees, his elbows, his fingers and palms, he even forced his chest against the rock in order to evenly distribute his weight. He easily climbed the first fifteen feet, using tiny protrusions as handholds and forcing his feet into thin cracks. Halfway up the rock, the wall became suddenly smooth and he had to hang on a tiny ledge while he searched for the next handhold. Scratching over his head, he felt for a crack that he could hold on to.

Ammon watched, all the time looking up. He kept the rope tight enough to break Luke's fall, but not so tight as to interfere or help support his weight. He watched his brother search in vain for a handhold, then called up, "Luke, there's a place to put your foot a couple of feet to your right."

Luke stretched out his leg and tried a place or two, but couldn't find anything that would support his weight.

"Higher up," Ammon shouted. "If you can get your right foot on that tiny ledge beside you."

Luke stopped and scowled down at his brother. "You must mean this ledge beside my ear!" he shouted in sarcasm.

"Come on! It's not *that* high. You can do it, buddy, if you get your knees high enough."

"I'm not a contortionist Ammon. How many people could lift their feet above their chest?"

"You're exaggerating, Luke. Now come on, you can do it!"

Luke stared at the tiny ledge by his waist, hesitating. He lifted his leg a time or two, measuring the height, but his other foot almost slipped. He looked at Ammon. "Would you like to come and demonstrate?" he called down.

Ammon started to answer but Luke ignored him. After several more minutes of searching, he descended the rock a couple feet, moved two arm lengths to his right, then started climbing again. There was a better route there, with handholds enough for him to sink his fingers onto. Fifteen minutes later he had climbed up to the overhang that extended out over the face of the cliff.

"How you feeling?" Ammon asked as Luke studied the overhang directly over his head.

Luke took his free hand and dipped it in the chalk bag strapped to the back of his harness. "Little tired," he called back. "That wore me out, getting stuck halfway up. Took a lot longer to get up here than I thought it would."

Ammon glanced at his watch. Luke had been on the rock for almost thirty minutes. He knew Luke had to be exhausted. A less experienced climber would have fallen a dozen times by now. A beginner wouldn't have made it ten feet up the wall. But Luke was just getting started. The most difficult part of the climb was directly over his head.

Luke craned his neck back as he held on with his fingers, his feet turned sideways to fit on a one-inch crack in the rock. Above him, the face of the cliff jutted outward at a sixty-degree angle, extending behind him for five feet or so. His hands trembled and his calves were beginning to cramp from the constant strain of holding his weight on his toes. He had to move quickly to find a way to get over the ledge or he wouldn't have any strength left to pull himself up. He searched in frustration, dribbles of sweat pouring down the side of his face.

*******

Roth stood in the air beside him. "*You can do it!*" he whispered into the exhausted man's ear. "*Ammon doesn't think you're strong enough, but you know that you are! Samuel could do it. Is he that much stronger than you?*"

Luke passed an exhausted hand over his eyes as he thought.

"*Sam has always been stronger,*" Roth hissed bitterly. "*He's better at everything! But you know you can do this. Now prove that you can do this.*"

Luke looked down. His brother stared up. He clenched the fingers on his left hand against the tiny cracks in the wall, then leaned back. He clung there, suspended, barely hanging on the cliff. He moved his hand across the overhang, feeling for the crack they had identified from the ground, searching for anything he could sink his fingers into. His shoulders ached, his arms trembled, and his neck muscles cramped.

"Luke," Ammon warned. "Be careful up there."

"I'm okay," he shouted.

Luke moved a few inches away from the wall and the safety rope went slack. "You got me!" Luke called as he glanced down.

"I got you!" Ammon answered as he put pressure on the rope to tighten it up. Bracing himself, he planted his feet and leaned back, anticipating Luke's fall.

Luke gathered his strength and reached back again. He put more weight on his toes and his leg muscles cramped with excruciating knots. He stretched out his fingers and lifted one leg. *He . . . couldn't . . . quite . . . reach . . . it!* He huffed in exhaustion, then shifted his weight to his left foot, and lifted up on his toes again. He clawed overhead and behind him. He could see the crack there, but it was two . . . inches . . . too . . . far.

Two inches. Might as well be two feet. He wasn't going to make it.

*******

*"Jump!"* the dark angel told him. *"Let go of the wall. You can do it, Luke! You have the rope to catch you. Jump! You won't get hurt even if you fall!"*

*******

Luke stretched out again, almost at the end of his strength. He extended his fingers. *Just . . . a . . . few . . . more . . . inches!* He dropped his head and looked down, relieving the cramps in his neck, then gathered his strength and repositioned himself on a tiny ledge on the cliff.

"You got me, right?" he called down to Ammon.

Ammon looked worried. "Come on, Luke," he answered. "Let's call it quits."

Luke shook his head. Not when he was this close!

He looked back up and stretched a final time for the handhold he had been reaching for.

It was simply too far.

He only had two choices now. It was jump or climb down.

He made his decision and swallowed hard.

He braced himself against the wall as he gathered his strength, then leaped for the rock while twisting in midair, extending both hands, stretching them as far as he could reach over his head.

He grasped the crack with the fingertips of his right hand, and he hung there, suspended, his feet swinging wildly through the air. He flailed with his other hand, forcing it against the crack in the wall, scratching and pawing desperately for something to grab.

Ammon braced himself below him, waiting to absorb the weight of his fall.

Luke almost screamed from the pressure on his arm. The adrenaline shot through him and he clawed like an animal with his free hand. As he pawed at the rock, tiny pieces of sandstone and dust tumbled into his eyes. Hanging by one hand, he scratched with the other, then felt a tiny crack in the rock. Stretching, he grabbed it with all the strength he had left.

He was slipping. He was exhausted.

He caught his breath as he hung there, four stories above the ground, then moved his right hand for a better handhold. He pulled himself upward and moved his left hand. Inch by inch, hand by hand, he moved upward toward the tip of the ledge. Another inch, another handhold, he moved on the overhang.

His arms ached. It was agony. He could hardly breathe. His fingers trembled with exhaustion and his shoulders knotted in pain.

He wasn't going to make it. He couldn't hold on any more. It took everything he had just to hang on the rock. He was growing lightheaded. His entire body was shaking and his arms were cramped in pain.

Just a few inches more. But he did not have the strength.

It was time to let go. He had tried, he had failed. Now his body was done.

He huffed in pain and disappointment, then reached desperately for the rope, while hanging by one hand.

The instant he put weight on the rope, it started sliding through his fingers. He watched in terror as it snaked from the overhand above him and through the air, falling toward the rocky ground so far below. As they passed in front of his face in slow motion the carabineer and safety bolt flashed in the sun. The rope fell with a light *whisp* before the metal devices clinked against the hard rocks below.

*******

Ammon saw the rope fall and almost threw up on himself. The bolt had broken free from the crevasse! It couldn't be! His mind flashed and he rushed to the wall. He legs turned to jelly and his gut crunched in a sick knot of dark fear.

He glanced up at his brother who hung from the edge by one hand. "*Oh God!*" he frantically whispered. "*Please, don't let him fall!*"

He dove on the rope in a panic, as if it could help him now. He laced it through his fingers, finding the bolt. The carabineer was still attached and he grimaced in pain, then stared at it blankly, a disbelieving look on his face. He turned for the trail, rope in his hands, and started to run, then stopped. He did not have enough time! Luke could not hang on long enough for him to get to the top of the rock and secure the rope again!

He looked up in horror.

He did not want his brother to die!

Then the bitter truth hit him like a baseball bat in his chest. He exhaled in pain, almost doubling over with guilt. He clenched his teeth and looked up, his eyes wide in gut-wrenching fear.

He *thought* the bolt was safe. But he hadn't been sure.

His brother was going to die. And it was his fault!

He looked up, his mouth agape, his throat too tight to scream. "I'll catch you, Luke!" he tried calling, but his voice only croaked.

*******

Luke knew he was dead. He simply couldn't hang on. He had drained all his energy, every ounce of his strength. His fingers were slipping and his arms cramped in pain. He tried desperately to hang on, but there was nothing more he could do.

He felt his grip slipping and he closed his eyes for the fall.

Time stopped, the world froze in place. He heard his heart beat and felt each pull of breath in his chest. He thought clearly and precisely as his mind raced ahead.

He opened his eyes and looked below him where Ammon was waiting in terror, his face sick and grim. It seemed as if he was trying to call to him, but his voice didn't come. His brother reached up as if waiting to catch him when he fell. The rope lay curled at his feet, completely worthless now.

Lifting his head, he looked up to the overhang. *He was so close.* Just another few inches. But he simply did not have the strength. He was hanging by one hand now. His fingers slipped again, and he held on by his last knuckles.

He listened to his heartbeat. Then he started praying. "Please, I do not want to die."

He closed his eye. Numbing pain in his arms. A sickening fear in his chest. "I don't want to die!" he cried again.

*"Then fight!"* something told him.

He opened his eyes and looked around.

*"Fight! This is your choice!"*

The voice was so clear, it was as if someone had whispered in his ear. He blinked in confusion, feeling sudden strength in his arms.

*"This is not your time,"* the unseen voice whispered. *"You have more work to do. Now, are you going to fight so I can help you or are you going to let go?"*

Luke tightened his grasp on the rock.

*"Look to your right! There is a firm handhold there."*

Luke turned his head and saw a large protrusion in the rock he had not noticed before. How could he have missed it? Was it *really* there before? He reached out and grabbed it. It fit like a glove in his hand and he curled his fingers around it, a perfect handhold. He felt a sudden rush of strength and he reached with his other hand. Another crack in the rock provided another handhold and he moved slowly upward on the ledge. He reached the edge of the overhang and hung, still suspended, then started swinging his legs while pulling himself up with his arms. He got one knee up and clawed at the overhang with his feet while pulling up with his arms. His other foot brushed the rock and he felt another rush of strength. He pulled one final time and his feet caught the top of the ledge. With strength beyond his own, he heaved himself over the top, then collapsed in a heap of quivering flesh.

He couldn't move his fingers. He couldn't move his arms. He was so numb and exhausted he barely had the strength to breathe. His head dropped to the side and he saw bloody scratches on his arm. His stomach turned to water, bitter and tart, and he rolled to his side and threw up a gush of clear fluid. Then he lay back, exhausted, barely able to think.

Below him, he heard his brother's desperate sobs.

*******

Ammon had fallen to his knees, then rolled onto his side. He pulled his arms to his chest and held himself tight while great tears of horror and relief rolled down his cheeks to dribble across his neck.

He had almost killed his brother. The whole thing would have been his fault! He shuddered again as his face went pale. A cold sweat drenched his face, his lips almost turning blue.

*God had saved him!* He had reached down from heaven and pulled Luke up and over the ledge. Ammon had watched it. There was no doubt in his mind. Someone had saved him, someone from above.

He looked at the rope that lay curled at his knees, one end still attached to Luke's harness, then picked up the bolt and carabineer and felt sick again.

He sobbed with emotion, overcome with guilt and relief.

*He had almost killed his brother!* How could he have gone on if Luke had fallen? Would he ever get over this moment? Would the dread ever pass?

He felt sick and alone. And he knew in his heart he would never be the same man again.

*******

A long moment passed. How long, Ammon didn't know, it felt like only a few seconds, but it could have been much longer. He finally pushed himself to his feet, untied the rope from his harness and ran up the trail to the topside of the rock. Looking over the ledge, he saw Luke waiting there, leaning against the cliff, his arms hanging weakly at his side. Ammon looked down at his brother a moment before Luke noticed that he was standing over his head.

Ammon couldn't speak. His mind was a haze.

"Hey, that was kind of exciting." Luke said with a smile.

Ammon shook his head. "I'm so sorry . . . so sorry . . . ."

"What for?"

"The rope. The bolt! It was my fault."

Luke shook his head and waved a dismissive hand, barely lifting it from his lap. "Come on, Ammon. Don't go soft on me, brother. It's one of those things. Anyone who climbs knows that it could happen. There was no way you could know. Just one of those things."

"I should have known the bolt wasn't sure. The rock was starting to crack. I should have stopped you."

Luke pushed himself up, leaning into the rock. "That's a crock! There was no way you could know. Now don't go girly on me, brother! Besides, I'm OK. And now I can say I made it over the ledge. Without a safety rope even! Let's see Sam beat that!"

Luke smiled, but his voice trailed off and both of the young men were silent.

After a moment of quiet, Luke said, "I heard something." His voice was solemn, almost reverent.

Ammon's eyes narrowed. "I saw something," he replied.

"I felt such strength."

"It was as if a hand lifted you up and over the ledge."

They both fell still for a very long time. Then they looked at each other and Luke lowered his eyes. "Can you secure the rope? I want to get off of this ledge."

Luke stood weakly. He barely had the strength to gather the rope from where it dangled over the side of the overhang, coil it up loosely and throw it up to Ammon, who secured it to the tree before pulling him the last ten feet to the top of the rock.

The two young men drove in silence the entire way home. "Should we tell Dad when he gets back from his trip?" Ammon asked as they pulled into the drive.

Luke shook his head. "I don't think so," he said. "Maybe someday, but let's not mention it for now."

# SIX

The prince's family was returning to the city. There were two young teenage boys and a daughter who had just celebrated her tenth birthday. Princess Tala hurried them forward and they moved smartly into the long limousine, a black BMW with bulletproof windows; steel rails in the side doors, surrounding the battery and the radiator; blast-proof metal plates welded underneath the floor; and run-flat tires.

Princess Tala, first wife of Crown Prince Saud, followed her children into the limousine's backseat. She moved carefully, her hand subconsciously protecting her stomach. She was just weeks away from delivering her third son, another prince for the kingdom, and she had developed a habit of resting her hand on her abdomen as she walked. Dropping into the back seat, she adjusted herself, smoothing her white dress and blowing away a stray curl of hair from her eyes. Tala was slender and beautiful, with deep green eyes and rich chestnut hair hidden under a silk scarf and thin veil. She sat gracefully, every move elegant, her eyes soft and wide like her ancestral mothers, the ancient Egyptian queens. Her dark skin was perfect and flawless, and the sight of her long neck and green eyes revealed enough beauty to command the attention of any man.

The Crown Prince had chosen wisely. Tala was a princess in every sense of the word. Which was both a great blessing and a weakness. Depending on how long she lived.

The three children sat across from their mother in the long sedan, their backs facing their bodyguard and driver. The princess nodded to the men in the front seat and the convoy began to move down the circular drive that led from the villa to the front gate that protected the grounds. The Royal Family's modest summer palace, a mere forty-five rooms and three pools, fell behind the line of cars, and the princess sighed deeply and looked out her bulletproof window to see the receding summer palace.

Built on the highest peak on the western side of the mountains that looked down on the Red Sea, the summer palace was a refuge from the brutal hot desert below. Here the mountain air was cool and tangy with the smell of juniper and pine. Ancient Joshua trees lined the private drive, their heavy branches hanging over the pavement and breaking the sunlight into shadows that flickered through the windows of the passing cars. The princess glanced back at the retreating villa with sadness. She spent more time here than anywhere else in the kingdom and it was always hard to leave. To her, all of the other palaces, magnificent as they might be, were no more than hotels where she might spend a few nights. This palace felt like home, the one place she was truly comfortable, and she would have stayed here forever if the Crown Prince would allow it.

Tala's daughter watched her peer through the back window as the stone villa grew smaller. She knew her mother was happier here than anywhere else in the world. In this matter they agreed. "When will we be back?" the little girl asked as the villa fell behind a line of conifer trees.

"Soon," her mother answered. "But we have other obligations. Our lives cannot be only pleasure, we have other things we must do."

"Can we come back next week?" her daughter asked.

The princess cocked her head and smiled. "El-Tasha, if we came back next week, what would you do about school?"

"I would rather be here on the mountain than go to school. Did you know I saw a mountain goat yesterday! It was way up on the cliffs. You should have seen it climbing, I thought surely it would fall. Can we come back next week and see if it is still there!"

The oldest son eyed his sister. "She's just looking for an excuse to get out of her studies," he teased. "El-Tasha would rather sit on a rock in the middle of the Euphrates surrounded by eel snakes than go to school."

El-Tasha shook her head. "That's not true!" she answered. "I like school. Sometimes. Well OK, I don't like the academy, but that's not the reason I want to come back . . . at least it's not the *only* reason."

The oldest son laughed again and Tala turned to him. He had the dark eyes of his father and was filling out in the chest. He looked so much like his father, it was almost uncanny, it was like a younger prince Saud sitting there. although he was just fourteen, he looked older. Something about the future responsibility of the kingdom made a boy grow quickly and the princess could almost see the subtle weight of the kingdom begin to settle on his shoulders. He was the next link in the transition of the kingdom. He'd been told to prepare from the time he was a child. Difficult as it was for him to comprehend, he was doing his best.

Princess Tala patted his knee then glanced through the bulletproof window at the road ahead.

A twelve-foot brick wall surrounded the mountain retreat. The only access to the villa, which was set back half a mile from the security wall, was through a heavy steel gate. Thick trees lined the road and the convoy of five vehicles sped along the hardtop toward the gate. The first vehicle in the convoy was a black military van containing the heavy weapons and surface-to-air missiles. A black SUV followed the black van with the royal family's personal bodyguards. Princess Tala and her family were in the third car, the long BMW limousine, followed by another SUV with her physician, the family pediatrician, a personal assistant, secretary, trainer and masseuse. The chief of security rode in the last vehicle, a heavy truck crammed with military officers and security police.

From his vantage point in the convoy's rear, the chief of security could watch their progress while observing the road ahead. After years of training (and some painful experience), the chief had grown accustomed to riding in the back of the convoy where he could more accurately observe the situation and measure the threats.

The chief shifted uncomfortably in the front seat of the truck. As head of security, the princess and her family were completely his charge and he would happily give his life if it were ever required to save them. The truth was, if harm were to ever come to the princess, Prince Saud would have him killed anyway. Better to die with honor than to die in disgrace. And though he had always felt pressure, he felt it increasingly morew. The radicals in the kingdom had grown bolder and more vicious. Like a dog crazed with hunger, they smelled the sweet tang of blood.

The chief moved anxiously to the edge of his seat as the convoy passed through the main gate and onto the descending mountain road.

The road leading down the mountain was smooth and well kept, but it was also cut with deep switchbacks and very steep grades. There were few guardrails or retaining walls and the security chief knew the road was a dangerous place. From the compound at the top of the mountain the road descended more than six thousand feet, turning and dropping along sheer canyon walls. The terrain was rocky and steep and the trees gradually thinned out as the road descended until the landscape merged with the barren desert floor.

The convoy moved quickly, the drivers braking expertly at each curve in the road before accelerating again. The princess watched the road tensely, then pulled out a cell phone. She punched her husband's private number and the call was relayed to a central switchboard in Ad Damman where a sophisticated GPS tracking system kept constant tabs on the location of the crown prince. The switchboard automatically transferred her call to the palace on the outskirts of Riyadh.

Prince Saud's personal assistant answered the phone, his voice all business. "Yes, Princess Tala," he said.

"Is Crown Prince Saud available?" the princess asked.

"I'm sorry, Your Highness, Prince Saud is in a meeting."

It never occurred to either the princess or Prince Saud's assistant that he might offer to interrupt. One did not interrupt the prince. Not even his wife.

"Is he still with the American general?" Tala asked.

"Yes, Princess Tala."

"General Brighton, as I recall?"

"I believe that is right."

"Do you know how long he will be?"

The older man huffed. "No, Your Highness, I do not." Princess or not, she was still a woman and the affairs of the heir to the kingdom were not her concern. "I will have him get in contact with you at the first opportunity," Prince Saud's assistant offered.

"Tell him we are leaving the mountain and will meet him in Riyadh."

"I will tell him," the man answered and the princess ended the call.

"Are we going to see father tonight?" her oldest son asked. Princess Tala nodded and all of her children smiled.

The limousine sped slowed for a particularly sharp curve in the road. The princess reached for the handhold over her window then felt her child kick, a strong thump against her abdomen, sturdy and swift. Placing her hand on her belly, she smiled. "Be still, my young prince," she whispered. "We are almost there."

*******

The five assassins had concealed themselves in the brush on the uphill side of the road just before one of the last switchbacks. Behind them, on the other side of a crest in the mountain, their helicopter hovered, keeping out of view. The men were dressed in identical black uniforms, leather boots and thin gloves. The fingers had been cut out of the gloves to allow them to maneuver their weapons with precision and their faces were concealed behind black masks.

The team leader listened to the earpiece he had shoved in his ear. "Two minutes!" he hissed to his team. He glanced down the line. The men were expertly concealed, spread out twenty feet to his left and right. The gun-blue barrels of their Soviet-made weapons protruded from the brush.

The team leader listened again, then gave his final instructions. "Call ready," he whispered into the microphone at his neck.

"Two's ready," the second sniper positioned to his right replied.

"Two, you've got the first truck in the convoy," the team leader instructed. "Repeat to me your instructions. You have number one."

"I do. Two has the lead truck."

"The first vehicle has the .50-caliber machine guns and missiles. You've got to take it or this whole thing is off. Understand, Two? We're depending on you!"

"Got that, colonel!" the other sniper replied.

"Three, you take the second vehicle, a black SUV," the team leader continued. "The target is in the third car, a BMW limousine. Repeat that . . . target is in the third vehicle. Leave that car alone!" The lead assassin scoffed in his mind as he thought of the lone BMW limousine. No decoys or deceptions. Which car contained the princess was almost comically clear. Fool of security! He was worthy of death.

He glanced at the two men to his left. "Four and Five, you've got the last two vehicles in the convoy. It is just like we planned it." He looked down the line. "Any questions?" he demanded.

His men remained silent and the team leader crouched lower in his hole then glanced down the line, checking their positions a final time. He saw the four barrels of the RPG-7 shoulder-launched missiles protruding from the brush and smiled. The RPG-7, a recoilless, shoulder-fired antitank weapon, was effective against fixed emplacements or moving targets. It has a five-hundred-meter range and could penetrate most conventional armor. Proven repeatedly in combat, RPG-7s had been successfully employed against armored vehicles, bunkers, and American helicopters.

Taking out these lightly armored vehicles would prove easy to do.

The sniper nodded with approval, then turned back to the road.

"All right then, my brothers," he said into his microphone. "Prove yourselves worthy or die in the cause. That is the only choice you have now. You must not let me down."

Twenty seconds passed. The convoy came into view. "Praise be to Allah," one of the soldiers whispered and the team leader glared. This wasn't about Allah! This had nothing to do with religion or faith in God. This was about power. And the kingdom. And the man they would have as their king!

*******

The convoy was nearing the bottom of the mountain. There were two more sharp curves below them, then a straight line to the electronically controlled gate that blocked access to the road. The line of cars decelerated for a curve, the vehicles bunching together as they slowed.

Inside the limousine, Princess Tala laid her head back and closed her eyes. Her daughter was asleep now, the two boys playing an electronic game. The BMW bounced lightly as it hit some gravel then pulled into the sharp turn.

*******

"Stand fast!" the lead assassin whispered into his microphone, sensing the evil eagerness in the air. The vehicles were almost directly below them, not more than eighty feet away. "Two, are you ready?"

"Ready!" the second assassin replied.

"Ready . . . ready . . . NOW!" the team leader screamed.

The four RPG-7s fired in a hiss of white-hot smoke and flame. The missiles trailed forward, reaching their targets in a fraction of a second and the four vehicles exploded in bright orange and yellow flames. The lead truck rocked up on its front wheels, crushing its bumper against the asphalt then nearly rolled onto its back. The black SUV with the doctors simply disappeared, swallowed in a fireball of black smoke and orange flame. The other two vehicles exploded a hundredth of a second later. The heat was so intense it started melting the asphalt, the oil-based road catching fire and spewing black smoke. The second assassin reloaded quickly and fired again at the lead vehicle, which was instantly blown in two, secondary explosions bursting from its cargo bay and blasting the air.

The black BMW limousine screeched as the driver slammed on the brakes. The road forward was completely blocked by a fiery wall of melting steal and flame. The limousine didn't move for a moment, the driver momentarily confused, then he threw the car into reverse, the tires screeching as he began to back up until he crashed into the hulk of the burning car behind it. The men in the limousine's front seat jumped out with guns in both hands and tried their very best against evil desperate men. They failed valiantly.

Another explosion rocked the hot air as the gas tank in the last car burst into flames. A single soldier stumbled from the second automobile, his clothing on fire. He rolled in the dirt then fell still, his arms reaching out, his face slowly baring his teeth as his lips were burned off. Fire and thick smoke billowed from the burning vehicles, the flames curling around the shattered windows and half-open doors. A single soldier crawled from the largest truck, pulling himself on his belly toward the ditch. The lead assassin fired. The barrage of heavy machine gun fire nearly cut him in two.

The assassins had already picked up their other weapons and, with a machine-gun fire burst through the air, jumped from their hiding places and ran down the hill. Behind them they heard the dull *whop, whop, whop* as their evacuation helicopter crested the saddle in the mountain and swooped toward the rising smoke. The assassins reached the road in a matter of seconds and came to a quick stop. Charred bodies, burning tires, blackened pieces of metal and melted weapons were scattered everywhere. The air was heavy with the stench of burning flesh and fuel.

It was a perfect hit. Not a soldier was left living. It was all that they could ask.

The team leader turned to the black BMW, the only vehicle in the convoy that had not been destroyed. The royal family was in there. He started to move.

*******

Crown Prince Saud put a hand on Brighton's shoulder. The waterfall gushed around them, cooling the air with its mist. Then he heard hurried footsteps approach from behind a cluster of palm trees and looked over to see his personal aide running toward them. "Your Majesty!" the servant was crying as he ran.

The prince took a step toward him. The servant came to a stop and bowed quickly, touching his forehead with his fingers. "Your Majesty!" he repeated as he lifted his head. The prince saw the panic in his eyes and his heart slammed in his chest. The servant grabbed the prince and started pulling him up the path. Behind him, other palace guards began to race into view. "Your Highness, come quickly!" the servant hissed.

"What is it?" Saud demanded.

The servant's eyes bulged. "A Firefall!" he whispered.

Prince Saud's knees grew weak. He knew the code. *Firefall!* An assault upon his family. "When?" the prince demanded.

Several bodyguards appeared from out of nowhere and started pushing him up the trail, pressing close, protecting him from all sides. Prince Saud reached out to the servant. "What is going on?" he cried.

"Princess Tala hit the panic button!" the servant told the prince. "That's all that we know. Now, please, you must come with us, NOW!"

*******

Princess Tala sat upright, her jaw tight in horror, her eyes wide and glaring in gut-wrenching fear. She reached under her seat and hit the panic button again. Her daughter was screaming in terror and the princess reached over and pushed her head toward the floor. Dropping to her knees, she fell onto the floor beside her. Peering over the seat, she looked out the front of the car and saw the bullet-shattered bodies of the men who swore to protect the princess and her children with their lives.

"Get down!" she screamed as she turned to her sons. The oldest one stared blankly past her, looking through the back window at the carnage behind, where a burning body hung out of the front windshield of the trailing car. Princess Tala smelled the smoke and felt the tremor of a smaller explosion behind them. She felt the car rolling backward then suddenly bump to a stop as the searing heat and smoke began to seep into the car.

The princess glared at her son, her eyes terrified. He reached for the door handle. "We've got to get out!" he cried.

"No!" Tala screamed as she slammed the locks on the rear doors. "Whatever is out there, they can't get in! We must stay inside the vehicle. It is the safest place we can be!" She reached for her crying daughter and pulled her close, then thrust her fingers under her seat and hit the satellite-monitored alarm again. She heard the dull whoop of an approaching helicopter and almost cried in relief before realizing the helicopter could not be friendly. She pressed against the front window, desperate to see through the blood and gore, then heard voices and saw shadows approaching through the smoke to the side. She pushed her daughter down and lowered her head.

"Get on the floor!" she commanded her terrified sons.

The children dropped to the floor and Princess Tala positioned her body to protect them from the horror that was walking toward their car.

The horror stopped at the door, and rapped the bulletproof window with something metallic, then stepped back. Princess Tala raised her head and barely peered through the glass. She saw the walking horror pointing at something cradled in his arms.

Tala focused on what he cradled: a RPG-7 rocket tube. Her eyes traveled up the tube and saw it was loaded with a rocket-propelled grenade. The dawning realization and terror drained all rational thought from her brain, leaving her unfeeling and calm. *"Don t you dare touch my children!"* she tried screaming but nothing came out.

The walking horror took a step toward her and pulled off his mask. Tala pulled a quick breath and her heart nearly burst.

No! It couldn't be!

*She looked into the dark eyes of one of her husband's brothers!*

He smiled at her, stepped back thirty big steps, waved at her, and shouldered the RPG-7.

"Please, Allah, save the kingdom!" were Princess Tala's last words.

The rocket-propelled grenade did not miss.

*******

The garden came alive with security forces and military police. Like ants from an anthill, they seemed to appear everywhere.

General Brighton took a step toward the prince, but a bodyguard pushed him back. The prince stared at him with glaring eyes. "It has started," he whispered hoarsely as his bodyguards pulled him away.

"What's going on, Prince Saud? What is a Firefall?"

"Stay here!" the prince demanded. "Don't move from this place. Don't move a foot or they might shoot you. I have little control over any of them now. When I can, I will send men who will escort you back to your compound. Go with them and do *exactly* what they say! I must go, I must go!" The prince turned and disappeared down the path.

\*\*\*\*\*\*\*

Twenty minutes after leaving his palace, Prince Saud's motorcade screamed through the gates at King Khalid International Airport outside of Riyadh. The line of black Mercedes and American SUVs rolled onto the tarmac where his aircraft was parked. A huge 747-400 taxied by, but the motorcade didn't hesitate to race in front of it, forcing the *Air Saudi* airliner to come to a sudden halt. Prince Saud's personal jet was waiting near the taxiway, its four engines running. Mobile stairs had already been positioned next to the aircraft and the prince took them two at a time. The side door was closed and the aircraft began to taxi the instant the stairs were pulled away.

Inside, the prince's chief of staff was waiting to give him the news. Saud listened while staring straight ahead, then dismissed his staff. Pushed up from his chair, he walked to his private office at the back of the jet.

Later that night, Crown Prince Saud was escorted into a large chrome and tile morgue in the royal family's private hospital in Medina. What remained of the bodies of his murdered family were placed on steel tables and positioned side by side. He walked to them, crying, then demanded to be left alone. The physician nodded and bowed before leaving the room.

The crown prince fell to his knees between the four gurneys where his family had been laid. He wept for three hours, crying out to Allah, cursing and pleading and begging to die. He made outrageous promises if Allah would bring them back, then fell in exhaustion and slept on the tile floor. Sometime later, the physician carefully entered the room to see the prince kneeling by his wife's body again. He held her hand tightly as he looked down at the floor.

"*Get out!*" the prince hissed and the doctor withdrew.

*******

*Lucifer watched Prince Saud suffer from the upper corner of the room. Lucifer stood still, his arms limp, his eyes staring down. He smiled as he watched, almost laughing with glee, the pleasure of the prince's suffering causing a cold glint in his eye. He was gloating just a little, a rare moment of evil joy.*

*He had accomplished by himself his act of murder, for killing the family was far too important to leave to any of his slaves. But his work was not yet finished. There was one more thing he had to do.*

*Lucifer knew he had to get the prince while he was desperate, before he had any time to think. He had to get him while he was consumed with bitterness, before he had a chance to settle down. So he moved quickly beside the mortal and began to hiss in his ear.*

*******

The prince remained in the room for almost twenty-four hours. When he emerged, he was unshaven, smelly and frayed as old cloth.

He knew who had killed his family. They were not far away. And they were not finished with their killing. There was more they had to do.

So he had come to a decision.

Then he had figured out a plan.

Forget everything he had ever promised his father about freedom or democracy. Forget all of his dreams. It was a different world now. A new battle. A new war.

Although brothers had escaped injury, there would be no unwounded soldiers in this war.

# SEVEN

It was almost six hours before Major General Neil Brighton's military aircraft was cleared to takeoff because of the emergency hold put on all air traffic in and out of King Khaled Riyadh International Airport. As he waited for clearance to leave the kingdom, the general fidgeted anxiously in his seat. As the evening sun settled, his C-20 was finally cleared for departure, the first aircraft in a long line of civilian traffic that was cleared to takeoff. The aircraft quickly climbed to thirty-nine thousand feet and leveled off. Brighton undid his lap belt and settled back in his seat. A young servicewoman dressed in her Air Force skirt and blue sweater served the general a light dinner, then brought him a secure telephone and encryption cable to so he could plug his laptop into the aircraft's satellite communications system.

"Anything else?" the servicewoman asked after helping him plug in.

The general shook his head. "No thanks, Sergeant Rice."

"You look tired, sir."

"Maybe a little."

"I'm sure you're eager to get home."

"Always eager, Sergeant Rice."

"We'll be changing crews at Ramstein, sir, but I'll make certain they bring on some hot oatmeal for your breakfast. And fresh grapefruit juice and oranges. Did I forget anything?"

Brighton shook his head and thanked her, then turned on his laptop and started typing everything he could remember from the meeting with Prince Saud. He closed his eyes, trying to remember every word. Then he concentrated on the chaos he had witnessed. *Firefall?* What was a *Firefall?* What was going on?

He had witnessed something important, but he did not understand.

It was a six-hour flight to Ramstein where they would refuel and change pilots for the long flight back to the United States. As the aircraft approached the Mediterranean Sea, the air became heavy with humidity and haze. Looking down, Brighton could see a solid cloud layer forming beneath him, and ahead there were growing lines of thunderstorms, huge angry monsters reaching up to sixty-thousand feet. The shadows from the thunderstorm cells cast purple, gray and blue hues across the lower layers of white. He saw the first bolt of lightning flash from one of the cells. He knew the small jet would have to weave its way between the storm cells and the pilot inside him wanted to climb into the cockpit and push one of the young captains aside. Fighting the temptation, he turned back to his work.

Behind him, his two aides fell asleep while the security officer stared out his window on the other side of the cabin. Another flash of lightning lit up the interior of the cabin and the security officer grabbed his armrest in a death grip. Brighton felt the aircraft begin to climb, trying to get a little higher to get over the storms, then turn a few degrees to the north.

Closing his eyes, he leaned back in his chair.

He thought of the stark-raving terror that had fallen across the crown prince's face, the guards milling in confusion around him, the tension in their voices, their weapons and radios, their determined urgency as they had pulled the prince away.

He knew it was likely he would never know what had happened today. The flow of information out of the kingdom was extremely tightly controlled. And the doings of the royal family of the House of Saud was the most highly guarded secret of them all. Personal information was completely nonexistent. He knew there would be nothing in the press, nothing over the wires, nothing in any intelligence reports.

But something had happened, something dangerous and deadly. He knew it, he felt it somewhere deep in his bones. He thought of the warnings the prince had given, the most frank and disheartening conversation with a world leader he had ever had, then sat back and shivered from a fear he didn't understand.

# EIGHT

Prince al-Rahman stood at the window of his Dhahran penthouse atop the Royal Saudi Oil company headquarters and gazed out on the ports of the city. The office was an enormous room filled with leather and rare woods from the far corners of the world. Racks of various game animals hung on the wall, some of them legal, most of them not, many of them endangered African animals shot by the Prince himself. He was good with a knife and he was good with a gun, the blood of his warrior ancestors running thick through his veins. He loved to track game, he was good at it, and he loved to kill. He loved to butcher his meat—gutting the animal and smelling the blood—there was something about it that was appealing to him. Like his Bedouin ancestors, he hungered to hunt though he never brought the meat home, but left it on the prairie for other scavengers to feed.

To Al-Rahman's right, a large plaque hung on the wall that was engraved with words from the *Covenant of the Islamic Resistance Movement*, sometimes called the *Covenant of Hamas*:

*"Israel will exist and will continue to exist until Islam will obliterate it, just as it obliterated others before it . . . ."*

. . . .

*"The Day of Judgment will not come about until Moslems fight the Jews (killing the Jews), when the Jews will hide behind stones and trees. The stones and trees will say O Moslem, O Abdulla, there is a Jew hiding behind me, come and kill him."*

. . . .

*[S]o-called peaceful solutions and international conferences . . . are in contradiction to the principles of the Islamic Resistance Movement.*

. . . .

246

*There is no solution for the Palestinian problem except by Jihad.*

The prince loved the words from the *Covenant.* They inspired him by reminding him of his comrade's convictions to improving the world through the spread of jihad.

As for himself, his battle was anything but a holy war. Indeed, it was very unholy, he would freely admit. He was not into God or religion, leaving such concerns to other men.

Al-Rahman stood at the floor-to-ceiling window. His younger brothers stood behind him, letting him think. The setting sun cast long shadows across the city, casting the office in a natural glow. He peered out the window to where the gray-blue waters of the Persian Gulf glimmered in the setting sun. The city was busy, the port alive and bustling with men, equipment and machines. Enormous oil tankers moved toward the sea docks where they would take on their loads of rich Saudi crude. After filling their enormous holds, the tankers would turn for various ports in the West and East where the Saudi oil would help to quench the insatiable thirst for energy that drove the economic machines of the world. Prince al-Rahman glanced down and imagined the reservoirs of oil that lie ten thousand feet under his feet, huge underground pools that stretched a hundred miles in every direction. A quarter of the world's known oil supply lay under the Arabian sands; four hundred trillion dollars worth of underground liquid gold. And the oil guaranteed not only the wealth of the Royal Saudi family, but the wealth of their subjects, providing each Saudi citizen with one of the highest standards of living in the world. For generations ahead, their wealth and well-being was assured.

*But not if . . . But not if . . . .*

The prince shuddered in anger and raised his eyes to the coast.

Once loaded with oil, the tankers would steam out to sea, passing huge cargo ships on their way to Saudi ports. Al-Rahman turned to the docks on the east side of the city and watched the multicolored container ships unloading their wares; luxury cars, electronics, food, soda, clothing, frozen meat, furniture, steel, plastics, wood and cables, heavy equipment, office supplies, golf clubs and boats, cotton balls, medicine, cement, and scientific equipment. The list of imports was as long as the docks that paralleled the sea, for his nation imported almost everything they needed to survive. He was reminded again that this was where the cycle was complete. Oil for cash. Cold cash for things. Oil revenues in exchange for the beautiful things of the world.

The kingdom was in order. There was peace and prosperity. His subjects were well-fed and happy. It was as it should be.

*So why did his idiot father insist on screwing it up?*

He turned quickly and examined his two younger brothers, weak men whose only assets were that they always did what he told them to do: two evil and cold-hearted babies who hated the thought of losing their power almost as much as he.

He studied their faces; twentyish, handsome, identical dark hair and mustaches, fine teeth and round shoulders. Yet they were so needy, so dependent, it was almost comical. Neither of his younger brothers had worked a day in their lives and it disgusted Al-Rahman that they were so incapable of taking care of themselves. They didn't know how to drive, how to cook, or even how to make their own beds. They hardly knew how to get dressed without their valets selecting their clothes and neither could draw a bath without screaming in frustration when the water flowed too hot or too cold. And they certainly didn't know how to fight, that's what their bodyguards were for, though they seemed to fight and scream at each other at the drop of a hat.

Still, Al-Rahman had learned his younger brothers weren't

entirely stupid. Indeed, they had proven that they were capable of learning if they were motivated enough. And the plans of their father had motivated them now.

"Are you here alone?" Al-Rahman asked the younger of the brothers.

The youngest prince had recently taken to traveling with a young woman he had met in Greece, dragging her around like a security blanket. It seemed she was always around, lurking in the next room and Al-Rahman didn't like it. He would have to get rid of her soon.

His youngest brother snorted. "Of course I'm alone. I'm not stupid," he replied.

Al-Rahman eyed him with a cold-hearted smile. Yes, he *was* stupid. And when he started a sentence with "Of course," one couldn't presume that was necessarily what he meant.

Al-Rahman turned away from the window and sat down at his gold-accented, mahogany desk. His brothers watched him carefully, sitting on the edge of their seats. Al-Rahman lit a cigarette while they waited, took a long drag, then leaned back and held the smoke in his lungs.

The older prince smiled almost sadly. Sometimes he wished his brothers could be more like him. But they weren't. Motivated by short-term pleasure and money, they couldn't see beyond the next day. So he would use them, then kill them. It was the order of things.

Al-Rahman glanced at his cigarette, letting the smoke drift from his nose. He bit on his lip, feeling a piece of stray tobacco there. "Did you show her your face like I told you?"

"Yes, brother, I did."

"And what was her reaction?"

The younger prince shot an anxious look toward his brother.

"I'm not certain. It happened pretty quickly."

"Did she die quietly?" he demanded. "Did she say anything?"

The younger brother lit his own cigarette and pulled a nervous drag. "She said something . . . I don't know, something about Allah and the kingdom."

Al-Rahman smiled. That sounded like Tala, always praising Allah. "All right, brothers," he concluded, "you did a good job. That will be all for now." Finished with them, he wanted them out of the room.

The two princes stood up together. The youngest one turned for the door, then glanced back to Al-Rahman. "And Crown Prince Saud?" he wondered quickly.

Al-Rahman waved an impatient hand. "That is not your concern."

The younger prince stared at his brother. "You know our father, the king, will figure this out. That will not be a good thing. We have to be ready to defend ourselves."

"The king is a coward," Al-Rahman shot back. "He will not do anything."

"But he still holds great power . . . ."

"Which is *exactly* my point! He holds to the same power that he wants to rip from our hands! He plans to dismantle our kingdom and turn it over to *them*." Abdullah shot an angry hand toward the west. "But does he pay the price of his decision? Of course not! We do! He waits until he grows old, enjoying a life of great ease, then commands his oldest son to take our kingdom apart. But I will not allow it." Al-Rahman cursed. "I swear that on his grave! It is he who betrays us! He is disloyal to Mohammad, and disloyal to me! He has been planning our destruction since before we were born!"

The older prince slapped both hands on the table, then pointed a finger at the younger men. "Remember this, my brothers," he hissed a final time. "We are trying to save the kingdom. That is all that we do. We are trying to save the kingdom from this selfish king, save it from his stupid son!"

The youngest prince lowered his head in subjection as he backed toward the door.

*******

The door swung close behind them and Al-Rahman touched a button on his desk to lock it. Seconds later, a side door to his office swung back. The old man stepped into the office. He walked painfully, shuffling between the chrome handles of a walker and it seemed to take him forever to make his way to the couch. He sat down wearily, then looked at the prince.

The old man's skin was so thin and waxy, he almost looked dead. Al-Rahman noted the sick eyes and hollow face then glanced to the side door that led to a private study, knowing the old man's doctor was waiting there. The old man coughed deeply, bringing up the collected phlegm from his chest.

Al-Rahman waited for him to spit, then reported. "They are dead," he announced.

"Good," the old man answered weakly. "You have made me proud."

Al-Rahman waited, unconsciously gripping a gold pen in his hand.

"Now we must take care of Crown Prince Saud," the old man struggled to breathe as he talked. "Then we will be ready to take the next step."

The prince relaxed his grip on the pen. After all of these years, it was what he had been waiting to hear. "I have your permission then?" he asked quickly.

"Yes, yes, of course. Do what you will. But remember, Prince al-Rahman, you must do something first. If you don't take care of all the offspring, then you will leave us a mess. You've got to cut out all the cancer or it will kill you one day." His eyes seemed to narrow. "The crown prince has another wife. Another son."

"I will take care of them."

The old man coughed again, then took a crackling breath. The prince knew he was dying—he had but a month or so to live. Al-Rahman thought back on that spring day in Monte Carlo, a little more than eighteen years before. Through sheer force of will, the old man had done what he promised, living to see their success. And here it was, so close. Everything was in place. In a very few weeks he would pull the trigger and the final war would begin.

"When will you do it?" the old man asked between gasping breaths.

Prince Al-Rahman thought a long moment. "Soon," he finally answered. "He's still mourning over the bodies. He's been there for hours. By now, of course, he knows that it was me. And he will act, I am sure; a few days, a few hours. We just killed his family, do you think he will wait? But he has a mountain to sort through before he can do anything. If he can't trust his brothers, then where can he turn?"

"Before he turns against us, he will see to his last son. He will take care of his heir and ensure he is safe. And he will do it alone; he won't trust anyone else. He knows there are snakes in the nursery and he will want to kill them himself. Until then, he is vulnerable, so we have a few hours."

The old man rasped, and then warned him, "Crown Prince Saud is no fool. It would be a mistake to underestimate him. So be careful, al-Rahman. We've come too far, been far too patient, and we've worked too hard and sacrificed too much to let this slip through our fingers this late in the game."

The prince pressed his lips. "Yes," he answered simply. "It is a dangerous time."

"Then take care of Prince Saud before he turns his attention to us."

Al-Rahman started to answer when the personal phone at the side of his desk buzzed quietly. He picked up the receiver and listened, then grunted a few instructions and hung up the phone. The old man peered at him and Prince Al-Rahman smiled. "Crown Prince Saud is on his way to the airport," he said.

"Where to?" the old man questioned, a hint of concern in his voice.

"I don't know," Al-Rahman answered. "But we are going to find out. He has requested his private helicopter. They are completing the pre-flight now."

# NINE

Princess Tala and her children were buried in a secret and private funeral at the royal family's ancient cemetery on the outskirts of Medina. Only Crown Prince Saud, his father and a few trusted kin stood over the dark graves as the gold-plated coffins were lowered into the dry ground. There was no press release, no public offering, no notification to the world that the princess had been killed and incredibly, word of the assassinations didn't leak to the international press.

When it came to interfamily homicide there was good reason to be silent. The kingdom had been thrown into chaos. And it was about to get worse.

\*\*\*\*\*\*

Seven hours after the private funeral, the Crown Prince of the House of Saud was moved to one of his personal helicopters that always stood on alert. The helicopter's blades were spinning when the crown prince showed up and the helicopter took off in the darkness without turning on its navigational lights.

The prince watched through the window of the American-made Sikorski S-92, a four-bladed executive helicopter that had more gold and leather than could be found in any executive suite looking down on midtown Manhattan. The highly modified cabin, originally designed to seat seventeen passengers had been modified into a six-passenger configuration, with opposing leather couches running down each of the sides of the cabin, a fully stocked bar, a small office and lavatory and two massive reclining chairs just behind the bulkhead wall. The carpet was a deep maroon and so thick it felt like one was standing on grass. Highly polished teak and mahogany accented the trim, and the seats were white leather, soft as velvet, and emblazoned with the royal flag.

Crown Prince Saud watched in silence as the warm waters of the Persian Gulf passed underneath his helicopter, but the night was so dark it was nearly impossible to get a sense of their speed. The winds had picked up, moving down from the north and the ocean was white-capped with rippled lines of foam reflecting the light of the yellow moon. The helicopter flew east, toward the Iranian border, and with each passing mile the emptiness inside him grew more dark and intense. He leaned against the helicopter's starboard window and felt the vibration of the rotors spinning over his head. The helicopter passed the first of the many offshore oil rigs that dotted Iran's western shore and he knew they would soon be "feet dry" over land. The Crown Prince could imagine the view from the cockpit—the miles of whitecaps below them, the enormous oil derricks casting shadows under the moon, the deep black sands and rising foothills of Iran's western shores, the moon in the pilot's faces and the enormous saucer of stars overhead. He glanced at his watch. A little after one in the morning. They had been in the air for an hour and would soon land.

The prince took a breath and turned in his seat. The helicopter was silent except for the sound of his second wife crying, a soft and heartbroken tremble that she tried to hold in. The prince looked lovingly at her and she wiped her eyes quickly to hide her tears. He reached out and took her hand and held it to his chest then placed his other hand very gently on the four-year-old boy who was sleeping beside her. "Do you want our son to live?" he asked simply.

The young princess nodded and squared her shoulders in reply.

"Then be strong," the prince demanded, his voice strained but firm. He pressed her hand against their sleeping child's head. "Be strong for him. Be strong for our family. Be strong for the kingdom. Be strong for me."

The princess wiped her cheeks as she stared at her lap.

The prince saw a vision of the four charred bodies, their barely recognizable faces peaceful now in death. He glanced at his last son, a four-year old who slept on his young mother's lap. His face too was peaceful. The prince's heart broke again.

His family. His honor. Their future. Their king. That was all that mattered. The prince knew that was true.

He studied his young wife, reading the pain in her eyes. She looked as if she were dying, as if she were already dead. She looked so lonely, so abandoned. "Are you certain?" she pleaded. "Is there no other way?"

The prince shook his head. "I have decided. We will discuss it no more."

The young princess sat back, her eyes fearful and wet. Her lower lip trembled. She was *trying* to be brave, she was *trying* to be strong . . . but this was so unexpected and so frightening. She looked straight ahead, her face strained with fear.

"Why can't I go home to my family?" she muttered. "Why can't I stay in Saudi Arabia? I know nothing of Iran!"

"Which is why we must do this! Are you so blind you can't see? Your life is in danger and so is my son! Now quit crying of your suffering! Would you rather be dead? Would you rather I have to bury him like I buried my other children?"

The princess stroked the sleeping boy's face. "But my husband . . . Iran? Why not the southern providence? My people are from that region. I want to live among them and . . . ."

"That's right! *You want to live!* So you must do as I say!"

"But it is so far away!"

"Pray it is far enough!"

The princess fell silent knowing she should not say any more.

Prince Saud leaned his head back and stared blankly at the darkness. She glanced at him quickly and saw the trail of his tears.

Minutes passed, then the prince leaned toward her. "You are strong, Ash Salman," he whispered firmly. "There is a determination, a wisdom inside you which is rare in my people. You have already shown more courage than most men I know. I will not leave you alone. I do have a plan! But there is a scourge in the kingdom. We suffer a deadly disease. It will take me some time to hunt my enemies. This threat, these assassins, I know who they are, but I don't know how deep it goes or who is involved. It will take me some time to figure out who I can trust and who I should kill. And until they are dead, I need to know that my last son is safe. It is he they are after, for he will be the next king. So until this the danger passes, you *must* hide."

The princess took a deep breath then turned back to her window to watch the darkness outside. The helicopter passed over the Iranian border and climbed to five-hundred feet. She saw a dark ribbon wind along the foothills to the south—the Khorramshahr highway that ran to the heart of the oil fields. She tried to remember the map she had studied the night before. The tiny village of Agha Jari Deh was but a little farther inland.

The helicopter leveled off, then descended.

The mountains rose up to meet them.

The princess was almost there.

\*\*\*\*\*\*

Rassa Ali Pahlavi lay still in his bed, awake but unmoving. The bedroom was cool in the mountain air. Something had woken him, something far in the distance, the low sound of beating rotors passing over a hill. He lay there and thought, then pushed himself out of bed and pulled on a thin shirt and dark trousers.

He walked silently out of the bedroom. Moving into the kitchen, he set a blackened copper kettle on the stove and turned on the propane, setting the flame on high. He moved carefully, making no noise, knowing the walls that separated the kitchen from Azadeh's bedroom were paper-thin. The water boiled quickly under the oversized flame and he sprinkled in two measures of black tea, stirred quickly, then poured the tea into a ceramic mug and held it tight, letting it warm his hands. He sipped once. The tea was bitter and he pressed his lips appreciatively as he sat down at the table.

A beautifully framed embroidery hung on the wall, an angular inscription consisting of three words; *Allah, Mohammad* and *Ali.* The name of Ali in the embroidery identified his household as a member of the Shi'a, or Shi'ites, those Muslims who consider Ali the legal successor to Mohammad. All around him were other reminders of his religion, along with verses from the *Qur'an* designed to chase evil away.

But evil *was* coming! Rassa felt a cold chill. *Something* was coming. He had felt this before.

Studying his meager surroundings, he felt restless and on edge. He sipped at his hot tea, seeking its warmth. Standing, he walked quietly to Azadeh's bedroom and pushed the door open a crack. She was sleeping soundly and he sat down in the kitchen again. Picking up a copy of the *Qur'an*, he repeated the cleansing phrase, *"In the name of Allah, Most Gracious, Most Merciful."* Cleansed, he started reading, choosing at random a verse.

"It is righteousness to believe in Allah and the Last Day; and the Angels, and the Book, and the Messengers; to be firm and patient in pain and adversity, and throughout all periods of panic. Such are the people of truth, the God-fearing . . . ."

He read the verse again, then looked up in thought.

"To be firm and patient in pain and adversity . . . ."

He thought of the sound that had startled him out of sleep. A helicopter. On the western side of the hill.

Helicopters flying toward the village? That was never good news.

"Pain and adversity." His village had had their fair share.

\*\*\*\*\*\*

Crown Prince Saud unstrapped his seat belt and moved to the small door that separated the passenger cabin from the cockpit and pulled it open. He was met by the dim, multicolored lights of the cockpit; four eight-inch computer displays, a terrain-following radar, and rows upon rows of digital gauges and multifunctions switches. The two pilots sat side-by-side, both of them Saudi air force colonels, old friends, trusted and worthy, their faces an unearthly green in the reflected cockpit lights. Saud stood in the doorway and studied the ALQ-162 defensive/countermeasures CRT, an automated system that searched out ground threats—ground-to-air radars, shoulder-fired weapons and other heat-seeking missiles. With the exception of the Operations Normal symbology, the screen was a pale, silver blank. Satisfied, he raised his eyes to look through the cockpit window. The world appeared crooked, for the pilot had rolled the helicopter into a steep bank. The horizon tilted across the windscreen at an uncomfortable angle, the moon and stars filling the right window, the coastline and lighted highway filling the left. His head spun a moment and he adjusted his weight to balance himself, then turned to the copilot, who gestured to the north. "Agha Jari Deh," the pilot said, pointing to a tiny collection of mud and brick houses nestled tightly against the rising mountains.

The prince watched anxiously. Even in the moonlight, the village was surprisingly small; so small, the helicopter would overfly it in a matter of seconds. There was only one road leading to the village and except for those who traveled to its market the village was almost completely unknown.

Saud studied the passing huts and small homes. It was so small. It was perfect. Allah had prepared a way.

******

The helicopter rolled level and began to slow down. The copilot lifted his hand to the helicopter's collective grips, which controls the helicopter's ascent and descent, and pressed his radio switch to answer a radio call. "Transportation is waiting," he announced to the prince.

Saud nodded and watched as the helicopter turned to line up on a grassy field, two or three kilometers south of the village. The circle of grass appeared as a dark bowl against the reflective rocks of the mountains. The village was quiet, less than a dozen lights shining to the north. He picked out the headlights of the waiting vehicles as the helicopter descended through three hundred feet and slowed below one hundred twenty knots. A powerful *whoop* emitted from above his head as the blades slapped the air, taking less of a bite as the aircraft slowed down. The pilot switched on the landing light and the tips of the spinning blades reflected the powerful lamp. Saud nudged the pilot on the shoulder, then stepped out of the cockpit and closed the door.

Moving to the princess, he sat down at her side. In the dim light of the cabin, he saw a single tear glisten on the edge of her chin. She stared ahead, unmoving, her determination building inside. The prince didn't speak to her as he slipped her lap belt on.

The helicopter landed with a bump on the uneven field and the pilot brought the twine turbine engines to idle and disengaged the rotors. Saud stood and worked the exit door, which dropped into the darkness, the folding steps exposed as the door slipped into place. He turned back to the princess who was waking their son. The three of them stepped out of the aircraft and into the cold mountain air.

*******

Rassa heard his neighbor's dog. The Afghan Hound bark urgently from behind the fence that followed the narrow trail that led up to the mountains. He stood up and moved to the window and looked out on the courtyard that surrounded his backyard where the moon cast deep shadows that wavered as the clouds passed overhead. The air was calm now, and cold, and he saw no movement in the dim light. Twenty seconds later he heard the sound of an automobile engine and the soft crunch of tires against the rock and gravel outside.

A sudden chill ran through him. He thought of the whoop of the helicopter blades and the roar of the turbine engines. Out here, in the most remote parts of the country, where the warlords and tribal chiefs ruled, a helicopter could only mean one of two things; warlords from the south, coming up to collect recruits for their bloody turf battles, or the jihadist—the lawless Islamic fanatics who had adapted to the presence of Western forces in Iraq by hiding out in the Iranian deserts where they planned their battles against the Great Satan and Jews.

Standing in the middle of the kitchen, Rassa felt his heart sink. He had seen many men disappear, pulled away in the night. Some had been suspected collaborators. Some had been hauled off to fight. Many were never heard of again. Fewer still returned to their homes.

He listened to the sounds of the car doors shut, then soft footsteps on the porch. He glanced in a panic to the bedroom door, thinking of his daughter, Azadeh, then considered the old rifle stuffed behind the ancient cedar armoire in corner of the room, a beat-up Lee-Enfield .303 that had been used by his grandfather during the First World War. The rifle was his own deadly secret, for to have a rifle, any weapon in fact, in Iran was strictly forbidden. Yet Rassa made no move toward it. If they were coming for him, be it the warlords or mullahs, it would be dangerous to fight them, especially with Azadeh in the next room.

So he waited, unmoving, listening to the footsteps outside his door. The wooden door rattled on its hinges but Rassa didn't dare to move.

# TEN

Rassa finally pulled the door open and peered out onto the dimly lit porch. Two middle-aged men stood in the darkness; both of them strong and well-dressed in dark western suits, though traditional turbans were wrapped on their heads. The nearest man blocked the doorway with his massive frame and moved one hand to his hip, exposing a thin, leather holster. The second man stood slightly behind the other and off to the side. Rassa glanced past the first guard to see two dark cars parked on the road, their engines idle, their headlights off. Without explanation, the bodyguards pushed into his home and swept through the room. Rassa stood speechless until one of them paused at the back bedroom. "Is Azadeh in there?" he asked Rassa in a deep tone.

Rassa moved toward the hall. "Who are you?" he demanded, his eyes flashing with rage.

"Is she in there?" the bodyguard repeated.

Rassa tightened in panic then shook his head. "You do not want her," he hissed, his voice husky with rage. It was the voice of a fighter at the edge of a war. "It is me you have come for! *Leave her alone!*"

He took a quick step toward the guard while glancing at the holster underneath the dark suit. If they had come for Azadeh then he would die in their way.

The leader ignored Rassa and nodded to the bedroom. "Check it out," he said.

The smaller guard nodded and slowly pushed the door open. Stepping into the room, he pulled a tiny flashlight from his pocket and flashed it inside. He saw the sleeping girl, her head buried on the side of her pillow. He swept the light quickly, taking in the simple bed, small chest, and white wicker drawer. A small collection of colorful dresses, silken hajib headscarves and full burkas were hanging from a rope tied across the far corner. A golden headband had been neatly arranged on top of the dresser. On the floor next to the bureau was a pair of sandals and leather shoes. He studied the room carefully, then stepped back and closed the door.

Rassa was waiting at the door, a look of rage on his face. He relaxed his glare only slightly when the guard closed the door. "Who are you?" he hissed. "What are you doing here? I have nothing to hide! I have nothing you want!"

The two guards didn't answer as they nodded to each other. The larger man moved to the front door, pushed it open and raised his right hand. The automobiles turned off their engines. Rassa heard the car doors open, then the sound of soft footsteps. He waited, then moved to the center of the kitchen, placing himself between Azadeh's bedroom and the front door.

A young woman entered the room, her dark eyes bewildered and red. She was dressed in a dark burka and leather sandals, and she pulled a deep blue shawl tightly over her shoulders. She moved to a position beside the wall, then pushed her burka back, revealing a long mane of dark hair. Another man followed, dressed in an exquisite dark suit. Rassa saw him and stepped back, sucking in a quick breath of air. The intruder walked into the room with the confidence of a king, his shoulders square, his head high, his eyes constantly moving with suspicion but still clear and sure. Rassa dropped to one knee as the prince moved through the room, the social chasm between them demanding he bow with respect.

The prince moved toward him and extended his hand. Rassa stood and the prince pulled him to his chest, kissing both of his cheeks in a display of respect.

Rassa dropped his eyes in confusion. What was this man doing here?

The prince stepped back and took in Rassa, measuring his appearance from his head to his feet. The woman remained near the doorway, her eyes dull with fright. The prince turned back to Rassa and gripped him by his shoulders. "Rassa Ali Pahlavi," he asked, "do you know who I am?"

"You are Crown Prince Saud, oldest son of King Fahd bin Saud Aziz, monarch of the House of Saud, grandson of King Saud Aziz, future Custodian of the Two Holy Mosques, keeper of the Holy Cities of Mecca and Medina."

Prince Saud nodded. Good. That was good. His cousin might have been raised in one of the most remote villages in the mountains, but clearly he was not an illiterate fool. He had read. He remembered. And he was aware. Some of the prince's own citizens would not have recognized him and only one in a hundred Iranians would have known who he was. He nodded with approval, then motioned toward the young women. "Do you know her as well?" he demanded.

Rassa kept his head low, afraid of meeting her eyes. "I'm sorry, Your Highness, I do not know who she is."

The prince nodded again. That was good as well. She mustn't be recognized if their plan was to work. And he had doubted she would be, not here in the Iranian mountains, so far from their home.

The royal sons were rarely photographed inside their own country, and it was strictly forbidden to photograph their children or wives. This wasn't England after all, with their maniacal fascination with the royal family. This was the House of Saud, the Kingdom of Arabia, Keeper of the Holy Cities. Theirs wasn't a monarchy of fairy tales and magic castles, a kingdom of tabloids, gossip and family secrets revealed.

The House of Saud was a kingdom of *power*, the kingdom of *Allah* on earth and paparazzi were simply not tolerated in their press. The royal wives and their daughters led luxurious but anonymous lives. It had always been thus and it would always be so, for it would have been demeaning to Allah and Mohammad for the women of the royal family to live public lives.

Which meant the princess could stay here *if* she would not be recognized.

Prince Saud nodded to the princess. "You do not know who she is?" he repeated.

"No, my *Sayid*. Should I recognize her?"

Prince Saud watched Rassa closely as he searched for any shadow that he was not telling the truth. Did he truly not know her? Would his eyes give him away?

Rassa's face didn't change. He did not know who the princess was.

The prince breathed a shallow sigh of relief.

It might actually work.

He studied Rassa again. His men had been investigating his cousin for almost a year, and there was little about Rassa that the prince didn't know. And though the final plans had been laid some months before, when the prince first became convinced they might actually come after his family, this was the first time he had seen him and he wanted to take his measure.

Rassa held the prince's gaze, never looking away. This man might be a prince, but *this* was his home. And no man was his master, a least not in *this* place.

Over the years the prince had learned how to measure a man. He had learned to distinguish between his enemies and friends, measuring secret ambitions and hidden desires, to recognize those who loved him and those who wished to bring him harm. Staring into Rassa's eyes, he saw no guile in him. This was a good man, straightforward and honest and for the first time in days, the prince began to relax.

He took a step toward Rassa. "We are not strangers," he said. "One of my grandfathers, your grandfathers, they were cousins I believe."

Rassa nodded. The genealogy was not unfamiliar to him. "That was many generations back. Maybe even five hundred years."

"Yes, but the bloodlines of royalty are extremely pure. We are far more closely related than you might at first guess."

Rassa thought for a moment, getting past his surprise and fear. "Our forebears were enemies," he added after reviewing the genealogy in his mind.

The prince smiled. "Yes, they traded a share of their men's lives in battles, there is no doubt about that. But they were not unfriendly, I think. They were sheiks fighting for their kingdoms and to protect their gold, but when the day was over, I suppose they were friends. That was business, that was then, and of course this is now. So you and I, we are family. And the bonds of our ancestors that tie us are far stronger than any blood that has been spilt in the past."

Rassa paused, then answered sadly.

*"When the battle is over,*
*And the evening winds come,*
*When spear tips glint in the twilight,*
*And the skirmish is done.*
*Then I hope I am standing,*
*And brother, I hope you are too*
*For on the other side of the war ground,*

*I will be thinking of you."*

The prince stood without moving. The ancient sonnet was familiar. Then he frowned, his eyes narrowing with heartsickness as he repeated the verse.

*"Then I hope I am standing,*
*And brother, I hope you are too*
*For on the other side of the war ground,*
*I will be thinking of you."*

He stole a glance at his woman, who stared at him in grief.

Not this time. Not his brothers. They only wished he was dead. He stood in mute silence, then suddenly shook his head.

Rassa stood close by, waiting, as Crown Prince Saud looked at him.

"Rassa Ali Pahlavi," he began, "I have come to you because I need your help. My life is in great danger. My wife is in great danger too. And the only son I have left is outside in my car.

"I am bringing him to you for protection. I bring him to you so he will live and one day be king. But his life is in great danger, for there are many around us who would not have it be so."

The room was deadly silent. Rassa gazed at the prince in disbelief, his mouth growing dry. Prince Saud nodded to his bodyguards, who motioned to each other and walked quietly from the house.

# ELEVEN

The men were seated on the wooden floor, their legs tucked underneath them as they leaned against cotton cushions. A cup of *chai* sat between them, thick as molasses, sweet as sugar, and strong enough to give an almost instant rush of energy. The smell permeated the room, warm and syrupy, and a thin wisp of steam rose from their porcelain cups. The young princess sat silently beside her husband. She reached out her hand and he squeezed it, then let it go.

The bodyguards took up positions outside the small home and Rassa could hear their footsteps through the thin glass windows as they moved around the house and through the courtyard. Rassa realized they were keeping to the shadows, never revealing themselves as they moved from the corner of the small house to the line of trees on the north and west sides.

The prince turned toward Rassa and folded his arms. "I'm going to ask you a question," he said.

Rassa's back stiffened and he drew a tight breath.

"Do you understand why you are here?" Prince Saud asked in a low voice.

"Why am *I* here?" Rassa answered, a puzzled look on his face.

"Yes. Do you know why you're here?"

Rassa stared at him blankly, confusion narrowing his brow. "I am here, Crown Prince Saud because . . . well because this is my home."

The prince shook his head. "No, Rassa Ali Pahlavi, that is not what I meant. Why are you *here*? Why did God give you life? For what purpose were you born?"

"The purpose of life is to surrender my will to Allah," Rassa answered automatically, repeating the words he had learned and repeated every day since he was no more than two.

The prince nodded impatiently. "Yes, Rassa, of course. But think beyond the *Qur'an*. I want you to tell me more."

Rassa thought in bewildered silence. "Your Majesty," he whispered, his voice trailing off. He looked at his *chai*, keeping his eyes on the floor. He finally shrugged his shoulders. "I do not know what to say."

The prince leaned toward him. "I have spent most of my life studying the holy teachings of the *Qur'an*," he said. "I am both by nature and training a deeply religious man. I have responsibilities to the kingdom, but more, I have responsibilities to Allah. Because of this, I have spent my life studying with the masters; the best educated Muslim philosophers anywhere in the world. And this is what I have come to believe. The *Qur'an* teaches that each man has a reason for living. Allah fates certain things, and he has brought me here, Rassa, to speak with you tonight. He has a purpose for you, Rassa and I know his will."

"Whatever you ask, I will do it," Rassa trembled in reply before he quickly added *Insha'allal.* If it is God's will.

Saud lowered his voice. "My kingdom stands on the edge of a precipice," he whispered. "We look over a terrible and deadly abyss. There are those within my country, even those within my own family, who want us to fail. There are those in my councils who crave a final battle with the West. There are those who believe we have a sacred obligation to join the *jihad* and are willing to do whatever it takes to make their dreams come true.

"They are dangerous. Extremely dangerous. They are a secret band of brothers, bound by blood oaths and lies. And they are not driven by a dedication to Allah! They are not driven by religion or a vision of a greater Islam!! They are driven by power! They are driven by hate! They are evil and deadly men who want to conquer our world.

"And like the shadows that spread when the sun sets, they grow even darker as the evening comes on. Yet no one notes their growing power, for the darkness settles so slowly it is nearly imperceptible. But their influence is spreading. I'm the only thing that stands in their way. And I am afraid."

Rassa stared openmouthed. It seemed impossible! The most powerful man in Saudi Arabia! One of the most powerful men in the world! He could not understand it! But as he gazed at the prince, Rassa saw a cold look of fear.

Prince Saud dropped his eyes and a shadow crossed his face. "Early this evening I buried my family," he explained. "My first wife and our children. A daughter. Two sons. Another son who was not even born yet also died in his mother's womb." He shot another pained look at his second wife, then slowly went on. "The only son I have left is outside in the car. I have brought him to you, Rassa, because you are my kin. I have brought my wife and child to you because I need you to keep them safe. There is nowhere in the kingdom that they could not be found. But here," he gestured, "in these mountains, in this tiny village in Iran, they will be safe for a few days. And that's all I need; a few days to destroy my enemies, that's all I'm asking for right now."

Rassa bowed in submission then gestured to his simple house. "But *Sayid*," he questioned, "look at my home. It is unworthy of the princess. It is unworthy of your son."

"*My poverty is my pride*," the prince quoted the *Qur'an* in reply.

"But I am a simple man, Your Highness. A simple man who is trying to survive on my own."

"Which is why this will work. They will never suspect! And Rassa, this isn't a decision I came to rashly. I have thought this through.

And I know in my heart this is the right thing to do."

"But *Sayid*," Rassa argued, "a young prince! In my home!"

"Listen to me!" Saud answered quickly, his voice growing strained. "You are Rassa Ali Pahlavi! The royal blood runs through your veins as it has run through your fathers for almost two thousand years! You cannot dismiss that! And they can't take it from you! We share royal blood, Rassa! That is why I came to you!"

Rassa was silent and the prince pointed a finger. "They will be looking for him," he prodded, his voice stained from fatigue and fear. "They will search through my kingdom, they will turn every rock, every reed, every reel. They will follow my movements, always searching for clues. But they will never suspect that I would dare take him out of the kingdom. And to Persia no less! They would not dream I would do this. And that is why this will work."

Rassa didn't respond. He did not know what to say.

Prince Saud watched him then stood quickly. He was finished explaining. It was time that he go. He nodded to the princess and she moved to his side. Turning to Rassa, Prince Saud made his final point. "The time is soon coming when Islam will rise from the ashes of the Ottoman Empire," he said. "It will rise and reclaim its rightful position of leadership in this world. For more than one thousand years, while the West rutted through the dark ages and wallowed in decay, the people of Islam stood as the military, economic and spiritual leaders of the world. And yet from the day Napoleon marched into Egypt, we have reacted like a stunned bull. One shot and we fell in a quivering heap to our knees. But the time is soon coming when we will rise again. There will be a Pan Arabia! But it will take a new way of thinking. It will take a new world. A new kind of leader to lead us there! A new king is required, someone who can purge Islam of the poison and lift it again as a symbol of wealth and peace to the world!

"I am that man, Rassa. I am going to change the world. And my son will follow in my footsteps. So we must keep him safe. Now do you understand?"

Rassa nodded gravely then pushed himself to his knees. "I will do as you command," he whispered as he bowed at the prince's feet.

The prince put his hands on his shoulders and lifted him up. "You must speak of this to no one!" he demanded. "Do you understand how important that is? You will call the princess a cousin who is visiting from Riyadh. Tell no one I have been here or we are both dead."

Rassa kept his eyes low as he nodded his head.

"Do you understand that, Rassa? Do you see how important our secrecy is?"

"I understand, *Sayid.*"

The crown prince gripped his shoulder, then looked at his wife. He nodded to the princess. "Go and get him," he said.

The princess left the house and returned with her son. The small boy stood shyly, holding tightly to his mother's hand. He had round eyes and dark hair and he looked around wearily. His father knelt before him and pulled him to his chest. Looking up, he nodded sternly to Rassa, looking him straight in the eyes. "Keep him safe," he demanded as he let his son go. "It will only be a few days, a week at the most before I come back for him. Keep them safe and I'll reward you beyond your wildest dreams. But if any danger befalls them, then I will hold you responsible. This is your charge, your great purpose and you simply can't fail."

Rassa bowed. "*Sayid,*" he replied.

"It could be dangerous for you, Rassa."

"*Sayid,* I will serve."

Prince Saud pressed Rassa's shoulder, turned sadly to the

princess and reached for her hand. "I will come back for you, Ash Salman," he whispered, leaning his mouth to her ear. "I will not leave you, not a day, not an hour, more than I have to. But for now we must do this. We must do this for our son.

"Now stay here. Be strong! Take care of my child and I will call for you soon."

The princess nodded, her face firm and proud. Saud leaned over and kissed her cheek softly then turned and walked out the door, leaving the young mother standing with the child prince in her hands.

*******

Rassa stared at her blankly, a dumbfounded look on his face. He didn't know what to say. He didn't know what to do. He opened his mouth, then shut it. Better to not sound like a fool. The young princess let her eyes drift to the floor. Her young son looked sleepily around the bare room. "Mother, why are we here?" he wondered. "Why did father go?"

The princess knelt. "Abd Illah, your father has gone for something very important. We are going to stay here for a few days."

The prince reached up for his mother, pulling into her arms. "I want to go with father. Why did he leave us?" The young boy started crying. The princess was not far from tears herself.

Then the bedroom door opened and Azadeh walked into the room. She shot a knowing look to her father and he realized she had been listening. "Azadeh," he asked her, "how long have you been awake?"

She ignored the question as she walked to the princess and her son. "Princess Ash Salman," she said as she bowed deeply with a graceful sweep of her arms. "My name is Azadeh Ishebel Pahlavi. I am Rassa's daughter. Welcome to our home."

The princess stared at her hopefully. Azadeh took the young prince's other hand and said, "We don't have a lot to offer, but anything we have is yours. It is an honor to have you with us, and we will do all we can to make your stay comfortable."

Rassa took a step toward Azadeh. "How much did you hear?" he whispered quickly.

"Everything," Azadeh answered. "I woke up when they knocked at our door."

"Then you understand?"

"I understand the princess has had a very long day. I understand the crown prince is in danger, and so is this child. Now we will make them safe and comfortable. We will treat them as our own."

Azadeh turned to the princess. She looked so young and vulnerable. An instant bond formed between them and the princess smiled wearily. Azadeh took the young prince and moved toward her bedroom door. "You are tired," she said. "Come. You two have my bed. I will sleep here by the fire. Come. You are tired. We will talk in the morning. It will seem brighter then."

Rassa watched in grateful amazement as Azadeh took care of their guests. She got clean sheets and clean towels and placed a bowl of warm water by their bed. She offered them tea and a biscuit, which both of them declined, then shut the door behind her, leaving them alone in her room.

Rassa smiled at Azadeh in gratitude. "Thank you," he said.

\*\*\*\*\*\*

Rassa waited until the others were asleep and the house had grown quiet, then slipped out the back door and through the yard, heading toward the center of town.

He found his friend Omar in the backroom of one of the dark warehouses he owned along the old docks on the river. Although it was after three in the morning, he knew Omar would be about his business. His friend often worked at night—some things were best done in the dark, and why should he sleep when there was cash to be made?

Walking through a side entrance of the old warehouse, Rassa paused for a moment to let his eyes adjust to the light and listened to Omar berate one of his lieutenants in the next room. Above him, in a hidden attic, Rassa knew he would likely find a cache of hand-woven Persian carpets on their way to illegal transport to Europe and the United States. He also knew Omar made more money on one pirated shipment of rugs than he made farming in a year. But he didn't envy Omar's money. He would have died from the stress.

Rassa knocked on the door before stepping into the room. Omar stood up to face him, his huge frame filling the semidarkness. "Rassa!" he demanded, "what are you doing here?"

"I need to talk with you," Rassa answered.

Omar glanced over his shoulder. "Could it wait?" he said.

"No, Omar, please."

Omar considered his friend then shot another look toward the back of the room. "All right," he said. "Let's go for a walk."

*******

The moon was just dropping behind the plains to the west and the lamps along the docks cast a dull, yellow glow. "What do I do?"

Rassa questioned after he had explained everything.

Omar gazed at Rassa, then shook his head in disbelief. His young friend was in deep water, in way over his head. The question now was, did he know how to swim?

Omar shook his head intently. "You've got a problem," he said. "And the truth is, good friend, you are too naïve to realize how big it really is."

Rassa looked at him, his eyes wide. "Just tell me what to do!" he pleaded.

"You have no choice," Omar answered without giving it any further thought. "The crown prince will not be trifled with. You must do as he asked. He is so desperate, he has played his last option, and that option, unbelievably, has led him to you. But you are also in danger. Are you wise enough to see that? The prince has powerful enemies, Rassa, he lives in an unforgiving and cruel world. It is harsh. It is mean. It is dog-eat-dog, or brother-kill-brother, then throw away the bones. It's a world that is difficult for you to understand. There is no good and no bad, only the weak and the strong. It is survival of the fittest and not a thing else.

"Now, is Prince Saud the strongest? We don't know yet. But those men who seek to destroy him will seek to destroy you as well. So if I have any advice for you, friend, it would be to stay out of sight. Keep your eyes open. The question is, did they follow the prince? One wouldn't think he would be so careless, or unlucky, but we really don't know. He was desperate, and his enemies are fearless and very powerful. So don't sleep too soundly, Rassa, not for a few days. The first forty-eight hours will be critical. If they are coming for you, I think they will be here by then."

Rassa looked confused. "But you don't think they would hurt . . . ."

"Absolutely they would. They are after the young prince, and you stand in their way. That makes you their enemy. The main question—really the only question—you need to consider is whether they will find him. How determined are they? How far will they go? Can Prince Saud protect his family? Did they follow Prince Saud? Do they have spies around?"

Rassa stopped and looked out on the river and slowly shook his head. "I would never do anything that would endanger Azadeh," he said.

"You are past that, Rassa. Everyone is in danger. You must accept that now."

Rassa didn't answer, but started walking again.

Omar watched him a moment, noting the slump of his shoulders and the drag of his feet. His friend was in trouble. So Omar committed to help. He would keep his eyes out, keep his own men in the square. He would watch the roads and highways and see what popped up. And he would warn Rassa if the wrong men showed up.

# TWELVE

The Sikorski S-92 flew low and fast over the water. The moon was setting in the western sky and a band of thick sea fog was developing below it. The moonlight cast shadows across the top of the fog, creating an illusion of flying over a landscape from the moon, endless miles of smooth and barren nothingness that stretched into the darkness of space.

Crown Prince Saud sat alone in the luxurious cabin. The lights were turned down and though his eyes were closed, he was not asleep. His body was numb with heartbreak and fatigue, but sleep was far from him. He was in too much pain. Over the past forty-eight hours he had lost everything he had ever loved; his wife and three children and his son yet unborn, his second wife and his last son, who were hiding now in Iran, his kingdom, his power, everything of any value to him—it was slipping away, a fistful of fine sand. He felt a blackness settle over him, a suffocating blanket of defeat, and he stared out at the darkness and sucked in a sudden, deep breath.

The helicopter vibrated around him, a smooth hum that developed from the rotors spinning over his head, a comforting vibration that settled into his bones. At the front of the cabin, one of the flat-screen TV monitors had been tuned to Arabic All News, but the sound was turned down and the prince paid no attention. The TV screen cast silver shadows through the cabin, causing his face to reflect in the oval window by his seat.

As the helicopter flew toward Saudi Arabia, the crown prince plotted in silence, his mind determined, the rage and grief mixing like a black storm inside. He wasn't thinking clearly and he knew it, but he didn't care any more. Patience was for cowards. *It was time to act!* Prince

Abdullah was the one who killed his family. He knew it, he had known all along. His private intelligence officers had warned him. Now he had to move quickly to protect what little he had left. His father. The kingdom. It all was in danger. They were not finished with their killing. Al-Rahman would strike again.

Unless he acted quickly to take him down first.

He balled his fists as he thought, his arms taut, his temples pounding with each heartbeat. He plotted in the darkness of the cabin and the darkness of his soul.

The enormous helicopter flew west, moving toward the low fog and the night grew thick and full as the moon fell toward the horizon. The Saudi coast began to shine in the distance, a silver shadow in the starlight where the fog broke and the seas hit the shores.

*******

The American-made F-15 Eagle fighter flew in a shallow circle at twenty-three thousand feet. At this altitude, the stars were clear and bright and the light of the moon glinted off the Eagle's composite wings. The pilot, a senior colonel in the Royal Saudi Air Force, had been in the air for almost an hour and was running low on fuel. In another fifteen minutes, he would have to return to base, which meant his career, and maybe his life, would be over. Prince al-Rahman had been very clear. Complete the mission, or die. And the colonel wasn't stupid. He knew his life was at stake.

He glanced nervously at his fuel readout, a sick knot in his stomach, then scanned his radar again. He had the APG-63 radar looking down, skimming the ocean below him, searching for his target. Why he had to shoot down the helicopter—who it was and why it was flying over the Persian Gulf toward Saudi Arabia at three in the morning—he didn't know. Bandits. Terrorists. A rebellious OPEC minister from Oman, an Iranian businessman who had crossed the young prince, he hadn't been told. And it didn't matter. All he knew was his instructions came from Prince al-Rahman himself. And one did not disobey the royal family, especially *this* prince. He was ruthless and cunning and, many speculated, on his way to the throne. So a smart man such as he would attach himself to the winner and ride with him for all he was worth, a calculation which made the situation before him very simple. Shoot down the helicopter and earn his first star. Fail and be shot. It was easy to be motivated with his life on the line.

The pilot flew the fighter aggressively, whipping the controls as he desperately searched the night sky. His digital fuel readout clicked again, decreasing to eighteen hundred pounds. The radar found nothing. The sky was empty and dark. The knot in his stomach grew. His readout clicked off another fifty pounds and he went through the numbers again in his head. Five hundred pounds of fuel to get back to base, a couple hundred pounds to fly his overhead approach, three hundred pounds for emergency reserve, two hundred to land. He had nine minutes, maybe ten, before he would have to turn back to base.

His palms had already sweated through his gloves, wetting the controls. "*Shoot down the helicopter or die trying,*" the prince's brutal instructions sounded again in his head.

The truth was, he didn't mind the thought of dying in combat. He'd give his life happily for the Kingdom of Saud, but he bitterly hated the thought of dying because he had run out of gas or worse, having the prince shoot him because he had failed.

He cursed, punching an angry fist on his knee.

Where was the target? What was he going to do? He glanced at his fuel gauge, then cursed once again.

Rolling the fighter up on its wing, he scanned the expanse of dark ocean almost five miles below him, staring through the side of his Plexiglas canopy. He counted no less than six oil tankers moving through the Persian Gulf, each of them trailing a long line of sea foam that shimmered in the moonlight. A couple enormous cargo transports moved parallel to the tankers, heading in the opposite direction toward the ports at Al Kawayt and Abadan. To the west, a bank of thick sea fog had developed and he watched as it drifted toward the Saudi coastline a little more than fifty miles away. He flew his aircraft north and then east, keeping it constantly banked up on her side, and the enormous oil derricks along the Iranian coast slipped into view, their dark towers rising over the shimmering waters of the Persian Gulf. He rolled the nimble fighter level then jerked the stick to the right and pointed the nose toward the Saudi coastline.

His radar swept across the horizon, hitting a couple targets, civilian airliners moving toward Riyadh and Al Manamah, but it was almost three in the morning and the civilian airline traffic was light. He commanded the look-down, shoot-down radar to search low once again, knowing the helicopter would stay near the water. His radar reflected a deep green shadow on his facemask as he focused on the screen. Nothing. Empty airspace. No helicopter there.

He shook his head in frustration. The sweat had moved from his armpits to soak the flight suit on his back.

*"Kill the helicopter or die."* His instructions were clear.

But he couldn't kill the helicopter until he found it first.

He glanced at his fuel gauge as it clicked through fifteen hundred pounds. He reached up and adjusted his radar out to eighty miles. The Saudi coastline cluttered the display and the phase-array system sought to cut through the radar energy that bounced back from the rocky coastline. The computer automatically adjusted the beam to cut through the ground clutter and the radar display was cleaner on the next sweep.

Then he got it. A quick hit almost sixty miles away. It was low and moving quickly toward the coastline, just above the fog. He commanded his radar to hit the target again. It measured the distance and ground speed difference between them and began to click in his ear.

Target. Helicopter. Fifty-six miles off his nose. He yanked the fighter twenty degrees to the right and hit the afterburners for eight seconds to get a quick burst of speed. The Eagle accelerated very quickly, reaching almost Mach one. Lowering the nose, he armed up his missiles and the targeting computer instantly began to growl in his ear.

He had a lock on the target. In ten miles he would shoot. Ten miles. Fifteen seconds. From here, it was easy. His mission was almost complete.

*******

The Crown Prince had barely drifted to sleep when the Sikorski suddenly reeled on its side. Then he felt his stomach lurch as the helicopter fell toward the ocean. His eyes flew open, his heart slammed and the adrenaline surged through his body. The helicopter lurched again and nosed over. The airspeed picked up and he heard the building noise of the airstream slipping over the cabin faster and faster. The helicopter rolled left and then right and his stomach turned again. He caught a glimpse through the window and saw the sea shimmering but a few feet off the left side. They were right on the water, no more than four or five feet in the air. He cried as the aircraft lurched, then started climbing again. A sudden burst of light, bright as the sun and moving off the left side, cast a freak shadow under its light. The ocean lit up like at noonday as the flare burned across the night sky.

The helicopter's defensive counter-measures were kicking out anti-missile flares!

The crown prince knew what was happening.

And somewhere inside him, though he didn't acknowledge it yet, a small voice whispered that he was soon going to die.

Grabbing the side of his chair, Prince Saud stumbled toward the cockpit door. The helicopter lurched again and he was knocked to the floor. The aircraft rolled on its side to almost ninety degrees and he slid like a doll across the carpeted floor, smashing his head against the conference table as he slid by. He felt the warm blood in his eye, but wiped it away and struggled to his feet again. The helicopter groaned around him, vibrating and shaking like an amusement park ride. They were exceeding their main rotor speed limit, he could tell by the screeching sound. He reached for the cockpit door and jerked it open just as the helicopter rolled again, throwing him to the side. Cursing, he crawled back to the cockpit and pulled himself to his feet.

He saw the amber caution lights and heard the warning horns. The two pilots were in a panic, one of them rolling the aircraft left and then right. He heard the warning system growling, warning him of an imminent attack. "Coming around!" the pilot screamed as he rolled the helicopter again. The prince's eyes shot to the defensive display and his heart turned to a cold rock in his chest. A fighter had locked on with its radar and was about to attack. "Who is it?" he screamed to the copilot on his left side. The Saudi colonel turned to him, his eyes wide with fear. "F-15," he cried. "He is lighting us up with his radar!"

The night illuminated again as the copilot spit out another bundle of phosphorous flares. The flares ejected from behind the main rotors and lifted into the night, trailing above and behind the helicopter in a white-hot trail of heat designed to pull away any heat-seeking missiles. The copilot reached to punch the flare button again, but the prince slapped his hand back. "Stop it," he screamed. "That is not going to help!" He jammed a finger toward the threat display. "He's hasn't fired a missile yet. And when he shoots, it will be a radar-guided missile, not a heat-seeker anyway. All you're doing is lighting us up like a flashlight, showing him where to shoot."

The copilot only nodded, ready to panic again. The pilot flew the helicopter like a madman who had been shot in the eyes, jerking it left and then right, rocking her up on her side. The prince saw the ocean rise up to meet them as the pilot rolled the helicopter again. The rotor blades slapped the ocean and the helicopter lurched to the side. The pilot panicked and climbed and the helicopter shuddered toward the night sky.

The prince braced himself, grabbing the top of the pilot's seats, then looked at the counter-measures display. It was an APG-63 radar. Yes, an F-15. Forty miles behind them. Closing very fast.

His mind raced as he considered their options. They were over the water. Nowhere to hide. Nowhere to land. The helicopter's spinning rotors would bounce back enormous beams of the radar energy to the F-15's receiver. They had no guns, no weapons, only a few counter-measures. He grimly shook his head. He was a fighter pilot. He had targeted helicopters from an F-15 before. A helicopter, over the water, against an F-15 with its missiles and guns

He swallowed, almost crying.

Abdullah was about to kill him. Then he would kill his son. There would be no freedom for the kingdom. All of his dreams were dead.

The pilot continued flying like a crazy man, breaking right and then left, climbing and descending, trying to break the lock on the radar that was tracking them from behind. But the helicopter was enormous and no more stealthy than a Mack truck. The missiles couldn't miss it. They had maybe a few seconds left to live.

Saud's brain slowed down as a sudden calm filled his mind.

He was going to die. He knew that already. But he might yet save his last son, *if* he could just reach his friend.

He turned to the panicked copilot and tore the radio headset from off his head. "Tune up the VHF," he screamed.

The copilot stared at him blankly, his eyes glazed with fear. "The VHF frequency?" he repeated.

"Give me control of the VHF radio!" the prince cried again.

*******

The Saudi fighter pilot checked his airspeed and altitude. Five-eighty knots. Fourteen thousand feet. The target was forty-one miles in front of him, almost straight off the nose. He watched as it rolled left and then right, a lumbering giant in its final dance of death. As if any of it mattered! It could rock, it could roll, it could climb or descend—his radar couldn't miss it now that it was locked on. He lifted his eyes and scanned the darkness. Searching the open ocean, he saw a tiny trail of white light burning across the water. He squinted, saw another trail, then laughed to himself. The idiot pilot was shooting flares! He smiled under his mask. A real genius! He hadn't even fired his missiles. It was pure panic down there.

Then he startled, his mind racing.

*What kind of helicopter carried anti-missile flares?*

His heart stopped, his mouth growing dry.

No civilian helicopters would carry defensive systems . . . maybe a government aircraft . . . no, none of them . . . except for maybe the royal family!

He almost threw up in his oxygen mask.

He was about to shoot a member of the royal family!

He didn't know what to do!

The firing computer continued to growl in his helmet. He was in firing range. The system was armed and ready. Radar locked. Ready to fire.

*Am I about to shoot a member of the royal family?*

Then Prince al-Rahman's words shot like electricity through his mind, "*Shoot down the helicopter or I will kill you myself.*"

He wondered for half a second, then pushed the thought from his head. Royal family? Maybe it was. But what did it matter? His instructions were clear. If he failed, Abdullah would kill him. He didn't have any choice.

"*Insha'allal,*" he whispered as he decided what to do.

He checked the distance and radar lock, then moved his left hand across the throttles, flipped off the safe switch and fired two advanced medium-range air-to-air missiles into the night air. The missile engines fired together in a trail of white smoke and flame and accelerated before him, then began to track downward toward the target.

\*\*\*\*\*\*

The helicopter copilot reached for the radio console and flipped the selector to manual. The crown prince leaned over the center console and changed the frequency to 122.5 MHz, which is the emergency channel. Every U.S. aircraft in the air was required to monitor this frequency. The prince pulled on the headset and jerked the microphone to his lips.

"Mayday, Mayday, Mayday," he said into the mike. "This is an emergency call for any U.S. aircraft. Mayday, Mayday, does anyone read?"

The prince released his broadcast button and listened, but the radio was silent. "Mayday, Mayday," he repeated. "Any U.S. aircraft, this is an emergency!"

The helicopter pilot cried out and pointed toward the threat display. Two missiles had been fired and were tracking them. Twenty miles and closing. The pilot screamed in panic. He rolled the helicopter and climbed then threw the nose toward the ocean again. The copilot reached up and released another five bundles of burning flares. The missiles continued tracking toward the helicopter, accelerating as they descended through the night air. The pilot racked the helicopter into a tight left turn, pulling back toward the missiles, trying to throw them off his tail. The copilot saw the missiles turn toward them, then slowly bowed his head.

Prince Saud watched the missiles track toward him. In seconds they would strike. Yet he felt no panic. No fear. His mind was peaceful and calm. He was empty as a basket that had been turned upside down, the emotion having been drained from his body and his soul. He thought of Tala and his children. He believed they were waiting, and he was ready to go to them now. He knew it was over, but he was prepared to die. He'd done everything he could to win the battle. Now the war was left to someone else.

Then he thought of his son and the last thing he could do. He pressed the transmit button and started broadcasting again.

"Mayday, Mayday," he said over the radio. "This is an emergency call to any U.S. aircraft in the region. This is Saudi Crown Prince Saud bin Faysal with an emergency message for Major General Neil Brighton of the national security staff. Neil, my friend, all of my family is dead. I have one son who is living and you must rescue him. The Agha Jari Deh Valley . . . you will find him there. He is there with my . . . ."

The missile hit the helicopter in the left engine bay. Prince Saud felt the fire and heat but only half a second of burning pain.

\*\*\*\*\*\*\*

The F-15 pilot saw the explosion lighting up the night sky, a yellow fireball with a billowing white and black core. He saw the smoke rising as the scattered pieces of the helicopter began to rain from the sky, pelting the ocean in a hailstorm of smoking metal and burning debris. The fireball disappearing quickly as the pieces fell. Then he smiled, satisfied, and turned his jet back toward his home.

# THIRTEEN

The hallways of the Pentagon are a wide, windowless and wondrous maze of interconnecting spokes and rings that start at the center courtyard and work their way out from there. They are crowded and dull and brightened only by the colorful assortment of Air Force, Army, Navy and Marines uniforms. The Pentagon has its own Metro station (one of the largest and most crowded in the city) as well as several cafeterias, its own shopping mall, bank and mail delivery operations. The services the Pentagon offers are equal to those of any small city—which, of course, is exactly what it is. More general and flag officers work in the Pentagon than any other single place on earth, most of them housed in the executive hallway along the outermost ring on the northwest side of the Pentagon. The building is always crowded and there is a sense of urgency that simply isn't replicated in any other government building, with the exception of the White House or perhaps the CIA. Those who walk the Pentagon halls know they are the sword of the nation, the tip of the spear, and they are willing to die for their country and to keep their people free.

Major General Neil Brighton had a small annex office along the outer ring of the Pentagon, one hallway over from the Chairman of the Joint Chiefs of Staff. It was an understated and private affair, a single room with no reception area, secretary, or staff. A place to think where he came to get away from the ringing phones and constant meetings and appointments that plagued his White House office. Inside the wood-paneled room, he had a small desk set against the back wall where he could turn in his chair and look out a large window onto one of the huge parking lots that surrounded the Pentagon. In the distance, the buildings of Washington, D.C. rose, punctuated by the Washington Monument's pearly white spire sticking up in the air. Unlike his White House office, which was decorated with pictures of him with two presidents, a vice-president, the secretary of defense, several senators and congressmen and various foreign leaders. The walls of his Pentagon office were decorated with his real love, which certainly wasn't politics, but fighters and fighting men. There were pictures of him as a lieutenant standing in front of his first F-15, pictures of him flying in formation along the Korean DMZ, over the Egyptian pyramids, and the Brandenburg Gate of the old Berlin Wall. There were pictures of him as a captain and a major, always in olive or desert camouflage flight suits, posing in front of a fighter jet. There were pictures of him with his squadron mates in various locations around the world; deep sea fishing in the blue waters of the Mediterranean Sea, riding camels in Iraq, eating sauerkraut at Lelas, and fighting wars in Kuwait, Bosnia, Iraq, and Afghanistan. A stranger could trace the general's career by looking at the pictures on the wall, from his flying days as a lieutenant to his first staff job at the Pentagon, the wing commander at Langley to another staff job with the Joint Chiefs of Staff. It was here that the transition to a political animal became complete—where he started having more pictures of him with ambassadors and presidents than military friends.

The general had been back from his trip to Saudi Arabia for less than a day. The sun had set over the Washington, D.C. and the parking lot lights had clicked on. Brighton sat alone in his office and stared out the large window, lost in his thoughts. Then came an urgent knock and his aide pushed back the door. "Sir," a colonel said as he rushed into the room.

Brighton turned wearily. "What you got, Dagger?" he asked.

Colonel "Dagger" Hansen took a quick step toward his desk. "Bad stuff in Saudi."

Brighton stood immediately. "What is it?" he asked.

"Crown Prince Saud bin Faysal is dead, sir. His helicopter was shot down a few hours ago."

Brighton's knees almost buckled and he took a quick breath. He felt like he had been hit in the stomach and he almost grimaced in pain. "Are you certain?" he demanded. "How do you know it was him?"

"We know," the colonel answered. "And that's not all, sir. The news gets much worse. Now come, I'll explain while we walk. The National Security Staff is assembling in the Situation Room and the president wants a briefing in an hour."

Hansen turned for the door and Brighton followed. The colonel explained what he knew as they jogged down the hall.

\*\*\*\*\*\*\*

Twenty minutes later, Major General Brighton was sitting at the Situation Room conference room table, surrounded by national security staff. He read the transcript of the radio call:

> *Mayday, Mayday . . . this is an emergency call to any U.S. (UNREADABLE) in the region. This is Saudi Crown Prince Saud bin Faysal with an emergency (UNREADABLE) for Major General Neil Brighton of the (UNREADABLE). Neil, my friend, all (UNREADABLE) . . . I only have one son (SIGNIFICANT UNREADABLE) . . . living? You (UNREADABLE) (rescue/rescued/resist??) him. The Agha Jari Deh Valley. (SIGNIFICANT UNREADABLE) . . . He is there with my . . . .*

Brighton checked the time of the transcription, then the time the interception took place. He studied the UNREADABLE portions of the transcript, trying to fill in the blanks, then turned to the communications specialist on the NSC staff. "Who picked up the message?" he asked.

"One of our receiving birds out of Baghdad," the staff member answered.

"It wasn't broadcast to any particular receiver?"

"No, sir, it was not. It was a call in the blind. A couple dozen other U.S. aircraft reported hearing the broadcast, including several receivers inside of Saudi Arabia. The reconnaissance aircraft had its recorders activated and was able to get the transmission, but the helicopter was so low it impeded the range of the broadcast. As you can see, there are significant portions that are unreadable."

"It wasn't broadcast using Have Quick secure radio?" he asked.

"Negative, sir," the young lieutenant replied. "No secure means of encryption were employed. Quite the opposite, the radio call was broadcast on the civilian guard frequency. It was the crown prince's intention to get the message to as many people as he could, hoping it would eventually make its way to you. Clearly, that was his intention. He mentions you by name, that much of the broadcast came through loud and clear."

"But if he was trying to send me a message, why not use his satellite radio?"

"Time, sir, or lack of it. It takes a couple seconds to synch up to a satellite. And when Prince Saud made this radio call, he was already under attack. It was amazing he had the presence of mind to get this much out. We've gone back and looked at some of the reconnaissance information from one of our Looking Glass IIIs. When this radio message was broadcast, the crown prince's helicopter was deep into evasive maneuvers. Missiles had already been fired. They were six, maybe eight seconds from impact. The broadcast was terminated when the missiles impacted the target."

Brighton sat back and thought, imagining the chaos in the helicopter in the last seconds of the prince's life as they tried to evade the inevitable. He considered the courage and calm the prince had displayed. He was a good man. A friend of America. He was going to miss him deeply. The world was not as good without him, as well as much less safe.

"And the unreadable portions of the transcript?" he then asked, pushing his personal anguish aside.

"We're still working on that, sir. There were a couple times when Prince Saud slipped into Arabic, so our translators have been going over the recording, trying to complete the transcription, but as I mentioned, the helicopter was low and portions of the transmission didn't come through. It might be this is the best transcription we ever get."

The general laid the transcript on the table and stared at the far wall. The staff worked busily around him, but his mind drifted back. The crown prince had warned him. But did he have any idea he was so close to death? A sudden chill ran though him. How much did the prince really know? He thought of the codeword. Was this Firefall?

He turned back to his staff. "Who was with him in his helicopter?"

An intelligence officer stepped forward. "So far as we know, he was alone."

Brighton shook his head. The Crown Prince of Arabia. Alone. In his helicopter. In the middle of the night. Out over the water. It was more than unusual, it was completely absurd. Turning to the transcript, he read it again. "*I only have one son.*" He looked up from the transcript and stared again into space.

Colonel Hansen moved to the conference table and sat down as a small group of staff members gathered around them. The colonel's face was taut and he nervously wet his lips. "Sir, we've been poking around since we intercepted this message," he said. "Our consul in Riyadh has been trying to talk with King Faysal, but hasn't been able to get through. However, the king managed to send us a message. We are still trying to confirm its authenticity, but it appears to be real." Hansen paused and wet his lips again.

"Yes?" Brighton demanded.

The colonel looked around anxiously. "I'm sorry sir, but we think Crown Prince Saud's family has also been killed."

"Killed?"

"Assassinated. A political hit."

"His family?"

"His sons from Princess Tala, Prince Saud's most senior heirs. And maybe Princes Tala and their daughter as well, all of them killed a little more than forty-eight hours ago."

Brighton's face drained of color and he blinked his eyes suddenly. He shook his head in doubt. "I don't believe it," he said.

"I'm sorry, sir. I know you and Crown Prince Saud bin Faysal were good friends. It's a kick in the gut, especially with his family . . . ."

"I don't believe it!" Brighton repeated, his voice growing sour. His thoughts came to him slowly, thick tar in his mind. "Why would anyone kill his family? With the security that's around them, I don't see how they could!"

His staff members stared at him, none of them willing to reply. Hansen tapped a finger on the table, pointing to a line on the transcript. He didn't say anything, but his growing impatience was becoming clear. "I'm sorry, sir, but it happened," he finally said. "I know he was your friend, but the old guy was bopped off, along with his wife and kids. We know they've been killed. Now we have to figure out what it means, why it happened and what's going to happen next."

Brighton turned toward him and Hansen tapped the transcript again, the surety of his action enough to cast Brighton's disbelief aside. "We are seeking confirmation, turning over every stone," the colonel continued, "but from what we are hearing from our friends at the Israeli Mossad, as well as our guys in Syria and Iraq, it looks like one of King Faysal's sons is making a move."

The general's face drained of color.

A power struggle in the kingdom! It was impossible to overstate the danger this would create. The instability in the Persian Gulf would send the price of oil through the roof. It would cripple western economies at a time when they were already on the edge. The hard cash it produced would be used to breathe money and life into al Qaeda and several other terrorist regimes. It would destabilize the entire region, including the fragile Iraqi government, while bringing out all the snakes and spiders in Syria, Iran, and Lebanon. It could shut down the Persian Gulf to international shipments of oil while increasing the opportunities for nuclear proliferation in the most dangerous part of the world. It would mean the military forces in Israel would be on hair-trigger alert. It would mean . . . . He felt a sick knot in his throat.

He took a deep breath. All right. It was here. He would deal with it . . . they would deal with it . . . they would do what they had to do. He rubbed his face, then his hair, then took a deep breath. Staring at the transcript, he started thinking clearly for the first time since walking into the Situation Room. "The prince's son," he wondered, "the Agha Jari Deh Valley?" A light began to flicker inside his head.

"Princess Tala?" Brighton asked. "She was killed, along with all of her children."

"Yes, sir. That is what we have been told."

"But there were no other assassinations?"

"Not that we know of right now."

"You know that Prince Saud had another son. He had a second wife. Another child."

The colonel didn't answer. *That* was something he didn't know.

"His enemies are trying to kill Prince Saud's heirs," Brighton said. "He is claiming stake to the kingdom . . . ."

"Sir?" Hansen questioned, then stopped and let Brighton think.

Brighton shook his head in frustration. Then it hit him like a slap on the head. "Get me a map," he demanded.

A map was laid out before him and one of the specialists pointed at the crash site in the Persian Gulf. "Was the prince's helicopter fly east or west?" Brighton asked.

"West, sir. Toward Saudi Arabia."

The general considered, thinking of what the crown prince had said, the warning in the garden, the fear in his voice. "Where is Agha Jari Deh?" he asked. Hansen pointed at the map. The general drew a line with his finger between Saud's personal heliport in Riyadh . . . the border . . . across the Gulf to Iran . . . through the mountains to Agha Jari Deh. The line was almost perfectly straight. He swallowed hard. "He hid him!" he said.

Hansen looked at him, not understanding.

Brighton pointed again. "He was hiding his last son, his last heir. He took him to Iran." His voice was so certain, no one dared argue with him.

Brighton moved toward an illuminated map on the wall. The small group of advisors followed, Hansen staying at his side. "Prince Saud knew it was coming," Brighton explained. "He tried to warn me."

He pointed to the small village with his finger. "He was over the Persian Gulf, on his way back from where he had hidden his son in Iran."

Hansen stood in silence, then cracked his knuckles. Brighton turned away from the wall map.

"If we know it, the killer knows. If we know where Prince Saud was going, then the assassin knows it, too. He has to kill the last son to ensure the kingdom doesn't fall to Prince Saud's heir. If that's the case..."

Hansen started nodding.

"We've got to help him," Brighton said as he turned to his aide. "What's the closest Special Operations unit?"

"You know how thin we are in Special Forces, sir. All of our Spec Ops units are committed to ongoing operations. I'm not sure if we have anyone available . . ."

"There's got to be someone!"

"Special Forces are stretched to the point of breaking three hundred and sixty-five days a year. None of them are idle. And we'll have to use an SF unit. This isn't the kind of mission we can send someone else."

"Find someone!" Brighton commanded sternly. "I don't care what you do or how you do it. Find us a unit we can task. We've got to get them to Agha Jari Deh before it's too late. We're looking for a young boy, four, maybe five years old. And Princess Ash Salman will be with him. Agha Jari Deh looks like a tiny village. If Saud took them there, then we can find him. But we've got to move quickly. If we picked up the radio broadcast, then Prince Saud's enemies inside Saudi Arabia certainly picked it up as well. They will be moving. They *are* moving now. We have to get there before they do."

Hansen turned to an Army liaison who had been standing with

the circle of advisors a few feet away. The army colonel stepped forward. "We've got a Delta Team R&Ring in Germany," he said. "They were supposed to get another couple days' rest, but we could load them up and get them in-country if we had to. If we can get airlift from the Air Force, they could have them in Iran within twelve hours or so."

Dagger turned to Brighton. His face was suddenly even more intense. *Sam's unit was in Germany. That was the Delta unit the colonel was taking about. He was ordering his son into combat. It was a lousy thing to have to do.*

"Sir?" Hansen prodded.

"Do it," Brighton said. "Coordinate with the Chairman, the SecDef, and the CINC to get the orders in place. We need their support to authorize a mission into Iran. The president will have to pull the final trigger. I'll lay the groundwork with him. Meanwhile, authorize all support and combat SAR assets. Who knows what our Deltas will run into once they get there. This is going to be a very dangerous mission, with no time to plan or prepare. Move other SAR assets if you have to. We can't leave these guys out there without support. If anyone gives you pushback, send them directly to me. Emphasize to the Deltas that this is a rescue mission only. They need to avoid a firefight if possible, but they need to be ready. We might meet up with hostiles and we have to be prepared to accept casualties." He stopped and scanned his staff. Most were scribbling notes. "I want the talking papers within an hour so I can brief the president."

The army colonel nodded and moved toward his console. Hansen went with him, all the time talking in his ear. Brighton looked at the other members of the staff. "Any questions?" he demanded. No one spoke. "OK, get at it."

The group sprang to life.

*******

Prince al-Rahman listened to the young communications specialist intently, boring his dark eyes into him. "You are *certain?*" he demanded, his voice deadly but calm.

"*Sayid,* yes I am."

"He said the Agha Jari Deh Valley?"

"I am certain, Prince Abdullah, that is what he said."

"That's in Iran?"

"Yes, my *Sayid.*"

Prince al-Rahman closed his eyes and looked up at the ceiling. "My older brother has been murdered," he said carefully. "I need to know everything. I need to know every detail of the radio call. Now, try to remember! Did he say anything else?"

The young soldier didn't move as he thought intensely. "I have told you everything," he finally answered. "Everything that I can recall."

"His helicopter was shot down?"

"It seems that way, *Sayid.*"

"And there were no survivors?"

"No, my *Sayid.*"

"No survivors . . . no survivors . . . ," Al-Rahman's voice choked with pain. He forced a look of grief and deep sadness that pulled the corners of his lips into a tight frown. His eyes teared, his lip trembled, it was a spectacular display, with just the right mix of rage, shock and sadness at his brother's death. Every head bowed in respect for his pain. Always emotional, his fellow Arabs recognized Al-Rahman needed a private moment to grieve.

The young prince wiped his hand across his eyes, then dismissed his staff with a wave of his hand. "Leave me," he whispered. "I need some time alone." His aides left without comment, the last one closing the heavy door to his office.

The room was silent a moment before Al-Rahman lifted the phone. "He went to Iran," he said when his chief of security picked up the line. "Agha Jari Deh Valley."

A long moment of silence followed. "Iran?" the general finally said.

"Yes," Al-Rahman answered, "Now I want you to go and get him."

"Sir, Iran is not a friend, they are an enemy. We have no assets in Iran."

"I don't care what you do or don't have. We may not have Saudi assets in the country, but many powerful Iranian officers are indebted to me. Start with General Sattam bin Mamdayh. Get him on the phone. He'll know *exactly* what to do."

"Prince al-Rahman," the general began to plead, "we have eliminated Prince Saud. His son is no threat to us. By the time he is old enough, it will be far too late!"

"You will do as I tell you. I want all of his children killed!"

"But *Sayid*, he is but a child. He poses no threat to you. Why can't we just let him be?"

"Because he will grow up, you fool! Because he knows who he is! He will remember his father and he will come after us. And his mother is with him. Do you think that she won't act? Are you stupid, my friend, or have you just lost your mind? I want all of them killed. None of Saud's children can live."

"But my Prince, if you will just consider for a moment . . . ."

*"I want them dead!"* Al-Rahman screamed like a madman into the phone. *"Now, are you going to do it, or do I need to have you replaced?* There are others who will follow my orders, general. You are not irreplaceable. Now you either bring me the son or I'll mount your head on my wall like the female sheep that you are. Choose now, but choose wisely, for I am not in a good mood. And I don't want to hear anymore whining about how he is *just a child!"*

\*\*\*\*\*\*

As director, Iranian Internal Special Security Forces, Iranian General Sattam bin Mamdayh was one of the hundreds of powerful and evil men who either owed Al-Rahman, feared him or were dependent upon his money.

When Prince Al-Rahman called the general on a secure satellite phone, he got right to the point. "I need your help," Al-Rahman instructed. "And I need it now."

"Anything," the general answered. "I will do what I can."

"There is a small village on the west side of your country, not far from the sea. Agha Jari Deh. Are you familiar with it?"

The general thought a moment. Yes, he was familiar. There was a young man who lived there, a grandson of the traitor Pahlavi, friend of the Great Satan himself. All of the Pahlavi offspring were under surveillance by his men, though Rassa Ali Pahlavi had spent a meaningless life of herding and farming, so far as he knew.

"The grandson of Pahlavi lives there."

Al-Rahman breathed upon hearing the name. "Are you certain?" he demanded, his voice strained and tight.

"Absolutely," the general answered. "I have observed him

myself. He is a dirt farmer, a peasant; my dog lives better than he. He lives in a shack I wouldn't stable my horses in. He is nothing, I assure you of that."

Al-Rahman was silent, his breathing heavy. "Pahlavi," he repeated like it was a bad taste in his mouth. "Pahlavi, grandson of the Shah . . . ."

"You know of him?" the Iranian general wondered.

Al-Rahman didn't answer. A long moment passed in silence, the phone humming softly between the two men.

Al-Rahman was impressed. It made perfect sense! His brother was brilliant. He *never* would have looked anywhere outside of Saudi Arabia. If his brother hadn't made the mistake of making the desperate radio call . . . if his people hadn't heard it . . . all might have been lost.

The Iranian broke the silence. "You know him, Al-Rahman?" he repeated.

"I know him," Al-Rahman answered. "He is a distant cousin, if you traced our lines back many generations."

The general filled the phone with laughter. "I could kill him," he offered. "I could send him to prison or I could bring him to you. Tell me what you're after. What do you want me to do?"

Al-Rahman answered quickly. "There is a boy. No more than four or five years old. He is a problem for me. I want you to eliminate the problem. Can you take care of that?"

The general snickered, drawing his own conclusion in his mind. A young lad? Sent away? One of the prince's wild oats. And now the princess didn't want the competition around her legitimate sons. How many times had he seen this? It was the same everywhere. "This will be easy!" he snickered. "I will see it is done."

"Yes, you will," Al-Rahman answered. "And you will do it

today."

"I'll have one of my personal units up there within a few hours."

"Yes, that is good. Before the sun goes down."

"*Sayid*," the general snapped. "But you realize, of course," his voice softened now, "this task you have asked of me, it is outside the official responsibilities of my office. I do this as a favor. A personal favor to you."

"I understand, Sattam bin Mamdayh." Al-Rahman knew how the game was played.

"I do it at great personal risk and sacrifice."

"I understand that."

"Then perhaps we could talk when I have completed this task."

"Yes, that will be fine."

"I will report my success."

"And, general," Al-Rahman added before he hung up the phone. "I don't need to state the obvious, but we don't want any leftovers. We don't want any talkers. No eyes. We don't want any children spouting wild tales to their friends. It would be better if there were no witnesses to tell of this tale; this Pahlavi, his wife, his kin. When you take care of the child, you need to take care of them. Otherwise we will have residuals, if you know what I mean."

The general only snorted. "I know, Prince Al-Rahman, how to do my job. You let me take care of your problem, then we'll talk again."

# FOURTEEN

A distant thunder rumbled down from the mountain and the air was heavy with the smell of rain. Azadeh and her father were working in the kitchen, preparing their evening meal. The young prince was asleep, nestled under the covers in Azadeh's bed. The princess worked beside Azadeh, helping to peel potatoes before dropping them into a boiling pot of salt and chicken.

Rassa heard his name being called from the backyard and he stopped, then grabbed Azadeh's hand. Azadeh held still and the princess watched them, her eyes growing wide. She had been in their home for less than twenty-four hours, and though she and Rassa had hardly spoken she didn't have to speak to understand the fear in his eyes.

Rassa moved to the back window. The sky was dark with heavy clouds. The back courtyard was slippery with mud and the animals were hunkered down under the olive trees that lined the back wall. Rassa saw a flash of movement as Omar Pasni Zehedan pushed his enormous frame over the back fence. He stopped and looked around, then ran toward the back door.

Rassa moved to meet him on the porch. Azadeh followed her father, but the princess stayed back. Omar, soaked with perspiration and out of breath, stood at the foot of the stairs, his curly hair hanging in front of his eyes. He was puffing and sweating despite the cold air.

"Rassa," Omar said, his eyes darting around. "There are soldiers in the village. They are looking for you."

Azadeh felt her heart crush as she gasped for breath. She reached for her father, but he pushed her aside. Moving onto the back porch, he drew the door half closed. Azadeh ignored his unspoken instructions, staying close enough to hear.

"What soldiers?" Rassa demanded.

"I don't know," Omar shot back. "I don't recognize their uniforms. Special Security Forces I think, but I've never heard of the unit and I don't know where they're from. But they are asking for you, Rassa, and they are only minutes away."

Azadeh moved to her father's side and grasped his hand. The princess had heard and she backed against the far wall, then turned and ran to the bedroom where her son was asleep.

Rassa turned to Azadeh. "Listen to me," he told her, "we've got to get out of here." He fell suddenly silent. Too late. The crunch of heavy trucks on wet gravel could be heard from the front of their house.

Rassa turned to Omar. "Thank you for the warning, but you can't help us now. Go. Get away while you can!" Without waiting for an answer, Rassa slammed the door in Omar's face.

Azadeh looked up at her father, her eyes wide with fear. He pulled her close and she felt him shudder. "Stay here," he whispered.

Azadeh pulled on his fingers, not letting them go. "Don't leave me," she begged him but Rassa pulled away.

"Stay with the princess," he told her. "Get into the back room!"

*******

The rains had quit just twenty minutes ago and a heavy mist hung from the orchard, dripping and wet, moist fingers that sifted through the trees but never quite reached the ground. The fog moved silently, almost as if it were alive, searching for something among the tall leaves. The surrounding mountains cast shadows through the thick underbrush, bringing on darkness before the sun had fully set. Far in the distance, somewhere east of the river, the roll of thunder echoed back through the trees as the rain squall moved away, pushing up the mountains to the east.

The army trucks sloshed to the center of the road and stopped. After years of Soviet oppression, Rassa recognized the sound of the trucks. Soviet-made APC-30s. Heavy. Armor plated. Twelve troops apiece. He listened and counted. At least three . . . maybe four trucks came to a stop outside his house. Two full squads. Fifty troops. He sucked in a quick breath.

Azadeh moved to the back bedroom and huddled with the princess below the window. The young boy remained sleeping in his mother's arms.

Rassa moved to the front door and glanced through the lace curtains. Two trucks had rolled to a stop in front of his house. One was farther up the road, one at the base of the hill. The road was deserted, all of his neighbors having rushed into their houses, though he knew they would be watching from behind their curtains, too. The soldiers spilled from the trucks and Rassa studied their uniforms: black combat fatigues, dark berets, flak vests and high, leather boots. He pulled away from the window as the soldiers approached. He shot a terrified look to Azadeh's bedroom, his mind reeling in fear.

*******

The soldiers weren't truly soldiers; at least most of them weren't, but brutal mercenaries who worked for their commander as his personal army of secret police, an off-the-books unit that reported only to the general and nobody else. The conscripts were commanded by cruel, glaring and arrogant officers.

The senior officer, a captain, emerged from the second truck, swatting the flies and smoking a thin cigarette. He was a squat man, with a thick neck and well-muscled thighs. His nostrils flared as he breathed and his glare was intense. His job was simple. Do what the general told him; nothing less, nothing more. And *never* ask questions.

The captain stuffed his hands into his front pockets, then barked out an order, pointing to Rassa's home. "Empty the house. Bring them all out here!"

His soldiers jumped at his voice. They moved to the door and blew it off its hinges with a burst of machine gun fire then rushed into Rassa's house. The kitchen was empty. They moved through the room, opening the small armoire, spilling the dishes from the counter and knocking the chairs to the floor. They ran to the first bedroom and kicked the door back. No one was there. At the end of the hall, the bathroom was obviously empty. Which left the last bedroom. Four men gathered around the door, their guns at chest level. Their leader gave a quick signal and one of the soldiers kicked in the door.

They burst though the doorway and looked quickly inside. The bedroom was empty. The bed covers had been thrown on the floor. The window was open and a cool breeze blew the curtains back.

*******

Omar grabbed the princess and pulled her over the brick wall. She held to her son, grasping him in her arms. The boy cried and the princess pressed her mouth to his ear, whispering to him silently, "Don't be afraid. Go to sleep!"

Rassa followed, and then Azadeh. All five were over the back wall.

Omar glanced at the stranger and the young child in her arms.

"The princess, I presume?"

Rassa nodded, pressing his body against the rock, then started crouching toward the old barn.

"There," Omar hissed as he nodded toward the trail that led up to the mountains.

Rassa stopped and looked up at the rain-shrouded peaks that rose over the village, studying the rocky trail that disappeared in the cold mist. He heard voices, then the crash of gunfire as the soldiers shot the front door. He threw a desperate look toward Omar. "You have to save them," he said. He nodded to the princess and her son who was clutching to her arms. "Take them," he whispered. "Go to the mountains. You know that trail as well as anyone. The mist is heavy. It will hide you. Now go! Get away!"

Omar didn't hesitate. He motioned toward the young stranger. "Come," he hissed and she moved to his side. Omar reached for her young child and took him in his arms. Crouching, he ran through the orchard and slipped behind the barn. Rassa listened for a moment, hearing their footsteps fading away as they moved up the rocky trail. Then he turned to Azadeh. "Stay here!" he said.

"Please don't leave me, Father."

"Do as I tell you. Stay here. Out of sight."

"Father, you can't leave me!"

"It is the princess they are after; the princess and her son. They don't want you or me. I think that we will be all right."

"But Father . . . what are you going to do?"

There came a loud crash from the house as one of the bedroom doors was kicked open. They heard the banging of footsteps and then the soldiers curse.

Rassa turned back to Azadeh. "I have to give them time to

escape."

"But Father, if you leave what am I supposed to do?"

"Stay here, like I told you. Everything will be OK. They aren't going to hurt me, it is the royal family they want."

Rassa glanced toward the mountains. Omar and the princess had disappeared in the mist. Another crash sounded from their house, this time from Azadeh's bedroom. More cursing, more yelling, and Rassa stood up. He glanced quickly to Azadeh. "I love you," he said. "Stay here. I'll be fine. But stay out of sight."

Rassa jumped the fence to his courtyard, then ran toward the house. Azadeh peeked over the fence, then started to cry. She reached out toward him, but she didn't call his name.

Azadeh crouched against the wall a moment, then sprinted to the orchard and hid in the mist. She heard her father's footsteps and the guards calling out, then a warning shot being fired before the guards dragged her father down.

*******

The guards worked quickly. They were brutal, but well-trained, and they knew what to do. First, they searched Rassa's house, tearing it almost to pieces, knocking holes in the walls and tearing up the floors, looking for a hiding place or a secret trap door. Other soldiers gathered Rassa's neighbors, everyone who lived on the hill, herding them like sheep into a circle. The guards stood over them, sneering at their countrymen, ready to shoot the first one who dared to move. Other guards spread out. It only took minutes to search every house on the hill. They found Azadeh hiding in the orchard and they dragged her to the circle of cowering villagers.

Azadeh looked down on the village. The streets were deserted. The market was empty and every shade had been pulled. "Soldiers in the village!" The call had gone out. The village looked like a ghost town. Everyone knew what to do.

Azadeh cried in her heart. "Please, help us!" But Azadeh had lived long enough to know that help would not come.

The captain of the guard approached Rassa. "Name!" he demanded.

Rassa swallowed hard, his Adam's apple bobbing. "Rassa Ali Pahlavi," he said.

The captain nodded, his brown teeth protruding from receding gums. "The woman!" he demanded. "We want to know where she is!"

Rassa stared at him blankly. "I don't know what you mean."

The captain smiled a sick grin. "Someone came here last night," he demanded in a raging tone. "They brought a young woman and a child. That much we know. Now tell us where they are if you have any hope to live."

Rassa shook his head weakly. "I don't know, my *Sayid.*"

The officer turned to the group of women and children that had been herded into the circle. He studied them carefully. Most of the women were old, the young ones having left the village for a better life somewhere else. A few children cowered at the back of the crowd, the older women gathered around them like mother hens. The foreigner was not among them. And neither was the child.

He turned to the captives. "All right," he said. "We are looking for a young woman and a boy. It is *very* important we find them. Do any of you know where they are?"

The villagers were silent. The silence was heavy and long.

"If you do not help us find them, we will have no alternative."

Again, only silence. The villagers kept their heads low.

He turned back to Rassa as he considered what to do.

His instructions from the general were simple. Find the woman and child. Make sure they were dead. Who they were or why they had to die did not matter, for he was not even curious. Following orders was all he had been trained to do. And he had seen what had happened to other officers who had dared question the general's commands. It was ugly, painful and far too long had they lived the process.

He would not make the same mistake. He would not think too much. Find the targets and kill them. It was a fairly simple job. But there were only a couple ways that he could do it. He thought awhile, then turned back to Rassa. Although he kept his head low, Rassa stuck out his chest. "Rassa Ali Pahlavi," he said, "you know why we are here?"

Rassa shook his head in terror. "No *Sayid*," he lied.

"We will find them, Rassa. They have to be here somewhere. We will tear down your entire village if we have to. All of your friends will suffer if you don't tell us what we need to know."

Rassa lifted his eyes. "*Sayid*, I swear . . ."

The captain swung violently, striking him on the head. "Don't lift your eyes to *me*, pig!" he screamed in a rage.

Rassa forced his head down to his chest. The officer stepped to the side, clearing a visual path between the terrified man and the group of huddled women and children. "Rassa," he asked, "do you have any family in this crowd?"

Rassa shuddered visibly, his shoulders slumping now. He looked across the clearing toward the huddled group from his village. Azadeh cowered, seeking refuge behind the wall of human flesh, but she still caught his eye and Rassa turned away. "I have no family, captain," he lied again.

The captain snorted. "We know you do, Rassa Ali Pahlavi. We just don't know who it is. But it doesn't matter. We don't care. You see, Rassa, there are other ways that we can do this. Now this is your last chance. Where is the man-child?"

Rassa lifted his eyes, knowing it mattered not what he said. The officer had made his decision and his fate was now sealed. He knew from experience, from watching others die, that there was nothing he could say now that would change the outcome. Yet he felt almost calm, as if a blanket of peace had settled over him. He lifted his head and looked at the captain, staring him right in the eyes. "Look around you," he taunted. "You can see he's not here. And I doubt you will find him. He is gone. You have failed."

The captain snorted in rage, then turned and screamed to his sergeants, "Tie this man to the tree!"

Four of the conscripts came forward and pulled Rassa by the arms, dragging him through the wet mud as he struggled to stand. Lifting him by the neck, they threw him against the nearest tree. The groups of villagers were quiet as Rassa was tied and bound.

There was no trial, no words, not even a condemnation of death, nothing to mark the decision that had already been made. The captain walked to the army truck that had carried him to the village. Reaching behind the front seat, he pulled out a small leather flask. He had come prepared for something new, something different today. The liquid sloshed in the flask as he approached the condemned man. Pulling the soft cork, he doused Rassa with diesel fuel. After soaking his hair, head, shirt and trousers, he poured the last cup of fuel around on and around Rassa's bare feet.

A young lieutenant came forward, his rifle in hand. "What are you going to do?" he hissed under his breath.

313

The officer didn't answer.

The lieutenant stepped between the captain and Rrassa. "This was not our instruction," he said.

The captain reached into his trouser pocket. "Step aside, lieutenant," he sneered, "or you will find yourself also tied to the tree."

The captain pulled out a small box of matches, then heard a faint cry of despair. Turning, he saw a wide-eyed girl. He smiled at her happily, cocking his head to the side. "Your father?" he mouthed to her.

Azadeh stared in terror, then nodded her head.

The captain extracted a match from the box and struck it against the knife sheath strapped to his thigh. The wooden match sizzled to life and he let it burn a moment, staring at the flame, then looked at Azadeh and dropped the match at her father's feet.

The fuel was slow to catch for the diesel had mixed with the rain and soaked into the mud. Several seconds passed before anything happened. Then a thin stream of black smoke began to billow from the ground. A yellow flame flickered, quickly catching Rassa's clothes.

Azadeh screamed. An old woman cried from the back of the crowd. Rassa took a deep breath and turned away from his daughter. The flames caught at his trousers, then the coattails of his shirt. Deep yellow, almost orange, the flames began to lick higher. Every eye, every head, was turned to the fire now. Smoke began to waft through the low trees.

Rassa cried out in anguish and Azadeh bolted from the crowded, running desperately toward him. A conscript stepped forward, but she pushed through his grasp, tears streaming down her face as she ran toward the tree. Tripping on a low stump, she fell at Rassa's feet. "No, Father! NO! You promised you would not leave me!" she sobbed.

The fire grew higher and she was forced to back away from the heat. The flames crackled and burned, reaching ten feet into the sky. She reached again for her father, leaning into the flames. "I want to come with you!" she cried. "Don't leave me, Father. Please, I want to be with you."

Rassa looked at her, let out a faint scream, then closed his eyes. The officer watched, a satisfied evil smirk on his face. The fire burned with a bright yellow flame.

Azadeh rolled onto her back, swallowing the sickness inside. The captain looked down and their eyes met briefly again. She lay there, unmoving, tears brimming her eyes, then moaned once in anguish and curled into a tight, little ball. She pulled at her knees and her eyes slowly closed. Her breath became heavy, as if she were asleep.

The captain turned to his men. "All right," he yelled. "There is a young boy in this village. Our instructions are clear. Find every boy in the village who is younger than five. Round them up and shoot them, then let's get out of here."

\*\*\*\*\*\*

Thirty-nine children were murdered in the village that evening. Those who opposed the soldiers saw their homes and property burned. Those who fought them were murdered along with their sons. Those who sought to hide their children were eventually found. The carnage was sickening to even the most bitter heart, the smell of death and smoking buildings filling the dim, evening air.

The Iranians were working through the last few blocks of the village when they heard the echo of helicopter blades bouncing off the steep mountain walls. They looked up to see American Blackhawks coming over the hills to the south. Black machines. Door gunners at the ready. Twin machine guns protruding from each open door. Their escorts swooped before them, Blackhawk gunships that were armed to the teeth. One of the gunships let off a quick burst, sending .50 caliber bullets bursting into the ground around one of the APCs.

The Iranian captain froze, his mouth open, his eyes wide in shock. He wiped the blood from his hands, then shading his eyes. Some of his men gathered around him as his mouth grew tight with fear. "American soldiers," one of the conscripts cried. "We've got to get out of here!"

The officer didn't move. Americans! In Iran! This was their homeland! *Their homeland!* It simply couldn't be!

The conscript screamed again, his voice piercing the air. The sound shook the captain into action. "Go!" he cried. "They *are* Americans! We've got to get out of here!"

The spell broken, the NCOs turned to their soldiers and started shouting instructions. "Load up. Leave your gear. Evacuate the area. NOW!"

The Iranian security forces in their special black uniforms, those brave men who killed children while in their mother's arms, the highly trained soulless attack dogs of General Sattam bin Mamdayh who had so valiantly walked and strutted among the civilians barking orders just a few minutes before, fell into a panic as the American helicopters passed over their heads.

The killers ran to their armored carriers. The engines started, spewing diesel fumes, and the troops ran up the small ramps into the machines. The sound of helicopters beat against the canyon walls as the U.S. helicopters set up to land. The APCs revved their engines and lurched away, moving toward the narrow road that led through the mountains, away from the village to the plains in the west.

# FIFTEEN

Army Special Forces Captain Samuel Brighton moved slowly through the village dressed for battle: black fatigues, tan leather boots, leather gloves, full flak gear, belts of ammunition, a first aid kit, grenades, radios, GPS receivers, emergency rations, binoculars. He wore a Velcro nametag, but no other insignia identified him as being from the United States. The sun had set now, and the light had grown dim. He looked slowly around him, feeling the contents of his stomach rise to his throat. He had seen combat and death, he had seen destruction and loss, he had seen blood and horror in close up and gory detail, he had seen men that he loved blown to bits before his eyes, but he had never in his life seen anything equal to this. He had never imagined such a scene straight from hell—the burning buildings, the smoke, the smell of spent rifles and blood. And the carnage concentrated on the children! His mind tumbled and reeled.

He held a gloved hand to his nostrils and prayed he would one day forget. He counted the bodies, most of them young boys. Young boys and their mothers. It was a gut-wrenching sight. His heart ached, twisted in two. He stopped and looked down, hearing a muffled cry at his feet. A young mother, her face revealed from the thin veil that had been pulled away, held a child who had been shot in the chest. The boy was no more than three, with tangled hair and fat cheeks. He appeared to be sleeping, but Sam knew he was dead. His mother rocked back and forth in the grass that lined the road and sang to him softly between her deep sobs. Sam didn't speak Farsi, though he understood a bit, and the tune was familiar, for he had heard it before. She sang slow and in rhythm, so he picked up most of the ancient words.

"*I have loved you so deeply*

*I have held you so tight*
*Go to sleep little baby*
*Rest in God,*
*Close your eyes."*

Sam turned away, gripping the handle of his rifle, the barrel pointed up, his thumb on the safety. He turned his back to the young mother, listening to her cry. He wanted to help her, to comfort her if he could, but what does one say to someone holding a dead child in her arms? How does one explain something so utterly evil, so utterly useless, so utterly cruel?

All the dead children? How could he ever explain?

But he wanted to listen; he wanted to hear her soft cry. He wanted to remember the pain she suffered, he wanted to share it and keep it, like a hot flame on his chest.

Whoever shot these children, he would find them one day. He swore that he would. He didn't know when or how, but he would find them one day. Then he would remember this tormented mother and the song that she sang.

A soldier didn't fight battles for personal reasons or revenge; it was a job, a duty, defending freedom was a call. But this scene of carnage, it drove him. He was a different man now.

Finally, he turned and walked toward his team leader who was making his way from a small field on the south side of the village where the helicopters had set down. The other captain came to a stop before him and the two men stared grimly, measuring the displeasure in each other's eyes. "Report?" the team leader asked, his voice businesslike.

Sam shifted his feet. "A lot of dead babies." He gritted his teeth. The other officer was his best friend, a man he trusted with his life, but he was angry at him now, and it showed in his eyes.

CHRIS STEWART

The leader nodded to his right, toward a hill on the western side of the village. "It started up there," he said. "The locals said there were soldiers . . . ."

"I told you!" Sam shot back, his voice seething with rage. "Bono, I told you I saw old Russian APCs. We could have gone after the soldiers and taken them down in their tracks. But no! That's not our mission, you said! We are here for the child. Well, what is our mission now? You want us to bury these children? Is that why we're here? We could have taken the soldiers, but what can we do now?"

"Sam," the leader answered calmly. "I'm not the enemy here."

Sam took a step back and sucked a deep breath. He pressed his lips and looked around, then slowly shook his head. "I'm sorry," he answered. "That was out of line. I was venting on you, Bono, and there is no excuse for that."

The leader watched him closely. "Apology accepted," he said, but his voice still firm. "And I made the right decision," he continued. "We did the right thing. This *isn't* an op. It's a rescue mission only. We could have gone after the APC, but they were already pulling away. What were we going to do, chase them all the way to Tehran? And we *did* do some good here, we interrupted their work. More importantly, we followed orders. Now come on, get a grip, we don't have much time. Let's do what we can, then beat cheeks out of Dodge. We're still in enemy territory, in the middle of a freakin' foreign country, let's not forget that."

Sam moved his automatic rifle to his other hand. "Roger," he answered. And though his eyes still burned with rage, it was directed at the carnage around him, not at his friend. He slipped his hand down the butt of his rifle, bringing the short-barreled machine gun to his chest. "And the boy we are looking for? What do we do there?"

320

The captain worked the wad of gum in his mouth, a stony look on his face. "Any suggestions?" he wondered.

Sam hunched his shoulders around him. "It's possible he might still be alive."

"Yeah. Possible. Not likely from the looks of it, but possible perhaps. But who is he, where is he? I doubt we'll ever find out. We don't have the men or the time to sort this thing out."

Sam snorted in disgust. "Freakin' mess," he said.

The captain nodded gloomily, then cocked his head to the hill. "Your squad is almost finished sweeping up there," he said. "Have them talk to the people. Find out what you can. I've got Alpha squad working the other homes near the square. Let's get an estimate on the damage, then get out of here. I'll give you five minutes, then I want your squad in the helicopters so we can get in the air."

Sam pressed his jaw. "Aye, aye," he said.

"Five minutes," the captain warned him as he walked away. "Not one second more. I want your squad ready when the helicopter blades roll."

*******

Sam jogged to the burned-out homes on the hill. The smoke hung low in the trees, heavy and still, like a deep gray and black blanket that had nowhere to go. The air was deadly still and the thick smoke burned his dry eyes.

His squad had done everything they could to clean up the mess. The medics had treated a few of the wounded, but the Iranian attackers had been good, if not kind. They were efficient with their weapons and almost all of their targets had been killed. The children proved an easy target, for their bodies were fragile and they didn't fight back.

Sam jogged to his waiting squad, who stood grim-faced and angry, their eyes dull with rage. The shock was universal. None of them were prepared to see such a thing.

"OK," Sam said, turning to his Farsi interpreter. "Anything to report?"

The sergeant tucked an unlit cigarette between his lips. "The stories are pretty consistent," he said. "Four APCs moved into the village sometime late this afternoon, probably not more than an hour, maybe an hour and half, before we got here. They asked for Rassa Pahlavi—that's his house over there." The interpreter nodded to a small cinder block and mud house to his right. "The Iranians were looking for someone, a young woman and a child." He stopped and cleared his throat, knowing the Iranians had beat them to the target and then continued. "When Pahlavi didn't help them, the soldiers freaked out. This is where it ended, with what you see here."

Sam wet his lips, then turned and surveyed the area. All the villagers had retreated into what remained of their homes. They were as terrified of the U.S. soldiers as they were of the Iranians assassins. "Did you notice?" he asked the sergeant while motioning to the remains of the village below.

The interpreter hesitated. "Yeah," he replied.

"All of their targets were children. All of them boys."

The other soldier was silent. It was painfully obvious.

"Which meant," Sam continued, "that they didn't find who they were after."

The interpreter swallowed. "So they made a sweeping generalization. All the male children must die."

Sam shook his head. "A rather harsh method to accomplish their mission."

"But effective," the sergeant muttered in a cynical voice. "You've got to give them that. When it comes to the mission, these guys are a dedicated bunch."

Sam wiped his face in frustration, then turned back to his men. "This Pahlavi," he asked. "Any information on him?"

The interpreter nodded toward a smoldering tree. "That's him over there," he answered. "They burned him alive."

Sam took a step to the right and his shoulders slumped as he looked at the smoking tree. The lower branches had been scorched, all of the leaves burned to ash. The corpse lay in a heap at the base of the tree "Anything else?" he demanded as he looked away.

"No, Sam, that's all."

"All right then, let's go. There's nothing more we can do and the Honcho wants to get out of here. Move to the helicopter. Let's get out of this hell."

"Roger," the soldiers muttered. They all wanted to leave. There was too much death, too much darkness, too much destruction and despair. And it seemed to be for nothing. None of it made any sense! His team gathered their gear and moved down the hill in a run. Sam watched them go, standing alone atop the hill.

A slight wind picked up, blowing up from the valley and lifting the smoke to the tops of the trees, bending it over the branches like the long, misty fingers of an enormous, dark hand. Sam turned his face to the breeze, hoping the wind would remove the stain from his memory and the smell of smoke from his clothes. He closed his eyes and listened, feeling the breeze on his face and the weight of his gear pressing against his shoulders and chest. The radio receiver beeped in his ear as the other squads announced they were ready to go. He pulled out the earpiece and let it hang at his neck. He needed a moment of silence, a moment of prayer.

He bowed his head slowly. "Dear God," he began, then paused for a time. He wanted to say something, and he felt that he should, but try as he might, he didn't know what to say.

He didn't feel like praying. He felt like kicking someone's head in.

He paused, then finally mumbled the only thing he could think of. "Please help them," he muttered, then lifted his head.

Turning, he started to walk down the muddy road. He had only walked twenty paces when something spoke in his mind. He tried to dismiss it, but the feeling remained. He paused, then peered back at the smoldering tree.

She crawled from the high grass on the other side of the road. She was young, wet, and muddy, with long hair and a tan dress. She moved toward the body at the base of the tree, and knelt beside it, holding her hands over her mouth. Watching her, he saw her shoulders heaving and heard her muffled cries.

*"Go to her,"* an unseen voice seemed to say. *"She is your little sister and she needs your help."*

Sam stared in frustration. *"But what could I do?"* he thought in desperation to himself.

The voice didn't answer and Sam didn't move. The sound of the helicopter blades began to beat from behind him as the pilots spun the rotors up to operating speed. He turned to the landing zone to see that his squad had loaded up in the helicopters and were ready to go. He heard his name being called through the tiny radio earpiece that hung at his neck. "Captain Brighton," his team leader called him. "Sam, let's go!"

He eyed the helicopters, then glanced back at the girl who wept by herself in the mud.

"*Go to her*," the voice repeated.

The helicopter blades spun, ready to lift in the air. Bono moved to the side of the lead helicopter and stared up at Sam. The leader motioned to his radio and pointed to him. Sam slipped in the earpiece and heard the captain's voice. "Sam, come on, man, we've got to get out of here."

"*Please, Sam*," the voice pled. "*I can't do this alone!*"

Bono's voice broadcast again into his earpiece. "Let's get out of here, Sam! Come on, man, let's go!"

Sam reached for the transmit button. "Stand by," he said.

"What are you doing up there, Sam?"

"Stand by!" Sam replied.

He turned away from the helicopters and looked at the girl near the tree. She kept her head bowed and her hand at her mouth. Sam took ten steps toward her and she finally looked up, her eyes wide with fear. She started to back up, pushing herself through the mud and Sam lifted his hands, holding them away from his body in a gesture of peace. She cowered, her head low, almost bowing to him.

Sam took another step forward and she slowly raised her head. She looked at him and his heart seemed to wrench in his chest. She was so young and beautiful; vulnerable as a piece of ash in the wind. Her eyes were brimming with tears, which left a small trail on her cheeks.

Sam caught a sudden breath. The feeling so strong it was like a kick in the chest. "I know you," he said.

She watched him intently, then cocked her head. Her face softened and she quickly wiped a rolling tear from her cheek. Sam saw the pain and desperation and he felt his heart wrench again. He felt breathless and hollow, his chest growing tight.

He moved to her slowly and she backed up in the grass. She kept her eyes low, too terrified to look at his face. Sam stopped a few paces from her, then knelt down at her side.

He shot a quick look over his shoulder. His boss and two soldiers had come up the road and were watching in silence from twenty paces away. They didn't move toward him, letting him talk to the girl.

Sam moved a few inches toward Azadeh. "I'm sorry," he said. He spoke slowly in English, hoping she would understand.

She forced herself to stop weeping and lifted her eyes.

And Sam saw it, a flicker of recognition, as if *she knew him too!*

He gestured to the charred body. "Your father?" he asked, locking her eyes with his.

She nodded in despair, then turned away from the tree.

"Where is your mother?" he asked her.

She only stared back.

"Mother?" he repeated.

Azadeh shook her head.

"You are . . . alone?"

"Now . . . I am."

Sam leaned slowly toward her and reached for her hand. "Look at me," he told her.

Azadeh kept her head low and Sam lifted her chin to look into her eyes. "Khorramshahr," he asked her. "Do you know where I mean?"

She backed away from him slowly, her face uncertain with fear.

"A refugee camp," Sam repeated, pointing with one hand to the north. "Khorramshahr," he repeated. "Go there. They will help you."

Although she nodded slowly, Sam could see she did not understand.

"Khorramshahr!" he repeated. "If you can make your way there . . ."

"Sam," Brighton heard his friend's voice. Bono had moved to his side and he placed his hands on Sam's shoulder. "Sam, we have to leave. Come on, man, let's go." He pulled on Sam's shoulder, then put a hand under his arm, lifting him up and pulling him toward the road.

"Khorramshahr!" Sam repeated. "I will have someone waiting, they will be looking for you."

Azadeh backed away in fear, moving away from the other officer who was pulling on Sam's arm. Sam reached for her desperately as he was pulled to the road.

"Khorramshahr," he called, but she disappeared in the grass.

******

Forty seconds later, the helicopters took to the air, flying over the village to keep away from the rising mountain peaks to the east. Sam sat at the open door in his helicopter, his feet hanging over the side. And though they flew directly over the village, the smoke was too thick to see if she was still there.

# SIXTEEN

Azadeh remained hidden in the grass until long after the sounds of the helicopters had faded away. By then it was dark and the smoke had cleared from the air, though the sky overhead was still obscured by high clouds. The night turned cold. Her muddy clothes clung to her skin and she started to shiver. Forcing herself to her feet, she walked in a daze toward her gutted house. Their furniture, their dishes, their books and their clothes, everything they owned had been tossed through the windows and the broken front door. She peered at the scattered belongings, then passed into her home, her teeth chattering from the cold and despair.

She walked to her bedroom, her eyes adjusting to the light, and looked around desperately, feeling a sudden sense of panic. Her room was in tatters, her mattress and clothes on the floor, but under the broken dresser she saw the golden headband. She picked it up quickly and shoved it deep into her pocket, then fell on the mattress and buried her head in her arms.

She was alone. Completely alone. She had no mother, no father, no family, no friends. Even the house wasn't hers, a woman couldn't own property, so the house would be taken and sold, and she would left on the street.

"Father," she whispered in her crushing despair. "I want to come with you. I want to be with mother. How can I survive by myself?"

In that black moment, Azadeh felt all the pains of her world: the aloneness of her breaking heart, Satan's evil laughter as he cackled in her ear. She felt the agony of spirit as she remembered the past; the happy days with her father, the warm home, the warm bread, and the sadness of knowing that it was all gone. She felt a crushing doubt and deep

328

anguish as Satan and his angels laughed at her.

Did any of it matter? Was there *any* sense in the world? Was there any good, any love, *any* devotion at all? Her father had spoken of hope, he had used the word *faith,* but none of it mattered, for it all was gone. None of it made any difference. None of it was real.

The only thing that was real was the darkness and the tattered remains of her home. The only thing that mattered was that she was alone.

"Please, Father," she whispered, "please don't leave me here by myself."

She wept in the darkness for a very long time. "I did everything you've asked me. I have tried to be good. But now you have left me. So tell me now, Father, what am I supposed to do?"

Then Azadeh rolled to her knees and started to pray, a universal reaction to what she had been through, a human reaction, not Muslim, not Christian, but something deeper, more permanent than the religions of the world, a reaction from her spirit that hovered within.

"Great Allah," she prayed as she pushed herself to her knees. But that was as far she went, as far as her teachings could take her. She didn't know what to say or how to ask any more. "Dear Allah...dear Allah... ." she repeated again.

Then her mind started drifting, thinking of her father again, the best example of love she had ever known in her life. But she didn't think of his burning or how he had died: she thought of his living and how she wanted to see him again, she thought of her longing to look in his eyes, to feel his arms round her and see his kind smile. But mostly she thought of the words he would say. He had a way of making her feel better, of making her feel strong, like life was worth living and everything would be okay.

"You were always proud of me, Father," she cried to herself. "You made me feel better. Can you comfort me now?"

\*\*\*\*\*\*\*

Rassa Ali Pahlavi knelt beside his daughter at the side of her bed. He stroked her face lightly, feeling the softness of her cheek. And though he looked at her sadly, the hurt in his own eyes had passed, the pains of the mortal world could not touch him any more. The world didn't hurt him, he had completed his mission and passed his great test. "I *am* proud of you, Azadeh," he whispered in her ear. "You are strong, you will make it, and God will be at your side."

He stroked her face gently, then looked up at the sky. "I love you, Azadeh," he repeated. "And we will be waiting, watching and caring for you." He stroked her cheek lightly, then gently kissed her brow.

It was time that he left, at least for a short while. Sashajan was waiting. And there was other work he had to do.

\*\*\*\*\*\*\*

Azadeh felt a soft touch on her temple and she opened her eyes. And though she didn't see her father, she knew that he was near. Then an unseen voice whispered to her, *"Your father still lives. He still loves you. He cannot stay with you, but I can, and I will comfort you now."*

Then she felt a warm, soft and gentle blanket falling over her soul. It was. It wrapped completely around her, from her head to her feet, and kept the piercing arrows of Satan from touching her heart.

She slipped away into sleep, where a deep comfort waited. She slept peacefully through the night, dreaming of a better world.

# SEVENTEEN

## Dhahran, Saudi Arabia

Prince Al-Rahman, now the oldest prince in Saudi Arabia, sat in the center of his office, an opulent and oval-shaped room with gold-plated walls, mural ceilings and diamonds imbedded in the molding around the windows and floors. His desk was huge. Three computers and a row of telephones were positioned to his left. An one hundred forty-inch flat screen television was tuned to CNN, was built into a wooden console to his right. A wall of tall windows, twenty feet high, looked out on the expanse of desert to the east. The sun beat through the windows, forcing the air conditioner to run constantly.

Prince Al-Rahman noted his reflection in the glass. Although he was middle-aged, he was still strikingly good-looking and well manicured. He was also as cold, hard and evil as any man in the world. More, far more, *he was the future king,* patriarch of the world's great family, a great empire builder like the sultans before. He knew that he was chosen. That was obvious to him now. His father didn't believe him, nor did all of his kin. But he had proven them wrong. And he would prove it again.

*******

There was a soft knock at his office door and, after a respectable pause, one of the most recognized and wealthiest people in the United States was escorted into his office.

"My friend, good to see you." The prince extended his hand. The venerable American walked toward him and shook it firmly. "Abdullah," he greeted him, his voice raspy and thin.

The Crown Prince studied his guest. He is growing tired, the

331

Saudi thought as the man approached. He looked wrung out and defeated. We need to keep a close eye on him.

He pointed to an arrangement of couches and leather chairs and the two men sat down. Black coffee was ready, and the prince poured for his American guest.

"You are ready?" the American asked as he sipped at his coffee.

"Yes, my good friend." The prince sat back and relaxed against his leather chair.

The two men gazed at each other, each playing his best poker face.

"Before we get started, I've got something to show you," Abdullah began. He opened a packet and threw half a dozen photographs on the table: mothers wailing in front of a smoky wall, children in various poses of death, small boys, even babies, all of them shot in the head or the chest. The American picked up the photos, his face unemotional. "Ugly work," he offered. It was the only thing he would say.

Al-Rahman held another collection of photographs in his hand and he tossed them on the table as well: American helicopters. U.S. soldiers. Weapons. Hard faces. Smoke and burning houses. The Americans walked through the village and stood over the dead. Although grainy and tilted, the images were clear.

"This is the story I want you to put out," Abdullah said. "U.S. soldiers are to blame for the assault on Agha Jari Deh. They were looking for al Qaeda. When the villagers didn't cooperate, they punished them. We have witnesses. Testimony. Everything you will need. Al-Jazeera will run with the story when I give them the word. You take it from your side. You know what I want."

The American studied the photos. "They'll deny it, of course."

"Of course they will. And eventually they'll prove they weren't involved. But the damage will be done. The truth doesn't matter that much anymore. Those who hate the United States will believe it, not matter what evidence is eventually revealed. The *New York Times* will front page the story for weeks. It will weaken the administration and divert them from their work; there'll be hearings in Congress, special investigations, the whole bit. And remember, all we're after is another chip in the wall, another crack in the foundation, another scandal to weaken your country, and this will give us that."

The American picked up a photo showing a dead child on the street. A U.S. soldier stood behind him, smoking a cigarette while talking to his comrade and pointing away. The image was clear enough, he could read their nametags. Sanchez and . . . Brighton? Maybe Bingham? Either way, it didn't matter, they were about to be famous, their images slapped across every newspaper in the world.

"I'll get some people on it," he said, tossing the photograph on the table. "When will the story break?"

"Later in the afternoon tomorrow."

"That isn't much time."

"It's a big story. It's My Lai again. U.S. military atrocities make very good press so it will be hard to sit on a story, if you know what I mean." Abdullah's voice was curt and sarcastic, but he smiled as he spoke.

The American sipped at his coffee. A few moments passed in silence. "On the *other matter*, you know, I've been thinking," he finally said. "Asking around, getting a few opinions, talking in the abstract, of course, but trying to get a feeling for how this will be received. And I have to tell you, Your Majesty, that I believe you are walking on very tenuous ground."

"We know we are. But you will take care of everything."

The American was clearly uncomfortable. "I don't know, Your Highness. We can do many wonderful things, we've done miracles for you in the past. We are very powerful, our partnerships span the whole of the globe, our friendships very personal, our contacts cultivated and nurtured through the good and the bad. But there is, after all, only so much we can do, and this plan is far more than we had ever envisioned. Destroy an entire nation! How would you suggest we manipulate the political consequences of that?"

"We won't destroy them. We will move them. There is an enormous difference, my friend."

"But they will not be moved."

"That is their choice. If they stay, they will die, but I cannot choose for them. We can't make them be reasonable, though Allah knows we have tried."

"They will not go away. They have nowhere to go. And even if they did, even if they were given other options, they would choose to die in their homeland. They have made that very clear. It is that important to them."

"Again I will say it; I cannot choose for them."

The American sat back in frustration. Although he had sanctioned human suffering many times, this was crossing the line! He pressed his lips together and his heart beat in his chest. "How many people will die?" he asked in a low voice.

The crown prince adjusted in his seat. "It is not your concern."

"But Prince Abdullah, if you really want us to represent you, then you must. . ."

Abdullah lifted a hand to cut him off. "I would be careful not to confuse our relationship or overestimate your input. You are to advise and represent, not to interfere or give counsel when it is not asked of you."

The American understood and bowed his head.

"All right, then," the prince continued, "now, if it would make you feel better, I will tell you that it probably won't be as bad as you think. Two of the nuclear weapons are tactical in nature and are relatively small. What we are proposing isn't much different than what has been done before."

The American shook his head. "How can you say that?" he cried.

The prince leaned forward and narrowed his eyes. He spoke with indignation, his voice sharp and on edge. "Dresden," he sneered, "twenty-five thousand civilians firebombed. London; two hundred thousand; twenty thousand dead in a single attack. Leningrad; three hundred thousand civilians killed in combat, another half million starved. Berlin; two hundred eight-nine thousand killed in the last month of the Bolshevik advance alone, and who knows how many in the months before that? And let's not forget what your own nation has done. Hiroshima. Nagasaki. *Poof!*" The prince brought his fingers together and blew them apart. "A hundred thousand gone. *Poof!* Just like that.

"So get my point? This is nothing new. War isn't for the weak. And we've seen this many times before."

The American frowned and swallowed. The prince's eyes flickered yellow and his co-conspirator pulled back. Something stirred inside him! Where had he seen that evil flicker before? He swallowed again, forcing himself to relax. "I would like to know how many people will die," he said before he lowered his eyes.

The prince shrugged his shoulders. "Maybe twenty-five thousand in the initial attack. Perhaps another twenty from the radioactive fallout."

The American looked at his coffee and tried to steady his hands.

"And your target is Jerusalem?"

The crown prince sat back and laughed. "Jerusalem!" he snorted while shaking his head. "Do you think I'm stupid? Don't you understand me yet?" The Crown Prince whistled in disgust. Did this man understand *anything?*

The American started in confusion. "But if not Jerusalem . . . ?"

The prince waved an impatient hand. "My target is Gaza."

The American almost choked. "Gaza! You're kidding! It doesn't make any sense! That's a Palestinian area! A hundred thousand refugees live in Gaza."

"I know they do. And those who die will die as martyrs. Allah will receive them unto his own.

"But Israel is the nation that you want to destroy!"

"No, my good friend, *we want to destroy the United States*. But to do that, we have to sacrifice Gaza. Israel will be the second step. Once we have destroyed these two nations we can turn our rage on you. And by the time we are finished, a hundred million of your people will lie dead in your streets. Your nation will lie in ruin." Abdullah's voice had risen to a rasp and his face seemed to darken like a shadow across the moon. "The world will be changed forever," he almost seemed to hiss. "Leaving it ripe to be taken. And *that*, my friend, is why you and I are here."

26859954R00184

Made in the USA
Lexington, KY
18 October 2013